*Beverly*

## THE FIGHT FOR FINGERHOOD

Once Robert Fingerhood, author of the bestselling sex manual, *The Fingerhood Position*, was the greatest single stud in the world of joyful sex—and the ultimate erotic answer to every lusting lady's passionate prayers.

But now Fingerhood has announced his retirement from the swinging scene. Fingerhood is getting married—to a girl young enough to be his daughter and old enough to be all the woman he wants.

There are four ladies, though, who have different ideas—four ladies who are crazy to show Fingerhood that they aren't taking his desertion lying down . . . not when there are so many more interesting positions to try. . . .

### *RETURN OF THE CRAZY LADIES*

Ø

## Great Reading from SIGNET

# RETURN OF THE CRAZY LADIES

by
*Joyce Elbert*

A SIGNET BOOK

NEW AMERICAN LIBRARY

## PUBLISHER'S NOTE

This novel is a work of fiction. Names, characters, places, and incidents either are the product of the author's imagination or are used fictitiously, and any resemblance to actual persons, living or dead, events, or locales is entirely coincidental.

NAL BOOKS ARE AVAILABLE AT QUANTITY DISCOUNTS
WHEN USED TO PROMOTE PRODUCTS OR SERVICES.
FOR INFORMATION PLEASE WRITE TO PREMIUM MARKETING DIVISION,
NEW AMERICAN LIBRARY, 1633 BROADWAY,
NEW YORK, NEW YORK 10019.

Excerpt from *The Prophet*, by Kahil Gibran, by permission of Alfred A. Knopf, Inc. © 1923 by Kahlil Gibran; renewed 1951 by Administrators CTA of Kahil Gibran Estate and Mary G. Gibran.

SIGNET TRADEMARK REG. U.S. PAT. OFF. AND FOREIGN COUNTRIES
REGISTERED TRADEMARK—MARCA REGISTRADA
HECHO EN CHICAGO, U.S.A.

SIGNET, SIGNET CLASSIC, MENTOR, PLUME,
MERIDIAN AND NAL BOOKS
are published by New American Library,
1633 Broadway, New York, New York 10019

First Printing, July, 1984

1  2  3  4  5  6  7  8  9

PRINTED IN THE UNITED STATES OF AMERICA

*for Eliza Dove*

*I wish to thank my editor, Andrea Stein, for her invaluable help.*

# I

## THE INVITATION

# 1

The sun rose earlier and brighter at Malibu than anywhere else in the world. Especially in June when it seemed to bounce off the beach like yellow gold lightning, with a few pavé diamonds thrown in for *bonne chance*.

At least that was what Simone Georgette Lassitier Omaha thought, and she should know (she arbitrarily decided), since she'd been living in the supersnobbish Colony for the past four years. And sitting out on the upper deck of the magnificent glass-and-redwood house almost every morning, trying not to get a suntan or worry about her career or wonder when her sex life was going to improve. If she stayed with Jimmy Newton, maybe never. He came in six seconds, then resumed work on whatever screenplay happened to be in his typewriter at the moment.

Simone sighed. It was undoubtedly her fault. Because even if Jimmy took six weeks to come, she didn't think she ever would. Not through intercourse, anyway. That was the reason for her spectacular lack of success with men. Oh, they were intrigued at first, but it didn't last long.

"You're a cute kid," her last co-star said, after he screwed her against a wall in her dressing room. "Let's be friends."

"*Friends*?" She was outraged. "How dare you? I don't want to be *friends* with you. I want you to adore me, worship me, threaten to kill yourself over me."

He laughed. "You've got to be kidding. Men don't kill themselves over chicks like you. No way."

"Why not?" Since her secret ambition was to be a femme fatale, that was the worst possible thing he could have said. "What did I do that was so terrible?"

"It's what you didn't do, honey. Next time, fake it." He slapped her on the ass. "You've really hurt the old ego."

"I come in other, more baroque ways," she said, departing in a huff. "An orgasm is an orgasm is an orgasm."

Jimmy didn't have much of an ego, at least not a sexual one, and maybe that was why he was still around. In dreamland at the moment, as were most of the others. Only Colin had already left for Burbank to shoot another episode of his highly rated private-eye series, *Arizona Pete*. The silver Yamaha that Colin zoomed across the Southwest desert on (when he went on location) was as well known to the American public as the Lone Ranger's horse once was. And Colin seemed equally attached to it.

Simone never watched *Arizona Pete* if she could help it. As far as she was concerned, it was bad enough that she had to live in the same house with the cokehead who starred in it. If he weren't in Phoenix half the time, she didn't know how she could have stood it.

"I don't think cocaine is the reason you dislike Colin," Jimmy said in defense of his buddy. "I think it's because he never made a pass at you."

"Why would I want him to do that, *vieux schnock*?"

"To prove that he finds you desirable."

Simone crossed her eyes, sucked in her lips, and made her imbecile face. "You mean, there's a man alive who doesn't?"

In her own way she was attached to Jimmy and at times even considered marrying him, in the hope that once a firm commitment was made they could work out his premature-ejaculation problems. But mostly she was relieved that he'd never popped the question. Perhaps it was better to go on as they were: sometime lovers, business associates, each of them concentrating on a career. The fact that Simone had a career to concentrate on still startled her. She not only never wanted one, she was easily the most unambitious person she knew, and what happened to her four years ago was a miracle.

Only Kate, her astrologer, confidently predicted that thanks to the Sun conjunct Jupiter in her tenth house a big job change was coming her way. Simone scoffed, but Kate said, "The stars never lie, Libra."

That didn't begin to describe it. Overnight she went from selling roller skates on the Venice boardwalk to being an acclaimed movie star in her first acting part ever. With all the odds stacked against it, *Charmer* racked up eight Academy Awards and turned its leading lady into a hot property. Jody

Jacobs of the Los Angeles *Times* was quoted as saying that Simone's was the most dazzling success story to come out of Hollywood since Lana Turner had been discovered at Schwab's Drugstore.

The telephone was ringing. She couldn't imagine who would be calling so early.

"Good morning, Libra." It was Kate, her astrologer. "I have some interesting news for you. It has to do with your house of travel, you lucky creature."

"Travel? But I'm not going anywhere."

"That's what you think," Kate chuckled. "The Sun trine Venus in your ninth house says otherwise. So get ready for travel, adventure, and a brand-new life, because they're definitely on the horizon."

"A new life?" She didn't think she could withstand another metamorphosis. "What kind of new life?"

"I'm an astrologer, not a fortune-teller," Kate replied sharply, hanging up.

Two years ago Simone was voted Europe's most popular actress, which brought her smack into the international-star category. Three years ago she won an Oscar nomination and lost wretchedly to Diane Keaton. And for almost four years running she had been the darling of the media, to whom she told the most outrageous lies. Like when a reporter from *People* asked how she happened to end up with lavender hair, and Simone said that the colorist mistakenly used too much toner—or something. It was no mistake at all. It was a shrewdly calculated move on the part of Jimmy Newton to make her mousy brown hair so weird and unique that the media would sit up and take notice.

They'd taken notice all right, and so had everyone else. Within a month of *Charmer*'s release, women all over America were dying their hair incredible shades of lavender, purple, and violet and crimping it in ringlets to achieve what had come to be known as "The Simone Look."

From then on everything she did became an instant fashion trend. Such as her habit of wearing angora berets into which she would stuff her lavender hair, while sitting out on the deck in the cool early-morning hours. After she appeared like that on a July cover of *Vogue*, department stores in major cities began to report an astonishing out-of-season demand for angora berets.

"*God morgen*, Miss Simone." It was the Swedish house-keeper carrying her breakfast on a gold lacquered tray. "I thought you would want to know that Mr. Newton didn't come home until after two A.M. Harold and I heard his car pull into the driveway. Normally, I wouldn't mention it, but you did ask me to keep my ears open."

Simone could have kept hers open forever and not heard a peep, since her bedroom faced the ocean. "*Merde.* I mean, thank you, Hilda. You did the right thing by telling me."

She would kill the crazy son of a bitch yet. Even though Jimmy had warned her from the start that he had a weakness for all-night poker games, Simone underestimated the power of their allure. She thought the only reason he threw his money away gambling was that his life was lonely, empty, sexually unfulfilled, but that after he lived with her he would no longer need seven-card stud.

Events proved her wrong. Jimmy needed it, all right, at least four times and God knew how much money a week. He was the counterpart of his buddy Colin McKenna, who needed women and coke with the same frequency and urgency. While Simone disapproved of drugs, she could understand Colin's obsession with sex (even if it didn't include her). Everyone in Los Angeles seemed a little gaga in that department; leave it to her to find the one man who couldn't have cared less.

"Aren't you going to eat your breakfast?" Hilda asked, concerned because her employer was forever on a diet.

Simone observed the steaming cup of café au lait, freshly squeezed orange juice, one beautiful brioche with a pat of marmelade, and gagged. How could she eat after hearing Hilda's disturbing news? Only a few days ago, Jimmy *swore* that he would steer clear of gambling and Gardena for at least a month.

"I'll spend a lot more time with you and the kids," he promised. "We'll go to Disneyland and stuff like that."

Before, he *swore* he would ask Colin to find a place of his own.

"I'll tell Colin it's time to shove off," he promised. "I'll say he's in the way, now that I'm no longer a swinging bachelor."

Simone sighed. There was no use believing Jimmy's promises; he obviously just made them to try to calm her down. Instead his duplicity had the exact opposite effect. She picked up the gold lacquered tray and threw it over the side of the redwood deck, then screamed hysterically at the top of her lungs.

"*Jag förstär inte*," Hilda said, never having resigned herself to the destruction of private property. As she went downstairs to retrieve the pieces, Jimmy Newton emerged on the deck. Undressed as always, his penis curled into a tight little flower (Simone liked to think of penises as flowers—they seemed less threatening), he had the usual glass of Pepsi Light in his hand and an out-of-sorts expression on his face.

"What gives with all the shrieking and yelling? They can probably hear you in Oxnard."

"I don't give a damn if they can hear me in New York. I want to know when you're going to do something about our two major problems."

"Which problems are those?"

"The disappearance of the sabertooth tiger and the plight of the starving masses in Djakarta."

"What?"

"*Colin and gambling, you fucking idiot.*"

"Oh."

"Oh?" she said, mimicking him. "Oh? Is that all you have to say for yourself?"

"What did I do now?" he sheepishly asked.

"It's what you *didn't* do. Hilda told me what time you rolled in this morning and I don't need anyone to tell me that Colin McKenna is still living in this house. If I didn't know better, I would think the two of you had a sex thing going."

"Oh, we tried that once when we were stoned on ludes. But if you'll pardon the pun, homosexuality really sucks."

"I suppose you consider that funny."

He managed a wan smile. "It's not bad for a guy who's had less than five hours' sleep."

"You want funny?" She pulled off the angora beret to reveal her hair saturated with a mashed-avocado-and-yogurt conditioner, then topped by a clear plastic shower cap. "Is that funny enough for you?"

"Last week it was walnut oil and ground sesame seeds," he said with disapproval. "I don't know why you torture your hair like that. It never gets a chance to breathe."

"You're a fine one to be talking about torture. What do

you think you're doing to me with your gambling? I don't even understand *why* you gamble. I mean, what sense does it make—this business of sitting in a stuffy, smoke-filled room with seven other men who are all trying to escape the pressures of life? What does poker have that's so goddamned special and privileged?"

"Action. Suspense. You never know which card is going to come your way, you never know whether you're going to lose your shirt or walk away with a bundle. It's exciting."

"So is war, but most people try to avoid it."

"What do you want from me? I don't play golf or tennis, I don't belong to a country club, I can't swim, and I refuse to jog. So it's only natural that I should have some sort of diversion. Be glad it's poker and not women. Then you'd really have something to kvetch about."

"At least I could compete with a woman. Who can compete with a deck of cards?"

He smiled at her. "Hey, it's not as bad as all that."

"That's what you think."

He ambled over, sat down on the edge of her chair, and kissed her on the cheek. "In spite of all my shortcomings, I love you, kiddo. Remember that."

For some reason, his attempt at reassurance had the exact opposite effect. "There's something you're not telling me, Jimmy. What is it?"

"What is *what*?"

"I don't know, that's what I'm trying to find out. What's going on?"

He looked around, behind, in front of him, trying to make light of it. "I don't see anything going on."

"You're hiding something. You can't fool me."

He raised his hands. "On my mother's life, I'm not."

"You never knew your mother, you bastard. You were raised in an orphanage."

"So what? I still had a mother, didn't I?" He smiled again, asking for a truce. "Everybody has a mother. Somewhere."

"You're cute, Jimmy." She detested his evasions. "Very cute."

He headed for the door before she could throw another temper tantrum. "Not as cute as you, kiddo."

Whatever he wasn't telling her had nothing to do with

cards, at least not directly. But she knew that the men he gambled with were all in the movie business and maybe, in between hands, he was slyly shopping around for another star—to replace her in his next movie. Simone was in professional hot water. Her last picture had bombed catastrophically at the box office and every finger in the industry was pointed straight at her.

Not the script, she thought resentfully, not the direction, not the editing, just her and her "tired performance," as a certain influential L.A. critic put it. While the public would forgive a favorite star for appearing in one crummy movie, the studio responsible for its financing would not. Especially when that movie cost over twenty-five million dollars and had to be yanked out of theaters after its first week in release. Fear and trembling surfaced in high places.

*She's getting too old.*
*She's caricaturing herself.*
*She's still kooky, but it's no longer fresh kooky.*
*She has to change her image.*
*She can't, that image is all she's got.*
*She's had it.*
*She's dead.*
*She must be replaced by a younger model.*

Simone cried for days when Jimmy repeated the rumors, trying to pacify her by saying he was on her side and didn't believe a word those studio dummies said. But whether he believed them or not, he needed them to back his next movie, tentatively titled *Rockabye Princess*. It was about a Danish princess who ran away to the United States and became a rock star. Simone loved the script and was dying to play the unconventional princess, but what if she weren't allowed to? Aside from the fact that she had become used to success and all the adulation that went along with it, she had no idea of how else to support herself and the twins. She couldn't count on flaky Jimmy and she couldn't go back to working behind the counter at CheapSkates. Even when she was a nobody, she hated that job. Imagine how she'd feel now, what a comedown!

What was she to do? How was she to manage? Her clothes bills alone had become astronomical. Why, one beaded Bob Mackie gown cost the equivalent of a year's salary at CheapSkates. The possibility that she might never again be able to afford Bob Mackie brought tears to her tired eyes. The ocean blurred along with her uncertain future and she lit her first Gauloise of the day, wishing she'd never set foot in California.

"Mommy! Mommy!"

The twins came squealing and running toward her, dressed in their crisp navy-and-white school uniforms, the Lycée crest on their darling blazers. The sight of them made Simone's heart melt and her maternal spirit rise. How could she be worrying about sequined Bob Mackie gowns, when she had the twins' education to think of? Their father was contributing a measly fifty dollars a week, which didn't cover the Lycée's yearly tuition for *one* child. But that was Steve Omaha, blithe and devil-may-care to the end.

"Darlings," she said, hugging her two Gemini offspring. "Did you eat your breakfast?"

Prince stared at his shoes, while Rima giggled.

"Prince spit out his Flintstones," Rima finally offered.

"And Rima poured Kool-Aid all over her Crispy Wheats 'n Raisins," Prince retaliated.

"And I threw my breakfast over the side of the deck," Simone couldn't help adding. "We're three of a kind."

"You shouldn't encourage them to misbehave, they're naughty enough as it is," Hilda said disapprovingly. "Time to go, children. Harold is waiting for you. *Skynda på.*"

Simone released them after one more wet kiss and one more fierce hug. "Hilda is right, you don't want to take after me. I'm a bad example. In the future, you want to *swallow* your vitamins and pour *milk* on your cereal. Is that understood?"

"Yesh!" they laughed in unison, knowing full well that their mother would never discipline them and that they would never listen to poor old Hilda. "We love you, Mommy!"

And they were gone, to be driven to Le Lycée Français de Los Angeles by Harold in the Rolls. Two such tiny little things in that huge car, Simone thought, touched by the image. The twins had no idea it was an unusual way to go get their education. They assumed that all children were driven to school by a chauffeur in a long black limousine with bullet-proof windows, had the use of an Olympic-size swimming pool during play periods, associated with the multiracial offspring of diplomats, movie moguls, and oil tycoons, and graduated bilingual. Just as when Simone was seven years old, she assumed that all children sat in a one-room school-house in Normandy and learned to read in French.

A couple of hours later, having successfully avoided the perils of another aging suntan, she was dressed in puckered silk stripes by Missoni, her lavender hair washed and blow-dried into a glamorous tousle, her mood bleak. All she had to look forward to was her Beverly Hills exercise class to work on her gluteus medius (ugh), lunch with her agent at Michael's to discuss her faltering career (double ugh), and then the long drive back to Malibu to try to find out what Jimmy was hiding from her (triple ugh). Simone's heart wasn't in any of it. She yearned to run off to Upper Volta, she felt so hemmed in and fettered. As a movie star she didn't have the freedom to just *roam*, she was too damned visible, too damned vulnerable, being in between pictures was too damned boring.

She checked three mirrors in the bedroom to make sure that her Orlane foundation was evenly applied over her milky face and neck, then double-checked the magnifying mirror for traces of a wrinkle. Although she did this about twenty times a day, she never found anything to worry about. Simone worried, anyhow. In October she would be forty, how much longer could she continue to ward off the inroads of time? Forty! It seemed impossible. She didn't look or feel that old, she hadn't grown up yet, how the hell could she be turning forty? She gave her wrists and earlobes another morale-boosting blast of Volage.

"Harold," she called downstairs. "I'm ready to leave."

"*Det är bra*, Miss Simone. I'll get the Rolls out."

That somber funereal vehicle. Suddenly she couldn't face it. "Never mind, Harold. I'll take the Porsche instead."

When she descended the stairs, Hilda and Harold were staring at her in dismay. Simone was one of the worst drivers in the world and they remembered what happened the last time she took the Porsche. There was a five-car pileup on the Pacific Coast Highway and the police marked her license with a second traffic violation. One more, they cautioned her, and her license would be revoked altogether.

"I promise to drive carefully," she told Hilda and Harold, whose eyes were filled with apprehension. "Has the mail arrived yet?"

Hilda handed her one letter with a New York postmark and

Simone uttered a soft cry of surprise. It was from Robert
Fingerhood, her kinky ex-boyfriend, the first man she'd ever
loved, the first man to break her heart, and the only man she
knew who had turned his personal obsession with erotica into
a professional windfall. Yes, it was the same Fingerhood
who'd become a nationally famous sex counselor and reputedly
helped millions of people find fulfillment by assuming what
he immodestly called "The Fingerhood Position." He had
even written a book by the same title. What she couldn't
understand was why he was writing to *her*. Their only
correspondence these days was the terse exchange of Christmas
cards, sometimes with a monosyllabic note at the bottom.

Simone giggled. What if Fingerhood had lost his hair?
What if he'd gotten fat and paunchy? She couldn't imagine a
fat, bald, paunchy Fingerhood, although it would serve him
right for being such a bastard. When they'd met fifteen years
ago at Anita Schuler's party, Simone hadn't realized he had a
sinister reputation for singling out beautiful women and breaking their hearts. She was working as a fur model on Seventh
Avenue then and Fingerhood was working on his Ph.D.
thesis, entitled "The Relationship Between the Rate of the
Subject's Maternal Heartbeat and the Rate of Sexual Intromis-
sion That Is Optimal in Orgasm."

"I never come," she told him. "Not even through digital
or oral stimulation. Let alone intercourse."

"Never?" he croaked.

"*Non.*"

And she continued not to despite his dedicated and sincere
efforts, just as she continued to bake meatloaves in plastic
bowls that dissolved, run up astronomical department-store
bills that she had no intention of paying, and imagine she
would be twenty-four forever.

"You're irresponsible, immature, and scatterbrained,"
Fingerhood said one day. "Take your unpaid-for clothes and
move out."

Tearfully, she did. When she learned that he'd replaced her
with one of her best friends, Beverly Big Boobs Northrop,
Simone tried to kill herself. She didn't really want to die, just
make the two of them miserable, but she couldn't even
manage that. Beverly, a tall busty redhead whom men whis-
tled at (before the feminists screwed up everything by saying
it was sexist), was Simone's idea of a femme fatale. She used

to look at Beverly's voluptuous curves and feel like a broomstick in comparison. To add insult to injury, Fingerhood told her that Beverly had "a cunt that never stopped."

"What does *mine* do?" Simone asked in despair.

"Lies there, rolls over, and plays dead."

"I sound like a cocker spaniel."

"If the shoe fits . . ."

In spite of all the positive experiences that had befallen Simone since then—marriage, children, a glamorous career—it still hurt to remember Fingerhood's crass rejection. It hurt a lot. When her husband said he was leaving her, she thought of Fingerhood leaving her. Because he was the first man she ever loved, his rejection hurt the most and scarred the deepest.

"Miss Simone, are you sure you don't want Harold to drive you in the Rolls?" Hilda asked. "It's one of the things you pay him for, you know."

She hugged them both, fished in her purse for the keys to the dusty-pink Porsche, and waved them giddily in the air. "Don't worry about me. I'll remember to use my directionals." Halfway out the door, she heard strains of *Norma* coming from Jimmy's room. "Please give Mr. Newton a message. Tell him that I've run off to Upper Volta to farm karite, and to take care of the twins until I return."

"Upper *where*?"

But she was already heading for the garage, a smile on her upturned lips, Fingerhood's letter clutched tightly in her hand. The minute she got into the Porsche, she ripped open the envelope. She couldn't wait another second to find out what Dr. Sex had to say for himself after all these terse, monosyllabic years.

The mail had not yet arrived when Anita left her stylish house on the Chelsea Embankment, but half a block later she ran smack into her postman.

"Letter from the States, madam." He beamed and handed her a familiar-looking airmail envelope. "Ta."

Certain it was another condemning missle from her mother in Cleveland, she tucked it into her snakeskin purse and went to catch the Underground. Three stops later she was at Oxford Circus.

"Hallo, love. Give us a kiss?"

Anita didn't see who said it, the words were whispered in

her ear so fast, the station was so crowded. But she did notice that a few men's heads turned as she went by in a cloud of Calandre (her perfume of the month), their eyes clicking in silent admiration. She wet her lips, tossed her newly frosted blond hair, and smiled to herself. It was gratifying to know that in spite of her very casual and very English attire, she still projected a very sexy and very glamorous American image. Then again, she damned well should, she worked hard enough at it. From her baby-pink Mary Quant fingernails to her sheerest Pretty Polly tights, Anita didn't leave anything to chance.

Today she was dressed rather warmly for June in an A-line tweed skirt (to hide her double Kotex bulge), a twin sweater set of Scotland's finest cashmere, her Russell & Bromley walking shoes, and an Aquascutum raincoat into which she had tucked a clear plastic rain kerchief. The first time Michael saw her wearing the kerchief, he chuckled and said it looked like a fridge bag for lettuce, but she let him sneer. When it came to anything the least bit feminine, Englishmen were utter ignoramuses.

She felt like informing him that she bloody well hadn't spent half a day acquiring a pre-Raphaelite look at Moulton Brown just to have it ruined by a thunderstorm; still, she held her tongue. Michael didn't much care for her backtalk (except in the sexual arena, when he loved it); he said he got enough bitching and complaining from his wife, Lady Harding, whom he SWORE he hadn't screwed since the day Princess Anne married that nincompoop.

"Damn damn damn!" Anita muttered to herself.

She had gotten out at the wrong end of the tube station and was walking toward Regent Street when she realized her mistake and whirled around, nearly knocking over a startled Arab. The noise and bustle of the West End were unnerving. A red double-decker bus whizzed by in a heavy stream of traffic while hordes of shoppers, office workers, and cinemagoers hugged the pavement. Anita's appointment with the liver specialist was at three and she was late already, according to the Patek Philippe that Michael had given her two Christmases ago. Since his gift to her this past Christmas was an electronic pillbox, was it any wonder that her liver condition was getting worse? Instead of rushing to keep her appointment, she deliberately slowed down.

After years of punching a time clock as an airline stewardess in New York and then as an airline reservation clerk in Chicago, Anita found it deliciously sinful to thumb her nose at punctuality now that she'd become a lady of leisure. At least that was how she liked to think of herself. Her mother's description was far less flattering. *You're nothing but a kept woman* (she accused Anita in a recent letter), *and that's not much better than a whore. When are you going to wise up and stop letting that married limey support you? Get rid of him, become independent again, and start looking for what you really want: a nice American husband!*

Anita bristled. She could tell her mother a thing or two about how she'd risen to sophisticated heights since moving to London. As the mistress of Sir Michael Harding, she was treated to the very best—a lovely home on historic Cheyne Walk, charge accounts at the finest Bond Street shops, winter vacations on the sunniest islands, and most of her time free to do with as she wished. Michael rarely saw her more than two evenings a week, although he did demand that she be at home every night in case he decided to call or stop by unexpectedly. The point was that when Michael entered her life, so did *style*, plus a few other things she wasn't too crazy about, undoubtedly stylish among London's sexually elite, yet sickening too. Sometimes she wondered what would happen if she refused to do those things, but she was too intimidated to find out.

So she did her ostrich act, refusing to face the fact that for Sir Michael Geoffrey Harding (the eighth Earl of Gloucester, chairman of Harding Aerospace, Ltd., graduate of Eton and Oxford, husband of Lady Philippa, father of Andrew and Alexandra, esteemed participant in the weekend fox hunt, and molded product of the archetypal British nanny who wheeled him in a Millson perambulator so he would get off to a fine upper-class start) his girlfriend's major appeal was her willingness to erotically entertain some of his closest friends while he watched behind a gold filigreed screen and jerked off. . . .

The West End crowds were behind her now; lovely Georgian houses loomed up ahead. She could see the medical building jut into the sky. The liver specialist's office was very quiet and imposing, with overstuffed chairs, prints of fox hunts on the walls, and copies of *The Tatler* and *Manchester*

*Guardian* lying about. Nobody spoke above a whisper, including the nurse who asked her not to smoke.

"Smoke? I never smoke!" Anita was horrified by the idea; in restaurants she always asked people to kindly extinguish their cigarettes. "Between my chronic active hepatitis and my irregular menstrual cycle, not to mention a lingering pain on the right side of my face which no one on either side of the Atlantic has been able to diagnose, I have more than my share of health problems. I don't need lung cancer, too."

"No, Miss Schuler, of course not," the nurse said thoughtfully. "The doctor will be with you before long."

Anita tried to make herself comfortable but she felt wet and soggy, thanks to the unexpected arrival of her period that morning.

"Oh dear," Michael said, as his prick came out all bloody. "What hath nature wrought?"

"The curse, it would seem."

He propped himself up on one elbow, his sky-blue eyes fastened upon her. "I thought you got rid of it a week or so ago. Am I dreaming?"

"No, darling, it seems to have gone haywire recently."

"This is a bit awkward, I'm afraid."

"What's awkward?"

"I've invited Dickie Wembley over tonight. You know." He floundered euphemistically. "For a drink."

She could feel her temper rise, but she'd trained herself not to let it show; her livelihood depended on it. "You'll just have to cancel him, then," she said, her voice steady, silky. "Won't you, darling?"

"I thought you liked good old Dickie."

"I adore him." She detested the gross son of a bitch. "But my feelings have nothing to do with the matter, not when I'm bleeding like a stuck pig."

"On the contrary, my dear. Your feelings have everything to do with it. Liking someone means making concessions, extending oneself, being a sport about it all."

A *sport*? she thought with contempt. She hadn't gone ω one of those stoic English schools where the girls learned how to wield a hockey stick and be a sport at the age of six, jolly good, chin up. She felt like saying that where she came from nobody expected a menstruating woman to engage in extracurricular sexual activities. But that wasn't quite true. In

America (as in England and all over the world) women in her line of endeavor were expected to do all the distasteful things that wives, girlfriends, and so-called "respectable" women weren't called upon to do. That was why she was allowed to sleep late, lunch at the most popular restaurants, have tea at the Ritz, stock her boudoir with the most costly perfumes, have a masseur come to her home twice a week, and go to Champney's twice a year.

"Even if I could bring myself to tell Dickie that it's off for tonight, I wouldn't know where to reach him," Michael said as a conciliatory gesture. "He's going to be showing a maiden aunt the sights of London. Sorry, darling."

Anita cursed the fact that she owned a diaphragm, which held back the menstrual flow and would permit her to take part in tonight's bacchanal. But when she thought of her best friend, Lucy Pickles, struck down by a stroke at the age of thirty-four, she thanked her blessings. A team of medical experts had unequivocally linked the stroke to Lucy's use of birth-control pills over the past decade. Once an active energetic woman with her own radio show on the BBC, Lucy was now paralyzed on the right side and could barely pronounce her own name.

"How can I refuse you, sweetheart?" Anita said with a charming smile of capitulation. "What time is Dickie due here?"

"That's my darling, I knew you wouldn't let me down." He tweaked her right nipple, pleased that she'd surrendered without too much of a fuss. Michael didn't like fusses. "You just have your diaphragm in by seven-thirty and no one will be any the wiser. There's a good girl."

Dr. Smythe-Kitson's private office looked like an extension of his outer office, except that the horses on these walls weren't chasing foxes. They were still being readied for the hunt. The sight of them made Anita wince. Michael had stables in Gloucestershire and was obsessed with the foul beasts. Not only did he subscribe to *Horse & Hound*, compete in the trials at Badminton, have a box at Ascot, but he once admitted that being able to go galloping on his favorite mare, Queen's Ransom, made everything else pale by comparison.

"*Everything*?" Anita had pressed him.

"Within reason, darling."

She would not be so easily pacified and refused to go to

bed with any of his perverted friends until he bought her a pair of gold-and-sapphire ear clips at David Morris, apologized profusely, and explained that he hadn't meant to include her in the unfortunate statement. She insisted that he make the disclaimer on bended knees. Watching Sir Michael grovel made Anita feel as though she weren't the only victim in the relationship. Michael could be a victim too, and a damned abject one at that. The only problem was that he liked being abject, it gave him pleasure, whereas all it gave her was another pain—in the liver, in the stomach, in her head, ovaries, on the right side of her face. And resulted in yet another trip to the doctor's office.

"How have you been keeping, Miss Schuler?" Dr. Smythe-Kitson rose and shook her hand. "Feeling a bit better, are we?"

"Quite the contrary, doctor. I regret to say that I'm feeling worse. Much worse."

"Sorry to hear that." He was a portly man in his early sixties, red-faced and apoplectic-looking. "What seems to be the problem, hmmmmm?"

"The usual. Lots of nausea, indigestion, pain around my liver, lassitude, exhaustion. I don't have any energy, it's all I can do to get out of bed in the morning."

"Have you been checking your elimination? Stools still white, urine still that nasty brown, hmmmmmm?"

She nodded. "I'm afraid so."

"And you've been taking your cortisone pills, as directed, hmmmmmmm?"

She nodded again. "I've been taking them, but they don't seem to be working. Maybe I need a higher dosage, although they do give me the most dreadful symptoms. I wake up every morning sweating like a pig and feeling as though the top of my head is about to blow off."

"Unfortunately, those are a couple of the side effects of the drug." He consulted her medical records. "You had your last blood-chemistry tests just about six weeks ago. Why don't you go into the examining room and we'll do another series? Then we'll know exactly where we stand on this stubborn little ailment of yours, hmmmmm?"

She resented his patronizing tone—he made it sound as though she were *willing* a dysfunctioning liver on herself. Nobody could be that self-punishing; it was one of the most dismal illnesses to befall her. And according to Dr. Smythe-Kitson, one of the rarest. Chronic active hepatitis wasn't the infectious kind that one got from eating bad shellfish or from people who already had the disease, nor was it the toxic kind of hepatitis one developed from the overconsumption of alcohol. But it was a serious inflammation of the liver just the same, albeit autoimmune in her case. What that meant, in laymen's terms, was that she seemed to be mysteriously rejecting her own liver.

"Maybe you don't fancy it," her best friend, Lucy Pickles, said before her stroke. "People have been known not to like their noses or legs—I had an aunt who abhorred her knee-caps—so why can't you dislike your liver? You should ask your doctor whether it was very ugly or deformed before you became ill."

"This is no joking matter," Anita sternly reprimanded her. "You have no idea how much I suffer."

When she left Dr. Smythe-Kitson's office, she headed straight for Boots with her new cortisone prescription. The blood tests had shown a distinct disintegration of liver function since her last visit, and Dr. Smythe-Kitson decided to increase her medication to ten milligrams. He told her to come back next month for more tests and warned her that if no improvement was made, he would be forced to perform a blind autopsy to determine why not. Anita had been putting off this horrendous procedure for months now, praying she might be able to avoid it altogether. The reason it was called "blind" was that a huge needle (with a light at the end of it) was plunged straight through the skin blindly, hopefully into the liver. If it missed the liver, it could cause the lungs to collapse.

She wondered what Lucy would have said to that, if only she could speak. Anita missed Lucy's dark humor. For the truth was that chronic active hepatitis had been known to lead to cancer of the liver, even though Dr. Smythe-Kitson tried to steer clear of the subject for fear of frightening her. As though she weren't scared out of her wits already. The prescription paid for, she marched down Oxford Street and over to South Audley, where the most expensive china shop in all of London was located. Thomas Goode's. It was Lucy who introduced her to Thomas Goode's and said that it used to make crested Wedgwood china for Queen Victoria and other monarchs. Anita had purchased her own place settings there, choosing time-tested traditional blue.

It didn't take her long now to select a perfectly garish ceramic flower in yellow and cerise, with avocado-green buds, and ask for it to be sent along to Mrs. Anthony Pickles in Hampstead. While Lucy may have lost her power of speech, she hadn't lost her sense of humor and this ceramic atrocity was bound to give her a giggle. Anita enclosed a card promising to come visit soon; then with her conscience assuaged she walked to the corner and hailed a taxi on Mount Street. Before getting in, she spoke three magic words to the driver.

"The Ritz, please."

Feeling sufficiently fortified to face her mother's latest condemnations, she took the airmail letter out of her purse. To her surprise it wasn't from her mother at all, but from Robert Fingerhood. The rest of Western civilization might know him as the madly clever therapist who'd saved millions of people's sex lives by having them fornicate in hammocks ("The Fingerhood Position"), but Anita knew him fondly as her tarnished prince.

He once helped her through one of the worst periods of her life and for that she would never forget him. Unfortunately, she hadn't loved Fingerhood as much as he loved her and she aborted their affair by asking the airline for a transfer to Chicago. It was a stupid and self-defeating thing to have done, but she used to be the world's biggest romantic, and romantics didn't compromise—they held out for true love. Well, she'd held out all right and look what she ended up with: Michael and Dickie Wembley. Had she stayed in New York back then, Fingerhood would have undoubtedly asked her to marry him and she would be a happy matron today.

Maybe it wasn't too late, she suddenly thought, recalling that in his last Christmas card he said that he was still single and remembered her with great fondness. She eagerly tore open the letter, but seconds later her face fell.

*Darling Anita* (he'd written). *You're never going to believe this* . . .

It was midmorning when Beverly woke up. Thank God the art museum was closed today and she was off from work, she thought as she dragged herself into the kitchen to heat the coffee that her husband had brewed earlier.

She'd pretended to be asleep when Dwight got up, and he made no effort to wake her. Obviously, he didn't want to confront her any more than she wanted to confront him, last night's episode already another bitter wedge between them. She drank two cups of coffee, scanned the Casper *Star Tribune*, then looked at her list of "things to do":

1. Supermarket
2. Post office for mail
3. Women's Support Group
4. Swimming pool—exercise!

The town's swimming pool was indoors, heated, and usually half-empty by the time she got there after her weekly meeting of the Women's Support Group (by far the most interesting item on the list). It was still too cool in northern Wyoming to swim out-of-doors in June, unless you were the stoic adventurous type. Beverly's friends in New York thought she was exactly that when she announced she was moving to Wyoming ten years ago right after her divorce from Peter, but she knew better. The move was her way of hiding from the world and specifically from Peter—hiding her drinking, that is. Her greatest fear was that he would legally take the children away from her if he found out how serious her alcoholic problem was, and she hoped that in a peaceful small-town Western setting her drinking would taper off. It didn't. Not for a long time, anyway.

The ringing of the telephone made Beverly's heart leap and the usual thought race through her mind. *Maybe it's Sally*. But it wasn't Sally. It was Eunice, the counselor who ran the Women's Support Group.

"I have a favor to ask of you," Eunice said quickly. "I won't be able to supervise today's session—problems at home—and I wondered if you would take over for me."

"Me?" Beverly stared dumbly at the painting that hung above the sofa: it was of Don Ameche and Alice Faye on horseback. She had bought it from Simone's ex-husband years ago, when they all lived in New York. "But I'm not professionally qualified, Eunice. I wouldn't know what to do."

"You let the other women start talking about what's on

their minds, and if someone goes off on a detour, you gently steer the conversation back on track.''

"You make it sound so simple." In the painting, Alice Faye had the mustache—not Don Ameche. Beverly smiled in spite of herself. ''I'm sure there's more to it than you're admitting.''

"Of course there is, but who says every session has to be a paragon of group therapy? It's better than canceling altogether. don't you agree?''

Beverly did, especially since she'd decided to tell the group about Dwight's sexual coercion and physical abuse. Until now she'd kept it to herself, ashamed to admit what she had been putting up with, but after last night she was afraid to go on holding it all in. It was too much to deal with alone; she needed help, advice, guidance. But without Eunice, how much guidance could she expect?

"I don't run the group," Eunice said, as though reading her mind. "The group belongs to you and every other woman who participates. The real interaction is among you women, that's where you get your strength: from each other. I'm just the lady who makes an occasional suggestion. I'm sure you'll do a fine job.''

By the time Beverly drove into town that afternoon, the sky was overcast and it had grown colder. She was glad. Her long-sleeved green sweater didn't seem inappropriate and nobody would suspect the number of bruises it covered.

Considering last night's tussle with Dwight, she looked pretty good and it wasn't because of heavy makeup either. Except for a dab of Touch Stick to cover some of her more prominent freckles and a light layer of Revlon's Silk-On-Velvet lip gloss, her face was as innocent as a baby's. She never bothered with her hair. Red, naturally curly and thick, it cascaded over her shoulders with all the freedom and abundance of hair that hadn't been damaged, stripped, dyed, bleached, frosted, permed, highlighted, lowlighted, straightened, set, stretched, or heat-dried most of her life. Beverly wasn't chic and she knew it, but she had something that many chic women didn't: a smoldering sex appeal. Even when she lived in New York, she hadn't dressed in the latest styles or tried to camouflage her unfashionably large breasts. That was why other women seldom gave her a passing glance, whereas men spotted the sensuality right away and managed to communicate their desire. They had been communicating it for as long as Beverly could remember, except for her first husband, who preferred skin and bones.

She parked the Ford at the corner of Main and Boysen and crossed over to Janeway's Supermarket. Janeway's and Simpson's were the two supermarkets in town and Dwight had given her firm instructions to divide her grocery money between them as evenly as possible. That was because both stores ran ads in the Williams *Independent Herald* and it wasn't a good idea to antagonize a regular advertiser. After what happened yesterday, Beverly was more afraid of antagonizing Dwight than anyone. When he returned home around midnight he was not only drunk, but enraged with the proprietor of the local hardware store for having canceled his half-page ad in the *Herald*, of which Dwight was editor, general manager, and twenty-five-percent owner.

"The son of a bitch said his ad wasn't pulling in any new customers, because there *aren't* any new customers in a town this small," Dwight angrily reported as he staggered to the liquor cabinet for another shot of bourbon. "The son of a bitch said that the only other hardware store within fifty miles of here is so badly equipped that it doesn't even sell building supplies! So if he doesn't have any goddamned competition—he barks at me—then why the hell is he wasting good money on a half-page ad every week?"

"It sounds logical," Beverly made the mistake of replying.

"Oh, it sounds *logical*, does it?" He stared at her with sneering contempt, his lips white, clenched. "What you mean is that I'm not a good enough salesman to hang on to a lucrative advertiser, don't you?"

"No, that's not what I meant at all. Honestly, darling. I meant that if you look at it through his eyes, he has a point."

"And *I* don't, I suppose? Trying to make a go of this lousy hick paper so I can support my elegant wife in the style to which she's long been accustomed isn't a valid enough point for you?"

"I didn't say that."

"But it's what you meant."

"No, Dwight, it wasn't." Fear began to rise within her as she saw the flush of hatred on his face, saw the vein throbbing in his neck, felt his hot anger. "I swear it wasn't."

"Don't bullshit me, Beverly, I can see right through you.

It's interesting how you stick up for everyone except your own husband, it's fascinating how you're able to understand everyone's point of view except mine. It's absolutely unbelievable how you think everyone is right, but not yours truly. That's quite an opinion you have of me: ineffectual, incompetent, a real loser.''

"I don't think you're a loser." She suddenly realized that *he* thought so, and that terrified her even more. "I never said you were a loser, Dwight."

"You don't have to, it's written all over your pathetic face. You're sorry you married me, aren't you? You probably wish you were still married to your first husband, Mr. Moneybags. Peter may have been a faggot, but at least he knew how to rake in the old do-re-mi. Isn't that what you're thinking? How much better off you were with Peter Northrop than with me? Peter would have known how to keep that hardware-store proprietor from canceling his ad, wouldn't he? Peter might like to screw young boys in the ass, but he wouldn't lose a good advertising account. Isn't that what's running through your mind? Admit it!"

"Stop torturing me, it's not true." She lit a cigarette to help ease the shaking. "I haven't thought of Peter in years. Why do you bring him up every time you've had too much to drink?"

"I may have had too much to drink but I'm not deaf, dumb, and blind," he said, throwing back another bourbon. "I know when my own wife is so sexually turned off that she can't bear for me to touch her. I'm not that stupid, Beverly."

"No one said you were stupid. No one said you were a poor salesman. I don't know why you have these terrible opinions about yourself."

"Oh, it's all in my mind, I suppose? I'm denigrating myself for no reason at all, is that it? Well, just tell me something, wife of mine. How long has it been since you've wanted to make love to me? Six months? A year? Ever since you stopped drinking two years ago and turned into Mary Poppins? Isn't that when you became disgusted with me? In other words, without the numbing effect of alcohol, you're sexually revolted by me. Isn't that a fact?"

Before she could refute his accusations, he knocked the cigarette out of her hand and ground it into the rug with his heel. Then he grabbed her by her long red hair and tried to

kiss her. Beverly writhed in his tight hold, she tried to avert
her head, she couldn't stand the smell of bourbon, the poison-
ous smell of his rage, of her own sickening and mounting
fear. He couldn't stand her fear either.

"*What the hell are you afraid of?*" he shouted angrily.
"I'm your husband, not some mad rapist. Or maybe that's
what you'd like. Is that what turns you on? Violence?"

"No, no." She was trembling, shaking. "No, Dwight,
no!"

"Yes, I can see it in your eyes." He cracked her across the
face. "Don't tell me it doesn't excite you, you bitch. You
love it, you're begging for it."

She was too terrified to refute him and too terrified to agree
with him. No matter what she said or did, he twisted it
around to suit his own tormented needs. She tried to look
firm and assertive, not frightened; she tried to stare him down
and pretend she wasn't afraid. It seemed to work, a little bit
anyway, because he didn't hit her again. Instead he managed
to pin her against the wall; then he kissed her with a furious
urgency as though by the sheer force of his will he could
drown out those voices of anxiety and insecurity that had
plagued him for so many years. Afterward he dragged her up
to the bedroom, ripped off her clothes, threw her across the
chenille spread, and made her submit to him. His hands were
hard against her soft and pliable flesh.

"You bitch," he muttered, just before he came. "You
damned cold, rich little bitch. One of these days I'm going to
fuck you unconscious." Then he pulled it out of her and
came vindictively, drunkenly, all over her face. . . .

"Good afternoon, Mrs. Kirby." The produce clerk came
bounding over as she was selecting peaches and tried not to
stare at her well-filled sweater. "That was a wonderful idea
of Mr. Kirby's—to use a photograph of a different clerk in
Janeway's ad each week. Kind of makes the shoppers feel
like they know us personally and can trust us to suggest the
best buys. He's a smart businessman, your husband."

Beverly nodded, wondering why she had married two men
who were undeniably clever and undeniably difficult.

"Avocados just in from California." The produce clerk
pointed proudly to a bin at the far end. "Thirty-nine cents a
pound. Ripe."

Despite the fact that neither she nor Dwight was crazy

about avocados, she selected two of the dark green lumps and smiled back at the clerk. Anything to keep Janeway's and their employees happy, she thought, aware that Dwight was trying to get them to increase their advertising from one to two pages. She hoped he succeeded. Maybe if he had more tangible evidence of his own worth, his self-confidence would grow, his alcoholic consumption would decrease, and his violent outbursts would come to a halt. Or maybe his problem had deeper roots than either of them suspected.

Beverly knew so little about the subject of wife abuse that up until her own experience she assumed it only existed among the lower, badly educated classes. And yet neither she nor Dwight fell into that category. He was from a solid middle-class ranching family who lost their money during the Depression, yet managed to send their only son to college. And Beverly was from a wealthy Salt Lake City family, where violence was unknown. She had never seen her father or older brother raise a hand against a woman and would have been shocked if either one had done so. She was shocked the first time Dwight raised his hand to her, appalled, confused. Yes, she'd been all of those things but she'd never been furious. Did she feel so guilty about her loss of sexual desire that she secretly believed she *deserved* to be struck?

After putting her groceries in back of the Ford, she realized that she barely had enough time to pick up the mail before heading for the counseling center. The FBI's "Ten Most Wanted" still adorned the bulletin board at the post office, as did a large black-lettered sign which read: "WE IN WILLIAMS BELIEVE IN GOD, AMERICA, AND THE FLAG." Can't argue with that, Beverly thought, wishing she didn't get a fluttery feeling every time she set foot in here, and prayed there would be a letter from Sally. There hadn't been one for the last two years, not since Sally disappeared from Radcliffe in her freshman term.

Beverly was stunned when she learned the news, grieved, inconsolable, for in a way it was more like Sally's disappearance from the world. One minute her daughter was a conscientious student who'd gotten straight A's, made the dean's list, and was one of the most popular girls in the quad. And the next minute she was gone, after telling her roommate that she was meeting somebody for dinner at Locke Ober's. No one could understand what happened.

Dwight had been wonderful throughout the ordeal, support-
ive and consoling. So had her ex-husband and her son,
recently admitted to Harvard. But nothing could console
Beverly. She blamed herself for Sally's defection, felt certain
she'd run away to punish her for being a drunk and irresponsible mother. And when Dwight offered her a brandy for her
nerves, she pushed the glass away revolted. She hadn't touched
a drop since. Nonetheless she still woke up in the middle of
the night, heart thumping, wondering if tall, slender, dark-
haired, dark-eyed Sally were alive or dead. And if alive, how
was she living?

To the best of Beverly's knowledge, Sally had never voiced
any particular career ambitions, and whenever Beverly asked
her what she wanted to do with her life, Sally grew whimsical,
often defiant.

"Maybe I'll become the first woman president of the United
States," she once said. "Or maybe I'll start swimming in
Scotch, like you. Who knows? Who cares?"

"I care," Beverly said, frightened, hung-over. "You really hate my drinking, don't you?"

Sally looked at her with disgust. "What do *you* think,
Mother?"

"I don't understand how someone so intelligent can have
so little interest in the world around her," Beverly persisted,
trying to ignore her daughter's reproach. "Surely, there's
something you want to do."

"Yes. Turn twenty-one, so I can dip into my trust fund
and get the hell out of Wyoming." She was seventeen at the
time. "The sooner I leave this two-horse town, the better."

Beverly sighed. Her only consolation was that Sally still
had four years of college in which to change her mind, shape
up. "Perhaps you'll make a successful career out of marriage
and motherhood," she lamely suggested.

"That will be the day!" Sally sneered.

Sally was twenty now, and Beverly wondered how she was
supporting herself. Did she have a respectable job? Had she
become a prostitute? Joined the Moonies? Was she on drugs?
Was she working in pornographic movies? (She'd seen
*Hardcore* and shuddered.) Maybe, despite her disclaimer, she
had gotten married or was living with someone.

Beverly prayed she was well. Once, on a false lead, she
had to try to identify a female victim who'd been murdered in

a nearby town, but the minute they drew back the sheet she knew it wasn't her daughter. Sally had a prominent beauty mark on her left cheek.

"What on earth?" Beverly now said, aloud.

For mixed in with the latest issue of *Field & Stream* and a bill from Pacific Power & Light was a letter from Robert Fingerhood! Beverly couldn't imagine what he wanted, but she was curious, since he never sent more than an annual Christmas card. Certain people affect our lives so deeply that they're never the same again and Fingerhood had affected hers that way. He was indirectly responsible for the dissolution of her first marriage. If not for him, she might still be married to Peter Northrop, still be living in New York (or Paris, where Peter now made his home); she most certainly would not be buried in a small town in Wyoming with an abusive husband and a runaway daughter.

At the bottom of his last Christmas card the tall, dark, wildly attractive Fingerhood had written: "Have you read my book? It sold over half a million copies in hard cover and is going to be made into a movie."

While she hadn't gotten around to reading *The Fingerhood Position*, she'd heard enough about its revolutionary theory (who hadn't?). *Newsweek* claimed that Fingerhood was farther out on a genital limb than *The G Spot*, while *Time* magazine playfully dubbed him "Dr. Sex," and all because of his suggestion that couples make love in hammocks to achieve what he called "transcendental orgasm." Beverly found it hard to imagine anyone actually filming *The Fingerhood Position*, although if they could film David Reuben's *Everything You Always Wanted to Know About Sex*, maybe she was wrong.

She glanced at her watch, stuffed the mail into her shoulder bag, determined to read Fingerhood's letter before the Women's Support Group got under way. Then she all but ran to Bald Eagle Street, where the counseling center stood. It was a yellow one-story structure built in the late forties and had originally housed the Chamber of Commerce, but as the town grew and prospered, the Chamber of Commerce moved to larger quarters and the counseling center was formed.

The room was light, cheerful, its walls covered with crayon drawings done by children in the kindergarten classes. The women sat on folding chairs in a circle, their purses on the floor next to them, ashtrays in laps, a few knitted, most wore blue jeans and sweaters or T-shirts. Beverly counted eleven women including herself. Someone was missing.

"Where's Martha?" she asked.

"Ladies' room emergency," a brunette in a red windbreaker replied. "She'll be back in a sec."

A sec was all Beverly needed. She ripped open Fingerhood's letter and took out a sheet of white embossed stationery. The first words brought a smile to her Silk-on-Velvet lips.

*Hi, Toots. Guess what? I'm finally getting married.*

Lou stood in the kitchen of her rambling West End Avenue apartment looking seriously sophisticated in a padded shoulder Norma Kamali jumpsuit, trying to make Lobster en Bellevue Parisienne for twenty-eight people, and fuming because Vanessa hadn't bothered to come home last night or had the decency to call this morning to say she was still alive.

God knew whose bed she was in doing what lascivious things, Lou thought, torn between the greenest jealousy and the blackest outrage. While the jealousy was a gut-wrenching personal matter, the outrage was strictly professional and undeniably justified. She and Vanessa had started their catering business together and were supposed to be equal partners all the way down the line, but whenever it suited Vanessa she simply disappeared overnight, leaving Lou to mop up whatever culinary chores there happened to be.

"It's not fair," she said to her cat, Liberation, who sat on a window ledge watching birds. "It's thoughtless, inconsiderate, amateurish, and I'll be damned if she gets away with it!"

Lou felt like screaming. She felt like banging her head against the array of skillets, saucepans, roasters, griddles, and chicken fryers that covered one entire wall of the efficiently designed kitchen. Tonight was the night they were catering a sit-down dinner for twenty-eight of New York's most beautiful, kvetchy, hard-to-please people. The dinner was being given by a famous evening-wear designer whom Lou had met when she was a roving reporter for *The Rag*, covering New York's most prestigious events. Those years spent working for the arbiter of world fashion had had a lasting effect upon her.

A trim brunette whose weight never fluctuated more than a pound or two in either direction, Lou may have traded in her secure salaried job for risky self-employment, but she never traded in her pride in looking chic and pulled-together—even if she was only helping Vanessa make a batch of cream-puff swans for the freezer. At the moment she was straining four and a half quarts of fish aspic through a sieve lined with flannel. Later, she would pour the aspic over chilled medallions of lobster.

The telephone buzzed.

"Some Like It Hot," Lou said, trying to sound cheerful and unperturbed. "Can I help you?"

"I wanted to make sure that everything was running on schedule," the evening-wear designer mumbled in a nervous French accent. "Not that I don't have absolute confidence in you, Lou darling, but one does tend to become a bit *inquiet* before these damned sit-down affairs."

Jean Pierre Mallarmé had recently been written up in *W* and lived in an all-black Angelo Donghia duplex, with all-white marble bathrooms. He pretended to be from Lyons (actually he was from Fargo, North Dakota) and for as long as Lou had known him he managed to get at least three French words into the conversation. She always counted.

"Stop worrying, Jean Pierre." She turned her attention from the aspic to the lobsters, which had been boiled and chilled into angry red submission—all ten of them. "It's going to be a gorgeous dinner, smooth as silk. I promise."

"Then I can expect you and your friend at four *avec* all the goodies, can I not? Please say yes, before my skin dries up again. It always dries when I'm anxious."

She had one lobster on its back and was trimming around the inner edge of the shell. "Yes," she said.

"What about the bartender?" Jean Pierre's voice had risen an octave. "You didn't *oublier* that I need a bartender tonight, did you? I liked the one you brought last time, so sweet and efficient and such a cute ass. Wherever do you find them, darling?"

The conversation was over, she thought, his three French words were up. "Just relax, Jean Pierre, and leave the worrying to me and Vanessa. We're going to overwhelm you with a simply fabulous dinner. See you later, sweetie."

Unlike ninety-nine percent of their clients Jean Pierre never wanted to select the menu himself, he wanted to be surprised. And he paid handsomely for the privilege (they would clear about a thousand dollars on tonight's meal). Lou looked at the menu Scotch-taped to one of the huge stainless-steel refrigerator doors:

- Lobster en Bellevue Parisienne with Salade Russe (to start)
- Crown roast of lamb filled with sautéd mushrooms and cherry tomatoes
- Rice pilaf with pine nuts
- Julienne of endive & watercress salad
- Whole-wheat crescent rolls
- Vanessa's special strawberry chiffon pie

Vanessa had baked six pies with the secret ingredient she perversely refused to divulge to anyone, including Lou, and would complete their decoration once they got to Jean Pierre's. They always served the pie on entrée plates, so that extra whole strawberries could be piled alongside each slice for a spectacular glistening red effect which clients seemed to adore.

One of the first lessons Lou had learned when they launched Some Like It Hot a couple of years ago was that presentation counted for as much as culinary expertise. In order to flourish in the cutthroat world of New York catering, both qualities were necessary in abundance and that was probably why they had become so successful so quickly: because Vanessa was a gifted, imaginative, top-notch chef whose creations were enhanced by Lou's aesthetic and discerning eye. The combination was pure magic.

Tonight, Lou had decided, the waiters would wear red cummerbunds, red carnations in their tuxedo lapels, and serve dinner on red linen tablecloths using the whitest bone china she could rent. The effect would be gloriously dramatic against Jean Pierre's ebony apartment. Flower displays on each of the four round tables would consist exclusively of red and white roses. And for the *sine qua non*, she had dug up an art-deco black marble fountain and was going to fill it with more roses. Jean Pierre Mallarmé (a.k.a. Johnny Miller) would plotz when he saw the *Flying Down to Rio* fountain and probably offer to buy it from her afterward. If not, she would install it right here in her country kitchen and fill it with lemons and oranges, which Vanessa used tons of in her cooking.

Lou took a swig of cold breakfast coffee and went back to

extracting meat from the ten lobsters, lined up on a long butcher-block worktable. Aside from the fact that she was stuck with an unfamiliar recipe, no help, and no culinary talent of her own, she felt morbidly jealous at the thought of Vanessa being in bed with another woman, a stranger whom she'd picked up at one of those dike bars she liked to frequent and which Lou abhorred. Vanessa claimed that that was because she hadn't committed herself to being a lesbian.

"There's a part of you left over from the straight world that is horrified by the switch you've made," Vanessa recently informed her. "It hasn't yet accepted you as a lover of women, and maybe it never will. In fact, that other part thinks that what you're doing is downright disgusting, perverted, ugly, demented, and neurotic. It's still hoping that one of these days you'll shape up and go back where you belong— the world of men. You remember men, don't you, Lou? Those funny broad-shouldered people who shave and have been victimizing us since time began."

The awful part about the accusation was that on a certain subterranean level which Lou felt deeply ashamed of, Vanessa was right. Not that she ever intended to go back to that world, but every once in a while when they were making love a cloud of despair would settle upon her and shriek, *What, in God's name, are you doing?* She told herself that was only natural, since she'd been thirty-seven when she came out of the closet, as opposed to Vanessa, who'd never been in and was technically still a virgin. Unsullied by a man's prick.

The telephone rang twice more by the time she finished garnishing the goddamned Lobster en Bellevue Parisienne with stuffed hard-boiled eggs, artichoke hearts, and chopped aspic, covered it with plastic wrap, and put it in the second refrigerator along with the rest of Jean Pierre's fare. Just as she was debating whether to have lunch first or wash forty-two cups of salad greens, a familiar voice rang out behind her.

"Look who's home!"

She whirled around to face Vanessa, radiant and smiling, her hair woven into a long thick braid that hung down to her waist. Vanessa didn't care whether the style suited her, any more than she appeared to care whether her truancy had caused Lou any pain or anguish. If only I didn't love her so much, Lou thought, if only I weren't so grateful to see her back unharmed.

"I guess you forgot about Jean Pierre's dinner party tonight," she said.

"Not at all. My apologies for leaving you with the lobsters."

Lou felt like throttling the slim figure wearing yesterday's duck pants, crumpled T-shirt, and the afterglow of lovemaking. In sheer self-defense, she began to wash the forty-two cups of salad greens.

"Guess who you've got a letter from?" Vanessa had picked up the mail. "Your old flame, Robert Fingerhood, sex counselor to the masses. Do you really think that making love in a hammock is a way of transcending the earth's boundaries?"

"I wouldn't know. I haven't been in too many hammocks lately."

"Okay, okay. Mea culpa. I walked out without telling you where I was going. I left you with the lousy lobsters and now I'm not giving you a hand with the salad. But I'll make it up, I promise." Vanessa opened the refrigerator and poured herself a glass of milk. "Aren't you curious about what Fingerhood wants?"

Actually, Lou was more curious about where Vanessa had been and who she'd been with than why Dr. Sex was writing to her after so long. The last time they laid eyes on each other was fifteen years ago, and as far as she was concerned, another fifteen could go by. She never understood why he continued to send Christmas cards every year when she continued to ignore them. Perhaps he kept an index file on all his old girlfriends; it wouldn't have surprised her one bit. Except that he would need an entire room—if not a building—for such a file.

"I would have called to let you know I was okay," Vanessa said, awkwardly trying to make amends. "But believe it or not, the phone was disconnected."

"You should try associating with more solvent people."

"No, it wasn't financial. The lady in question happens to be moving today. I'm sorry if you were worried."

She looked so guileless, Lou thought, so innocent with those big hazel eyes fringed by golden lashes, not a speck of makeup on her lightly tanned face. She looked like a schoolgirl home for lunch, rather than a twenty-eight-year-old woman who had just spent the night with another woman and left her lover holding the bag in more ways than one.

"I'm not interested in your explanations, Vanessa. I'd like some consideration for a change. This is getting to be a habit with you, a bad habit, leaving me with all the dirty work while you're off chasing lanky strangers. And I want you to know that I don't intend to put up with it."

"She wasn't lanky," Vanessa maliciously replied. "She was five-feet-four and quite curvaceous. What are you trying to do? Make me feel guilty?"

"Yes, goddammit, you *are* guilty. Of being unfaithful to me and of shirking your responsibilities. You might have told me that you planned to stay out all night. I would have prepared the lobsters yesterday and then slept late this morning. We won't be finished at Jean Pierre's until well after midnight and I'm half-bushed already, thanks to you and your thoughtlessness."

"Try taking vitamins and try telling the truth." Vanessa had turned sullen. "You're not upset about the lobsters, you're upset because I was with someone else. You're jealous."

"You bet I am. Is that so unnatural? I love you. Why shouldn't I be jealous?"

"Oh no you don't. Don't try to justify your possessiveness on the grounds of love, because I refuse to be drawn into that fishy net. You think you're some paragon of virtue because you never pick strangers up at bars, don't you? Did it ever occur to you that you might be too tediously faithful for my taste? That it might not bother me one iota if you didn't make me the center of your life? That I might actually feel relieved? I love you, but you can be smothering at times. I'm going to take a shower and cool off." She marched out of the kitchen, her resentment echoing down the long corridor. "It's claustrophobic living with you, Ms. Forever Faithful."

Lou felt like throwing the salad greens after her, all forty-two cups of them. *Ms. Forever Faithful.* What a dismal picture that phrase conjured up. She shuddered to think it described her accurately. It couldn't, she wasn't like that, she was better than that (wasn't she?). But because she had nobody to turn to for a second opinion, there was a tendency to believe the accusation. It was one of the perils of working so exclusively with the person she loved, and she wondered whether it had been a mistake to go into business with Vanessa.

Although starting Some Like It Hot had been Lou's brainstorm, of course she couldn't have done it alone. She may have had the financial shrewdness, social contacts, and flair for dramatic presentation, but Vanessa had the indispensable and ingenious cooking skills. Still, maybe it was time for a change. Maybe she should buy Vanessa out and find herself another partner, one with whom she wasn't romantically involved.

Lou toyed with the idea. She didn't much like it, she felt superstitious about fooling around with a winning combination. She felt as though she would be cutting off her nose to spite her face. Was she approaching this all wrong? Perhaps instead of getting rid of Vanessa the cook, she should get rid of Vanessa the lover.

"I've always put work first," she said to Liberation. "I'd rather save my business than my love life. Does that make me a monster?" And yet if she were a man her decision would seem admirable, commendable, enterprising. Lou smiled bitterly and opened Fingerhood's letter.

*I'm getting married at the end of the month. Can you come to the wedding? Better yet, can you cater the wedding?*

Aside from learning that the biggest playboy she'd ever met was relinquishing his precious bachelorhood, she was struck by another inconsistency. Nowhere in the letter did he mention the name or identity of his bride-to-be. It was a glaring omission, egocentric and thoughtless, almost as if he were planning to marry himself. Typical of him. Her first reaction to both requests was to tell him to go screw himself. Her second reaction was to go for a fast jog. She changed into her Jogbra, running shorts, and Nikes. There wasn't time for the park; she would have to settle for the Drive.

The minute Lou hit the street, she felt better. There was nothing like air, even the putrid New York variety, to put things in perspective. She ran north for a while, then cut across Ninety-sixth Street. A man waiting for a bus tried to pick her up by tagging after her and asking her to have dinner with him. He was husky, blue-eyed, not bad-looking, and had a Leica over his shoulder.

"I'm a free-lance photographer." His shirtsleeves were

rolled up and he had blond hair at the wrists; it glistened in the sunlight. "I adore brunettes with trim bodies."

"Sorry, but I'm otherwise involved," she said, frowning. "Thanks just the same."

She left him standing in front of the Second Presbyterian Church and then headed south on Central Park West, zigzagging her way home. She was sweating and out of breath when she let herself into the apartment, but she'd changed her mind about Fingerhood's wedding. "I'm going to cater it, get paid for it, and dig up a new lover all at the same time," she told Liberation, who was still sitting on the window ledge.

Somewhere on Riverside Drive it had hit her that a new lover didn't necessarily mean a permanent long-range one; maybe all that was needed (to throw the fear of God into Vanessa) was a sizzling short-lived romance. With a man. And since all the men she met were either married, fell into the Jean Pierre category, or possibly were mad rapists lurking at bus stops, what better hunting grounds could she ask for than an old-fashioned June wedding?

Lou grinned, poured herself a glass of wine, and toasted her own ingenuity. She had forgotten to eat lunch, and the wine went straight to her head. It felt good being tipsy at two in the afternoon, it felt lovely in fact. She looked at the clock again, appalled. *Two!* She hadn't finished washing Jean Pierre's salad greens. In a few more hours she and Vanessa had to have the van loaded, ready to drive across town to Park Avenue and Sixty-third Street with tonight's dinner. They would never make it unless she sprang into action right now. She poured out the wine, started to make coffee, decided to wash the salad greens in the bathtub. And meanwhile, where the hell was Vanessa? How long could a shower take? What sins of last night was she scrubbing away?

Lou marched down the corridor and pushed open the door to Vanessa's bedroom, without knocking. As usual, the sign over the bed unnerved her: LIB MEANS NEVER HAVING TO SAY YOU CAME. But right now she was too angry to think of its ominous implications.

"Goddammit, Vanessa, this procrastination of yours has gone far—!"

To her surprise, Vanessa lay on the blue-and-white-checked gingham spread sound asleep, her arm curled around a blue-and-white-checked gingham pillow, her mouth slightly open,

her clothes strewn on the floor. Simone floated into view.
Not the real-life Simone, but her celluloid counterpart asleep
in a scene of *Charmer*, her arm similarly curled. Lou wondered whether she'd been attracted to Simone years ago, but
she doubted it. Women never used to interest her that way
and she would have laughed if anyone had said that she
would change her tune. She sure wasn't laughing now.

She looked at Vanessa's slender, small-breasted body. It
had never seemed so vulnerable, so lovable, so seductively
available. Her anger melted into desire, quick and pulsating,
her throat felt dry, and a vein throbbed in her neck. Moments
like this were worth everything, she thought in a frenzy,
everything. She got out of her clothes and slid into bed next
to Vanessa, who still hadn't moved. Lou put a finger on her
left nipple and kissed her lips at the same time. Vanessa
opened her golden-lashed eyes and smiled teasingly.

"I wondered what was taking you so long," she said,
spreading her tanned legs and kissing Lou back.

*What, in God's name, are you doing?* an inner voice
screamed.

# 2

Simone felt so excited by Robert Fingerhood's invitation, so giddy and delirious at the prospect of going to New York to attend a real honest-to-goodness wedding, that she nearly had three automobile accidents on her way to Beverly Hills. They were all caused by her proclivity for kamikaze lane changing and infuriated other motorists to such a degree that she was showered with insults as she went racing by.

*"Learn to drive, lady."*

*"Wake up, asshole."*

*"Where'd you get your license? Tijuana?"*

People were so infantile, she thought as she swerved into the left-hand lane without looking behind her or signaling. A man in a passing Mercedes gave her the finger, his face blue with fury.

*"Crazy dumb broad."*

Simone waved at him and continued on past the Sunset Boulevard exit, having decided to skip her exercise class today. She could work on her gluteus medius some other time; what she needed now was a good clothes fix. Like an alcoholic heading straight for the nearest bar, Simone, the compulsive shopper, turned off on Wilshire and headed straight for her favorite department store, gleaming Neiman Marcus, determined to buy out the place. Her appearance caused a minor sensation among the salespeople, who weren't used to seeing movie stars come charging in at eleven in the morning (in Beverly Hills nobody of consequence was visible until after lunch) unaccompanied and unescorted, snatching up everything they could lay their hands on.

*So the fuck-up was finally getting married*, she thought as she grabbed velvet jumpsuits and Charmeuse evening dresses, crocheted bed jackets and carioca-sleeved nightgowns, satin shirts and cotton chambray skirts, silk tunic sweaters and pleated linen pants. *So he finally found someone tall enough, gorgeous enough, smart enough, and dumb enough to say "I do."*

The fact that he hadn't announced who that someone was didn't surprise Simone. The poor girl would be lucky if she got a taste of her own wedding cake, with an egomaniac like that for a husband. Simone giggled on the escalator. Yes indeed, this was going to be one ceremony where the bride-groom would steal all the honors, hog the limelight, and was conceivably having *his* hair done for the big event.

"Aren't you Simone?" a saleswoman gushed after she had ordered bikini panties in every shade they came in, which was eleven. "Or am I dreaming?"

"*C'est moi, madame.*"

Simone gave her a big-celebrity smile, pleased by all the attention she was getting. She loved being looked at, she loved being a movie star, at times like this it was more fun than anything she could imagine, and the terror of losing her exalted position engulfed her again.

"You're my favorite actress," the saleswoman declared. "I saw *Charmer* three times. You were wonderful in it, captivating. Are you going to make another movie soon?"

"Don't tell anyone because it hasn't been officially announced yet, but I'm going to star in *Rockabye Princess*," she said, throwing caution and truth to the winds. "I play a Danish princess who gets bored with all that stuffy palace rigmarole, runs away to America, and becomes a famous rock star. I'm not sure whether I'll use my own voice or whether they'll dub, but either way I get to sing some sizzling new songs." The fact that she couldn't carry a tune to save her life didn't stop her from making this outrageous statement.

"Who's your leading man going to be? What kind of part does he have?"

"We're hoping for Ryan O'Neal or Donald Sutherland. He plays a small-town disc jockey who discovers me and then becomes my manager-lover. I mean, he discovers my singing talent but has no idea of my true identity until the Danish secret police come looking for me."

"Colin McKenna."

"Excuse me?"

"That's who your leading man should be." A dreamy expression spread over the saleswoman's middle-aged face.

"In my opinion, Colin McKenna is the sexiest actor on television. You and he would make a sensational movie team, has anyone told you that?"

"No one."

Simone gagged at the prospect of having to kiss Colin, even before a camera and crew of technicians. His breath stank of Pernod, which he guzzled like water whenever he wanted to come down from coke. And coke made his nose drip. Kissing Colin McKenna would be like kissing a dirty, germ-laden handkerchief. But those weren't her only objections to America's most popular TV star. Far from it.

When she moved into the Malibu house four years ago, she had tried to make friends with Colin. At first she was simply awed and overwhelmed by him, and wanted him to like her. Later (after she stopped being awed), she continued trying because he was Jimmy's buddy and she wanted to keep the peace. She'd heard all the nostalgic stories of Jimmy and Colin's early days in Hollywood and how they both had struggled to make it big, while working at menial jobs and often sharing the same pair of shoes. Jimmy said that if not for Colin, he could never have survived those lean and painful years.

"Colin saved my ass," Jimmy told her. "I was ready to throw in the sponge on more than one dismal occasion, but he wouldn't let me. He boosted my morale, assured me I had talent, said he'd beat the shit out of me if I gave up. And he would have, too. Then, when he got his big break in *Arizona Pete*, he assumed all expenses for the house so I was free to write. I mean, suddenly he was a *star*—he could have bought himself a gorgeous mansion in Bel Air, but he didn't. The loyal son of a bitch stayed right here and, in effect, supported me until I could support myself."

"Like a wife."

"Yeah, but without the headaches."

In time Simone found herself growing jealous of the bond that existed between the two men. It seemed to her that even though Colin and Jimmy were basically heterosexual, they were far closer than she and Jimmy were. *They* were the couple, *she* was the third party. And no matter what she did to try to usurp the hold that Colin exerted over Jimmy, she couldn't make a dent in it. Then one day she overheard Colin telling Jimmy to get rid of her. It sounded like a conversation they'd had before.

"She's an old bag," Colin said in his usual crude manner. "This town is crawling with gorgeous, sexy, *young* chicks who would give anything for a roll in the hay with a hot screenwriter like you. Simone is dynamite on screen, I grant you, but off screen she's strictly from dullsville. What do you need her and those snotty twins for? Give her her walking papers, man, and latch onto a little swinging freedom. Between the two of us, we'll turn this place into a pleasure palace."

"It's not as simple as that," Jimmy said uncomfortably.

"Why the fuck not?"

"I'm in love with her."

"Don't shit me, this is your old buddy you're talking to. The chick's history, man. Since when did you start getting hung up on chicks with gray-haired cunts?"

"It's not gray, it's lavender—same as the hair on her head. We dyed it together with vegetable dye." His voice took on a wistful tone.

"I don't capish," Colin jeered. "You're either never home or you're holed up writing, you barely see her as it is, you don't seem to *want* to see her. So what's this love business? All she's doing is cramping our style. If she weren't here, you wouldn't have to shlep to Gardena for poker. You could have an all-night poker game right here on the premises. You'd be dealing in one room and I'd be banging my brains out in another, just like the good old days. Remember?"

"Only too well," Jimmy said, sounding more uncomfortable by the second. "That's what I'm afraid would happen again. Anarchy. Simone and the twins give me a sense of family, stability, discipline. They keep me from totally burying myself in poker. You know how addicted I am to the game, it's a disease with me. If Simone and the kids left, I'd be eating, sleeping, and drinking cards twenty-four hours a day. Don't you understand, Colin? She's my *control*."

"She's your fucking *funeral*," Colin said. . . .

Simone now smiled at the lingerie saleswoman with all the goodwill she could muster. "I'm sure you mean well by suggesting that I co-star with Mr. McKenna in *Rockabye Princess*, but he's never made a movie in his life. A feature movie, that is. And then there's his age: he's only twenty-five." She thought of his crack about her gray-haired cunt, and winced. "Don't you think he's just the tiniest bit too young for me?"

"A few years here and there don't matter if the magic is right. Remember those famous movie teams? Spencer Tracy and Katharine Hepburn, William Powell and Myrna Loy, Rock Hudson and Doris Day, Humphrey Bogart and Lauren Bacall. Those combinations were magic. Do you know why?"

"You left out Fred Astaire and Ginger Rogers. No. Why?"

"Because of the way the particular actor *looked* at the particular actress. There was something in his look that made the actress seem far more glamorous and alluring than she would have been with another leading man. When Spencer Tracy gave Katharine Hepburn one of those insinuating glances of his, you immediately suspected she had hidden sexual depths that weren't obvious to the naked eye. Do you see what I mean?"

Simone saw. It was an intriguing idea. Without debonair Fred Astaire to lavish attention on her, who the hell would want to screw Ginger Rogers? "And you think this applies to me and Colin McKenna?"

"I certainly do. Not that you aren't sexy or glamorous all by yourself. You're even more attractive than you appear on screen, which is why I can't help feeling that your leading men haven't brought out your sensuality."

Her personal dislike of Colin should not be allowed to color her professional judgment, she told herself. She'd heard legendary stories about actors who hated each other's guts, but registered hot steamy sex on screen. Maybe the hatred even helped. Maybe in the arms of that nose-dripping, breath-stinking shmuck, she would become a femme fatale yet.

"If anyone can bring out your sensuality, it's Colin McKenna," the saleswoman declared. "When he looks at you with those smoldering green eyes of his, you'll turn into a woman with those hidden sexual depths. Just the way Lauren Bacall did in *To Have and Have Not*."

The idea of having hidden sexual depths appealed to Simone no end. "I will?"

"Absolutely. You and Colin McKenna would burn up the screen. You'd make Lauren Bacall and Humphrey Bogart look like chopped liver. Take my word for it."

But as much as Simone wanted to, she couldn't. She and

Colin McKenna on the silver screen not only made no sense, it would be her Waterloo. The saleswoman wasn't a pro, she didn't understand the camera's harsh and unrelenting truth. Colin was fifteen years her junior and boyishly *looked* it. The cameraman could smear Vaseline on his lens from here to Twentieth Century-Fox and she would still end up photographing like Colin McKenna's mother (talk about gray-haired cunts!). She smiled politely at the saleswoman.

"It's a very interesting idea. I'll be sure to mention it to the producer."

When she left Neiman Marcus, her euphoria was gone and her career anxieties (most of them age-related) had returned full force. All she could think of as she drove to Santa Monica to meet her agent for lunch was whether he would have good news for her. The best news would be that she'd gotten the part in *Rockabye Princess*. Not-so-terrible news would be that the studio still hadn't decided. Terrible news would be that another actress had gotten it.

Simone didn't know what she would do if that happened. Become a middle-aged finger painter. Sign up for unemployment insurance. What with Jimmy's gambling debts and her own spendthrift ways, they barely had a dime between them. The recollection of her last bank balance made her careen into the middle lane without signaling.

"*Stupid broad,*" a passing driver shouted.

Simone accelerated. She hated business lunches, she hated real food, and she triply hated having to go to Michael's to eat it. Her agent pretended he booked at Michael's because it was convenient for her to get to from Malibu, but he didn't fool her. Michael's was chic, haughty, typically Southern California in its fascistic snobbism, definitely a restaurant to be seen in. *Nouvelle cuisine* places like Michael's, with no sign on its unobtrusive door, made her think of *nouvelle cuisine* places like Ma Maison with no telephone listing in the directory.

It was at Ma Maison that she met Jimmy Newton, her sixty-second lover and resident genius. The reason she considered Jimmy a genius was that a few minutes after picking her up, he announced that she was going to become a superstar. Since she'd spent most of those minutes with her hands over her face, sobbing and moaning how her husband had left her for a young compliant cocktail waitress, she wondered how he could be so certain.

"A superstar?" she said in amazement. "But I'm not even an actress. Do you, by any chance, happen to have the Sun in Leo? Because that could explain your showman's instinct."

"I think so."

"You mean, you don't know where the Sun was when you were born?" As far as Simone was concerned, that was tantamount to not knowing about World War II.

"Sure, I know," he barked. "It was hiding under a rock. I was born in the rainiest August anyone had seen in forty years. Now stop this astrological crap, I'm busy."

He turned her head from side to side and looked sharply at her body, which she'd never gone to any pains to hide. She still remembered what she was wearing that day: a tight tight tight black cashmere sweater, even tighter black pants, and spiky red alligator heels that she'd charged at I. Magnin's months before and still hadn't paid for. At the age of thirty-five, Simone's body was a nice, compact, wiggly little thing that slid here and there naturally.

"Yes, it's sliding all right. Still, in my opinion, older women are the wave of the future, wait and see." He whipped out a notepad from his Hawaiian shirt pocket and wrote, reading aloud as he went. "Breast lift, thigh lift, face lift, and removal of front lower ribs. That should do it."

"What's the last one for?" she asked suspiciously.

"To make your waist appear smaller. Thought you knew about that old Victorian procedure, it was very popular in its day."

"It sounds gory. And why do you assume that I need my thighs lifted? You haven't seen them." She would not argue about her face, which could use a couple of tucks here and there, nor about her breasts, which had been fighting a losing battle with gravity for the past few years.

"Don't have to see them," he said matter-of-factly. "Something tells me you aren't exactly into exercise or jogging or any of that stuff."

It was true, all too true. She had never exercised one day in her life, not even out here in the Land of the Stay Trim & Keep Fit. As for jogging, forget it. The last thing she needed was to have her uterus bobbing up and down like a puppet on a string. Simone suspected that all over Southern California there were women walking around with loose uteruses. Maybe that was why panty shields had become so popular recently—to keep all those loose uteruses in place.

"I assume your legs are okay," Jimmy said, peering at her trousers. "No veins or anything yucky like that."

"Certainly not." She felt pleased to be able to defend one area of her anatomy without reservation. "Men have been known to die for my legs."

"Good. Then we won't have to do any vein stripping." He put the notepad away and smiled at her in a cool businesslike fashion. "Guess that's it, then, in the op department. I'll take care of the arrangements, UCLA Medical Center, wonderful cosmetic surgeons there, they can perform miracles."

Simone's tears dried up on the spot and she began to eat her duck salad with tremendous urgency, as though anticipating the cardboard food she would soon be served in the hospital. Provided she had the appetite to eat after everything was lifted and/or removed.

"So you see, you've got nothing to worry about," Jimmy said, trying to be sociable now that practical matters were dispensed with. "But just out of curiosity, what made your husband take a walk?"

"I listened to people like Gloria Steinem. I told Stevie that unless he used a foot deodorant, I was through washing his smelly socks. Then I stopped cooking and began serving take-out food from Kentucky Fried and McDonald's. I also criticized him for going down on me every time we made love. I said he had no imagination. In other words, I *asserted* myself like the feminists claim you're supposed to. Only it didn't work."

"Real men don't use foot deodorants," said the voice of masculine authority. "I'll bet that cocktail waitress he left you for doesn't mind washing his socks, smelly or not. And I'll doubly bet she doesn't object to a steady diet of muff-diving, either. She probably cooks gourmet meals, too."

It was true, painfully true. What a fool she had been. "Women's lib ruined my marriage and made me miserable, but I thought if I went someplace expensive today I might feel better. Instead, I ordered nearly a hundred dollars' worth of lunch and was feeling lousy until you came along and saved me."

"A hundred dollars!" Jimmy stared at her duck salad and

solitary cup of coffee. "What the hell did you eat before I got here?"

"Drank. An entire bottle of Krug Grand Cuvée. Normally I don't touch the stuff, but champagne is supposed to be good for the nerves." Farrah Fawcett and Ryan O'Neal glided by and were seated across from them in the sun-dappled garden. "My nerves were going haywire because I have barely any money in my account at American Savings and Loan. Plus, a set of twins at home."

He didn't bat an eyelash at this mention of children. "You can all move in with me, I've got plenty of room." He signaled for the check. "I'll even spring for your lunch, then we'll go back to your place and you'll pack your bags. How old are the twins?"

"Nearly three."

Tears came to her eyes as she wondered what the future held for her poor children. Something told her that Steve Omaha wouldn't take his parental obligations very seriously. Sagittarians, the free spirits of the zodiac, weren't known to.

"I've always wanted a ready-made family," Jimmy said. "How are you in bed?"

"*Pas bandeuse*."

"What does that mean in plain English?"

"Not so wonderful."

"I'm not so wonderful either. In fact, I've been told I'm pretty awful. Not that I give a damn, sex is overrated as far as I'm concerned. Next to making movies, what I like to do best is gamble."

Simone had never known a gambler; it sounded very romantic and Dostoevsky to her. As for his disinterest in sex, why should she care? She didn't find him very attractive, that Hawaiian shirt was a real turnoff.

"What do you gamble at and where do you live?" she asked.

"Poker and Malibu."

She barely heard his first reply, she was so dumbstruck by the second. "The Colony?" she gulped, having expected him to name someplace dumb like Tujunga.

"You look impressed."

She sure was. Anyone who lived there had big bucks, which was the next best thing to a big you-know-what.

"What do you do for a living? Are you a producer? You seem so young."

"I'm twenty-seven and a producer is what I'm looking for—to help me get a movie I wrote off the ground. It's called *Charmer*. I'm going to direct it and after you've had all those little ops I mentioned, you're going to star in it."

"I hate talking about ugly, creepy, crawly money, but won't those operations cost a bundle?"

"A friend of mine will lend me the dough in exchange for a piece of the movie." He turned her head. "Anybody can have a sensational profile, it's no big deal. But there's something about you that's different, unpredictable, I can't put my finger on it. And that's what stars are: *people who can't be conveniently labeled*."

Simone was flattered, although confused. "It sounds as though you don't have much money and yet you live in one of the richest, most exclusive areas of Los Angeles. How come?"

"I inherited the house from a famous rock star who drank herself to death. She left it to me in her will, free and clear. Also, I don't live there alone. I share it with Colin McKenna and he pays me rent. Driving-around money. Today I decided to drive to Ma Maison and inhale some energy, I was running low." He gave her a reassuring smile. "It's a real cozy little ménage. You'll be happy there."

She was happy already. Just the thought of getting out of that crummy pad in crime-infested Venice and giving up her boring job at CheapSkates made her feel like singing the "Marseillaise." Simone didn't yet believe that she would star in a movie, let alone become a superstar, but so what? She believed that Jimmy believed it, and right now that was good enough for her. She stood up to face her mentor, who was only an inch or so taller than she. A mini mogul.

"I can hardly wait to start packing," she said, grinding her hips and rolling her eyes. Madly.

It was a gesture that Jimmy would ask her to repeat months later when the cameras were finally rolling, even though neither of them could have guessed the impact it would have. Like Goldie Hawn's delectable giggle or Cher's wise poker face, the mannerism would become embedded in the minds of moviegoers all over the world as the unique property of a new and magnetic star named *Simone*.

*    *    *

Beverly anxiously cleared her throat and gazed at the eleven women seated in a semicircle.

"I have a problem that I need to share with you. A very serious problem." She lit a cigarette to help ease her nervousness.

"It's about my husband. I think that originally our relationship could be described as one of boozy sex. Even when Dwight used to knock me around a little—'love pats,' we called them—I was secretly titillated and went back for more. I'm ashamed to admit that now, yet it's true. And we continued that way for years. But when Sally ran away from college and I stopped drinking, I suddenly lost the desire to make love. That's when our problem began "

Beverly wondered if she were making some of the women uncomfortable; most of them had grown up in small Western towns and weren't used to sharing bedroom secrets. She had gone to college in the East, honeymooned with her first husband in the South of France, lived in New York, vacationed in Greece and Europe, skied in Gstaad, but did that make her any different *emotionally* from these women? She suspected not. Love at first sight was something they could all relate to, and love at first sight was what she had felt when she saw Dwight Kirby that long-ago Sunday in June.

It was at Mass at Holy Trinity Episcopal Church and she almost didn't stay for the service, feeling ridiculously out of place in her sophisticated clothes, high heels, and Eastern suntan. How foolish to have come here dressed for St. Patrick's on Fifth Avenue, she chastised herself, resolving to tone down her appearance in the future. More than anything she longed to be accepted in Williams, assimilated into the lifestyle of the small Western town. She had discovered Williams years before when she and her first husband were driving through on their way to Jackson Hole, Wyoming's chic ski resort, for a holiday on the slopes. They stopped for lunch at a friendly café and later stretched their legs by walking around the pretty, tree-shaded park. Beverly liked what she saw. The town struck her as a haven of peace and tranquillity, with none of the noise, clamor, or irritations of New York. If ever she wanted a retreat from the world, she thought at the time, Williams would surely be it.

But as she looked around at the Sunday congregation, she

wondered if her move here had been a mistake. The people who looked back at her were pale, withdrawn, and seemed to have been outfitted by Sears, Roebuck. Except for one man in the opposite pew. He had a deep bronze tan, coal-black eyes, an expensive custom-made suit, and seemed as uncomfortable as she. In a way he was, having just returned to his hometown after an absence of many years to take over as editor of the local weekly newspaper.

Dwight Kirby had been living in San Diego with an ailing wife, Beverly soon learned, but thanks to a recently deceased aunt he now owned twenty-five percent of the lucrative Williams *Independent Herald*. He could have owned an ice-cream stand for all the difference it made to her. What an attractive man, she thought, what a powerful-looking man. Their eyes met and locked. She was going to marry him. She knew it immediately. There was only one problem: how to meet him.

She solved that a week later by driving to the office of the *Herald*, which was located around the corner from the courthouse. It was an uncharacteristically hot day in July and even though she wore a thin cotton dress, her underwear was sticking to her skin. When she parked the car across the street, she could see Dwight's profile through the large old-fashioned plate-glass window. He was pounding away on a typewriter, a lock of coal-black hair hanging over his forehead.

"Good afternoon," Beverly said nervously as she entered the messy but otherwise deserted office. Stacks of old newspapers were piled everywhere and Dwight's rolltop desk was overflowing with correspondence, ads, bills, artwork, photographs, press releases, subscription orders, stories written in longhand by local stringers. "I hope I'm not interrupting you. I'd like to place an ad in next week's paper."

He stopped typing, looked up and smiled. It wasn't a very wide smile or a very friendly one, but his lips were parted and his teeth gleamed. Beverly thought of a fox.

"Here, write it out on this." He handed her a form pad. "As clearly as possible."

She did as she was told and then handed the pad back to him, aware that her hands were trembling and her throat felt dry. "Can you tell me how much it will cost?"

Instead of answering the question, he read the ad aloud. "*Baby-sitter wanted Wed & Fri evening. Two children 8 & 10 years old. Call 555-1873.''* He gazed at her curiously. ''I realize that it's none of my business, but what plans have you made for Wednesday and Friday evenings?''

He was right, it *was* none of his business, and ordinarily she would have told him so. Instead she found herself answering the question. ''I'm going to take an art-appreciation course at the high school. Now that I'm living out West, I want to learn more about Western painting.'' It was only a little white lie, she told herself; she'd been meaning to sign up for that course for ages.

''Can't your husband baby-sit those two nights?'' he asked.

''I'm divorced.'' Why did she feel so uncomfortable beneath his audacious gaze? So awkward and faltering? ''Maybe I should mention what I want to pay the sitter. Do you know what baby-sitters get these days?''

''Me?'' He laughed. ''I haven't the foggiest.'' He opened last week's paper. ''Perhaps someone else has run an ad and is listing rates. Yes, here we go. This woman is offering a dollar-fifty an hour, which doesn't sound like a big deal. But on the other hand, you'll probably get high-school girls replying, so maybe it's a big deal at that.''

''Put in a dollar-seventy-five,'' Beverly said, suddenly feeling reckless.

Except for the railing that separated them, she was standing very close to him. She could smell his after-shave lotion, she could see the tiny dots of four-o'clock shadow on his face, could imagine his arms around her, the strength of them. His shirtsleeves were rolled up, his arms were tanned, muscled, the hair bleached from the sun; they were powerful arms. For a moment, she felt as if she would faint. It was all she could do to continue standing upright without swaying.

''A dollar-seventy-five an hour,'' he said, jotting it down. He sounded amused. ''I see we have a sport here.''

She knew that she had to get out. And now. Otherwise something would happen that she might later regret. ''How much will the ad cost? I'm in a bit of a hurry.''

He glanced at her again, then counted the number of words. ''Three and a half dollars.''

She opened her purse and gave him a five-dollar bill. The touch of their hands was like electricity, she could feel it down to her toes. ''That's very reasonable,'' she said idiotically.

''Is it?''

He was staring into her eyes now; his own eyes had a flickering light deep inside them that she would never forget. What was he staring at so intently? What did he see?

"I'd like to buy you dinner tonight," he said. "May I?"

"Yes," she heard herself reply.

Didn't he think she knew about his wife, or didn't he care? Was he so arrogant, or was her own desire so clearly visible?

"What time is convenient for you?" he asked.

"Anytime after seven." Her voice sounded like a croak. "Provided I can get the cleaning woman to stay with my children."

"And if you can't?"

"I'll find someone."

"You're sure?"

She nodded. "Positive." To her astonishment, her panties were soaking wet.

"*Positive*?" he said in a teasing voice.

She nodded again, like a robot. "Yes."

Then an amazing thing happened. He stepped over the railing, grabbed her around the waist, pulled her to him, and kissed her with the kind of searing intensity that Beverly had only read about in books or seen in movies, but never experienced. Not once in her entire life, not with her husband or any man who came before him, after him, or in between. Not even with Fingerhood, she thought wildly, kissing him back. When they drew apart, she was out of breath and her senses were inflamed.

"I'm positive too," Dwight Kirby said, sticking his hand right up under her dress and feeling her wet panties.

After that they met whenever he could get away. Beverly waited for his calls like a drug addict waiting for her supplier, and felt the same frantic letdown if a day went by without hearing from him. For the fact was that Dwight Kirby proved to be the kind of accomplished and exciting lover she had dreamed about for years. Attentive to her needs, he knew how to satisfy them exquisitely. He was by turns gentle, brutal, sensitive, demanding, and selfless—a combination of contradictions that exhilarated her and ultimately gave her the assurance to match him in erotic play. Her orgasms, which used to be fairly intense (even with less skilled partners) now became cataclysmic. At first she couldn't believe that she was capable of so many delicious and attenuated responses, but Dwight kept showing her over and over again how unlimited her capacities were.

"I feel so greedy," she once said. "Almost wanton."

"It looks good on you. You're beautiful, Beverly."

"That's how you make me feel."

"That's how you *should* feel."

With no other man (except Fingerhood) was she so proud of her naked female self. Peter thought she was a cow, and for years she lived with his unflattering remarks about her lack of chic, lack of sleek, lack of style. But Dwight seemed to adore everything about her large, buxom, Rubenesque body, right down to the freckles on her rounded arms. And never stopped telling her so.

It was heady stuff and as time went by she grew to depend on it, just as she grew to despise the stealthiness of their affair and all the sneaking about they had to do to avoid gossip. She wanted to be with Dwight full time instead of grabbing her pleasure in bits and pieces, she wanted to make him as happy as he'd made her. Every so often she would remember that poor ailing woman he was married to and feel guilty, torn. But her major feeling was one of triumph and self-vindication: the cow had turned back into the peacock she used to be. *When*, Beverly wondered, would she turn into a wife? Two years later she attended the first Mrs. Kirby's funeral and shortly thereafter became the second Mrs. Kirby. . . .

When the counseling session was over, everyone agreed she deserved better than the indignities and injustices she had learned to live with, and that both she and Dwight could benefit from individual counseling.

"You're a battered wife, that's what you've been busy denying," a woman said to her. "Hell, it ain't an easy thing to admit, but now that it's out in the open, you'll be able to handle it."

Beverly nodded. "I used to think that Dwight had all the answers and I could turn to him for guidance. But when your husband starts slapping you around, who do you turn to then?"

Although some of the women thought she should get a divorce, others respected her desire to try to work out the problem. Beverly had tears in her eyes as she thanked them for their support. She'd never known how important it was to have other women on her side, she'd never realized how comforting and helpful they could be.

"If that motherfucker takes another poke at you," a cowgirl said in parting, "you just give me a ring, honey, and I'll make mincemeat out of him."

Beverly hugged her.

Minutes later she was driving south through the Wind River Canyon, not having the faintest idea where she was going or why. She only knew that she had to get away and clear her brain. The road was empty, the skies overcast, and once she was out of town, there wasn't another human being in sight. Just the river, sky, and imposing canyon whose towering rocks revealed formations for each major era of the earth's development, going back to the Paleozoic age nearly three hundred and fifty million years before. Beverly liked continuity, she still suffered pangs of dismay over her first divorce, she liked the fact that these rocks had stood in this very same place for all those millions of years, just *stood* there through rain and snow, day and night, heat and cold, Indians and white men, peace and battle, watching the progress of humanity.

*What* progress? she wondered, pressing down on the gas until she was going eighty miles an hour. People were so frail and fallible, they made mistakes—often the same ones, repeatedly; they floundered, they tried again, they persevered, they survived; people were so goddamned admirable and yet sometimes spent a lifetime not learning much of anything except how to go on from one day to the next. As she and Dwight had been doing and getting nowhere fast. As she hoped Peter Jr. and Sally would avoid doing.

"Don't think of Sally now, or you'll have an accident," she warned herself.

When she got to Shoshoni, she slowed down and parked in front of a luncheonette. "I'd like a cup of coffee and a doughnut," she said to the waitress. "Please."

Then she lit a cigarette and inhaled deeply, almost happily. One of the nice things about living out West was that since nearly everyone smoked, she never felt guilty about her own habit. People back East (she'd read somewhere) were rapidly giving up everything in their zeal to be healthy—smoking, drinking, eating, and even sex.

She couldn't imagine Robert Fingerhood giving up anything pleasurable; he was too militantly self-indulgent for that. The luscious meals he used to prepare, the vintage champagne he served, the intense and yet languorous way he approached a woman all attested to his hedonistic nature. It was a nature that Beverly wholeheartedly approved of and thought the world could use more of. She herself had been seeking it when Simone introduced her to the handsome clinical psychologist. The way he stared right into her eyes and smiled told Beverly that he would be wonderful in bed. And when they finally did get together, she realized how unhappy she was at home.

She stirred her coffee now. No sugar, no cream.

"You're the creamiest woman I've ever met," Fingerhood whispered one cold rainy night, jamming it into her as hard as he could, panting for breath. "You . . . are . . . *the* . . . creamiest."

She still remembered how she used to look forward to those weekly trysts in his Mexican jungle apartment in the East Twenties, how she was able to muddle through the rest of her life in deadly Garden City knowing she had that one night to dream and wait for. And what made it even more delicious was that Fingerhood seemed to have been waiting as impatiently and greedily as she. He acted as though he would have hung himself from the ceiling fan if she didn't show up and let him make love to her in his hammock (without realizing it, they were assuming "The Fingerhood Position" even then!). There was nothing she had to say, he knew what to do, he seemed to intuit her slightest inclination and was happy to satisfy it. No, more than happy, *thrilled*. Like the time he began tying her to the bed, when she hadn't uttered a word.

"What are you doing?" she asked, wondering how he guessed the thoughts racing through her feverish brain.

"Pretending I'm the leader of a South American revolutionary gang who's never seen a red pussy before."

"Close," she admitted. "Very close."

One evening another couple stopped by Fingerhood's apartment for a drink, an airline pilot and a blond stewardess, a real honest-to-God beauty. Her name was Anita Schuler and she was so golden that she *shimmered*. That was the only word Beverly could have used to describe it; there was an aura about her that Jean Harlow and Marilyn Monroe must

have had too. Beverly saw the tension between Anita and
Fingerhood and felt frightened, threatened. He's going to fall
in love with her, she thought with a sickening thud, unless
he's in love with her already. About a month later, Fingerhood
said their affair was over.

"You drink too much," he told her, "and your mentality
is too suburban."

"Is that all?" she asked with a forced smile.

"No, if you keep up this boozing your kids will hate you."

"Do you hate me?"

"Of course not," he said softly. "It's just that . . ."

She suspected it was just Anita Schuler. "You needn't
explain."

Unlike Simone, who nicked her wrists in the bathtub when
Fingerhood dropped her (for Beverly), Beverly had no such
inclinations. She'd been brought up by an elegant mother
who considered displays of emotion to be cheap, vulgar,
tasteless. Beverly did what her mother would have done
under similar circumstances: she departed with as much élan
as she could muster.

Two days later she decided to leave Peter and move to
Manhattan with the children. Fingerhood's steady and all-
consuming brand of lovemaking had ruined her for Peter's
sardonically detached approach. Who needed those crumbs?
Not she, not anymore. She would build a new life for herself,
she vowed on the day of the move. She would make new
friends, meet new men, she and her children would be all
right, better than all right, they would *flourish*.

"It's okay, Mommy," Sally, then aged five, said. "I don't
want to move any more than you do."

Anita's taxi pulled up on the south side of Piccadilly and
she eagerly got out. Tea at the Ritz was one of those institu-
tions that made her feel like a princess. Well, at least a
viscountess, she thought as she strolled through the elegant
lobby past a wood-paneled reception area, rubbing elbows
with wealth and power.

She adored the Edwardian Palm Court with its thick rose-
colored carpets and gilt-crystal chandeliers, its dusty-rose velvet couches and tapestry-damask armchairs. Afternoon tea
was enjoyed here amidst a discreet level of chatter, served by
impeccable waiters who never looked you directly in the eye.

"Are you ready to order, madam?"

One of the reasons she loved living in London was that waiters and tradespeople called her "madam," as opposed to their counterparts in America whose salutation was the crude "miss" or the infinitely vulgar "lady." Another reason she loved living here was that women's lib hadn't gained the stranglehold it enjoyed in her own country. A stewardess she used to fly with dropped by recently on a layover and said that men back home had lost their balls and it was all the feminists' fault.

"They've killed off all the brash, sexy, aggressive, assertive, interesting men," the stewardess hotly declared. "What's left are househusbands, homosexuals, weirdos, and shrinking violets who are so threatened by the new brand of female that either they can't get it up or can't get it in, or if they manage to do both—by some miracle—they don't know what to do with it once they're there. I recently made it with a guy who asked my *permission* to go down on me."

"What did you say?"

"I told him if he was that insecure, to forget it. Who needs a bashful blow-job?"

But the English were still acting like Lawrence of Arabia, thank God, still clinging to their centuries-old traditions, whether it be etiquette between the sexes or tea at the Ritz. Anita languidly crossed her legs. What bliss just to sit here gazing at the large crested silver trays, Georgian teapots, fine china, and a list of the best Indian, Ceylon, Darjeeling, and Lapsang blends. She had just finished telling the waiter that she would have the Darjeeling and a plate of smoked-salmon sandwiches, when a stocky gray-suited figure loomed in front of her.

"Anita, I thought it was you. I say, this is a pleasant surprise." He looked furtively around. "Are you here on your own, darling, or have I caught you in the midst of a wicked indiscretion?"

She looked up and into the muddy close-set eyes of Dickie Wembley. His fat neck was stuffed into one of those new spread-collar shirts named after Prince Charles. "Sorry to disappoint you, Dickie, but I'm by myself. What brings you here?"

"Auntie from Hampshire." He indicated an elderly woman in one of the tapestry armchairs. She wore a dreadful floral dress and was piling jam on a scone. "I offered to squire the old girl around town today and it's damned tiring work. But not to worry." He gave her a broad smile, revealing large pink gums. "I'll be back to my usual energetic form by the time I see you and Michael *ce soir*. I'm looking forward to it, darling."

His "usual energetic form" was a polite way of saying that Dickie Wembley's appetite for masochistic sexual pleasure knew no bounds. The last time he'd been over, he stayed for five hours and left with a bleeding backside, smiling, deliriously happy. Michael was happy, too. The minute Dickie was out the door, Michael screwed her right through the soccer match on TV before coming in an old school sock.

"Don't you be late, now," she said with a teasing smile.

"And don't *you* forget to wear that naughty little black lace undergarment," he whispered, his breath redolent of whiskey. "You know the one I mean, love. It drives me wild."

As soon as he left, her tea arrived. She took it as the English did, with plenty of milk and sugar, and bit ravenously into one of the delicate sandwiches. She didn't know what it was—her liver scare or Dickie Wembley—but she felt as though she were starving. Ever since she was a chunky child, Anita had turned to food in times of distress, so after she had finished every last crumb on the plate, she ordered a slice of the Ritz's double rich chocolate cake and wolfed it down as though the end of the world were coming.

Perhaps it was, at that. *Her* world, anyway, where nice girls from Cleveland grew up, got married, had children, moved to the suburbs, and sublimated their sex drive at PTA meetings. Not the other way around, as she was doing, sublimating her PTA drive in sex. Fingerhood's wedding invitation made her remember when she came close to having a wedding of her own. So close. Tears stung her eyes. Jack Bailey, airline pilot of her dreams, was the only man she'd ever really loved, and it took her a long time to get him to propose. It took an abortion and a breakup and the move to Chicago, it took years in fact. But finally he asked her to marry him.

"Oh, Jack!" she cried. "I thought this day would never come!"

"Neither did I."

She suspected he meant it sardonically and didn't pursue it.

Men were strange creatures, whimsical, stubborn, moody, and none of them wanted to get married. To be married was to be tamed, an unnatural state for them. They had to be pushed or finagled or somehow threatened into it, and in the odd case where they came to the decision by themselves (as Jack had), it was invariably because they were too tired and worn out to play around any longer.

It wasn't a flattering theory, but it had been Anita's theory from the time she first discovered boys and realized that what she wanted more than anything in the world was to marry one of them. And yet before Jack, no one had asked her. She wondered why not. They asked other girls, less desirable girls, girls less suited for marriage, girls less intent on getting married, often girls who viewed marriage as a big confining bore.

Like her dizzy old friend Simone, who couldn't cook, sew, or balance a budget, who didn't believe in fidelity, didn't want to ruin her figure by having children, didn't like sex all that much (she once confided to Anita), didn't have a lot of money, a fascinating job, or an original idea in that birdbrain of hers, and who nonetheless managed to get herself hitched to a pop painter at the age of twenty-four.

Anita had been furious. The only sense she could make of it was that Simone had marvelous breasts. They were nowhere near as big as those of that rich (and married) cow, Beverly, but they were firm and stood up without a brassiere. Odd that she should think of Beverly after so many years, yet they were all intertwined whether she liked it or not—Simone, Beverly, Lou, and herself, the masculine common denominator having been delectable Robert Fingerhood. The first time Anita laid eyes on Fingerhood was when he crashed a party she was giving in New York.

"Did anyone ever tell you that you're an exceptionally beautiful girl?" he asked, his eyes filled with admiration.

But she only had eyes for Jack Bailey, fool that she was. She would have been better off settling for Fingerhood, because exactly two weeks prior to her wedding Jack suffered a massive coronary in the arms of a rival stewardess and was pronounced dead by the time they rushed him to the hospital. Anita was in Marshall Field's trying on wedding gowns when she heard the news, and fainted.

The minute she came to, she experienced a sharp pain in

the area she would later identify as her liver. No wonder she hurt! Not only was the love of her life gone, not only did she have to call the Ambassador East and cancel the Pump Room for the reception, but the goddamned stewardess was everything she'd always wanted to be—cheerleader and pompom girl at some rich Shaker Heights school, homecoming queen, Miss Machine Tool of Ohio, proud recipient of "Most Popular Stewardess of the Month" award, and even prouder recipient of Jack Bailey's sperm.

"He was a real bull," the stewardess whispered to Anita at the funeral. "I think I'm preggers."

Anita stepped on the girl's open-toed shoe and pressed down as hard as she could. "I hope you have Siamese twins," she said with a sincere smile.

Immediately afterward, she called a friend who belonged to the Playboy Club and asked if he would take her there for a drink.

"My life is ruined," she tearfully explained. "I need some pampering."

"Happy to oblige."

The chivalrous character of certain men had stopped Anita from giving up entirely on the opposite sex. From the minute the checkroom bunny greeted her friend by name, she could feel her anguish slowly fade away. Seated in the amber-lit, thickly carpeted top-floor bar of Chicago's Playboy Club, drinking brandy alexanders and gazing at the spectacular Lakeshore Drive view, while being surrounded by handsome men in designer clothes, she was almost able to forgive Jack Bailey his treachery. Her friend was sympathetic when she told him the appalling story.

"Poor baby." He patted her hand. "You've really been through the mill."

Afterward they drove to the supersnazzy Drake Hotel, where he'd reserved a suite for the night. Before going upstairs Anita suggested they stop off at the Coq d'Or for another brandy alexander. Then she went to the ladies' room and put in her diaphragm, which she always carried with her. As soon as they got to the suite they undressed and jumped into the shower, put on robes that the management provided, danced drunkenly to radio music, tumbled into the huge bed with a tufted peach headboard, and spent the entire night screwing their brains out in every position they could think of. His favorite was the spoon. Hers was the missionary, even if it had become fashionable lately to denigrate it.

"I love you, baby," he moaned in the darkness. "The way you move that ass, jeez!"

By the time morning rolled around, Anita was exhausted but less depressed than she would have been if she'd stayed home and cried herself to sleep. Jack Bailey, the love of her life, was dead, she was not going to be married after all, she might never fully recover from his cruel and incomprehensible actions, but it was nice to know that there was one man in Chicago who considered her the most sensational and desirable female walking. Even if he was only four-feet-eleven, weighed ninety-eight pounds, and was a familiar figure at the Arlington Park Racetrack. . . .

"Would Madam like anything else?"

"Only the check, please."

She had to get out of here, she thought, panicked. Suddenly her entire life seemed like a shambles, tea at the fucking Ritz or not. Her mother was right, she was nothing but a whore. How had this happened to her? She would be forty-one next month and what did she have to show for it? The jewelry that Michael had bought her, the clothes and furs in her closets, plus one thousand pounds that she managed to squirrel away, period. While Michael was more than generous in attending to her creature comforts, he point-blank refused to give her large chunks of cash. He was no fool, she thought bitterly. What he gave her was taxi and tipping money; everything else was charged to his accounts and the bills sent to his office. God forbid she should have to soil her hands or tax her brain dealing with that dirty, filthy green stuff.

A wave of hopelessness and futility washed over her as she paid the bill, overtipped the waiter (she loved to overtip with Michael's money), and ran out into the bright June afternoon. Her future had never seemed quite so grim, her security quite so precarious. Should anything happen to Michael, she might be left out in the cold. In Britain a mistress had no claim upon her lover's estate (palimony was unknown here), so her only hope was that he had actually provided for her in his will as he swore he'd done. If the son of a bitch were lying, she would be screwed but good.

She staggered down into the Green Park tube station, transferred at Victoria, got out at Sloane Square, walked briskly along the tree-lined streets of Chelsea until she reached an imposing house on the riverside of Cheyne Walk, and she was home, thank the Lord. She felt as though her legs couldn't have carried her one yard farther.

The first thing she did was make herself a good stiff drink and to hell with her liver. Then she sat down in the Empire swan chair and tried to watch sunlight playing on the manicured English gardens, but it didn't help. She couldn't bear to imagine who Fingerhood was marrying. She felt jealous already, unnerved by the thought that Simone, Beverly, and Lou might be at the wedding too. What if they all looked younger, thinner, happier than she did? She couldn't stand it. Her mother once accused her of having what the Germans called *Schadenfreude*, which meant the enjoyment of other people's tragedies. It was true, dammit! She was so miserable that she wished the worst for everyone. She hoped that Beverly's breasts hung to her waist, that Lou had become a bull dike, and that the movie director Simone lived with had just run off with Victoria Principal.

That made her feel a little better and she went upstairs to see what she had in the closet that was suitable for a June wedding. As she was riffling through rows of dresses, she had an inspiration. Maybe if she were extra-nice to Dickie Wembley tonight, she could finagle Michael into reserving a suite for her at the King Croesus on Park Avenue. It was New York's newest and most luxurious hotel and if she could stay there it would help compensate for a lot of things. Like the fact that she had no husband, no money, no career, and no prospects.

"Otherwise, I'm doing just fine," she said to her reflection in the mirror, holding up her new Chloe mousseline stripe over shepherdess pantaloons and imagining it with her black cultured pearls for the appropriate note of élan. "Chances are I'm doing a hell of a lot better than Miss Machine Tool of Ohio and her Siamese twins."

It was three-thirty. Vanessa was downstairs finishing loading the panel truck and Lou had just grabbed a Bendel's shopping bag containing Jean Pierre's crescent rolls when the telephone rang.

"Some Like It Hot," she said hurriedly.

"Lou, I need help." It was Doris, an old friend from the Movement, whose main area of interest was abortion. "Right-wing leaders are going to push the Human Rights Bill through the Senate this summer unless we do something to stop them. I'm organizing a team of people to go door-to-door handing out printed postcards asking for opposition to this bill—"

"Doris, you've caught me at a very bad time."

"What I want to know is whether you're willing to be part of this team," Doris went on, unperturbed. "Say *yes*, Lou, we need volunteers desperately."

"I'd love to help, but I can't tell you how busy we've become. There aren't enough hours in the day."

Lou hadn't been actively involved in the Movement for a long time and felt guilty, particularly when she received Ellie Sneal's letter a few days ago reminding her that the deadline on ERA was at the end of the month. To her shame, she'd forgotten all about it and promptly sent Ellie a personal check for five hundred dollars by way of atonement.

"If you're that busy, how about giving me half a day?" Doris pressed her. "Which day is best for you?"

"There aren't any good, better, or best days in the catering business," she said, torn. Signing up would not only help others, it would help convince Vanessa that she was serious about her radical feminism. "I don't see how I can spare the time."

"Abortion is life and death, Lou."

"Yes, I know but . . ."

She stopped, remembering how she'd gotten pregnant at the age of seventeen and had the baby out of fear and ignorance. Abortions were illegal then, immoral, and Lou had given birth to a beautiful healthy baby girl. Because of the censure and disapproval she would have been subjected to as an unwed mother, she agreed to let her parents bring Joan up. She agreed to let Joan think that those parents were her true parents and that Lou was her older sister.

How many years had she suffered because of that heart-wrenching decision? Too many to count. Fortunately, Joan turned out just fine. She was an accomplished musician and lead singer with an all-woman rock group, Mink & Sable, recently hailed by *Record World* as the biggest threat to the Go-Go's. Joan had called last night from L.A., where Mink and Sable were playing the Roxy, to say that their shows were a sellout and she'd be back in New York at the end of the week. Her last words were, "Give my regards to Vanessa." And Lou nearly blurted out, "We're lovers, you know." But as always, something stopped her.

"Are you going to relent and give me one afternoon a week?" Doris said.

"How about Monday?"

"You've got it. The postcards are already printed and—"

"Talk to you tomorrow. I have to run."

Lou drove crosstown. The traffic wasn't bad going through the park on Eighty-first Street, at least it moved. But Fifth Avenue (which she tried first) was all clogged up, and so was Park (which she settled for). Vanessa sat next to her in the panel truck, six strawberry chiffon pies in a cooler at her feet. The rest of Jean Pierre's dinner was in back, packed in everything from laundry baskets to huge Tupperware containers. The Lobsters en Bellevue Parisienne were in an ice chest. Delivery was a bitch.

"We packed so fast, I hope we didn't squash those gorgeous strawberries I bought for the pies' decoration," Vanessa said, nervously tearing at her cuticles. "I hope the champagne arrives in time to be chilled."

"They're *sending* it chilled."

"I hope the waiters show up. Remember what happened when we catered that Valentine's Day party for Jean Pierre last year? I shudder whenever I think of it."

Three of the four waiters they'd hired had come down with an intestinal virus at the last minute, but Lou knew some unemployed actors and managed to save the day. It was the kind of once-in-a-lifetime situation that would probably never ever happen again. Still, there was no telling that to Vanessa, who always worried herself sick at this stage of preparation. Lou stopped for a light on Seventy-first Street. To her surprise, the same man who tried to pick her up earlier was standing on the corner, the Leica slung over his shoulder. Was she imagining it or was he staring at her? Before she could avert her gaze, he began to smile and wave. Furiously.

"Who the hell is that?" Vanessa asked.

"I can't imagine."

The man was mouthing something now, but the street and traffic noises drowned him out.

"He acts like he knows you," Vanessa said suspiciously.

"Well, I don't know him."

Lou wished he would disappear (had he been following her?). She wished that the light would change. She wished that her favorite city in the world didn't have so many nuts running around in it.

"I can't tell you how much my children enjoyed that Easter-egg party you catered for Mrs. Greene's daughter." A woman in Halston chic had come over to chat, a not unusual occurrence inasmuch as their panel was instantly identifiable by its hot-pink color and gold lettering. "Do you people know how to make kedgeree? I was thinking of serving it for Sunday brunch, instead of the usual quiches or boring omelets."

"What an interesting idea," Lou said heartily. "Of course we know how to make kedgeree. In fact, I'm proud to say that we make one of the best kedgerees in town. Why don't you give us a call and I'll come over with the pricing?"

"Thanks." The woman pocketed Lou's business card. "I'll do that."

The light turned green and she took off. In her rearview mirror she saw that the man with the Leica was still standing in the same spot, looking after her. "What the hell is kedgeree?" she asked Vanessa.

"Flaked fish and boiled rice, with curry and cream."

Vanessa was a walking recipe book, Lou thought admiringly. "It sounds awful."

"It *is* awful but if you cover the center with sieved egg yoke and sprinkle chopped parsley around the edges, it looks great." Vanessa's cuticles were raw now, one of them bleeding. "I hope we got the sand out of those salad greens. I hope we didn't overcook the vegetables for the Salade Russe. That's all I need—mushy green peas."

Lou decided to change the subject. "I hope you know how to bake a wedding cake."

It worked. Vanessa blinked and abandoned her cuticles. "What for?"

"Fingerhood is getting married."

"Big deal. I thought you never wanted to lay eyes on the son of a bitch again."

"Business is business," Lou said breezily. "Besides, we've never catered a wedding, it might be fun. Maybe I can even talk Fingerhood into hiring Mink & Sable for the reception."

"Are you crazy?" Vanessa's anxiety was totally gone,

belligerence had taken its place. "Mink & Sable is a hot group, their single just went platinum, your daughter is a rock star—or have you forgotten? Why the hell would she want to perform at a *wedding*?"

"You make it sound like a funeral." Lou honked at a New Jersey car that was straddling both lanes.

"That's what marriage is for a woman. Marriage is based on woman's dependency, as you seem to have so conveniently forgotten."

Lou had married Zachary after his first wife (Vanessa's mother) died. "Are you sure you're not confusing me with your mother?" Lou asked.

"Don't be cute, you know what I mean. The only difference between you and Momma was that you had two jobs. In addition to being fashion editor at *The Rag*, you had to see to it that my father was properly fed, his clothes kept clean, his home kept spotless, his health needs attended to, his social life organized, his male ego catered to, and his sexual desires—which I prefer not to think about, if you don't mind—graciously fulfilled." Vanessa paused for breath and the definitive last word. "Wives are unpaid servants."

"I loved your father, Vanessa. I'm glad I married him. I'm sorry he died. And frankly, I'm not in the mood for your liberation speeches." The New Jersey car let her by at last. "As for Mink & Sable playing at Fingerhood's wedding, Joan might do it simply to please me."

"That's a good one," Vanessa snapped. "Why would you be pleased to see your daughter lower herself for the consumption of a bunch of sentimental, hypocritical, middle-class, marriage-obsessed morons? She's better than that, she's an artist."

"And artists need an audience." Lou refused to let Vanessa bait her. "Besides, I want to show her off. Fingerhood hasn't seen her since she was a messed-up ten-year-old and I'm proud of how she's turned out. Justifiably proud, I might add."

"Then you respect Joan?"

"Of course." Lou wondered what she was getting at. "It goes without saying."

"If you respect her, why aren't you honest with her?"

Lou pulled up in front of the service entrance to Jean

Pierre's building on Sixty-third Street. "What have I been dishonest about?"

"You and me."

Oh shit, Lou thought. "Vanessa, why do you always bring up difficult subjects whenever I'm trying to park this truck?"

"Because it's the only time you can't put on your warm-up suit and that hideous-looking Jogbra and go running out the door."

"What do you have against my Jogbra? It keeps my breasts from bouncing up and down."

"Your breasts aren't large enough to bounce."

Lou smiled. "You really hate it when I run."

"I only hate it when you use it as an excuse to avoid discussing something important, which is what's happening now. This reluctance of yours not to tell Joan about us is important, you know."

"I know," Lou said, feeling uncomfortable.

"You're afraid to tell her, aren't you, afraid she might slink back in disgust, consider you a pervert, never talk to you again. Parents!" Vanessa spit out the word. "They're so unbelievably corny."

Lou straightened the panel. "You must have thought your father was pretty corny, too. He went to his grave thinking you liked boys. As I recall, you didn't hang up your sign— LIB MEANS NEVER HAVING TO SAY YOU CAME—until after his death."

"That sign annoys the hell out of you, doesn't it, because of all the orgasms you used to fake in the old days?"

"Who said I faked orgasms?"

"You may not have said it in so many words, but you implied that you did. With my father, of course."

Although it was true, Lou would have felt like a traitor to Zach's memory to admit it. "Your father was a much better lover than you imagine, Vanessa."

"Sure he was. And I'm Anita Bryant. As for my having deluded Zachary, that's a hell of a lot different than your deluding Joan. Zach was older, part of a more conservative generation, he couldn't have handled it. Joan is young, hip, smart. Besides, I'm sure she suspects."

"Suspecting isn't the same as knowing. But you're right, it's long overdue." She turned off the ignition and put the keys in her skirt pocket. "I'll tell her the next time I speak to her."

"Promise?"

"Yes."

But Vanessa wouldn't let her off the hook so easily. "You're not just saying that to shut me up, are you? You'll really do it?"

Lou raised her right hand. "I *swear* it. What do you want from me?"

"I plan to hold you to this, Lou. I mean it."

"Jesus Christ, I mean it too. Now, let's go."

At this reminder of where they were, Vanessa's professional anxieties returned. "I hope we didn't forget the meat thermometer for the lamb. I hope Jean Pierre still has that bottle of grenadine."

"What do you need grenadine for?"

"I don't, but the bartender will. Tequila sunrises, remember? That's all Mr. Macho will drink."

"Who's Mr. Macho?"

"Jean Pierre's best friend. The one with the shaved head and riding boots. The one he invites to every party." Vanessa stared at her in dismay. "Are you losing your memory?"

"It's known as early senility."

"At forty-two?"

"They say that as people get older they find it easier to remember things that happened years ago, rather than things that happened recently."

"So what are you remembering?"

"So it's none of your business," she replied as she opened the back door of the panel and began to remove Jean Pierre's thousand-dollar dinner. . . .

"*One and a half jiggers tequila, five ounces orange juice, three dashes grenadine, and stir—not shake—over crushed ice*."

She could still hear Fingerhood telling a bartender in a Village restaurant how he wanted his tequila sunrises made, and she could hear it as clearly as if it were yesterday rather than back in the late sixties. She could still hear his toast.

"It's been wonderful, Lou." He clicked glasses. "I've enjoyed every fun-filled second. Skol."

She gazed at him in alarm. "You make it sound like it's over."

"It is."

"That's not funny, Fingerhood."

"Neither is this affair of ours. You must realize by now that we're on totally different wavelengths, that our tastes don't coincide any more than our needs do, that what you want in a man I could never provide."

"You seem to have thought it all out." How dare he dismiss her like this! "And what is it that I want? Since you pretend to know."

"Emotional security. The rock of Gibraltar."

"I'm not unique in that regard. Every woman wants emotional security, it's only natural."

"They don't want it as badly as you. You want it as a top priority. I'm not implying that's bad, only that I can't supply it. You've been through a couple of rough relationships recently—both with married men—so it's only natural that you should be looking for someone solid. I don't blame you. I'm just saying I'm not that someone."

She wished he hadn't reminded her of those relationships, particularly the one with Peter Northrop, which ended so dismally. Afterward she steered clear of married men and tried to remain emotionally detached from the unmarried ones as well. She started floating around the clubs, discos, and nightspots of New York and Paris, pretending to be ready for a fling with anyone who caught her eye, but the truth was that (like the girl in the Klopman ad), what she wanted was a man to lean on. An older man, someone not too handsome, who would be flattered by her part-time dependence and grateful for whatever crumbs of affection she had to offer. Because she worked so hard and competitively during the day, she didn't want to work at all in the evenings. She wanted to lie back and be pampered, indulged, catered to, waited upon.

Then along came Fingerhood fresh from his affair with that dopy airline stewardess, Anita Schuler, and Lou bit. But he was a bad choice, since he wasn't about to cater to any woman beyond the initial rush of courtship. He accused her once of being sexually passive and she supposed she was. Again, it was that end-of-the-day weariness when she wanted someone else to do all the work for a change (just like a male executive, she thought fleetingly). But Fingerhood was handsome, young, demanding, a prima donna himself; he required a lot more attention than she was willing to give.

She was too busy attending to her career to have that much left over for a man.

And sitting there in the flickering light of the Village restaurant, she realized she shouldn't be angry with him—they were mismatched. She was angry just the same, infuriated, frustrated. He filled a gap in her busy life and it was an important gap. He made her body come alive, he recharged her batteries, he made her feel like a woman. Without the erotic diversion he provided, she couldn't cope with her pressing workload. Now she would have to find a replacement for him, and that meant taking the time to look around, review, reject, select, and ultimately start all over again with a brand-new lover. She cursed. It was worse than breaking in a new secretary.

"I suppose you've met someone else," she said.

"No, I thought it would be better to make a nice clean break."

She felt desperate. "Please reconsider. I'll try to change. I'll take the initiative when we make love, I'll get on top in the hammock, I'll stop wearing that red nail polish you hate and let my hair grow." She searched his face. "Okay?"

"It isn't enough."

Panic set in then, anger, hatred pure and simple. She didn't want to marry him, she didn't even want to live with him, all she wanted—*all*—was to get laid a couple of times a week, and the bastard was refusing her that! "It's enough for me," she said bitterly.

"I'm sorry, Lou."

"There's another woman."

"There isn't. Cross my heart."

It was a lie, she soon discovered, thanks to Simone's friendly reporting. Fingerhood was not only racing through New York with a go-go dancer named Dixie (or Trixie), but he was making a fool of himself over her. People who ran into them agreed he was smitten. Simone had seen the girl perform at the Metropole and said she was really something with those tassels and that ass. Lou's anger came rushing back at the thought of being replaced by a go-go dancer, and she called Fingerhood in the middle of the night after drinking an entire bottle of Chardonnay.

"You're an intellectual lowlife," she shouted without preamble. "A cretin with a rabbit's hormones, you're the biggest jerk I've ever had the misfortune to become involved with. You and that nitwit deserve each other. Instead of brains, she has her tassels and you have your balls. I hope the four of you will be very happy together and don't ever speak to me again.''

After a slight pause he said, ''Who is this?''

She threw the phone across the room. They'd broken up only three weeks ago and he didn't recognize her voice! She immediately drank a second bottle of Chardonnay and went to work the next morning with the worst hangover of her life. To this day she gagged at the sight of Chardonnay. . . .

''Thank heaven you're here.'' Jean Pierre stood on the threshold of his all-black duplex wearing a red silk kimono and a white face mask, wringing his hands. ''The bartender just canceled. *Il est malade*. Whatever are we to do, darlings?''

''I never liked the way he made tequila sunrises anyway,'' Lou said, relieved that his three French words were up, and that it was time to get to work. ''I'm going to get you the whiz who used to tend bar at Fonda la Paloma. Just leave everything to me, sweetie.''

A minute later she was dialing one of her unemployed actor friends and telling him to get his ass over there. Pronto.

# 3

"Darling, you're a vision!" Eddie got up from under the restaurant's white garden umbrella to kiss Simone. "You should always wear Missoni. I've never seen you so radiant, so glowing, so sinfully beautiful!"

"Flatterer."

Still, she was attracted to the charming Gemini and liked to believe he meant all the outrageous things he said. Maybe the saleswoman at Neiman Marcus wasn't the only person who thought she had hidden sexual depths, maybe unpredictable Eddie thought so too.

"Who's here today?" she asked, looking around.

"Everyone. Smile."

She saw what he meant. Dustin Hoffman was at one table, looking serious. Sean Connery was at another table, looking virile. And the head of the studio that financed Jimmy's movies was at a third table, looking powerful. The possibility that he might be one of the VP's opposed to her starring in *Rockabye Princess* made her lose what little appetite she had.

"I sincerely suggest you try this Sauvignon Blanc." Eddie patted the bottle cooling beside him. "It's a lovely vintage, not as assertive as a Pouilly Fumé or a Sancerre, it contains a little Sèmillon to give it balance. May I pour you a glass, darling?"

"Not on your fucking life." He had been trying to turn her onto wine for as long as she'd known him, but Simone hated the stuff. "I'll have a Diet Pepsi."

"You little savage." He blew her a kiss. "I'll convert you yet."

Edwin Lee Drake, born and raised in Carmel, headed his own very successful talent agency which he'd inherited from his own very successful father. He was in his late thirties, had fair hair, freckles, two ex-wives, a Dalmatian named Muscadet, and a tendency to wax rhapsodic over grassy, slightly herbaceous wines with a lot of complexity. Simone didn't care about any of that shit; what bothered her was that in the four years he'd been her agent he had never once made a pass. He was very sexy, with milky white hands, beautiful sensitive fingers, and buffed nails. Today he was in silk and linen burnt wheat by Armani.

"Movie production is way down," he said over charbroiled saddle of lamb with red-currant sauce. "I've never seen the studios so idle, so many people out of work. We're in a recession and God knows when it will end."

"Does that mean they're going to shelve *Rockabye Princess*?" Despite his protests, Simone had ordered a Grand Marnier soufflé drowning in red-raspberry sauce and globs of whipped cream (she would diet tomorrow). "Is that the bad news, Eddie?"

"I don't have bad news and I don't have good news. I have what you might call 'no news.' The studio still hasn't made up its mind about who they want for the female lead, but the competition is getting rougher. They might be looking for a younger actress to play the Danish princess."

Simone felt her heart sink. Jimmy was right, they'd decided she was too old. "They think I'm over the hill, don't they? They're going to ask me to play Brooke Shield's mother next, aren't they? And after that I'll be doing those Bette Davis loco-in-the-attic parts, won't I? I'm finished, Eddie, isn't that the truth?"

He took her hand across the table. She watched those beautiful fingers caressing her own, and she wondered whether he would caress her breasts the same way. So light, so feathery, so exciting. A shiver ran through her.

"Of course you're not finished, darling. What an idea. You're in the same category as Jackie Bisset, Candice Bergen, and Jane Fonda. The problem is that the studio now thinks the male lead in *Rockabye Princess* should be younger than the way Jimmy originally conceived him. In which case they'll have to get a younger actress. It's all relative."

"How much younger? The last I heard, they wanted Ryan or Donald Sutherland. Charles Grodin's name was mentioned, too."

"They've changed their minds. They now think that *Rockabye Princess* should be a young makeout movie for next summer's release. So they're veering in the direction of Jeff Bridges, Robby Benson, and Timothy Hutton."

"*Timothy Hutton!*" Simone's voice rang out across Michael's impeccable garden, heads whirled around. "Timothy Hutton is only twenty-one years old. Who's going to play opposite him? Kristy McNichol?"

"Need I remind you that most movie audiences today are under twenty-one?" Eddie said, without missing a bite of lamb. "There's always the chance that the studio will return to the script's original concept—you know how they tend to seesaw—but as of now they want Jimmy to rewrite for young."

"*Rewrite*? I didn't know Jimmy was *rewriting!*" So that was what he'd been hiding from her, the two-timing coward. "I'm being sabotaged in my own home by the one person who's supposed to be on my side. This is the worst fucking news yet, Eddie."

"I'm on your side, too. And I wouldn't call it sabotage, exactly. All Jimmy is trying to do is get his movie into production. Nobody can afford to be a prima donna in these financially troubled times. Well, maybe Marlon Brando and Barbra Streisand still can afford to. The studio was considering Barbra for *Rockabye Princess*—after all, she can sing— but she can't play opposite Timothy Hutton either. So now they're considering Debby Boone and Marie Osmond."

They were young enough to be her daughters, Simone realized with a double anxiety rush. "What's this about Barbra Streisand being able to sing? I thought they were willing to dub."

"They're no longer sure that's a smart idea. They think it might be better if the princess were played by a real singer."

"Why don't they test Ella Fitzgerald?"

"Don't be bitter, darling. It's bad for your digestion."

"My digestion took off for Marrakech about ten minutes ago." His hadn't, but agents could always eat. They had other irons in the fire, other clients, other deals, whereas all she had was herself. "The twins will have to go to public school. I'll have to go back to work—real work, that is. I'll never be able to afford another Bob Mackie gown. I'll be lucky if I can afford a small house in North Hollywood. Oh, Eddie, you're one of the best agents in the business. What should I do?"

"Don't panic. I'm in there pitching for you and you could

try pitching at home. You sleep in the same bed as the screenwriter-director, don't you?''

''What good is it doing me?'' She refused to admit they had separate bedrooms because of Jimmy's sexual disinterest. ''He's rewriting the part for a younger actress and he doesn't have casting approval anyway.''

''He may not have the final word, but he has clout with the studio. How he's managed that, I'm not sure. Jimmy was as much to blame for your last picture laying an egg as you were, even though he walked out of the mess smelling like Steven Spielberg. Jimmy owes you, darling. He should be leaning on the studio to let you play the princess. Are the two of you having personal problems?''

''Sort of, but I'm going to New York at the end of the month so maybe my absence will make his heart grow fonder. An old friend of mine is getting married.''

''Now, why didn't *I* think of that?'' Eddie's eyes lit up. ''That's very interesting, especially since I gather you're going alone.''

''What's so interesting about it?''

''You never know who you might meet when you travel. Or who you might travel with after you've fallen hopelessly in love.'' He nodded at the studio head, who was leaving the restaurant. ''I think the time has come for you to have a hot affair, darling. And what better place to have it than New York, with all those nosy, pushy, greedy photographers floating around looking for tawdry gossip?''

Simone remembered her astrologer's prediction: *travel, adventure, a new life*. The woman was uncanny!

''Not only has Jimmy been taking you for granted, but more importantly, so has the studio,'' Eddie explained. ''They think all you can play is the same cute kooky gamine you've been playing up until now. But the Danish princess isn't that type at all. She's daring, wild, reckless, unabashedly sensual. Beneath her cool Nordic exterior that we see at the beginning of the movie lurks a fiery hot tamale.'' Eddie looked at her significantly. ''And after New York, that's how the studio will see *you*.''

''It sounds exciting.'' She thought of all those hidden sexual depths waiting to be unearthed by the right man. ''Except that I'd feel guilty splashing myself over the tabloids with a handsome stranger after everything Jimmy has done for me.''

"You can't go on feeling obligated to Jimmy for the rest of your life. I don't mean to sound cruel, darling, but he hasn't been very obligated to you lately."

And Eddie didn't even know about Jimmy's sexual neglect or all those nights she cried herself to sleep alone while he was gambling in Gardena. Jimmy said he needed her, adored her, depended on her, but he didn't act as if he meant it. He'd made love to her exactly twelve and a half times in four years. What kind of adoration was that?

"Who do I have the affair with?"

"Someone very young."

"*Young?* What do you mean by *young?* How *young?*" She thought of the saleswoman's grotesque suggestion about Colin McKenna. "I'm nearly forty years old, Eddie. You're my agent. What the hell are you trying to do to me?"

"Get you the lead in *Rockabye Princess*. If the studio thinks that someone young is banging your brains out in real life, they'll decide that it's okay for someone young to be banging your brains out on screen."

"That's the dumbest thing I've ever heard."

"Not to a studio executive. It makes perfect sense."

"I won't do it."

"Why not? It will work. I can practically guarantee it."

"That's what I'm afraid of. Playing opposite a young actor will make me look like a wrinkled hag." She shuddered. "No one will ever cast me as a romantic lead again. It will finish off my career, but good. Don't you understand anything?"

His hand touched hers. "I understand that you're a beautiful, seductive, gorgeous creature. You could play opposite a teenager and make the audience believe it."

His touch was like electricity. "I could?"

"You don't realize how youthfully you photograph."

"I do?"

"Have faith in me," he said, moving his hand up her bare arm.

"I don't know." She started to weaken. "I guess it depends on how much Vaseline they smear on the camera. . . ."

But hours later when she was driving back to Malibu, she knew she had been conned.

"I hate my agent!" she screamed out the window. "I hope he pisses Sauvignon Blanc until he needs a kidney transplant!"

The person she really hated was herself for believing that Eddie was attracted to her. What a gullible fool she was. She should have suspected that he had ulterior motives, business motives (what else?). After he ordered two more bottles of Sauvignon Blanc, some of which he talked her into consuming, he asked her to go home with him. She was bowled over.

"I didn't think I was your type," she said weakly.

"You're every man's type."

That was all she needed to hear. They jumped into their respective cars, raced to his house in exclusive Holmby Hills, and fell into the circular bed. Eddie was everything she had fantasized about since they met, and more. She adored the take-charge way he made love. Unlike six-second Jimmy, he was languorous, he knew how to tease and titillate. Oral sex seemed to be his special domain, and while Simone had enjoyed a fair amount of that in her erotic travels, she began to see that either she hadn't enjoyed the right kind (quality) or she hadn't enjoyed enough (quantity), or maybe both, because Eddie was driving her wild.

"Oh, my God," she moaned. "Oh, Jesus."

"Mmmmmmm, you taste good."

She giggled. Little did he know that what he liked so much was the yummy scent from her Cupid's Quiver douche, the silly adorable man. Her giggle broke the spell, so that when she climaxed it was nothing spectacular—just a faint release of tension. Simone reproached herself. If she was going to become a femme fatale (with a cunt that never stopped), she had to start acting more sultry, more Sophia Loren and less Goldie Hawn.

"I want you," she said in a throatier voice, fanning her hair on the pillow. "Hurry, hurry."

She hadn't asked a man to hurry in years (not since the midget); usually it was the opposite. Eddie didn't need much encouragement. He flipped her over like a pancake, pulled her ass up, and entered her from behind with one long fierce thrust that made her scream—half in pain, half in delight. Then he began pounding away, in and out, in and out, sometimes going higher and sometimes lower, each time going deeper until he was so far into her that she was afraid he'd burst out through her belly button. But just when she felt as if she were about to come, she didn't and he did. It made her feel decidedly inadequate.

"I gather that the earth didn't move for you," he said afterward.

"It never does that way."

He seemed to understand. "It's probably because your clitoris is so hidden."

"*Hidden*?" She didn't want her clitoris to be *hidden*, that's what her sexual depths were supposed to be (was it the same thing?). "You mean, it's not in the normal place?"

"It's a little high up, hard to connect with during intercourse. But don't worry, darling, we'll work something out."

She doubted it. She had failed again. Was she destined never to find a man to bring her to orgasm through intercourse? The feminists claimed that the man didn't matter, that orgasm was within every woman's own control, but Simone objected to the idea. She didn't want to be in control of her own orgasms, she didn't want the responsibility. She wanted to be spirited off on a magic carpet by a confident stranger who would lift her to dizzying heights of ecstasy she'd never known. Eddie was lifting her now, to her feet. And he was hard again.

"What are you doing?" she said hopefully. "Where are we going?"

"Out to the garden. I want to make love to you on my revolving lounger. It's solar-powered and rotates every five minutes for more even tanning." He led her out the back door. "I keep it under an umbrella, so don't worry about the sun. You'll like it, you'll see."

Since it was obvious that he had rotated-screwed with other women, Simone didn't like it already. She wanted to feel exclusive, cherished, but she also wanted to have a solar-powered orgasm. This could be the answer to her sexual prayers (it sounded even groovier than Fingerhood's hammock)! The garden was surrounded by high shrubbery and huge leafy trees and the air felt delicious on her naked body. She was eager to watch Eddie go at her in broad daylight; it turned her on like nothing else. But when they got onto the blue canvas lounger (which was mounted on a contraption containing the motor), she noticed that his erection was gone. Then he lit a cigarette and sat inches away from her.

"What's the matter?" she said anxiously. "I thought you wanted to make love again."

"I'd prefer to explain my publicity plan first. You're going to be very impressed, darling."

"I'd be more impressed if I came while you were inside me," she said coquettishly.

"You're cute." He ruffled her hair, as though she were a poodle. "Now, here's the way I see it. You show up in New York with a young, sexy show-biz type whom you're obviously having an affair with. The two of you check into the Regency, or better yet the new King Croesus on Park Avenue. Then you start doing the town—"

"You think I'm a lousy lay, don't you?"

"Don't be silly, darling. You start hitting all the hot spots where the media hang out. Studio 54, Xenon, Twenty-one, Joanna's, the Red Parrot, Sardi's—"

"It's because of my clitoris, isn't it?"

He blinked. "What is?"

"Why you don't want to make love to me again."

"Stop interrupting. Where was I? At Sardi's, right. Now, nobody has seen you two disparately aged lovebirds together and it's a dynamite story. The media cream in their pants over stories like this. It's as if Jane Fonda were to suddenly turn up drooling over Christopher Atkins."

"Jane Fonda is married."

"That's a hypothetical example," he said sternly. "You know what I mean."

She sure did. What he meant was that she'd struck out again, just as she had with every man she'd ever known: Fingerhood, Jimmy, her co-star, her husband, the movie composer she screwed in desperation the night she lost the Oscar, the cameraman whose only interest was her labia minora which he said resembled a pink tea rose, the construction worker she picked up on a dare and was let down by with a bang, even the midget—they all agreed she was a washout in bed.

"*Entertainment Tonight* will pick up the story and so will all the news services," Eddie enthusiastically continued. "If we're lucky, the *Enquirer* will splash it on their cover along with a sizzling photograph of the two of you glued together. Make sure you take lots of sexy clothes to New York, plunging necklines, naked numbers, the works. I want you to be photographed in something revealing while this young stud gazes adoringly into your eyes—"

"If my clitoris weren't so hidden, you'd be gazing adoringly into my eyes this very minute."

"Shut up. Then he'll be quoted as saying that you're the most exciting, desirable, tantalizing woman he's ever known. Maybe he'll even say that he's asked you to marry him and you're thinking it over." Eddie straightened. "That's good. *You're* thinking it over, not him. Get it? You're such a dynamite chick that this horny kid can barely stop himself from fucking you on the dance floor at Xenon. Darling, the studio will go wild. They'll sit up, snap their fingers, and collectively shout, '*Rockabye Princess*!' And you've got the lead."

He paused for her reaction. "Well? What do you think?"

"My life is ruined."

"What are you talking about? What's wrong?"

She would never have a solar-powered orgasm now. Chances are she would never *ever* have an orgasm through intercourse. Being a femme fatale was obviously not for her.

"Nobody wants me," she said, on the verge of tears. "Nobody desires me. Nobody in real life considers me a dynamite chick. Only in a trumped-up P.R. scheme. And you want to know what's wrong? You have the nerve to ask? Jesus Christ, isn't it obvious?"

He seemed perplexed. "Not to me."

"I'm a flop as a woman."

"But you'll be a hit in *Rockabye Princess*. If you go through with my publicity idea." He stopped, uncertain. "You *are* going to go through with it, aren't you, darling?"

"What difference does it make?" she said through her tears.

"The difference between eating and not eating."

She remembered her last bank balance. Eddie was right. "I'll do it."

"You won't be sorry. Don't cry, darling. You'll end up winning an Oscar for this one. Trust me."

Simone doubted if she would ever trust another man again. They were all a bunch of conniving, manipulating, scheming bastards. No wonder her clitoris was hidden—it was afraid to come out and face the enemy.

"Who do I check into the King Croesus with?" she said, drying her tears. "Who's the young, sexy show-biz type I shack up with?"

"I've saved the best part for last." Eddie gave her his most triumphant agent smile. "Would you believe Colin McKenna?"

Beverly drove down wide tree-lined streets until she reached a white house with a spacious lawn and awnings over the windows. Had it been daylight, she would have been reminded that the house needed a fresh coat of paint, but it was past eight and dark.

After reading Fingerhood's letter she sat in her car outside the Shoshoni luncheonette for what seemed like hours, wishing she could accept his wedding invitation. It would be wonderful to watch him march down the aisle with his mystery bride (she was probably half his age, skinny, gorgeous, and madly in love with him), do some shopping, take in a few plays, have fun. Maybe Simone would be there, not to mention Anita and Lou, and seeing them again after all these years would be fun too.

Beverly wondered how the other women had changed and if they were happy. Despite their differences in the past, she hoped so. But this wasn't the time to be leaving on a pleasure trip; this was the time to try to save her crumbling marriage. She would write Fingerhood tomorrow and send her regrets.

In the kitchen she found a scrawled note from Dwight. *Where are you? I'm worried. Call me.* Next to it was a fragrant pink rose that he'd picked from their garden and put in a bud vase. He must have come home for dinner, not found her there, and panicked. Was he afraid that she'd run out on him because of what happened last night? Maybe. She knew that deep beneath his crusty veneer lay a vulnerable little boy who feared abandonment. Sometimes in his sleep he cried out, "Don't leave me, Beverly, please never leave me!" And yet when morning came, he would put on his crusty veneer (like an old hat) and go on his detached way.

She decided to go over to the newspaper and speak to him in person. After his dinner break, he frequently worked until midnight. Being the editor of a small-town newspaper meant being overworked and underpaid. Except for a couple of part-time assistants and a full-time linotype operator in the pressroom, Dwight pretty much put out the Williams *Independent Herald* by himself, week after week.

Certainly no one would ever accuse her husband of being

lazy. Quite the opposite. He was industrious, ambitious, responsible, and a person of stature in Williams. The fact that he was born here, left in his early twenties to become a reporter on newspapers in major cities around the country, then returned to his hometown to settle down permanently, caused many people to look up to and idealize him. Especially those segments of the population who'd never set foot outside their own state. To them Dwight was the original hometown boy who'd made good, who'd had some of that urban glamour rub off on him, but not so much that he didn't remember—and value—his roots.

Although Dwight played up this image for all it was worth, underneath lay a core of bitterness because he hadn't made it as a big-name reporter on those dailies he used to work for. That's where the action was (at least where it used to be before the advent of TV news), and there was no substitute for the adrenaline rush that came when a reporter was breaking a hot story. Whenever he remembered the excitement of those days, it was with a mixture of poignancy and deep regret.

Weekly papers like the *Herald* were primarily a showcase for advertising and chatty items about local happenings. There were no news stories to be broken, no presses to be held, no thrills, no surprises, nothing in fact that had first attracted Dwight to his field of endeavor. Still, it was a decent living, particularly since his aunt left him twenty-five percent of the paper and the publisher promised him another twenty-five if he could triple the circulation—a challenge he was still trying to meet.

The fact that Dwight married his mistress shortly after the first Mrs. Kirby died of leukemia would have been a considerable strike against him in a town as religious and God-fearing as Williams. But even there he managed to emerge a hero. What he did as soon as he and Beverly tied the knot was run an editorial in the *Herald*, reminding the townspeople of the pioneer spirit of the old West, where it was gospel for a healthy, red-blooded, all-American male to march down the road of life with a healthy, red-blooded, all-American female as his wife, helpmate, and stabilizing influence.

And *that*, Dwight humbly proposed in print, was all he was trying to do. The memory of the first Mrs. Kirby would be forever with him, he pledged, an inspiration and source of divine guidance. He ended his appeal with the hope that he had the community's blessing in this second holy union of his, from which he expected to gain the strength to go on as God in his infinite wisdom intended.

The editorial received more enthusiastic letters than any other editorial run in the paper since its inception in 1903 and established Dwight Kirby as a combination of Will Rogers, Lou Grant, Jack Anderson, with a dash of Jimmy Stewart thrown in for good luck. Beverly wondered what those admiring and congratulatory citizens would say if they'd been present last night to see their folk hero turn into a drunken, violent animal. . . .

It was past nine and the streets of the business section were deserted when Beverly parked outside her husband's newspaper office. The swivel lamp above Dwight's rolltop desk was on, a beacon in the otherwise sultry and deserted street. She pushed open the door and went in. He didn't see her. He was huddled over his wreck of an Underwood, typing something with fierce concentration, mumbling to himself under his breath, cursing, the smell of bourbon drifting aimlessly in the warm June air. He wasn't dead drunk but he'd had more than a few—probably with dinner when he didn't find her home, or he might have had them anyway as a hair-of-the-dog cure for last night's excesses. Just thinking about what had happened last night made her wince.

"Dwight?"

The sound of her voice snapped him to. "Beverly! Jesus Christ!" He stared at her as though seeing the proverbial ghost. "I've been going crazy wondering what happened to you. I called Eunice, I called the woman next door, I even went over to the swimming pool, but nobody had seen you. For a minute, I thought . . ."

"You thought what?" she said softly.

"Nothing. Never mind." In response to her softness, he was gruff. "Where the hell have you been? You had me worried sick."

"You thought I walked out on you. Isn't that what you were going to say?"

He lit a cigarette, stalling, preparing his reply. He couldn't admit his own dependency, his immense need for her. There were needs and there were needs, Beverly mused, and some of Dwight's were so unsavory that he pretended they didn't exist at all. Of course. What man with any pride or integrity would want to confess that he needed his wife as a punching bag?

"No, I didn't think you walked out on me," he said irritably. "Why would I think something crazy like that? I was afraid you might have locked horns with a boozed-up motorist and had an accident. There've been a lot of car accidents this past year because of idiots who drive while under the influence. That's what I'm devoting next week's editorial to. More highway safety regulations."

He pointed to the page in his typewriter, which was headed: NO BOTTLES IN CARS! "What Wyoming needs is a state law prohibiting open containers of liquor in cars. Right now we don't have such a law, and until we do we're giving tacit approval to drinking and driving." He squinted in the yellow office light. "Why are you staring at me like that?"

"I was just wondering why you find it so hard to be honest with yourself. Here you are half-bombed, writing an editorial that raps drivers who drink too much, and yet by the time you leave here you'll be one of those drivers. Do you deny that that's hypocritical? Do you deny that you beat me up last night, raped me, and consequently were afraid I might have left you?"

"I didn't *rape* you. That's bullshit and you know it."

"Oh, you have another word for it?"

"Yeah, I was exercising my conjugal rights and there isn't a court of law in the land that would condemn me for it."

"There isn't a court of law in this land that wouldn't condemn one person for doing bodily harm to another person."

"Listen, I'm sorry about that, but when you give me the sexual cold shoulder I go berserk. I can't help it, goddammit. Did you ever stop to think how I feel each time you pull away from me? Like I'm some sort of creep or leper, that's how. Aren't I entitled to any affection from my own wife? Is it wrong for me to expect a little *loving* now and then? When I married you, you couldn't get enough of it. In fact, I used to worry about whether I'd be able to satisfy you. That's a good one, isn't it?"

He laughed hollowly. "But when you stopped drinking, you suddenly became a virgin. I've never seen anyone change like that. It was weird, Beverly—you went from nymphomaniac to Little Bo Peep overnight. Is it any wonder that I blow my stack every once in a while? Another man would have started screwing around, found himself a little action on the side, but that's not my style. I don't want anyone else, I want you, I'm in love with you. But you don't want me. That's the real problem.''

She marveled at his ability to twist and turn the situation—and she had no doubt that that was the way he saw it. He needed to see it like that in order to justify his reprehensible actions.

"No, Dwight. I do love you—if I didn't, I would have left you a long time ago. The real problem is that when you drink too much, you become violent and you abuse me. My body is black and blue from what you did to me last night. If you don't believe me, I'll show you the marks.''

He looked away. "I said I was sorry.''

"Sorry isn't good enough. There's only one way we can deal with this situation if we want to save our marriage, and that's for both of us to go for counseling. I'm willing. Are you?''

He seemed like a trapped rat. "No.''

"Why not? Don't you care about making our marriage work?''

"You know I care." He began to swivel in the chair. "But that doesn't mean we have to bring outsiders into this. This is *our* problem and we can handle it ourselves.''

"I don't think so.''

He stopped swiveling. "Why the hell not?''

Beverly took a deep breath. It was going to be even more difficult than she had anticipated. "Dwight, I know I've been having sexual problems since I stopped drinking. I know that I haven't been as responsive to you as I would have liked, but that doesn't justify your striking me. I can understand your resenting me, even hating me, but taking it out on me physically? No. That's never justified and that's what you don't seem to comprehend. I have the feeling you think I *deserve* to be hit.''

"Maybe I do," he admitted, his voice thick with alcohol and bitterness. "Maybe that's exactly what I think.''

"I realize that I should have seen a counselor before this to help me to get to the bottom of my own problems, but I thought that because I loved you our relationship would straighten itself out." She tried to take his hand, but he jerked it away. "Love all by itself can't solve every problem that comes along, sometimes love isn't enough. But there are people trained to deal with these matters, and that's what we need, both of us."

"You mean *you* need one," he said. "I don't. All I need is my sexy wife back, then I'd be fine. I've told you once and I'll tell you again. No counselors, no shrinks, no outsiders. This is nobody's business but our own, and I don't want to hear any more about it. Now I'd like to know where the hell you were this afternoon. What was it that kept you so busy you didn't have time to cook dinner?"

Beverly felt defeated, frustrated. She had counted on his being more reasonable, or she wouldn't have come here. "I drove to Shoshoni."

He looked at her with suspicion. "What for?"

"No particular reason. I just felt like it."

"Oh, I see. You just felt like taking a scenic drive to little old Shoshoni. Is that what you're saying?"

Having failed to admit his wrongdoing, having refused to go for help, he was now trying to put her on the defensive. She didn't like the tone of his voice, his attitude, his insinuating cross-examination.

"Yes," she replied. "That's what I'm saying. Is it so odd?"

"Damned right it's odd." He slammed his fist down on the desk and papers scattered over the floor. "It's not only odd, it's a lie. You were gone for over three hours, and Shoshoni is only about thirty miles south of here. What did you do? Go by way of Montana? No, you never went to Shoshoni."

Beverly suddenly felt nervous, a warning bell went off in her head. "What do you mean? Of course I did."

"I mean, you have a lover and that's where you were. With him. If he lives in Shoshoni, then all right, you did go there, but you went to get laid."

"That's not true!"

"The hell it isn't!" He was furious. "I may be just a small-town boy without your vast and sophisticated world experience, my dear, but I'm no fool. I know a ridiculous excuse when I hear one, and yours is one of the most ridiculous of all time." He reached into the top desk drawer, brought out a bottle of Wild Turkey, took a long swallow, wiped his lips with the back of his hand. "You think I'm some sort of hick asshole, don't you, telling me a stupid lie like that? Now it all makes sense. That's why you've been playing the ice maiden in bed, you're getting it elsewhere. What are you looking at? Haven't you ever seen a man take a drink before? Oh, excuse me," he said in mock apology. "I didn't use a glass, did I? How un-Emily Post, will you forgive me, my dear? I promise to bone up on my drawing-room manners the next time we meet. Truly I do." He belted down another shot. "Fucking unfaithful cunt!"

"You're wrong." She was trying to remain calm. "I don't have a lover."

He didn't appear to hear her. "What a sap I've been, dreaming up excuses for you, when all the time you were banging another guy. I used to think you weren't yourself because of Sally, because we didn't have more money, because I couldn't give you the same things that your first faggot of a husband did. I used to think you'd come around eventually, and it would be like the old days. I used to think I should be more patient and understanding. *Understanding!* My wife is shacked up with some stud, and gullible fool that L am, I'm trying to be *understanding!* Don't you find that funny, Beverly? Why aren't you laughing?"

"Please, Dwight, don't do this. You don't know what you're saying."

"Oh, yes I do. And maybe for the first time in our marriage." His eyes met hers with sheer hatred. "I know what I'm saying, all right. The next time, I won't hit you, you goddamned bitch, I'll *kill* you."

Beverly ran out of the office and jumped into the car, her heart thudding in her chest, her hands ice cold in spite of the warm June air. As she started the motor, she realized that she didn't know where to go, she didn't know where she would be safe. Maybe if she could stay at Eunice's tonight it would give her a chance to think, to plan. Right now she felt numb, frozen, her mind inoperative. The only thing she knew for certain was that she couldn't go back home, not now, maybe not ever, not if she valued her life.

As she rounded the corner, she noticed that she was nearly out of gas. It might be a good idea to stop and fill up, just in case. Just in case *what*? she asked herself. Just in case she couldn't stay at Eunice's. Just in case she had to go some-place else, farther away, someplace where Dwight couldn't possibly find her. Fingerhood's wedding invitation swam before her eyes. *Hi, toots.* Just in case she decided to drive straight through to New York.

Chantilly, Magie Noire, Flora Danica, Invoire, Nocturnes, Calandre, Armani, Dioressence, Fidji, Gianni Versace, Chloe, Femme, Polo, White Linen, L'Interdit, Anais Anais, Ombre Rose, Shalimar, White Shoulders, Bal de Versailles, Michelle, Bill Blass, First, Molinard de Molinard, Joy, Tea Rose, K de Krizia, Night Blooming Jasmine, Fleur de Fleur, Must de Cartier, Vanderbilt, Y . . .

The fading light played upon the golden pyramid of perfume bottles on Anita's Regency dressing table. She had been a perfume freak all her life, and just gazing at the costly array relaxed her tense muscles nearly as much as the heavy kneading work being done by Rupert, her masseur.

"You've been nipping at the sherry again, I can feel it," Rupert said as he pounded one of her thighs with retributive ferocity. "And after all my warnings on the subject, too. Whatever am I going to do with you, ducks?"

"This has been an unsettling day. I needed something to calm my nerves."

"In the future, try tea. Alcohol retains water in the body and builds cellulite. Cottage Cheese City is what we will soon have, if you don't behave yourself. *Comprenez-vous*, darling girl?"

Anita had come to have a high regard for Rupert, as did his other select clients whose bodies (and faces) were their fortune. Aside from being good at what he did, he was discreet, amusing, and unquestionably gay, which meant that the lord of the manor need never worry about his physical attentions to the lady of the manor, who was invariably starkers during his visit. Anita made only two requests of Rupert. One was that he wash his hands thoroughly after arriving, and the other was that he refrain from kissing her before departing.

She had no intention of lying awake nights wondering what insidious infection he might pass along, considering where his hands and mouth might have been since they'd last met. One couldn't be too careful about hygienic measures these days, Anita felt, what with that nasty herpes virus running rampant among sexually active people. She once refused to kiss Michael for two solid weeks when he showed up with a suspicious cold sore on his mouth. That was all she needed on top of her other ailments, an STD (sexually transmitted disease).

"How are my thighs doing?" she anxiously asked about her most stubborn problem area. "Tell me they're improving, Rupert, lie to me. I need all the support I can get."

"What's wrong, ducks? Isn't Sir Michael treating you nicely?"

"If you call a threesome with one of his old school chums 'nicely,' then that's how he's treating me."

"It rather sounds like fun to little old deprived me."

"Deprived and depraved, you mean. It's too bad you can't take my place tonight. That would make at least two people happy."

"Yes and they're both in this room." He chuckled with vicarious glee. "But what about the blokes who're shelling out for all the merriment? We can't forget about *them*, can we, now?"

Unfortunately not, Anita thought with sullen resentment. If only Dickie could have been postponed to some other evening, if only she didn't have her period, if only she weren't so anxious about the trip to New York, if only Fingerhood had said who he was marrying (the omission had been driving her crazy since that afternoon), if only *she* were getting married. To Michael, to Fingerhood, to anyone. No, not really anyone. She still had her standards.

It would have to be someone handsome, intelligent, accomplished, and disgustingly rich, someone who worshiped the ground she walked on and would gasp at her pristine loveliness as she glided down the rose-strewn aisle to Mendelssohn's "Wedding March" wearing a high-necked gown of white crepe de chine trimmed with Alençon lace and hand-sewn seed pearls, with a twenty-four-foot train (the same length as Princess Di's) and the most flattering mantilla veil that money could buy.

Anita had dreamed about her own wedding ceremony a million times, using different people to play the maid of honor, bridesmaids, and flower girl. She had imagined her father all gussied up in a rented tux giving her away while her mother, corseted into a peach silk number, would beam with joy. And the murmurs of the congregation would reach Anita's ears. *I've never seen such a beautiful bride, have you? He's lucky to get her even if he is one of the richest men in the Western world. He's bought her her very own island in the Caribbean, that's where they're going for their honeymoon. . . .*

"Can't you do that a bit more gently?" Rupert was using his hands like chopping blades on her waistline. "You're killing me."

"A bit more gently isn't going to help get beyond the tissue." He flopped her over and attacked her abdomen with rapid blows. "Sorry, ducks, only doing my job."

As she soon would be doing hers, she thought, stowing her wedding fantasies away for future reflection. The honeymoon island in the Caribbean was always the last image to disappear from sight, it was so very vivid to her with its blue tropical sea shining in the moonlight. *One day,* she consoled herself, *one day.* And meanwhile she had plenty to be thankful for. Things could be worse, she could be alone and without a man.

She shivered at the prospect. To be alone was Anita's idea of pure unadulterated hell. Any man was better than that. Even Dickie Wembley? Well, Dickie was work, this was work night, she mused, trying to put it all in perspective. Being nice to men like Dickie Wembley was what paid for her jewels, those sunny winter vacations on the Algarve and Cote d'Azur (when respectable girls were trudging through the damp cold of London), it was what would buy her that wild Barguzin sable cape she had her eye on. *Think sable,* an inner voice whispered, *think ruby and diamond clips, think Yves St. Laurent and Oscar de la Renta, think the King Croesus and shopping at all those gorgeous Madison Avenue boutiques.*

"Now, that's what I call a beautiful sight." Michael had entered the bedroom so quietly that he caught both her and Rupert unawares. "No, please don't stop," he told Rupert, who had one of Anita's buttocks in his hand. "Keep pounding away at the merchandise but remember to be careful, my boy. It's prime cut."

"Good evening, Sir Michael," Rupert said in his most respectful tone (another reason why lords of the manor liked Rupert—he knew how to kiss ass with the best of them). "I quite agree with you, sir. This is a very lovely lady."

"And a very sexy one." Michael reached down for Anita's breasts, which were pressed beneath her on the massage table. "Come on, darling, let me see those two little beauties. Oh, there they are." She had shaken off Rupert's grasp and obediently raised herself on one elbow. "I say, they look rather pale. They haven't had their tit makeup applied yet, have they?"

Michael loved to talk dirty in front of Rupert, he just adored it. So did Anita, it turned her on like nothing else. And both men knew it.

"Honestly, Michael, behave yourself." It was important that she go through the pretense of objecting. Michael expected it. "What will Rupert think?"

"Whatever he bloody well likes."

To Michael's mind, Rupert was little more than a servant and everyone knew that their opinions weren't worth a fig. He had begun to suck on Anita's nipples, as Rupert moved back, uncertain whether to stay or go. Above Michael's head, Anita motioned to him to stay and pointed to the bulge in his pants, grinning. Rupert covered the bulge with a towel, his eyes never leaving the naked woman with the fully clothed man who was now moving his hand down to Anita's pussy.

Thank God she had put her diaphragm in before Rupert arrived, she thought with relief, otherwise Michael's fingers would come out all bloody rather than just nice and dewy from her own scent mingled with the peppermint flavor of her newest douche, Royal Flush. Diaphragms were damned useful when it came to holding back the flow of blood, and she only prayed that Dickie Wembley wasn't good at smelling rubber, otherwise he might guess the unsavory truth when he ate her later tonight. He always did that after the saddle-and-whip routine, although sometimes Michael beat him to it. If that happened, Dickie would approach her from the other end and lower himself until he was in her mouth. After he came and Anita pretended to, the men would switch positions and Anita would pretend to come again.

Men were such gullible fools, she would think as she writhed and moaned and swallowed and screamed out her pleasure. They believed in their powers of sexual persuasion at the most unlikely moments. And yet when a woman was truly enjoying herself, they often didn't seem to know it or want her to continue feeling so good. Like right now. She was all steamed up thinking about faggy Rupert losing his mind watching them, and just plain having a dirty old time letting

Michael play with her in front of a third party—and in almost broad daylight. She even felt she might come (wouldn't that be an unexpected bonus?), but he suddenly stopped.

"Oh, darling, do go on," she tried to encourage him.

"That's quite enough for now." He gave her a resounding slap on the ass. "You won't get another token of affection from me until I see those tits wearing that lovely rouge I'm so fond of. Not the pink, darling, the bright crimson red. You know the shade I mean."

"Of course. Strawberry Frappé. I'll go put it on."

"No, my sweet, not now. After Rupert leaves. Let him finish his massage."

"But, Michael—"

He ignored the pleading in her voice. "Champagne? I was just about to go downstairs and open a bottle."

This was *work* night, she sternly reminded herself. Her own pleasure came second, fifth, last, it didn't matter if it came at all. That wasn't why she was here. Once when she and Michael were on holiday in Wales, they had to stop the car to let a flock of sheep cross a narrow country road, and Anita noticed that the sheep's fleece was marked with the insignia of their owner. That was how she felt, particularly on Monday and Thursday nights, as though Michael's insignia were burned into her flesh, branding her his own exclusive property, to do with as he wished.

"I'd love a glass of champagne," she told him. "And there's caviar in the fridge, a brand-new tin of it. Crackers from Fortnum and Mason alongside. Hurry." She smiled into his eyes with just the right amount of studied desire (she practiced in front of a mirror when he wasn't around). "I hate your leaving me so soon, you just got here. I've been missing you madly all day, you beast."

"We know what the lady misses, don't we, Rupert?" He winked at the masseur, who winked reassuringly back. "The lady misses something nice and strong and long and hard, doesn't she? But she can't have it just yet, it's far too soon. Right! One glass of champagne coming up." He moved to the staircase and glanced back over his shoulder. "Carry on, Rupert."

The minute he'd gone downstairs, Anita slipped off the table and let Rupert fold it up, put it in back of the closet, pack up his gear, and be off. He patted her pussy affectionately.

"There's a good girl. See you next week, ducks. And remember, don't drink too much champers or Rupert will be angry at you."

"How can I not drink it?" she moaned, wishing he hadn't touched her vagina, although surely his wash-up earlier would have killed any lingering germs (wouldn't it?). "Beneath all that upper-class *sang froid*, Sir Michael is hot as a pistol. This is going to be one hell of a long evening."

Rupert looked at her cascading blond hair and rosy curves with a mixture of envy and malice. He looked at the magnificent four-poster Chippendale bed in the background, with its hangings of gold silk and ivory damask, its Frette sheets ready for revelry. The whole shebang cost more than he earned in ten years, he thought, picking up his worn red satchel.

"Them that has, always complains, ducks."

While Michael was getting the champagne, Anita went into the bathroom to check her diaphragm and make a few cosmetic repairs. She rubbed some Charles of the Ritz's Age-Zone Controller into her fine skin, dabbed Vichy deodorant under her arms, Complete Care onto her hands, neck, and breasts. After years of being sneered at by American men because her breasts were too small, it was a relief to have finally found a lover who thought they were just fine. If not spectacular. Anita knew she owed a lot to Englishwomen, whose breasts for the most part were even smaller than hers and made her look curvy by comparison. It was a good thing she hadn't immigrated to Italy, she thought as she gulped down one aspirin, one Valium, one Naturitab, one of her new cortisone pills, and one Lomontil. Just in case she should be struck by diarrhea before the evening ended, God forbid, but champagne had a slightly laxative effect on her.

Anita's medicine chest resembled a small pharmacy, inasmuch as she never threw out a prescription. Not that she would dream of swallowing a moldy old pill, but they were good to have on hand in the event she had to remind a doctor what he'd prescribed for her condition last time (currently she saw four specialists). A few drops of Eye-Clear in her china blues and she was temporarily set. There was no point in bathing now, Michael might want to muss her up a bit before Dickie Wembley arrived, which meant that she would just have to bathe all over again afterward. Being dainty was superessential in her line of endeavor but so was being superorganized.

In the six years that she'd been Sir Michael Harding's mistress, Anita had learned how to conserve her energy and not waste time. She only had a few precious hours each week in which to keep Michael happy and panting for more of the same, so she tried to make that time count for as much as possible. Her motto was: *Whatever he wants he gets, his slightest wish is my command.*

"A man who's paying for a woman's upkeep has to be made to feel like a king," she once told Lucy Pickles, trying to explain her philosophy. "He must believe that the woman thinks of nothing else all day but him, and how she can please him."

Lucy laughed deprecatingly. "Why would any man believe such rubbish?"

"Because when it comes to sex, they're all idiots. They *want* to believe it. I act as though Michael's pleasure is of paramount importance to me and that I simply adore having sex with him, that I can't get enough of it, that it's what makes my world go round. If I didn't convey that impression loud and clear, he'd dump me tomorrow."

"It sounds like damned hard work."

"It's like everything else," she said philosophically. "Once you know the formula, there's nothing to it."

A flair for the theatrical and a strong desire to become Michael's wife was all it took, plus having once been an airline stewardess didn't hurt one bit. Anita often thought that going from stewardess to mistress was a logical progression, since the emphasis in both jobs was upon pleasing and serving. The only major difference, as far as she could see, was that she no longer had to wash puky baby bottles and she made a hell of a lot more money for smiling at masculine inanities.

When she emerged from the bathroom, she was wearing a plunging bra in royal-blue silk and short scalloped panties trimmed with luscious royal-blue lace. Underneath was a matching garter belt. She sat down at her dressing table and was fastening a garter to the end of an ultrasheer stocking when Michael reappeared carrying two frosty glasses of Taittinger Brut Reserve. He handed her one.

"Bottoms up," he said, clicking glasses. "And speaking

of bottoms, I do like yours. That shade of blue is absolutely super. Is it new?''

She nodded. ''I bought it just for you.''

''Well done, darling.''

''I'm glad you approve. You know how much I want to please you.''

''I always approve of your pretty undies,'' he said, smiling benignly. With whom else but one's mistress could a man in his position have the luxury to discuss something as frivolous as women's undergarments? His wife favored sturdy practical things that made him groan. ''Everything you wear is quite delectable. That garter belt peeking through, in particular. Don't put your stockings on, though, I want your legs bare for the moment.'' He patted her rosy smooth skin, which Rupert waxed periodically. ''Who knows? We might have a little tumble before Dickie gets here.''

''An appetizer before the main course?''

''Something like that.''

''It sounds delicious to me.''

''Greedy little wench, aren't you?'' His hand traveled down the front of her panties, as though to make sure that all the equipment was still intact. ''Yes, this little blue number suits you very well indeed.''

Anita spent a fortune on lingerie. It was important to titillate Michael with something different as frequently as possible, so that he didn't become bored. Tricks and magic and games were her department; she had to be ready at all times to chase away a bad mood or an occasional bout of ennui. One of her bureaus contained nothing but the most slinky and seductive lingerie sold in London, another bureau held the toys she amused him with when more conventional methods failed. She turned her body in profile now and crossed her legs so that he had a better view of her.

''Your bra is very pretty with all that blue lace, but I much prefer what's underneath it,'' he said, watching her apply makeup. ''Just leave those delicious bottoms on, at least until Dickie gets here.''

She unhooked her brassiere and playfully threw it at him, then began to brush Douceur et Eclat foundation on her cheeks. She loved the Rose Indien shade, it made her face look naturally pink and flushed—not artificially done at all.

''Don't you want me dressed when Dickie arrives?'' she

asked, taking another sip of champagne. She wished he had brought the bottle up, but didn't mention it for fear he would think she was eager to get plastered. "I was planning to wear my brocaded gold kimono, the one you bought me at Harrods Calypso Room. Remember?"

"No, I don't."

His voice sounded caustic, or was she imagining it? "Of course you remember, darling. It was that day you played hooky from work. We had lunch at the Dorchester and then you decided to take me shopping at Harrods."

"If my memory is faulty, as it would seem, so is yours, my dear."

She wasn't imagining it. "I don't know what you mean, Michael."

"I thought we had decided that after Rupert left, you were going to cosmetically enhance those beautiful breasts of yours. That *was* what we agreed upon, wasn't it?"

"I'm sorry, darling, it slipped my mind." Why was he making such a big deal out of it? she wondered as she picked up her lipstick brush. Dipping it into the little pot of Strawberry Frappé rouge, she proceeded to paint her nipples bright red. "There. Does that look better?"

"Much. And next time, please don't overlook something I've asked you to do." His voice was petulant, resentful. "I dislike having to repeat myself, particularly when I make damned few requests as it is."

She wondered why he was being so difficult. Business, no doubt. Maybe things were going badly on his favorite research product: a plane with a laminar flow wing. Whatever the hell that was. She wished that Dickie would hurry up and get here before Michael's mood worsened. She mustn't let that happen. She went over to the chaise, snuggled in beside him, and put a hand on his trousers.

"I won't forget something like that again, I promise," she said softly, kissing his cheek. "I don't know what I could have been thinking of."

"Not me, I shouldn't imagine," he sulked.

She gingerly unzipped his fly. "But that's the whole point, sweetheart. I *was* thinking of you, that's what distracted me. Or maybe I should say, I was thinking of this big fellow."

His expression of petulance disappeared as he gazed at his

rapidly swelling organ. "He is looming rather large tonight, isn't he?"

"Very large." She bent her head down, checked discreetly for any sign of infection, and kissed him. "Mmmmmmm. You taste good." It was something she always said, men loved to hear it. "Really yummy."

"You just can't wait to get at it, can you?" He was appeased, it never failed. "My little girl just can't wait to start sucking cock, can she?"

"No, I can't. I've been thinking about it all day." She took him into her mouth and made the appropriate sounds of enjoyment.

"You little whore," he grunted. "You're such a little cunt, you know how to suck cock, don't you? Who taught you? Where did you learn?" He pulled her up by the hair and kissed her lips as one hand stroked her rouged nipples, then himself. "I won't let you make me come now. Not unless you beg. Well?"

"Please, Michael, let me," she said in a tiny pleading voice, thinking about that gorgeous suite at the King Croesus. "Please. I love it so much."

"I know you do, you adorable little bitch, cockteaser. You know how to drive me out of my mind, don't you?" He was pressing her nipple very hard. "Don't you? Answer me when I talk to you."

"Yes, I do love to make you excited. You come so beautifully." She was trying to take him into her mouth again, and trying not to think about what she would do if he refused to let her go to New York. "Won't you do that for me? Won't you fill my mouth with your gorgeous taste, darling? I'm so excited, I don't want to wait any longer."

"If you insist."

"Oh, I do," she moaned. "I do."

She bowed her head again and went at him, moving around and pushing her ass in his face. She made loud sucking sounds, very loud, as loud as she possibly could, because she knew that it excited him to have her behave like an animal in heat. And meanwhile he had pulled down her lacy blue panties and started to do something he was very ashamed of, which was why it gave him so much pleasure. He was sucking like crazy at her asshole, he'd once told her that he wanted to do it all his life but never had the nerve with another woman. Anita was delighted to hear that, it gave her a pretty good hold on him, she felt, and hopefully it would keep him coming back for more. She wondered what his wife, Lady Philippa, would think if she could see her distinguished husband with his nose buried in his girlfriend's furry crack. His hands were squeezing her buttocks, squeezing and pressing, slapping.

"Move it for me, you bitch. You're mine, every part of you belongs to me. Isn't that right? Tell me I'm right."

"You're right," she said, coming up for air and thinking of those Welsh sheep. "I'm all yours, you're absolutely right."

Anita found it interesting that he always started their evenings playing the slightly sadistic role, when his true inclinations lay in the opposite direction. It was almost as though he went through the motions of dominance to atone for his subsequent passivity and need for punishment.

"Every last inch of you is mine," he panted, slapping her ass harder. "Isn't that true?"

"Yes, yes, it's true."

"And don't you forget it, you little whore."

The blue lace garter belt was cutting into her soft flesh. "No, darling, I won't."

"Swear it."

"I won't forget. I swear. I belong to you."

"Damned right you do. Give it to me, you bitch, give me all of you."

A moment later he exploded and she had to swallow several times to get it all down (he was a gusher), and when she emerged her eyes were gleaming, she was smiling, her mouth was wet and some of the semen dribbled down her cheek.

"You're shameless," he said, pleased that she would revel in her debauchery. "Go and wash, then finish putting on your makeup. Dickie will be here any minute. I'll go get us another glass of champagne." He looked after her as she moved toward the bathroom. "I hope you've saved something for old Dickie. We don't want to disappoint him, do we, darling?"

She turned, her rouged breasts staring him in the face. "I don't want to disappoint *you*. Not ever. I love you too much."

They liked to hear that, too. Then she went to wash her mouth, thinking that the evening hadn't even officially begun and her jaw felt tired already. After brushing her teeth, she did a few facial exercises, combed her hair, returned to the dressing table and selected Praline Touche d'Eclat blusher for her cheeks—it was the next best thing to having naturally high cheekbones. She combed her thick blond hair and smiled at her reflection in the mirror. It smiled right back, assuring her that all would go well this evening, that she had never looked lovelier or more luminescent. She might have been a bride waiting for her husband to make love to her for the first time, alone on their very own honeymoon island in the Caribbean. And if she tried, she could even catch a glimpse of that blue tropical sea shining in the moonlight. Right outside the window.

A moment later the doorbell rang and Michael's hearty voice broke the spell. *"You're a sight for sore eyes, Dickie. Come on, old chap, come in!"*

Lou sang "Get Me to the Church on Time" as she dressed for her eleven-A.M. meeting with Fingerhood. In the week since she'd decided to go shopping for a male lover, she had felt less irritated by Vanessa and more carefree than she had in ages. Basically she still loved Vanessa and didn't want to lose her (if she could help it); all she wanted to do was give the little bitch a taste of her own infidelity.

Action. Doing something about her problems. Taking steps to ease her pain. It never failed to produce a feeling of being back in the driver's seat, and it was a feeling that Lou liked. A lot. She had just chosen Perry Ellis' pink linen tank top over his longish white linen dirndl skirt that was just creased enough and just expensive enough to look as though it didn't give a good goddamn about anything, when Vanessa caustically spoke up.

"I see that you're still catering to the enemy."

"What's bothering you now?"

"You and that voguish outfit of yours."

"Did you think I would go in my Jogbra, Nikes, and warmup suit?" Lou regarded herself in the bedroom mirror. "What's wrong with this outfit?"

"The same thing that's wrong with those three coats of Vaselined mascara, or the fact that you don't have a hair or a lash out of place, only your eyeliner interestingly smudged. And you wonder why I don't think you're serious about your radical feminism.''

"If you expect me to apologize for caring how I look, I don't intend to," she replied. "*You're* the one who has to change, if you're coming with me.''

Vanessa regarded her cut-off jeans and old T-shirt with "University of Maine" lettered across the chest. "What's wrong with what I'm wearing? At least I don't use three tons of nail polish, hair conditioner, and matte foundation in a phony attempt to impress the enemy—like you do.''

"I've told you repeatedly that I don't consider men the enemy. Now, go and change, I'm leaving in ten minutes.''

"If I have to change, I don't want to go.''

"That's fine with me." She slipped into her Ferragamo sandals and transferred the contents of her red leather purse to her mauve straw purse. "I'd rather deal with this by myself, anyway.''

"I'll change. But only because I'm dying to meet the man who broke your heart.''

"He didn't break it, he dented it slightly.''

While waiting, she sprayed herself with Cabochard, toned down her blusher, and wondered whether showing up with Vanessa would lead Fingerhood to the conclusion that they were lovers. Ordinarily she didn't give a damn what anyone thought, but she did today. That wasn't the only reason she preferred to go alone, though.

Visiting a prospective client had always been Lou's exclusive domain and she resented sharing the fun with a second party. This end of the business was where she threw *her* weight around and got *her* jollies (as Vanessa got hers in the kitchen). Even moments like this before the initial meeting were precious. She loved feeling her competitive juices start to flow and her enthusiasm for deal-making brim over. Later when she was involved in the actual selling of Some Like It Hot, that enthusiasm would reach its peak.

"Do I look respectable enough?''

Vanessa now wore a modified mini with blue and white stripes, blue thonged sandals, and held a quilted red shoulder bag that Lou had given her for her birthday.

"A vast improvement. Let's go. We have a long crosstown ride." She grabbed the hot-pink folder. "I still can't believe that Fingerhood is living in a penthouse on Sutton Place. He always hated ostentation.''

When they reached the lobby their doorman, Raoul, struggled into his jacket and went to flag down a taxi. West End Avenue was sultry and airless, a heat wave having hit New York overnight. They rode in silence. Lou pretended to study some new menus she had recently added to her folder, but actually she was thinking of Fingerhood. She wondered if he was still so attractive or if he'd gone to the dogs like so many men his age, whose Dorian Gray excesses finally caught up with them.

"You know what would be great for a June wedding?" Vanessa said, interrupting Lou's thoughts. "A slew of striped bass in aspic accompanied by a cucumber mousse. Very light and refreshing. I hope Fingerhood has nothing against fish.''

"I hope he has nothing against spending money. I had no idea how much it costs to get married these days until I sat down and worked it out on paper.''

Lou had drawn up four different kinds of wedding parties for Fingerhood to choose from. One of the main considerations was whether he wanted a buffet spread where guests helped themselves, or a sit-down meal served by staff. That, plus the kind of food and liquor, as well as the length of the affair, would determine the ultimate cost. The least expensive reception she could come up with ran twenty-five dollars per person; the most expensive ran seventy-five. Music and flowers were extra. So was the cake.

"I just realized something," she said to Vanessa. "The last wedding I attended was my own.''

"Don't remind me.''

"Why not? I have very fond memories of it.''

She had eschewed conventional lace, net, and beading for a flowing blue tunic gown with deep kimono sleeves, its long skirt slashed thigh-high to show off her blue-on-blue patterned stockings. On her head was an arc-en-ciel wreath and around her neck a single rope of blue pearls. Zachary had tears in his eyes when he turned and saw her coming down the aisle on the arm of her father. The ceremony was performed at the Park East Synagogue (because she was half-Jewish, she qualified), the reception was held at the lovely Café Des Artistes restaurant with its leaded glass windows and sensuous Howard Christie murals. Joan was her maid of honor, Zachary was attended by a younger brother, while eighteen-year-old Vanessa who'd flown in from Maine looked askance at the happy couple.

"I never understood why you wanted to marry my father. He was so much older than you, so much more stodgy. I never understood what he had to offer. It sure as hell couldn't have been sex. I know he was wealthy, but money didn't seem very important to you. So what was the big attraction?"

"I was in love with him."

"Oh, come on."

"People fall in love with people who meet their needs. That's what love is all about, in case you didn't know."

"Maybe he met your needs because he wasn't too heavily into sex."

Vanessa couldn't reconcile herself to the idea that there had been a time when Lou enjoyed heterosexual lovemaking. It was an area in which Vanessa felt at a loss to compete, so she pretended it didn't exist. Lou smiled. Vanessa was about to discover that it existed, all right, and not just in the past.

As their taxi crawled across Fifty-seventh Street in the hot midday traffic, Lou remembered how happy and delirious she felt to have finally tied the knot at the age of thirty-two. Even though marriage was never her number-one priority, nonetheless Lou had been brought up at a time when it was considered de rigueur for a girl to find herself a husband sooner or later, or bear the stigma of being considered an old maid. Unwanted, unloved, unworthy. Despite her flourishing fashion career and the fact that she was financially independent, she believed that in order to complete the circle of her life she absolutely and positively had to get married.

Lester Lanin played at their reception, while she followed Zachary's uncertain step to "Seems Like Old Times" and "Somewhere, My Love." As she gazed at her gold-and-diamond Tiffany wedding band, she realized that she'd joined a sacrosanct legion of womanhood—perhaps one of the most exclusive and snobby female clubs in the world. Wives, Inc. Getting married had seemed like a very mature step, a step up, there would be no more of those frivolous girlish pastimes such as dating and waiting by the phone, wondering if he would call, wondering if he would fall in love with her, impregnate her, abandon her, or not impregnate her but abandon her anyway for someone else, someone more compelling.

And then missing him, crying over him, desperately trying to figure out what she had done to lose him, and never really knowing if her answers were right or not. And then (maybe worst of all) having to start out once more with a new man, facing new problems, new conflicts, new anxieties, and wondering the same old things all over again. There would be no more of that for her, Lou thought giddily on her wedding day; she was a wife now. Safe, secure, respectable.

The taxi pulled up in front of a towering brick-and-stone fortress on Sutton Place South, where the air felt richer, cleaner, and decidedly more rarefied than on the Upper West Side. A white-gloved doorman gave them an insinuating interrogation before deigning to admit them. The lobby was softly lit, Persian-carpeted, with lots of black marble. The elevator was walnut-paneled and boasted a small bench covered in wine velvet. And when Lou rang the penthouse bell, the door was opened by a four-foot-high robot.

"Good morning, my name is Jeeves." It bared its wire teeth in a simulated smile and extended a plastic hand. "Won't you please come in? Dr. Fingerhood is busy with a patient but he'll be free shortly." Its voice was chillingly warm and friendly. "Follow me, please."

The robot led them down a richly waxed corridor past the living room, furnished in shades of oyster, beige, and tan, boasting lots of smoky mirrors, modern paintings, one strategically placed hammock, and glimpses of a terrace lush with foliage, past two bedrooms en suite, to the very end of the hall, where it turned right and the decor changed from luxurious to functional. The robot gestured toward what was obviously a waiting room. The walls housed floor-to-ceiling bookcases, which seemed to hold every tome written by every author on the related subjects of psychology and psychiatry. One entire shelf was filled with books dealing with sex.

"Next time would you kindly come in the patients' entrance?" The expression on the robot's cathode-ray-tube face changed from welcoming to chastising. "That one over there."

"We're not patients, we're the caterers," Vanessa archly replied. "For Dr. Fingerhood's wedding."

Four lights went off in rapid succession on the robot's chest—blue, yellow, green, orange—followed by an apology. "Please forgive my error. I'm only human, ha ha ha."

Then a small vacuum cleaner shot out of its lower-right-hand side and went to work on some cigarette ashes that had been dropped on the carpet. Within seconds they were gone, the vacuum returned to its hiding place, and the robot started to leave the room.

"Wait a minute," Lou said. "Can you tell us who your employer is marrying?"

Five lights switched on (one of them a deep angry purple). "I'm sorry, madam, but I'm not allowed to reveal that information." It bowed and departed.

Minutes later the door to Fingerhood's private office swung open and a rangy girl with small, exquisite features emerged. She carried a large flat black model's portfolio and had been crying.

"It's so *awkward* in a hammock," she murmured unhappily to the doctor at her side. "The last time, I fell off and almost broke my nose."

Fingerhood topped the girl by a few inches and wore a reassuring look. "No one ever said it would be easy. But when you achieve your first transcendental orgasm, you'll know it was worth the effort."

Vanessa giggled. Lou was too busy observing the handsome face (she remembered so well) lined in all the right places, the thick dark hair still intact but sprinkled with gray, the button-down shirt striped in navy, white, and maroon, the silk paisley tie, navy twill trousers, loafers of the finest cordovan leather. He looks fantastic, she thought, wondering what to make of the parrot. Perched solidly on Fingerhood's shoulder, it seemed to be staring at her sideways.

"*Neurotic, exotic, erotic girls!*" the parrot shrieked suddenly, ruffling its feathers. "*Twirls, curls, I want Mikimoto cultured pearls!*"

The model shrank back in fear. "Don't let him touch me!"

"He's not trying to," Fingerhood said soothingly. "But I must apologize for his outburst. I got Miguel from a schizophrenic patient. They rhyme everything, you know."

Vanessa poked Lou. "Do you think he takes out the black eyepatch and wooden leg for special occasions? Or is this the whole act?"

"Shut up."

The minute the model left, the parrot flew off to perch on a bookcase shelf. Then Fingerhood and Lou fell into one another's arms with exaggerated cries of delight, profuse regret over having let so much time go by, and inflated compliments about how terrific the other looked. When they drew apart, Lou felt relieved that the worst was over, and she imagined he did too. At least she hadn't let herself go to pieces like so many women her age, she thought, surprised to realize how badly she still wanted his seal of approval.

"Lou, you've made a success out of a second career." He smiled his old seductive smile. "I think that's terrific, my compliments."

"And mine on your book." His presence was electric; now she remembered why she'd been so hung up on him. "I hear it's still selling like mad."

*"Bad, glad, sad sack!"* shrieked the parrot. *"Back, pack, I hate hack writers!"*

"Go away, Miguel," Fingerhood said, his gaze turning toward Vanessa. "Don't demean me in front of this lovely lady, the honor of which I haven't yet had."

Lou introduced them and thought, *Now he knows we're lovers,* then chastised herself for being such a paranoid and provincial jerk. But all Fingerhood seemed curious about was that both their last names were Greenspan, and after learning why, he changed the subject to cooking. Lou had forgotten how indifferent he was to anything that didn't directly affect him and how it only made her want to try harder to win his attention. She wondered whether he behaved that way on purpose and whether other women reacted as anxiously as she. Vanessa would have called it "Trying to please Daddy," and maybe that was part of Fingerhood's subliminal appeal.

"I gather you're the chef," he said to Vanessa. "As talented as Lou is, I can't conceive of her in the kitchen. When I knew her, her one culinary accomplishment was making the worst coffee I've ever tasted. Have you studied cooking formally?"

"Yes, at the Culinary Institute of America and also at Hot Wok, a wonderful Chinese school. But the main thing about cooking is that you never stop learning. There's always something new to discover, something you didn't know yesterday, and that's what makes it so exciting for me."

"You sound dedicated."

"I am," she said emphatically. "I think of cooking as an art, not merely a skill."

He lowered his eyes, gazed up through his lashes (a gesture that on almost any other man would have seemed fatuously effeminate, but managed to work), and gave her the full flashlight glare of his charm. "And I'm sure it's an art that you excel in."

Vanessa couldn't imagine what Lou had ever seen in him. "At the risk of sounding immodest, I'm not half bad."

"I don't doubt it for a second."

Lou observed her ex-lover in action. He still flirted with every woman who crossed his path (he couldn't help it, it was a conditioned reflex), he still looked sensational. Why did certain men get better as they got older, while most women just got older? Here he was in the prime of his life, a forty-eight-year-old reprobate who could pick and choose from a range of women between twenty and fifty, and here she was at forty-two trying to hold on to Vanessa. It seemed so cruel, so unfair. What did Mother Nature have in mind when she let the sexes mature so disparately? The only sense Lou could make of it was that Mother Nature was a misnomer. *She* was really a *he*.

"What do you think of Miguel?" Fingerhood asked Vanessa.

She wished he would ask what she thought of him: an asshole, if there ever was one. But she decided to be polite, for Lou's sake. "Miguel is beautiful and I'm partial to beautiful things."

He leaped on her reply with pleasure. "It's unusual for someone to pick up on the aesthetics immediately, but of course as a chef you have a trained eye for color, flair, coordination—qualities that Miguel possesses in abundance. A lot of my female patients are afraid of him, terrified in fact. You saw the model."

"Is that why you have him?" she said coldly. "To see how many women you can frighten?"

"Hardly. Although Miguel is an expedient way to get a fast reading on new patients. How they react to their shrink with a parrot on his shoulder is very informative, it can save everyone a great deal of time in therapy. And yet you'd be amazed how many people never mention him at all—not ever. They act as though he didn't exist. And it's not because they're indifferent to him—we discover that six months later."

"Then why all the silence, doctor?"

"Because not everyone is as communicative or sexually

fearless as you.'' His voice was like a caress. He seemed unaware of her contempt. ''A lot of people have trouble conveying their sexual hang-ups. And when confronted with a stimulus like Miguel that they find disturbing, confusing, fascinating, or repelling—as the case may be—they try to pretend that those hang-ups don't exist.''

''What makes you think I'm so sexually fearless?''

''Because you're not intimidated by Miguel. Birds are erotic symbols and parrots are the most erotic of all. They're wild, primitive, dangerous. They bite.''

''I bite back,'' she said with a curt laugh.

''I rather thought you would. Let's return to my living quarters, shall we? I'd suggest sitting on the terrace, but I'm afraid it's too hot now,'' he apologized as they entered the oyster-beige-and-tan living room. ''This part of the apartment faces east and gets the morning sun.''

Lou looked around. The room's wall-to-wall carpeting was thick, its abstract-expressionist paintings were expensively original. Except for a few Aztec sculptures and a familiar hemp hammock, the only similarity between this classic contemporary room and his old cluttered Mexican seduction den was that both were marked by a penchant for larger-than-life possessions. Even the pop-art wall clock, shaped like a daisy with twelve petals, loomed twice as large as any normal clock. Once when she and Fingerhood were kissing in this very same hammock, he told her that her teeth were too small. It was the weirdest criticism she'd ever received.

''I go for women with big teeth,'' he had said by way of explanation. ''Sue me.''

She wondered whether his fiancée had big teeth, too.

''I've decided that the terrace is where I want to have the wedding ceremony performed,'' Fingerhood declared as they made themselves comfortable. ''Do you think it can accommodate fifty guests, Lou? It's a wraparound.''

She surveyed the landscaped terrace, which looked down upon the sun-drenched river below. A big red tugboat was slowly chugging its way north, and on the other side the trees of Roosevelt Island were stationed like sentries. There was a feeling of airy splendor here, high up and removed from the smog, grime, and dirt of the city below.

''Getting married on the terrace is a charming idea. It's

definitely large enough," she said. "What time is the ceremony scheduled for?"

"Four o'clock on the last Saturday of this month." He shook his head as though he still couldn't believe it. "Frankly, I can't wait."

"She must be quite a woman to have tamed the elusive Fingerhood," Lou said. "I thought for sure your fiancée would be here today. I'm dying to meet her."

"You will. But meanwhile, let's continue."

Lou shrugged and consulted her folder. "Four is good, it means the terrace will have had a chance to cool down from the morning sun. We can start serving as soon as the ceremony is over. Do you know how long it will be?"

"Twenty minutes tops. We're keeping it short, sweet, and nondenominational. The minister will read passages from the Book of Ruth, *The Prophet,* and *The Fingerhood Position,* then after a few words of counsel we exchange our vows and troop back in here for the sit-down dinner."

"You've just answered one of my questions," Lou said, wondering which passage the minister would choose from *The Fingerhood Position* (the one that likened fucking in hammocks to sexual aerodynamics?). "If we move all this furniture into the bedrooms, we can set up the tables right here. I suggest seven tables of six people each, then a bridal table of ten."

"Ten?"

"Comprising the members of the wedding party and their escorts."

A shadow of consternation flickered in his eyes. "What about parents?"

"It's customary that they share a table with other family members and the clergyman." She made a note in her folder. "Is there an entrance to the terrace other than from this room? Because if not, we're going to have trouble. The processional might run into waiters carrying trays of champagne, that sort of thing."

"Don't worry about access to the terrace. Both bedrooms lead out to it. But I'm glad you mentioned champagne." He rang a silver bell on the coffee table. "I want the finest, Lou. *Of everything.* I've waited forty-eight years to get married and I'm going to do it in style. So whatever you do, don't skimp and don't worry about the bill. It can't be steep enough for me!''

Vanessa felt contemptuous of conspicuous consumers like Fingerhood. To her mind, they equated a show of money with a show of masculinity, the poor fools. ''What do you think of cold striped bass in aspic, with cucumber mousse?'' she asked him. ''As an appetizer.''

''It sounds delicious but I want only the freshest, firmest, most delectable bass. This is going to be a wedding that people will remember for the rest of their lives.'' He rang the silver bell again. ''Where the hell is that robot? And why do you suddenly seem so uneasy, Lou?''

''I hate to continue without your fiancée. Aside from the fact that I'm dying to meet her, I can't believe that any woman would intentionally miss the arrangements for her own wedding.''

Bitter experience had shown that when dealing with a couple, it was essential for the woman to participate in the initial discussion. Otherwise she often complained later on about her wishes being ignored or countermanded, which sometimes resulted in their having problems collecting the bill. Once they had had to sue.

''Sally should be back any minute, but we needn't wait,'' Fingerhood said. ''She and I are in total accord.''

*''Adored, afford, all aboard the train!''* The parrot had flown into the room and was circling the coffee table. *''Vain, cane, Lane Bryant's is for fatties!''*

''That's the last time I'll ever get a parrot from a schizophrenic with a weight problem,'' Fingerhood muttered. ''Go away, Miguel. Can't you see I'm busy?''

*''Dizzy, fizzy, I'm in a tizzy! Lizzie Borden took an ax, Saks Fifth Avenue is more my style!''*

He flew over to an Aztec sculpture, just as the robot came in and bowed in the direction of his employer.

''Three glasses of champagne,'' Fingerhood said sternly. 'And please don't forget to chill the glasses like last time.''

''I'm only human, ha ha ha.''

''Sally?'' Lou said after the robot had left. ''Sally who? Who is this mysterious fiancée of yours?''

''You'll find out.''

Lou leaned forward. ''Do I know her?''

''Not exactly.''

"Even *I'm* curious," Vanessa added.

"I don't know what all the fuss is about—"

Just then the outside door opened and a young girl came in, carrying a bunch of daffodils. She had the bearing of a model (maybe he specialized in them, Lou thought). Tall, slender, dark-haired, dark-eyed, a beauty mark on her left cheek, she wore red terry shorts, running shoes, and was out of breath, as though she'd been jogging. She blew a kiss at Fingerhood.

"Hi, sweetheart. Sorry I'm late." She smiled brightly at the two women, revealing very large teeth. "I'm Sally Northrop. You must be Vanessa and Lou Greenspan. It's so nice to meet you."

Vanessa was surprised by how young she was. A baby. Up close her face was strangely gaunt, considering her extreme youth. A dissipated baby model. "It's nice to meet you, too," she said, extending her hand. "Isn't it, Lou?"

But Lou had gone into shock. It couldn't be. It was impossible, ridiculous. It took her a moment to speak. "You're not . . . ?"

"Fingerhood's fiancée? I most certainly am." She seemed amused by Lou's discomfort. "Don't you approve? Do you think I'm too young and girlish for the old roué? Don't let my girlish looks fool you. Fingerhood didn't know what dissipation was until he met me."

Lou swallowed hard. The last time she'd seen her, Sally was five years old and having a birthday party. Sally's father had taken her to it. Sally's mother was smashed at it. Later the three of them drank opium and made love in a weird apartment with life-size George Segal sculptures. How strange that Sally should have referred to dissipation just now.

"It's your last name," Lou said, stammering. "Northrop. You don't happen to be . . . ?"

"Beverly and Peter's daughter? Yes, I regret to say I'm that, too." The girl's eyes had gone dark. "You used to know my parents, didn't you? Back in the good old days?"

*"Ways, plays, daisies are yellow,"* Miguel shrieked, starting to fly around the room. *"Fellow, mellow, I like to fuck Jell-O. Doesn't everyone?"*

Then he flew over to Jeeves (returning with a tray of champagne), perched on top of his head, and let go with a few more hysterical rhymes before Fingerhood threatened him into silence.

# II

---

# *THE REUNION*

# 4

When Simone and Colin McKenna checked into the glamorous, glorious, luxurious, newly opened, one-thousand-dollar-a-night triplex (pronounced try-plex) at the King Croesus Hotel on Park Avenue, Simone was wearing a billowy-sleeved black georgette dress cut down to her belly button, five-inch spike heels, a rope cluster of real Fred Joaillier pearls, and smiling at everyone in sight—who smiled and stared right back at her.

The truth was that she felt like shit, but a movie star had to keep up appearances. Even the trip from Los Angeles started off on a catastrophic note. The first thing Colin did was try to pick up a flashy blond seated across from him, oblivious of the attentive man at her elbow. The blond smiled a polite refusal, but not before asking him for an autograph for her daughter.

"Yeah, sure, you're welcome, anytime." It was Colin's robotlike response to autograph requests. "You don't look old enough to have a daughter. Are you sure it's not for yourself?"

"Quite sure, Mr. McKenna," she said coldly.

"I'm staying at the King Croesus. Give me a tinkle."

When Simone whispered that not only was he embarrassing her, but that they were on a publicity tour to prove to the world (and the head of the studio) that they were madly in love and couldn't live without each other, Colin's reply was: "Your mouth is as big as your cunt undoubtedly is."

The flight attendant heard him and turned away to hide her smile. Simone wanted to die. First of all, it wasn't true—about her cunt being so big—and secondly, it was one of the most humiliating things that had ever been said to her. She intended to read Colin the riot act as soon as they were inside the privacy of their hotel suite, and if necessary, call Eddie to complain about how the shmuck was sabotaging all their plans. She wondered whose side Eddie would take.

Whenever Simone remembered that afternoon in Eddie's garden, she turned green. Not only didn't she have a solar-powered orgasm, but she soon learned that the reason he was so anxious for her to team up with Colin was that the sneaky son of a bitch had become Colin's agent too! She nearly fell off the lounger when she heard that one.

"But Colin is signed to do *Arizona Pete* for another year," she mumbled after she recovered from shock. "How can he do a movie as well?"

"*Rockabye Princess* won't start principal photography until the winter and Colin will have finished shooting his twenty-four episodes by December," Eddie informed her. "He'll be free from December to May—that's how he'll be able to do it. What's more, darling, he *wants* to do it."

"He does?" she asked miserably, remembering his Pernod breath and drippy nose, thanks to all that cocaine.

"All television stars want to do feature films. They want the prestige, they want to go down in Hollywood's hall of fame with the rest of the heavyweights, and they want it bad. Movies are class, TV is TV." Eddie beamed, no doubt anticipating his combined commission if both she and Colin were signed for the picture. "Besides, I've gotten Colin a wonderful new clause in his *Arizona Pete* contract. It specifies three weeks' shooting each month and one week off."

"What's so wonderful about it?"

"He'll be able to go to New York with you, darling. Aren't you excited?"

"Thrilled. Will he ride his silver Yahama all the way?"

"You don't look well."

Simone dashed to the bathroom and threw up the Grand Marnier soufflé she'd eaten at lunch, red-raspberry sauce, globs of whipped cream and all. That's how thrilled she was at the prospect of shacking up for a week with Colin McKenna. . . .

She spent the rest of the flight time to New York worrying whether she had put enough Nutribul Emulsion under her makeup to counteract air-travel dehydration and wondering what it would be like to see the Big Apple again. Although she'd gone there right after being nominated for an Oscar, it had been a hurried and pressured trip. All she did was sit in her suite at the Sherry Netherland being interviewed by reporters, then a limo whisked her off at daybreak to do a segment of the *Today* show, and the next thing she knew she and Jimmy were on Air France headed for the Cannes Film Festival to get in a little more hype. So in a way this was her first real return visit since she left nearly fifteen years ago.

She had never wanted to leave; it was her husband's idea. He said that the winters were too cold, the art-gallery scene was too incestuous, and it was no place to raise the children they intended to have. Since it was useless to argue with Steve Omaha once his mind was made up, she packed her bags and they drove west in an old station wagon crammed full of oil canvases. Although Simone adapted beautifully to Southern California (she loved everything about it, from the funky palm trees to the pastel houses), there was a part of her that never stopped missing the mad energy of New York.

Fingerhood was part of that energy. Whenever she thought of the city, she thought of him simultaneously, and felt her heart quicken. Yes, even after all these years and all her international success, he still had an unsettling effect upon her and she wasn't the least bit surprised. As far as Simone was concerned, any woman who pretended to be immune to the first big love of her life was either a liar or an insensitive jerk. Although she'd been tempted to call Fingerhood from Malibu to RSVP his wedding invitation, she stifled the impulse and asked her secretary to send a note instead. She refused to give him the satisfaction of knowing that a glamorous movie star (whom he'd thrown over when she was a poverty-stricken nobody) could be so anxious to talk to him. Mostly, she was dying to know who he was marrying and what the mysterious creature had that she didn't. Beauty? Brains? Personality? The right zodiac sign? Well, she would find out soon enough.

"The King Croesus is proud to welcome you to one of our very special triplexes, where we hope you will find everything you need to make your stay an enjoyable one," the Tower. manager said as he ushered them out of a private elevator on the Sixty-seventh floor and into an elegant two-storied apartment with crystal chandeliers, a winding gold staircase, and a dazzling view of lower Manhattan. "In case you're wondering why this is called a triplex but looks like a duplex, it's because there's still another floor you haven't yet seen: the solarium directly upstairs. Your private elevator will take you there for a bit of sun, a swim in the heated pool, or just to relax in your own jacuzzi.''

He smoothed his small black mustache and drew himself up to his full height of five-feet-nothing, adding, ''It's a great honor to serve you, Miss Simone, and you, of course, Mr. McKenna. My wife and I are ardent fans of both your movie and television work.''

''Thank you,'' Simone said, noting the magnum of champagne, bowl of fresh fruit, box of Godiva chocolates, and obligatory vase of long-stemmed roses. ''You seem to have thought of everything.''

The Tower manager lowered his eyes modestly. ''We try.''

''Neat, very neat.'' Colin was pleased by the costly furnishings and silk-patterned walls, yet somehow imagined he was still on a surfboard. He should have cooled it on the coke he'd done in the limo from JFK. To orient himself, he now set his ten-thousand-dollar black-and-gold submariner Rolex three hours ahead to New York time. ''I think I could learn to rough it here, but before they send our bags up, how about showing us the bedrooms?''

''That's a good idea, darling.'' Simone put her head on his shoulder and gazed adoringly into his charley-alerted eyes. ''We want to make sure that the mattress is firm enough, don't we?''

''That wasn't exactly what I had in mind—''

Before he could finish what might be an embarrassing sentence, she turned confidentially to the Tower manager, who couldn't keep his gaze away from her cleavage. ''I think my fiancé is afraid of finding twin beds in the master bedroom. We'd prefer a double, you see.''

''*Fiancé?*'' The Tower manager's eyes began to cross at news of this heretofore unpublicized tidbit. ''There's been nothing in the papers, not a hint . . .''

''I realize that,'' Simone said, trying to look grave. This was her chance to start the P.R. ball rolling. ''Mr. McKenna and I didn't want to announce our engagement until we were absolutely certain of our feelings for each other. I think it's tacky the way certain movie stars flit from romance to romance, without a serious thought to commitment. Then after they've been photographed hugging and kissing and pledging their undying devotion, the affair suddenly ends and both parties are left with egg on their face. We wanted to avoid that kind of irresponsible behavior."

"I not only understand, I commend you on your discretion." The Tower manager felt as though he had stumbled upon one of the hottest Hollywood scoops of all time. "Does that mean we, at the King Croesus, might have the privilege of witnessing a wedding during your stay with us? Because if so, permit me to offer you the use of our lovely banquet hall for the happy occasion. It's called the Lydia Room. Croesus was the last king of Lydia before the Persians slaughtered the poor man, back in 546 B.C. A little Greek history, compliments of the management."

"How fascinating," Simone said with a coquettish smile. Colin had wandered over to a window and was staring at the skyline. "Strictly entre-nous, we're picking out the ring tomorrow at Cartier's but I suspect it will be a brief engagement. Don't worry, monsieur, as soon as the date is set you'll be the first to know."

"Most kind of you." He beamed in gratitude. "And now, if you and Mr. McKenna would follow me, I'll take you upstairs."

There were three bedrooms, all decorated in different color schemes. Simone could hardly wait to pick out the one she wanted for herself and lock the door behind her. The downstairs level was gigantic, with a full kitchenette, a formal dining room, and the dreamy gray-velveted living area, but it afforded no escape from that shmuck she was stuck with, so she planned to spend a lot of time alone in her boudoir. That is, when she wasn't shopping at Bendel's, Bergdorf's, and Bloomingdale's, attending Fingerhood's wedding, and making obligatory entrances with Colin at New York's hottest restaurants and nightstops in order to convince the studio that they were this year's odd couple.

In the week since Simone had agreed to go through with the publicity stunt, the studio had signed Colin for the male lead in *Rockabye Princess,* which made him extremely reluctant to embark on the trip, since *he* was home free. But then Eddie promised to get him an extra percentage point if he went to New York and helped Simone out—a bribe that greedy Colin grabbed and never stopped rubbing in her face.

Simone decided that if she did get to play the Danish princess, she would save her money and leave Jimmy. He not only had the nerve to categorically deny that he was rewriting *Rockabye Princess* for a younger actress, but he had the double nerve not to give a damn that she was leaving for New York the next day with his buddy.

"Colin and I are going to be joined at the hip for an entire week," she informed him. "In the same hotel suite. Aren't you the tiniest, eensiest bit jealous?"

"What's there to be jealous about? I trust you and I trust Colin. Just make the romance look good and you'll have the studio eating out of your hand."

"You mean, like they're eating out of *your* hand now that you've agreed to rewrite the part for some sweet young thing I can never play?"

"I wouldn't exactly call it rewriting," he said, looking uncomfortable. "You shouldn't believe everything your agent tells you. You know how agents are."

"How?"

"They're all connivers, manipulators, deceivers. You can never be sure what they're doing."

"Oh, I'm sure of what Eddie is doing," she said hotly. "He's trying to get me the lead in that lousy movie of yours, which is more than can be said of you, you rotten liar!"

"There's no need to get so worked up, Simone. I'm on your side, you should realize that by now." He pecked her on the cheek like a Dutch uncle. "Have a good time in the Big Apple."

"*A good time!* For all you know, I might be fucking your best friend starting tomorrow. Is that your idea of *a good time?*"

"Calm down, kiddo."

"Kiddo yourself!"

She picked up a Limoges plate and hurled it at him. Unfortunately, it missed him by an inch and shattered to pieces on the stainless-steel kitchen counter. "I hate you!" she screamed so loudly that Hilda came running. "You can play poker in Gardena until you're bankrupt, for all I care!"

"What are you getting so hysterical about?" he asked, unperturbed. "You should be pleased that I trust you with Colin. You should be happy that I have so much confidence in you."

"I'll give you confidence, you asshole!" She broke a

cream pitcher over his head. "I'll give you trust, you insensitive jerk!"

After that she cried for three days, hoping (in between wrenching sobs) that Eddie would call and renew her faith in the opposite sex. But when he did call, it was strictly business. He never once alluded to their little romantic escapade, nor did he ask to see her again. One fast screw and he'd reverted to his old professional role of agent, period. His callousness made Simone cry for three more days, during which time she resolved to find a new man. He would have to be loyal, devoted, passionate, think she was the greatest fuck in the world, and be ready to *kill* if another man so much as went *near* her. . . .

"Tell me something," Colin said to the Tower manager as he bounced around on the king-size mattress in the master bedroom, doing calisthenics and just generally behaving like a California bubblehead. "Don't any of these fancy rooms of yours have Water-Babies?"

"Excuse me, sir. Water *what*?"

"Water-Babies. They're a popular brand of water bed." He did a somersault across the heavily brocaded spread. "I'm not so sure I can fall asleep on a regular bed anymore, I've become so used to my Water-Baby. I even had one installed in my dressing room, so I can catch a little shut-eye when I'm not needed on the set of *Arizona Pete*—which isn't often, I assure you. But that's the price of starring in America's most popular series, so I'm not complaining. Except about this little number right here."

He patted the bed, then somersaulted back. "Water-Babies are great, man, really great. You haven't slept until you've slept on one. And you'll notice that I'm not talking about doing anything more risqué than sleeping." He pronounced it "risky."

"Yes, indeed, sir." The Tower manager's mustache looked as though it were going to fall off. "I'm sorry, sir, but none of our triplexes come equipped with water beds. However, I'm sure that the management of the King Croesus would be more than happy to provide you with one for a slight additional fee. If you want me to, I'll be delighted to check with—"

The Tower management never got to finish the sentence because Colin had leaped off the bed, and to Simone's horror, picked the terrified man off the floor before she could stop him. She had seen cocaine make him do a Dr. Jekyll–Mr. Hyde turnabout before, but never in public.

"Listen, fuckface," Colin said, nose-to-nose with the Tower manager. "I don't want to hear no crap about additional fees and how you'll be delighted to check with your superiors. I know that these lousy triplexes of yours go for a cool grand a night, and I know that you cheap bastards don't offer more than a five-thousand-dollar overall discount, not that I give a shit. I'm not paying for this bordello, my fiancée isn't paying for it. You realize who's paying for it, don't you, turkey?"

"No, sir." The Tower manager's voice came out in a tiny cramped whisper. "Truly, I don't. Those matters are handled by our reception desk."

"Sandler-Roma-Weintraub Studios, that's who's paying. And if you had half a brain, you'd be knocking off fees—not adding them on—in the hope that said studio, which is owned by one of the largest multinational conglomerates in the U.S. of A., might see fit to send you a few more heavyweights in the future. Maybe Farrah and Ryan, or how about Burt and Sally? You'd like that kind of patronage, wouldn't you? Sure, it would help you compete with class joints like the Pierre and the Helmsley Palace, wouldn't it, asshole?"

"Yes, sir. Please put me down, sir."

"If there's anything I hate, it's being ripped off. Maybe you think my fiancée and I were born yesterday to walk in here alone and deal directly with a no-style hustler like you, which shows what you don't know. Fact is, this isn't an official trip for us or we'd have been preceded by a slew of press agents, bodyguards, secretaries, hairdressers, personal managers, and every kind of gofer you care to name, the whole Hollywood shmeer. But we wanted this to be a quiet romantic interlude, no business, no publicity, no cheap shots, just the two of us—her and me, that beautiful lady and me—enjoying ourselves in the Big Apple before we start work on our new movie, *Rockabye Princess*, which happens to be budgeted at twenty million smackeroos, I might add. And our studio, kindhearted folks that they are, suggested we check into the King Croesus and they'd pick up the tab. Now, do you think that Sandler-Roma-Weintraub Studios give one good goddamn about a couple of lousy bucks for a water bed, when they have three of this year's top-grossing movies, not to mention their Las Vegas holdings, TV production company, record division, and video-disc operations? Well, do you, faggot?''

"Really, sir. I insist that you put me down.''

Colin dropped him to the floor. "Get lost, get me the Water-Baby, send up a case of Pernod and a couple of broads. I'm in the mood to get my ashes hauled.''

*"But, sir."* The Tower manager turned red and glanced at Simone, who wished she were in Sri Lanka. *"Your fiancée."*

"I said this was a romantic interlude, not a fucking one. Besides, where I come from in Shawnee, Oklahoma, we don't bang our women until the wedding night. It's not considered good manners, capish?''

"Yes, sir. Right away, sir." On his way out, he shook Simone's hand with a cold and sweaty palm. "I hope you'll be very happy at the King Croesus. Under the circumstances, that is.''

Simone didn't know whether to kill Colin or kiss him. Telling the Tower manager that the *two* of them had been signed for *Rockabye Princess* was a stroke of genius. It meant that the rumors would start circulating right away, and hopefully influence the studio in her favor. Also, she appreciated his having covered up the fact that she was paying for this trip entirely out of her own pocket. But she was appalled by his request for call girls.

"Why did you do it?" she demanded as he began toying with his coke paraphernalia. "The whole purpose of this trip was to convince people that you and I are a hot item. You've ruined everything, you idiot!''

"Relax, my little croissant, I'm not as dumb as I look." He laid out three lines of coke on a small mirror, then did one line, using a sterling-silver straw monogrammed with his initials. "First off, the Mustache will never believe that we aren't getting it on. He'll just assume that in addition to our standard A fucking, we want to have ourselves a standard B orgy before dinner." He pronounced "orgy" with a hard *g*. "And what's so terrible about him thinking that? Isn't that what we Hollywood folks are supposed to do the minute the grown-ups turn their backs—screw and suck in epic proportions? Hell, Simone, we don't want to disappoint the Mustache and ruin all his fantasies about how depraved we movie stars are. Now that he's seen what a shitheel I am and what a two-faced little lady you are (he's got you pictured in bed with those broads already, believe me), he won't have the slightest hesitation about spilling our whereabouts to the media, dig? Not that they won't discover us as soon as we start doing the town, but this way the Mustache will whet their appetites before we set foot outside this door."

Colin did a second line of coke and hooted. "He'll have the media creaming in their pants over all the raunchy goings-on in the King Croesus Tower, and you know that that makes for great publicity. You can't *buy* publicity like that, so relax, stop kvetching, take off your dress, and let's screw a little. We might as well play the game if we're going to take the blame. What do you say, Frenchie?"

Having spent the last four years denigrating Colin McKenna, she now found herself excited as hell. She couldn't believe it, but her nipples were standing at attention, a sure sign. Somehow his take-charge behavior, as vulgar and tasteless as it was, had turned her on despite her better judgment. But since when did sexual attraction have anything to do with judgment or logic?

*Never*, as far as she was concerned, and she didn't care if the feminists said it should. Equality between the sexes was a joke, it didn't exist, it never would, men ran the world and women ran after men—no matter how impossible they were. Simone stepped out of her dress to face Colin in black see-through panties, lacy garter belt, and butterfly-patterned stockings, her erect nipples staring him in the face.

"Not bad, Frenchie."

"Save the last line for me," she said, reaching for the monogrammed straw with one hand and the bulge in his pants with the other.

And later, when they were doing lustful unspeakable things, she found herself remembering the first time she'd made love to Fingerhood and how sensational it was. When they woke up the next morning, he told her she was beautiful (and she replied, "More beautiful than Anita?"). She wondered whether Fingerhood would still find her beautiful, or had time left its cruel and heartless markings, despite all those little ops that Jimmy insisted upon?

"What is it with you, Frenchie?" Colin demanded after he'd been pounding away for a few minutes. "Don't you ever reach the moon?"

Before she could explain about her hidden clitoris, the doorbell began to ring.

"And not a moment too soon," he cried, leaping out of bed. "That must be the hookers."

Anita had been actively miserable ever since she and Michael arrived in New York late that afternoon and checked into the Gramercy Regency, a quiet residential hotel with housekeeping apartments, that overlooked Gramercy Park.

"Charming and civilized," Michael said with approval, gazing out the window. "That's what this neighborhood is."

"I didn't come to New York for *charm*," she irritably informed her lover. "I came for a breath of glamour and excitement. Instead, here I am in a suite with a primitive kitchenette, one tiny bathroom, and not a boutique, department store, or art museum in sight!"

"But that's why I chose it, darling. It's so very discreet and secluded, not smack in the midst of all those vulgar shops and crowds and interminable noise."

She felt like punching the pompous bastard clear across the room. Having been his mistress for the past six years, she expected something far more luxurious than fading armchairs and draperies that had seen better days. She expected the King Croesus on Park Avenue, where (she'd had the misfortune to learn) her old nemesis, Simone, was staying. Not only was Simone ensconced in the hotel of her dreams, but she was ensconced in it with gorgeous, seductive, famous, and filthy rich Colin McKenna, whom Anita had been watching in *Arizona Pete* ever since ITV began airing his series each Thursday. It seemed to Anita that whatever she accomplished in life, Simone was destined to be four steps ahead of her.

"Besides, we can cook our own meals when we feel like it," Michael blithely went on. "You don't appreciate good solid value for money, that's your problem, darling."

"*Cook our own meals?* I thought this was supposed to be a holiday, I thought you wanted me to have a good time. Instead, no sooner are we through the door than you expect me to start cooking dinner. I don't even cook at home, for God's sake!"

Mondays and Thursdays in London were too filled with erotica to allow time for culinary accomplishments, of which she had none to speak, anyway. All those years spent warming and serving meals in the sky cured Anita of any romantic ideas she might have had about the pleasures of home cuisine. Still, in order not to appear totally unskilled, she taught herself how to make two dishes: chicken cacciatore and blanquette de veau. She figured they sounded complicated enough to impress any man who needed proof of her domestic abilities, although to date she'd prepared the chicken dish for Michael only once—when both the Indian and Chinese take-out restaurants were inexplicably closed on the same day.

"Now, darling, I wasn't suggesting you whip up a seven-course dinner." Michael couldn't understand her resentment. This was her big chance to show off for him in the kitchen; she should be overjoyed. "I merely thought we'd have breakfast in some morning, or you could concoct a delicious late-night snack, rather than relying on room service, which no doubt closes at some indecently early hour."

"It's open until midnight. I checked."

"As you wish."

"I certainly *do* wish." First that dreadful flight and now this. She was on the verge of tears. "Really, Michael, you might try to be a bit more understanding. God knows, *I've* been trying. I didn't say anything when you told me we were going coach instead of first class. I didn't say anything when you badgered me into eating that unsanitary salad on the plane—don't forget, I used to be a stewardess and I assure you, nobody knows *where* that lettuce has been. I didn't say anything when you expected me to drink coffee that was crawling with germs because it hadn't been properly boiled. I didn't say anything when you railroaded me into sitting in the smoking section and getting lung cancer. I didn't say anything when I went to the loo and they were out of toilet-seat covers and I had to pee standing up. All things considered, I've been damned agreeable until now. Even when I noticed that you drank from a water fountain in the terminal and then expected me to kiss you. We'll both probably come down with herpes simplex before this trip is over, but did you hear a peep out of me? No, I've tried to be a good sport despite the fact that I now have diarrhea (and probably food poisoning) because that cheap airline was out of beef stew and I had to eat those bloody shrimp croquettes for lunch—"

"You've made your point."

He was angry. Michael hated whiners, naggers, complainers.

All the English did; stoicism was what they liked, deprivation, war, tightening their belts. He would be happy if it were announced that famine had just overrun the entire Western world and everyone had to subsist on two crackers and a pint of polluted water a day. She could have screamed, she *would* have screamed if not for the sudden realization that she had to pull herself together or she would lose him. And then what? She would have to give up her leisurely life in London, move back here, and get a job—a dreary, boring, underpaid job that she might be saddled with for the rest of her life. It was easy for her mother to hand out advice about finding a nice American husband—as though she hadn't tried to do that just before she agreed to become Michael's mistress.

To find that husband now, at the age of forty, struck Anita as foolhardy. The odds were viciously against her. Besides, she prayed that in a few years, when Michael's children were older, he would divorce his tight-assed wife and marry her. In his own perverse fashion he was crazy about her, dependent upon her, indebted to her for having aroused him from sexual stupor and allowed him to indulge his deepest fantasies. To throw away her chances of becoming the second Lady Harding seemed ludicrous now that she had invested six difficult and turbulent years in the relationship. Surely her effort was meant to be rewarded by a ring on her third finger, left hand.

"Oh, darling, we'll be able to spend time together at last," she'd cried upon learning that Michael had to go to New York also. He was meeting with airline executives to try to sell them his pet research product: a plane with a laminar flow wing. "It will be wonderful to wake up beside you in the morning and know I'm going to see you again that same evening. It will be sheer heaven."

She planned to show her lover what a kind, caring, considerate, loving, and just plain marvelous person she was on a day-in, day-out basis, and thereby subtly persuade him to divorce Lady Harding *now* (rather than when their children were fully grown) and marry her. While she realized that very few Englishmen in Michael's position actually wed their mistresses, she'd begun to wonder whether her case might not be the tiniest bit different. She dated her newfound optimism back to the evening with Dickie Wembley. Although the festivities began in their usual disgusting fashion (with her seated on a Chesterford International spring tree saddle, inter-

mittently kicking Dickie with her Newmarket leather boots
and beating the shit out of him with a Whanghee riding cane),
it had not ended in its usual fashion (with Michael being able
to get it up long enough to fuck her, and then come in his old
school sock). Not that he hadn't done that just for good
measure, but after Dickie left the two of them sat in the living
room drinking cognac and coffee until daybreak, talking.
Michael confessed how bitterly unhappy he was at home,
how estranged he felt from his wife, who'd decided to go her
own way.

"What that means is that the damned fool woman has
taken an obsessive interest in birds," he said in a thickened
voice. "She's buying them in droves, all kinds of them—
toucans, cockatiels, cockatoos, mynah birds, parrots, canaries,
lovebirds, finches, macaws—and installing them in a room in
our house she calls 'The Bird Sanctuary.' I hate to tell you
what *I* call it."

"You poor darling," Anita sympathized. "How awful."

"You have no idea."

According to Michael, the room stank to high heaven, and
the shrieks and cries were bloodcurdling enough to dissuade
him from ever setting foot in there after his first exploratory
venture. Lady Harding's prize was a royal-blue macaw for
which she'd paid something like five thousand pounds, a
purchase she archly justified on the grounds that macaws
could be trained into becoming affectionate loving pets, and
besides, they were known to live for over a hundred years.
Unfortunately, the large bird had not been trained when
Michael went to visit and he ended up with a nasty bite on his
right index finger. He showed it to Anita.

"I'll make it well," she said, kissing it. "You were lucky
you didn't get an infection, birds are filthy little beasts,
germ-carriers of the worst kind. And they can't be housebro-
ken like cats or dogs, they *go* everywhere." She shuddered.
"I wonder why your wife likes them so much."

"She doesn't, actually, you know. It's her way of trying to
get even with me," he mumbled, pouring himself another
cognac. "She's paying me back for all the years she begged
and pleaded with me not to go grouse shooting in Scotland,
and I refused to listen to her so-called ecological arguments. I
still refuse to listen, damn her! I've explained that killing
grouse is what keeps the bloody species going. We don't

slaughter them, as she seems to think, we merely crop them so that a healthy stock can face the cold winter months and come back alive.'' He took a sizable swig of cognac. ''Besides which, I fail to see what grouse have to do with macaws. Different kettle of bird altogether, if you'll pardon the mixed metaphor.''

Seconds later he was asleep on her sofa, gently snoring. Anita felt very wifely as she removed his shoes and covered him with an old cashmere shawl of hers. Then she went upstairs to her bedroom and undressed, thinking that perhaps her hopes of becoming the second Lady Harding were closer to realization than she ever dreamed, much closer. . . .

''I have an idea,'' Anita said over coffee in the dull dining room of the Gramercy Regency, where she and Michael had just finished dinner. ''Why don't I call my old friend Simone and invite ourselves over for a drink? She and Colin McKenna are at the King Croesus and I'll bet they'd be happy to see us.''

''Why does that name sound so familiar?''

''Which name?''

''Colin McKenna.''

''Because you watch him every week in *Arizona Pete*, silly.''

''I do?''

''Darling, he has the *lead*. You know, the ex-Vietnam navy pilot who goes to Phoenix after the war to pay his respects to his dead buddy's family, and then becomes a private eye.''

''Oh, that chap.'' The series was infantile, but he found the desert scenery too exotic to miss. ''And who is this Simone person?''

''She's the actress I told you about, we used to be roommates.'' Anita stared at him condemningly. ''You don't pay attention to anything I say or do that doesn't involve sex.''

''Surely you don't mean Simone, the *movie star?* That sexy creature with the mauve hair?'' To his astonishment, Anita nodded. ''Good show, darling. I'd love to meet the lady.''

He sounded a little too enthusiastic to suit Anita. ''Frankly, I can't imagine how she managed to remember her lines long enough to become a movie star. Simone is one of the most scatterbrained people I've ever met."

Her brains could be scattered from New York to the Torres Strait for all he cared, she was such an irresistible piece of goods. "I imagine you two girls will have a lot to talk about," he added, so as not to appear overly eager. "Are you sure I won't be in the way?"

"What a quaint notion, darling." She would have cut off both feet before she marched into Simone's plush domain without a handsome, devoted man on her arm. "We took this trip to be together, didn't we?"

"That was the general idea, yes." He lit a cigar, wondering if he would be able to suffer through ten days in the company of this greedy, hypochondriacal, and chronically discontented creature. "How did you know where she was staying?"

"Fingerhood told me when I rang him from London. He and Simone used to be lovers and he's kept in touch with her. As he has with me and a few other women you'll meet at the wedding."

Until now Michael had no interest whatsoever in Fingerhood or any of the others he vaguely recalled Anita jabbering about. In fact, he'd been trying to figure out a way to avoid attending what he felt sure would be a hideously dull affair. But that was before he realized that Anita knew the tantalizing Simone. The actress's body, which he studied carefully in *Charmer*, was the kind he liked best: slender, high-breasted, girlish. To his chagrin, Anita's hips were beginning to spread despite the attentions of her faithful faggy masseur.

Michael had a phobia about women with large hips; they brought back chilling memories of his nanny, who had a seat on her a mile wide. Nanny had spanked him for years whenever she caught him "abusing himself," as she called it. He could still hear her shrill tones of chastisement.

"Oh, you're a naughty boy, Master Michael. You've been abusing yourself again. We shall have to punish you, won't we?"

Whereupon she would take him across her knee, pull down his pants, and slap him twenty times. To this day his erotic pleasure was in direct ratio to the degree of punishment being meted out, either in reality or in his feverish fantasies. It was one of the reasons he continually showered Anita with perfume and urged her to choose a different brand each month and wear it on their special evenings together. Only recently she had thanked him for being so generous, but he said that he received pleasure from her pleasure. What he failed to mention was the secret game he played: first he had to locate all the spots where she dabbed herself, and then kiss each and every spot or risk being severely punished. This month he had been kissing his way through Calandre, by Paco Rabanne, a very *wicked* scent.

"Were you and Fingerhood lovers, too?" he asked Anita.

"Let's just say that he wanted to leave Simone for me, but I turned him down." It wasn't the whole truth, but it wasn't a lie either. "So he settled for Beverly."

"Beverly?"

"She's an overweight redhead whose ex-husband had an affair with Lou and whose present husband has no money."

Michael's head was starting to spin. "Lou?"

"Why don't you give me a dime, darling, and I'll call Simone? I can explain everything in the taxi."

"Capital idea. I see I have a lot of catching up to do."

"So do I. I still don't know who Fingerhood is marrying, but at least it's not Simone, Beverly, or Lou. That would have been a tragedy."

A tragedy for whom? he wondered as he watched her wiggle off to the phone booth. For poor Anita, of course. She was so mean in her petty jealousies and rivalries, so grasping and insecure. Asking for that dime was such a giveaway, she was so afraid that life would single her out from the crowd and maliciously shortchange her. Didn't she realize that it usually did shortchange just those people whose fears were the most galloping?

Sir Michael Harding sighed and relit his cigar. Maybe this trip of enforced togetherness was a good idea at that. Up until now his view of Anita had been so narrowly sexual that he hadn't taken the time to look beyond her shimmering blond facade for a measure of the woman within. He'd just assumed that she possessed certain basic qualities he held dear. Good nature, decency, fair play. Perhaps he was wrong, he thought as he waited for her to come wiggling back. Perhaps he was seeing his mistress in her true light for the first time in six years.

* * *

About fifty blocks uptown, Beverly and her ex-husband were enjoying a reunion dinner after not having seen each other since Sally's disappearance from Radcliffe two years before.

Peter had taken her to a restaurant on one of the side streets in their old Lexington Avenue neighborhood, saying that not much had changed around there except for the closing of the Jaeger House some time ago. Beverly was glad that the famous Bavarian landmark was gone. It had bad associations for her inasmuch as it was the place where she'd done a lot of sneaky afternoon drinking, tucked away in a comfortable old leather booth watching ex-Nazis read *Die Staats-Zeitung* and wondering if her husband was gay. At least there was no longer any question of that, she thought, as Peter paid the check and suggested they walk over to the Stanhope for coffee.

After their divorce Peter moved to Paris, went into business with a talented young fashion designer named Georges Sorrel (quoted in *Marie Claire* as saying that his clothes were meant to inspire their passionate removal), and came out of the closet. Financially, both men profited from the liaison. Thanks to Peter's shrewd advertising and promotion campaigns, into which he had sunk a lot of his own money, Georges quickly moved into the higher echelons of international couture and *prêt-à-porter*, with franchising licenses in major cities. He and Peter had long since become a familiar couple at the snazzier nightspots and eateries on both banks. Now Peter told Beverly that Georges was a sexual *naif* with one recurrent fantasy: to be made love to by a man wearing a long black cape and nothing else.

"You would think he'd get tired of the same old routine, but *pas de tout*," Peter confided to his ex-wife. "If I didn't adore Georges, I don't think I could stand feeling like Batman every time we hit the hay. Still, it's a simple enough request. Mine tend to be more varied."

That hardly surprised Beverly. She was pregnant with Sally when Peter asked her to massage him with a combination of almond oil and special perfumed lotions while whispering obscene words in his ear. The massage part had been easy; it was the other she stumbled over. So he opened a bottle of champagne and a few glasses later she was able to let go. To her bewilderment, he had a series of violent orgasms (without allowing her to touch his genitals) and then never referred to what happened or asked her to do it again. Until this day, Peter was a mystery to her.

"Our marriage wasn't exactly geared to produce happiness, was it?" she asked as they cut west on Eighty-fourth Street in the warm June evening. "I was a woman who preferred my bottle of Cutty Sark to any man, and you were a man who preferred men. And we both were idiotically trying to live like the ideal young American couple. Why does it take some people so long to wise up?"

"We were brainwashed into believing we had to toe the line—*or else.*"

"Or else what?"

"That's the question nobody seemed to consider asking." He looked very Continental, very Louis Jourdan-ish, his features having mysteriously rearranged themselves to blend into his chosen European life-style. "You would think we faced the guillotine if we didn't force ourselves into the traditional, respectable roles that were expected of us when we graduated from college. One good thing came out of it, though. The children." He clasped her hand tight. "It's as though the earth just swallowed her up, isn't it?"

Beverly didn't trust herself to talk about Sally for fear she would break down altogether. She was exhausted, having driven clear across the country in six days. She was unnerved by finding herself with Peter, whose presence evoked all the sharp and painful details of their marriage. She was dying for a drink. It was the first time in two years of sobriety that she felt as though she would cut her hand off for a stiff Scotch, no ice, no water. The only reason she hadn't succumbed so far was the reminder that taking a drink would not bring Sally back.

Nothing seemed capable of doing that. Not her daily hopes and prayers, not the two private-investigating firms that Peter hired right at the start, not all the recriminations she'd hurled at herself for being an unfit mother, for uprooting Sally at an impressionable age, for saddling her with an unwanted stepfather.

When she married Dwight eight years ago, they moved into a less expensive house than the one she and her children had been occupying. Dwight promptly converted the basement into two attractive bedrooms, one for Sally and one for Peter Jr. They had their own wood-paneled living room with a fireplace and television set, but it wasn't good enough for Sally. She vehemently objected to sharing a bathroom with her brother.

"I don't see why *I* should lower my standard of living just because *you* married a poor man," she said to her mother.

"Dwight isn't poor. Merely less rich than your father."

"Even our housekeeper had a private bathroom when we lived in New York," Sally sulked.

"We don't live in New York anymore," Beverly tartly replied. "We live in the Cowboy State, or hadn't you noticed?"

"*Stop roaming, try Wyoming!*" ten-year-old Peter Jr. piped up.

"What happens when I have my period and Peter has locked himself in the john?" Sally was proud of the fact that she'd recently begun to menstruate. "You know how often I have to change my tampon. What will I do, Mother?"

"You will either come upstairs and use my bathroom or you will wait."

Sally's eyes grew dark with displeasure and she appeared much older than her twelve years. "I don't think it's fair to inconvenience a person who's menstruating. I need my privacy. Peter is still a kid, I don't want him fooling around with my intimate possessions."

"Then keep your Tampax in the bedroom and bring it into the bathroom as you need it, goddammit!" Beverly's nerves were on edge because of a fierce hangover. "You should consider yourself lucky that you only have *one* brother to share a bathroom with. It could be worse, you could have *five*."

Sally's lower lip trembled. "You're mean, Mother."

"And you're spoiled stiff, young lady. Now, stop bothering me with this nonsense!"

How many times since then had she wished she'd been more sympathetic toward Sally as she bridged those difficult years between adolescence and womanhood? Too many to count.

"I still can't believe that Fingerhood invited you to his wedding," she said to Peter as they passed the Bulgarian embassy. "You barely knew him."

"I don't understand it myself. And if I didn't have this

franchising deal to look into, I wouldn't even be here. God knows I didn't come for Dr. Fingerhood's long-awaited nuptials.''

"I'm rather looking forward to them. I could use a lift." She thought of her elaborate church wedding to Peter, contrasted to her no-frills elopement with Dwight to Billings, Montana, and smiled nostalgically. Weddings were delicious, no matter what. "Before I forget, I want to drive up to Harvard to visit Peter Jr., and I'd like you to come with me. I can't face going alone, not with Radcliffe five feet away.''

"Sure. Just name the day, but make it soon, Bev. I'm going back to Paris as soon as I wind up this deal. Georges has already started work on the fall collections and he needs my emotional support. Did I tell you that we had a great success at the Milan showings in March? Georges received a standing ovation when he tangoed out to the runway behind thirty of his most beautiful models at the end of the show. It brought the house down."

Although both she and Peter had been born with money, Peter's Brookline inheritance far exceeded her own. He would have been wealthy if he never worked a day in his life, which was one of the reasons Beverly admired him. He'd always worked, wouldn't have considered not doing so, and his ventures were invariably successful.

"You took a big chance when you went into partnership with an unknown like Georges," she said. "I'm glad that your instinct about him was right and that you're doing so well."

"I may not be creative myself, but I like to think I can spot the quality in others. There was only one unfortunate blemish on Georges's triumph in Milan. He decided that the models' faces should be chalk-white with violent slashes of color, and some of the American press referred to it as 'the bruised look.' They attacked us viciously for exploiting the battered-wife syndrome, which was never our intention at all. Poor Georges was crushed. All he wanted to do was create an asymmetrical face to blend in with his asymmetrical clothes. Strange how something so basically innocent can be so stupidly distorted by a handful of misguided do-gooders, isn't it?"

Beverly winced at this reminder of her own problem with Dwight. The more she thought about it, the more she realized that she had to stop assuming she had contributed to Dwight's anger or was responsible for his abuse. *It's not my fault,* she told herself as they rounded the corner on Fifth Avenue, *I'm not to blame.* That was the hardest step to take—absolving herself of guilt—but it was a step that the Women's Support Group agreed was essential for her peace of mind. Up ahead, the awninged café of the Stanhope Hotel beckoned.

"Two coffees, please," Peter said to the waiter. "And one cognac. Martell's." He turned to Beverly. "I hope you don't mind."

She minded like crazy, but it didn't seem civilized to say so. Be strong, she told herself, be brave. "I don't mind in the least," she replied, wishing she didn't like Martell's so much. She could smell it already. Maybe if she put a lot of sugar in her coffee, the craving would go away.

"I can't tell you how proud I am that you finally kicked booze," Peter said. "It couldn't have been easy."

"It wasn't. It isn't. But I can't help feeling that my drinking was one of the main reasons Sally ran off like that. It was her way of getting even with me. The strange thing is that I always wanted to stop for the children's sake—if not my own—but I never had the guts." Tears stung her eyes. "Oh, Peter, what if we never see her again?"

He put his arm around her. "Of course we'll see her. She'll turn up. Don't worry."

"If only I knew where she was, in which city, with whom, doing what. If only I knew she wasn't harmed. If only I could hear her voice."

Behind them a party of six was laughing, having a nice tipsy time. The café at the corner of Eighty-first Street across from the Metropolitan Museum of Art was pleasantly crowded with avid people-watchers, some of whom had a standing bet that within the hour Jacqueline Kennedy Onassis would walk past them from her apartment farther up the avenue. Others were just content to relax in the warm June evening at one of the few outdoors spots in New York that was located on a wide, clean, attractive street with no visible signs of refuse or decay. Beverly had forgotten what a pleasure it was to see well-dressed people again and inhale the aroma of spirited conversation. She was too drunk most of the years she'd lived here to appreciate her surroundings or take advantage of the attractions the city had to offer. She felt a wave of sadness wash over her now as she mourned all that time wasted by the demons of alcohol.

"Sobriety and Wyoming seem to agree with you, although I wish you would do something about your hair," Peter said. "You have such great hair, it's a shame to just let it *hang* that way." He touched the back of her head, where reddish waves billowed out. Like the masts of a ship at sunset, he thought. Extraordinary. "Why don't you go to Suga while you're here? You'd look wonderful in one of those upswept soigné styles."

"No, I wouldn't. I'd look terrible."

"How do you know? You've never tried it."

"Because every woman knows her own style. And mine is definitely not chic-sophisticate."

"Then what is?"

She winked. "Tousled-sexy."

He looked at her as though seeing her for the first time. "I guess you are at that."

"When we were married, you were forever trying to get me to lose weight and wear clothes that didn't suit me. Once you even suggested that I have breast-reduction surgery." She laughed. "Thank God I was too drunk to listen to you."

"I wonder what the hell I was thinking of."

"Probably the kind of boyish, skinny, high-fashion type I could never be." She watched a couple in evening clothes get into a limousine with blacked-out windows. "You have no idea how many years I spent being miserable because I knew that that was the only kind of woman you found attractive."

"I'm sorry, Beverly. I didn't realize what I was putting you through."

"The main point is that I survived. And I finally found a man who likes tousled-sexy."

Perhaps Dwight liked it too much. Was that why he kept abusing her? Because she hadn't lived up to his image for a long time now? *It's not my fault,* she hastily reminded herself, *I'm not to blame for his violence.* She had left Wyoming six nights ago, after packing a small suitcase and writing Dwight a note in which she said that she was going somewhere to think things over. She purposely did not explain where that "somewhere" was. She wanted him to wonder, suffer, and ultimately do some serious thinking himself. Then she got into her Ford and began the long drive east on Interstate 80.

Only once (in Council Bluffs, Iowa) did she phone to find out how he was. Dead drunk, incoherent, maudlin. She could barely decipher anything he said other than his slurred words of repentance. *Didn't mean it, didn't mean to hurt your feelings, forgive . . .*

Afterward she made another long-distance call, this one to New York. When Fingerhood answered she said she would be delighted to accept his wedding invitation, but their connection was so bad that he had trouble understanding her name.

"Beverly!" she shouted at the top of her lungs, as mechanics in the gas station smirked at each other. "Beverly Northrop Kirby!"

Had he forgotten what she once meant to him? Probably. It was all such a long time ago. Life was so different back in the careless sixties; they were so much younger, wilder, their expectations about the future were so fanciful and unrealistic. It was as though they imagined they would spend the rest of their days at a floating party, where sexual liaisons flourished self-indulgently and commitments didn't exist. Fingerhood's only commitment (now that she thought of it) was that he make passionate love to her every Wednesday evening, feed her one of his scrumptious charcoal-broiled-steak dinners, and then see her to her car preparatory to the tedious drive back to Peter and her children in Garden City. That he enjoyed her in bed, Beverly had no doubt. That she ever believed he was serious about her now struck her as the height of folly and she thanked God that the pink haze of the sixties had finally given way to the sobering reign of the seventies, or they would have all worn themselves out dreaming improbable dreams.

Did Simone, Anita, and Lou feel that way about the past? Beverly wondered. She tried to ask Fingerhood whether he'd invited them to the wedding, but the line became filled with static and she said good-bye. Her feelings about the three women were mixed. She smiled fondly at the thought of Simone, disliked Anita, and used to be jealous of Lou. Not until arriving in New York earlier today did she learn that Peter, of all people, had received an invitation too.

"I'm sure it will be an amusing event," Peter said, "if I remember the bridegroom correctly."

Beverly looked away. Peter had never forgiven her for

cheating on him with Fingerhood, even though he'd been cheating on her with Lou at the same time. His reasoning was that Fingerhood wasn't a "serious person," he was an embarrassment, and Beverly should have known better than to get involved with a fly-by-night nobody like him. She disdained Peter's snobbism. The fact that Fingerhood had saved her life by reassuring her she was still a sexually desirable woman (while her own husband seemed hell-bent on undermining her confidence) didn't impress Peter one bit.

"Never fuck out of your class," he warned her. "No good comes of it, believe me."

She now realized that he hadn't asked about Dwight, or why she was in New York by herself. Maybe he didn't consider Dwight a "serious person" either, or maybe he'd concluded that her second marriage was crumbling. The fact that it seemed to be doing just that was why she had driven clear across the country, using Fingerhood's wedding as an excuse to put two thousand miles between herself and her husband. That last angry encounter in Dwight's office, when he accused her of infidelity and drunkenly threatened to kill her, made her see how explosive the situation was. She knew then that she had to get away. For both their sakes.

To break up the long trip, she took a detour to her hometown of Salt Lake City for a reunion with her older brother, Howard, whom she hadn't seen in years. That was a mistake. As soon as she arrived, Howard accused her of having deserted her husband. It seemed that Dwight had called, frantic with worry, and Howard helplessly admitted that he didn't know where Beverly was. Upstanding citizens like Howard Henry Fields, III, who'd been elected state senator for sixteen years running, did not enjoy feeling helpless.

"Why did you leave your husband?" he beligerently asked her. "Don't tell me you're getting another divorce. What's the matter with you, anyway? Can't you hang on to a man?"

"Thank you for your deep concern, brother dear."

"Don't be flippant with me. I want to know where the hell you think you're going with that suitcase. And so does Dwight. He's out of his mind with concern."

Dwight was out of his mind, all right, Beverly thought, remembering his ugly threats. "I've obviously come to visit you, Howard."

"I mean, after you leave here."

She knew that if she told him, he would be on the phone to Dwight in one minute flat. "I have no specific destination. I thought I'd drive around, see the country."

Howard made a grunting sound of disapproval and marched out. The next disaster occurred that same night when her sister-in-law chanced to walk into her bedroom without knocking and gasped at the purple bruises on Beverly's arms and back.

"Good grief!" her sister-in-law said. "How did *that* happen?"

Beverly had no intentions of telling her the truth (her pride would never permit it), and she tried to wiggle out as best she could. "I was in a car accident before I got here. It's not as bad as it looks, they're only superficial bruises."

"A car accident? Have you seen a doctor? Are you sure you're not hurt internally?"

"Quite sure," she snapped. "Just forget you ever walked in here, okay?"

Her sister-in-law looked at her knowingly. "It wasn't a car accident. Dwight did that to you, didn't he?"

"What a preposterous idea!"

She could see that her sister-in-law didn't believe her and would report her suspicions to Howard. That meant Beverly could expect a lecture from him on why she had chosen to marry two highly unsuitable men in one lifetime. It was all she could do to get out of Salt Lake City and escape his dark glances, his wife's embarrassed ones.

Her second detour more than made up for that fiasco. She had heard about the Joslyn Art Museum in Omaha and a supposedly extraordinary but unknown Swiss painter named Karl Bodmer. Having accompanied Prince Maximilian on his North American expeditions up the Missouri River, Bodmer then proceeded to paint numerous scenes of daily Indian life. Beverly spent hours admiring their sharp, poignant simplicity. As a conciliatory gesture, she sent her boss a brochure and told him that she had to go east on family business but would be back at work as soon as possible.

She prayed she still had her job when she returned, although she wasn't going to worry about it. She was too worried about her shaky future with Dwight for that. Maybe while she was gone he would pull himself together and seek professional help. Beverly hoped so. It was what she prayed for every night on the road before she fell asleep in a strange motel room, alone. . . .

"I wonder whether Lou will be at Fingerhood's wedding," Peter said as they walked home along Park Avenue in the dusky twilight. They both were staying at their old apartment, which he'd held on to after the divorce. "I understand she runs a very successful catering business these days."

"In that case, you know more about her than I do." His extramarital affair with boyish, skinny, high-fashion Lou was one of those wounds that had never quite healed. "I've been out of touch with everyone."

"I hear she lives with a woman."

"Lives or loves?" Beverly asked.

"Both, apparently. It's her stepdaughter."

"Where's her husband?"

"He died some years back."

"You've certainly been keeping tabs on the lady, haven't you?"

Peter shrugged. "Gossip travels."

"Not to Wyoming, it doesn't."

"Maybe that's why you're here."

She looked at him. "What do you mean?"

"Maybe it's time for you to break out of that nice, safe, warm, little cocoon you've been holed up in for the last ten years."

She felt a sudden sense of panic, a renewed desire for a drink—stronger than the last one. "Why would I want to break out? I like it there."

Peter had a faraway look on his face, as though he were remembering something. "If there's one thing I've learned, it's that we often don't get what we like. Only what we *need*."

Meanwhile, other conversations were taking place throughout the city.

*Conversation #1. Anita & Simone:*

Anita: Three guesses who this is.

Simone (hopefully): Liz Smith?

Anita: Guess again.

Simone: James Brady?

Anita: Do I sound like a man?

Simone: Bob Colacello?

Anita: Who's he?

Simone: If you have to ask, I don't want to talk to you.

Anita: It's your old roommate, Anita Schuler, surprise surprise!

Simone: *Mon Dieu*, I'm stunned. How are you? Where are you? How did you know where I was?

Anita: Fingerhood told me when I called him from London, but he refused to tell me who he was marrying. Did he tell you?

Simone: I haven't spoken to him yet. What are you doing in London? Working for British Airways?

Anita: Boy, are you ever behind the times. I haven't worked in six years, I'm happy to report. I'm a lady of leisure, darling.

Simone: Does that mean you finally got married?

Anita (archly): It means I now make my home in London and I adore it there. It's so very sophisticated and elegant. As I said to Michael earlier, I can't believe how provincial New York is by contrast.

Simone: Who's Michael?

Anita: Sir Michael Harding, my lover. He's wealthy, charming, and handsome. To die over, as they say.

Simone: I get it. He's keeping you, but he won't marry you.

Anita: Don't be bitchy, darling. Just because you're a famous movie star and shacked up with Colin McKenna is no reason to assume you're any better off than I am. Remember, I knew you when you couldn't come.

Simone (giggling): I guess it means he won't marry you. *Pauvre* Anita, *toujours* the bridesmaid.

Anita: For your information, Michael happens to be trying very hard to get a divorce. He loves me madly, passionately, desperately. That's why he's in New York—because he couldn't bear to be separated from me for a second. So it looks like I'll be walking down the aisle sooner than you think.

Simone: I should hope so. Didn't you just turn forty?

Anita: Don't be gauche, I never discuss my age.

Simone: What's there to discuss? You're a year older than I am.

Anita: I'm going to overlook these carping remarks of yours because we're such old friends. Frankly, I'd love to see you. How about if Michael and I dropped over for a short visit?

Simone (caught off guard): That isn't a very good idea. Colin has an upset stomach and I'm not feeling so hot myself. [Background cries of sexual activity are heard.] Perhaps we can do it later in the week.

Anita: What was that?

Simone (innocently): What?

Anita: Those sounds I just heard.

Simone: Sounds?

Anita: Of explicit sex.

Simone: Your line must be crossed. I have to go now, it's been wonderful talking to you.

Anita: Don't you dare hang up, you depraved thing. You're having an orgy with Colin McKenna, aren't you?

Simone: What an absurd idea! Colin and I are in love, we don't need other people to stimulate us. [More cries of loud frenzied sex are heard.] Oh, I see what it is. Colin's watching an X-rated movie on cable. [Aside] Turn it down, sweetheart, I'm on the phone. [The cries become more pronounced.] I think he's a bit deaf, poor dear. As I was saying, Anita, why don't I call you tomorrow and we can—?

Anita (interrupting): We'll be there in ten minutes, don't bother to dress. Michael adores orgies. Do you have any S-M equipment lying around? Oh, never mind, we'll bring our own. See you.

Simone: Wait a minute. Anita? Anita, are you still there? [Hangs up.] Oh, shit. [Louder] Get rid of those call girls, Colin, I'm going to order tea and crumpets. The yenta of the century is coming over and she's developed a fucking English accent!

### Conversation #2. Simone & Fingerhood:

Simone: Why did you tell that bitch Anita Schuler where I was staying? You know that the two of us never got along, especially after you ditched me for her.

Fingerhood: Welcome to New York, Simone, you sound the same as ever. I didn't ditch you for Anita, I ditched you for Beverly.

Simone: Never mind the technicalities. You should have warned me that that pompous snob was going to call, I wouldn't have answered the phone. Who are you marrying?

Fingerhood: My lips are sealed.

Simone: You mean *no one knows?*

Fingerhood: Only Lou. I had to tell her, she and her girlfriend are catering the wedding. But don't get any ideas, Lou's lips are sealed too.

Simone: What girlfriend?

Fingerhood: Lou's become a lesbian.

Simone: I'd become one myself if I thought I could swing it. All you bastards are impossible, but I gather your fiancée doesn't think so. Is she young?

Fingerhood: You'll find out the day of the wedding.

Simone: I can't wait until then. I'll bet she's young, tall, gorgeous, and has big teeth. That's why you left me, wasn't it? Because my teeth were too small. You can admit it now, I'm over you at last. In fact, I plan to be getting married myself.

Fingerhood: Congratulations. Who's the lucky fellow?

Simone: Colin McKenna. He's a decent, kind, wonderful human being. [Background cries are heard: "Suck me, you cunt."]

Fingerhood: Who's the other woman?

Simone: What other woman?

Fingerhood: The one in bed with your future husband, or wherever they're doing it. For their sakes, I hope it's in a hammock.

Simone: No one else is here, it's a dirty movie on TV. What is it with you and hammocks, anyway? You have to be an acrobat to make love in one.

Fingerhood: What you have to be is united with your partner in your physical properties, united in your timing and rhythm, united in the way your bodies coordinate. One transcendental orgasm in a hammock and you're mated for life.

Simone: What the hell's a transcendental orgasm?

Fingerhood: The kind that surpasses anything imagined here on earth. It's the kind of orgasm that takes people beyond gravity, beyond boundaries known to mankind, beyond mere mortal ecstasy. There are no words for it.

Simone: *Mon Dieu!* I'm getting excited just hearing about it. Maybe Colin and I should try it. He'll do anything to please me, he worships the ground I walk on. [Background cries are heard: "Get down on your hands and knees, you bitch."] I wish he'd switch to another channel, that's the filthiest movie I've ever seen.

Fingerhood (chuckling): Sure it is.

Simone: There's no need to be snide just because you're

getting married and have gone beyond gravity. What's Lou's phone number?

Fingerhood: You're wasting your time.

Simone: No I'm not. Between me and that yenta Anita Schuler, we'll find out who your bride is. Why don't you be a nice guy and give me a hint? Just one tiny little hint.

Fingerhood: She's the most exciting seductive woman I've ever made love to. She has a cunt that never stops.

Simone (shocked): *Jesus Christ, you're marrying Beverly Northrop!*

Fingerhood: Close. . . . Close. . . .

*Conversation #3. Fingerhood & Lou:*

Fingerhood: Simone and Anita have arrived and they're dying to know who I'm marrying. If they call you, remember—mum's the word.

Lou: Why did you tell them I knew? You've put me in a very awkward position. You never should have said a word to those two blabbermouths.

Fingerhood: That's the point, they *are* blabbermouths. And I'm afraid if they learn the truth, they'll tell Beverly. My own mother has been irrational enough since she found out I'm not having a Jewish wedding. I don't need an irrational mother-in-law on my hands, too.

Lou: Not to mention an outraged father-in-law. Peter never liked you to start with. I can imagine what his reaction will be when he learns that you're not only marrying his darling daughter, but have been keeping her whereabouts a secret for two whole years.

Fingerhood: It wasn't my idea. I wanted to tell him and Beverly right away, but Sally refused. I even had to twist her arm to invite them to the wedding. I said that no matter what they did, they're still her parents.

Lou: What did they do?

Fingerhood: Sally won't talk about it. She's peculiar when it comes to her family. Otherwise she's a wonderful girl.

Lou: *Girl* is right. Doesn't it bother you to be marrying someone so young? You had an affair with her mother.

Fingerhood (chuckling): I like them young. Firm. Innocent. Adoring.

Lou: Sally doesn't look so innocent to me. And why is she so gaunt?

Fingerhood: All models are gaunt, you should know that.

Lou: But Sally isn't a *working* model. You said she prefers to stay home and cater to your every whim, you lucky pasha, you.

Fingerhood: Sally may not be gainfully employed at the moment, but she still clings to that skinny-model mentality. I suspect it's a way of rebelling against her mother's voluptuousness.

Lou: Vanessa has another explanation. She thinks Sally is on drugs.

Fingerhood: Only if you consider cigarettes "drugs." I'm trying to get her to quit smoking, but she's as stubborn as her mother. Remember when I couldn't get Beverly to quit drinking?

Lou: Beverly is going to hate me if she finds out that I knew about you and Sally all along. She'll wonder how I could have been so cruel as not to have told her. Oh, God, I feel guilty already.

Fingerhood (wearily): Please, Lou, don't add to my problems. Aside from my mother's craziness, Sally and I had a fight last night and now she refuses to wear a dress to her own wedding.

Lou: What does she want to wear?

Fingerhood: Who knows? Her blue jeans. A light bulb. Things are definitely getting out of hand. Would you do me a favor and take her shopping? She liked you. I'm sure that you can help her select something suitable.

Lou: I'd be glad to, but there's something I don't understand. Why did you wait until the last possible minute to make all these arrangements? Most brides pick out their wedding dress *months* before the actual event.

Fingerhood: Frankly, we didn't know we were getting married until a couple of weeks ago. The decision was very sudden.

Lou: Just promise not to tell Beverly that I knew about Sally.

Fingerhood: I won't. If you promise not to tell Simone or Anita.

Lou: It's a dirty deal.

# 5

Lou replaced the kitchen wall phone after talking to Fingerhood.

"The craziness has begun," she said to Vanessa. "Simone and Anita are cooking up trouble, Fingerhood's mother is making him feel guilty about marrying a Gentile, Sally wants to walk down the aisle in her blue jeans, and Beverly is going to strangle me when she finds out that I've known where Sally was all along. Help!"

Vanessa laughed smugly. "That's what I love about weddings. They bring out the worst in everyone."

"I wouldn't go quite that far, but they sure create chaos. I seem to recall that Zachary started to leave for the synagogue without his shoes and didn't realize it until the doorman pointed it out. As for me, I got into a fierce argument with my father, who suddenly wanted to know why I was being married by a rabbi and not a Catholic priest."

"I didn't realize your father was Catholic."

"Irish Catholic. And my mother was Hungarian Jewish. Talk about lively households."

Lou poured herself a glass of white wine. She was in the kitchen helping Vanessa prepare vitello tonnato for a picnic they were catering the day after tomorrow. Vanessa was browning veal in a Dutch oven and she was opening cans of tuna and anchovies. Having spent more years than she cared to remember at a nine-to-five job, Lou loved working in the evening. The telephone didn't ring as much and time seemed to slip by in a peaceful languid fashion. In a way, it was like not working at all.

"Have you and the happy couple decided on the entrée for the bridal dinner?" she asked Vanessa. "The last time I looked, it was a toss-up between Chicken Duxelles with Sauce Supréme and Turban of Chicken with Watercress Sauce."

"It's still a toss-up. Fingerhood wants the Turban and

Sally wants the Duxelles. I hope you got a deposit on this deal."

"I always get a deposit, it's standard operating procedure." She wondered what misguided gastronome was responsible for the combination of veal, tunafish, and anchovies which comprised vitello tonnato. "Why do you mention it?"

"I don't think Sally is going to marry him."

Lou put down the can opener. "Run that by me again."

"Don't look so shocked. Couldn't you tell there was something wrong between them the day we were there?"

"They seemed perfectly happy to me. Fingerhood just admitted they had a fight last night, but I believe that's known as prewedding jitters."

"I don't think Sally is in love with him." Vanessa started to add the onions, carrots, celery, and garlic that Lou had chopped earlier to the veal in the Dutch oven. "I think she has some sort of scene going with him that's important to her, and in order to sustain it, she agreed to marry him. Maybe in a moment of weakness or gratitude. But her heart isn't in it. And in the end, she'll chicken out."

"Duxelles or Turban?"

"Very funny."

"What kind of scene?"

"A drug scene."

"I just asked him about that. Didn't you hear me? He said the only thing she's addicted to is cigarettes."

"I don't believe him."

Lou was about to vouch for Fingerhood's honesty. Then she remembered how he'd lied about not leaving her for another woman, when all the time he had the go-go dancer lined up. "What do you think Sally's addicted to?"

"Something ominous."

"What are you saying—that she's a heroin addict? I admit she looks a little haggard, but so would you if you tried to keep up with Dr. Sex. Besides, did you ever hear of a heroin addict who jogs?"

"Merely because she wore running shoes and was out of breath that day doesn't mean she jogs. She could have just robbed a little old lady to support her drug habit. Cocaine, incidentally, not smack. Or else speed. Whatever she's on, it's an upper. Not a downer."

"I never realized you were so knowledgeable about drugs."

"I get around," Vanessa said mysteriously. "Besides, that gaunt look of hers is quaintly known as 'the coke look.' Cocaine is a very aging drug, provided you live long enough. It increases the blood pressure, heart rate, and respiration rate. In plain words, it's a killer. Not that I expect Sally to drop dead before the wedding, but don't be surprised if she calls it off at the last minute."

"You and your theories," Lou scoffed. She had finished putting the contents of ten cans of tuna and five cans of anchovies into a large bowl, which she slid across the counter to Vanessa. "You're merely projecting your own disdain of marriage onto Sally. As for her being addicted to cocaine, when I see it is when I'll believe it."

The telephone began to ring. "Some Like It Hot," Lou said, grateful for the diversion. "Can I help you?"

"Hi, Mom. It's me."

"Joan? Are you back?"

"Just got in from L.A. a couple of hours ago, and guess what? I'm in love."

"Who with?"

"A vibraphone player. He and his group, the Weirdos, were on the bill with us at the Roxy. He's wonderful, Mom, really terrific. I haven't been this happy in months."

"I'm glad to hear it."

"That's what I like," Joan said caustically. "Enthusiasm."

"Sorry."

Was she, though? In the last couple of years Joan had fallen in love with a record producer, a rock critic, a disc jockey, a country singer, a writer for *Record World* magazine, one jazz pianist, two drummers, and three guitar players. While Lou had been appalled by this slew of short-lived romances, she was so relieved Joan wasn't homosexual that she forgave her everything. But lately she'd started to worry about her daughter's promiscuity. Would it never end? It certainly showed no signs of doing so. Lou frowned. The vibraphone player sounded like the latest in a long line of one-week stands.

"I have a favor to ask," she said to Joan. "Would Mink & Sable consider playing at Fingerhood's wedding? I know it's an outrageous request, but before you say no, please think it over."

A long groan came across the telephone wires. "Are you serious, Mother?"

"Dead serious. Consider it: an all-woman rock group performing at a male chauvinist's nuptials. There's poetry there."

"Poetry or not, I doubt if I could get the others to agree. Who wants to play at a wedding? We're too professional for that shmaltz."

"I know you are, but it would mean a lot to me."

"Why?"

"I'm proud of you and I'd like to show you off."

Joan sounded embarrassed. "Oh, Mother."

"That's right, I'm your mother and I'm proud that you've turned out so well." Except for a little grass, Joan was clean. Pulled-together. Successful. Seemingly happy, despite her fickle love life and hazardous choice of profession. "You would only have to play for a couple of hours and I know that Fingerhood and Sally would love it. Just think it over, that's all I ask."

"Okay, but don't get your hopes up. Do you realize that the last time I saw Fingerhood I was ten years old?"

Lou remembered only too well. At that time Joan was living in Philadelphia with Lou's parents, whom she thought were her real parents. Their relationship was fraught with problems which were making all parties miserable. In desperation Lou consulted Fingerhood, then a child psychologist. He helped her see that she was standing in the way of Joan's progress by interfering and overriding her parents' decisions. He made her realize that she was confusing the child with *two* sets of authority figures and, consequently, turning Joan into an insecure and fearful young girl. On his suggestion Joan went for therapy, Lou's parents for counseling, and Lou retreated to the role she'd originally assigned herself: that of Joan's older, nonmeddling sister. It had been painful for her to let go, but she knew that if she didn't the person she would harm most was Joan. For the first time in her life she understood why there were so many accolades to the unselfishness of "mother love."

"I can't believe that Fingerhood is marrying Sally Northrop, she's younger than I am," Joan said as a doorbell rang in the background. "Got to go, Mom. Cooley and I are off to a recording session."

"Who's Cooley?"

"The vibraphone player. He's brilliant, a genius. I think this is love, Mother."

A dial tone buzzed in Lou's ear and she replaced the receiver, wondering whether she should have a little heartfelt chat with Joan. Maybe she'd been too silent about her daughter's indiscriminate love life, maybe it was time to sit down and talk things over.

"Didn't you overlook something?" Vanessa asked.

"What's that?"

"You said that the next time you spoke to Joan you were going to tell her about us. You promised. That conversation you just had was the next time."

"I'm sorry, I forgot."

"Think of a better excuse, Lou, because I'm not buying that one."

"But it's true. I became distracted listening to her go on about her new boyfriend. Frankly, I'm worried about her."

"I'm worried about *us*."

"Why?"

"You mean you have to ask?" Vanessa angrily stirred the tuna and anchovies into the rest of the ingredients in the Dutch oven. "Don't you realize how demeaning it is to me to know you're ashamed to inform your nearest and dearest that we're lovers?"

"I'm not ashamed. I'll tell her next time."

"No, you won't," Vanessa predicted. "You'll never tell her. You just can't deal with your radical feminism, can you?"

"Maybe I do go out of my way to play it safe with Joan, but it has nothing to do with my commitment to feminist politics. I'm terrified of losing her love—I came so close to losing her altogether years ago. You're not a mother. You can't imagine the incredible guilt trip I went through when I abandoned her—even if it was to my own parents."

"No, I'm not a mother and you're right about something else: it happened *years ago*. Why do you cling to it as an excuse for your cowardice today?"

"I don't mean to, but abandoning Joan was a scar I'll carry with me for the rest of my life. It's what keeps me bending over backward not to rock the boat, not to do anything that might alienate her. It's what keeps me trying to make amends."

"Amends?" Vanessa said indignantly. "No one is asking you to apologize for being involved with me. A simple statement of fact will do. Something like, 'Joan, I thought you should know that Vanessa and I are lovers.' Is that too much to ask?"

"No, it isn't."

"But?"

"I can't bring myself to say it."

"I'm afraid you'll have to."

"Or what?"

They looked at each other squarely. Vanessa had put down her spoon. She faced Lou in her green-and-white chef's apron, her long hair knotted at the nape of her neck, her face steamy from cooking. "Or we're through."

"Are you serious?"

"Very."

"Then it's an ultimatum?"

"That's one way of putting it."

"What's another way?" Lou asked quietly.

"Setting the record straight."

Vanessa was right, of course. "I see."

"Do you? I don't think you see much of anything when it comes to us. Only what you want to see, only what you want others to know. Namely, that I'm your partner, stepdaughter, friend, but God forbid anyone should find out that we've been sharing the same bed for the last four years! You were paralyzed with fear that Fingerhood would guess the truth. I'm not blind, Lou." She flung her apron on the floor and began to sob. "You're a coward and a hypocrite, and I'm fed up with it!"

The fact that Lou knew the accusation was true only made her feel worse. "I'm going out for a little while," she said.

"Sure, that's right, put on your Jogbra and run away from your problems."

"I'm not running away from them. I just don't see any point in staying here locked in a stalemate."

The Drive would be too dangerous at this hour, so Lou reluctantly settled for Broadway, which was crowded and maddening. After she'd had enough, she trotted over to a café known for its vin blanc singles scene. Columbus Avenue was even more congested than Broadway, due to the youth-with-money explosion that had hit the neighborhood some years back. Ordinarily she didn't come here, it was too kiddyville, too cutesyville for her taste, but the very lack of qualities she could identify with appealed to her now.

At the corner of Seventy-second Street a string quartet was playing Mozart. Passed out a few feet away was a drunk, his fly open. Four girls wearing Army fatigues glided by on pastel roller skates.

"Belushi really blew it," one of them sang out. "Speedballs. Dumb."

Lou thought of Vanessa's suspicions about Sally and kept walking. The café was crowded, its tables jutting out on the sidewalk. Waiters with skinny asses squeezed through tight spaces, their trays of drinks held high, their manner suggesting that this was a temporary frivolity before they hit the big time as actors/dancers/singers/musicians. From inside came the sound of hard rock and up above a full moon beamed down on the revelers, most of whom were in their twenties. The same age as Joan. She wondered whether they were blithely promiscuous too.

"White wine, please," she said to the waiter.

"I love your Kamali. I'm into draping myself. Days at FIT, nights here."

"There's going to be a Charles James exhibition at the Brooklyn Museum this fall. If you're interested in draping, you shouldn't miss it."

"Did you know Charles James?" He seemed awed. "He's my idol."

"I met him years ago when I interviewed him for *The Rag*. He was brilliant, but he had no business sense."

"Do you still write for the shakers and movers of *haute* Seventh Avenue?"

"No, I've gone into catering. Some Like It Hot."

"I'll get you some decent vino, not the pisswater they serve here. Pardon my French."

It was a very New York conversation, Lou thought, not knowing exactly what that meant (only that it couldn't have taken place anywhere else in the world), and it made her feel a little better, a little more centered. Even though she'd spent the first twenty years of her life in Philadelphia, she'd spent the next twenty-two right here and she communicated in the city's own abbreviated patois, which outsiders thought of as rude and abrupt. They didn't understand. They misinterpreted

New Yorkers' verbal shorthand for arrogance, when actually it was the most intimate kind of exchange that existed.

"It's a double, but I'm charging you for a single," the waiter said, presenting her with a large glass of cold white wine. "Enjoy."

She raised it to him, leaned back, and relaxed for the first time since she'd left the apartment upset over Vanessa's ultimatum. She had no doubt that Vanessa meant what she said, and still she couldn't bring herself to tell Joan about them. Why the hell not? Joan was hip, she wouldn't be shocked, she would probably say something like, "Oh, I knew it all along, Mother. No big deal." She could call her later tonight, spill the beans, and save her relationship with Vanessa. Yet she knew she wouldn't do it. Maybe she didn't want to save it. Maybe she was looking for more than a short-lived romance with a man. Maybe she was looking for the real thing.

A lover. A man. She tried to visualize him. He would have to be sexy, macho, and want her to stay overnight (it amazed her that she'd already decided to go to his place). Staying over would be the hardest part of all because of the possibility of early-A.M. sex, which men seemed to adore. Except for Peter Northrop, Lou never used to want to make love in the morning, the idea repelled her. She wondered what the difference was until one day it hit her. Smell. She liked the way Peter smelled in the morning (lemony), but most men's skin chemistry was too strong, too overpowering, as though in their sleep all their dark masculine powers had built up into one stockpile of scent that began seeping out at daybreak. If they smoked and drank to boot, doubly forget about making love in the morning.

She never had with Zachary, except for that one unavoidable time on their honeymoon in western Samoa (when Lou said she wanted to get away from it all, Zach took her literally and booked the Polynesian trip). Swaying palm trees and a blue Pacific were what they woke up to the first day, so jungle-movie-romantic, and before she knew what was happening Zach was on top of her thrashing away. It made her sick, although she did her best to control her distaste. But that night as they sat cross-legged on woven native mats at the *fia fia*, eating roast suckling pig and breadfruit, she diplomatically tried to explain that morning was not one of her better

times. And when they returned to the inn, she proved it by
making love with all the intensity she could summon up for a
man who'd never aroused passion or lust within her.

She married Zachary Greenspan for other reasons, cooler
and more logical reasons, for friendship and emotional support (Fingerhood had been right in his analysis, that was what
she wanted), for a shoulder to cry on at the end of a hectic
day at *The Rag,* for someone to escort her to the theater and
business parties, for someone to spend weekends with, for
someone to finally be a father to her illegitimate teenage
daughter. And wonderful, older, kindhearted, sentimental
Zachary had come through on every score. The plain fact was
that ten years ago, Lou wanted a husband. She'd never had
one, and she felt firmly convinced that every woman should
be married at least once, just to see what it was like.

Well, she had seen, and despite Vanessa's disparaging
remarks about matrimony, it wasn't bad. In fact, if Zach
hadn't died she might still be married to him. Not because
she was deliriously, romantically, ecstatically happy but because she didn't know enough to want anything more, anything better. She figured this was it: a flourishing career, an
understanding mate, and her daughter living with her after all
those painful years of separation. How much more greedy
could a person be? Lots, Lou learned at Zachary's funeral,
lots and lots more greedy. For it was there that she and a
now-grown-up Vanessa met again, and Lou began to feel
stirrings that frightened yet excited her, stirrings that threatened the foundation of the solid middle-class existence she
had grown so fond of.

Sexually, Lou hit her stride with Vanessa. Most men rushed,
they raced, they were in too much of a hurry to get to the
main course, whereas Vanessa lingered over the appetizers
long enough to satisfy Lou. The fact that with another woman
there was no "main course" as such had not escaped Lou's
attention, yet she was tired of all that, fed up with the
pressure that men exerted to get on with it, to get to it, to
ultimately *fuck.* Sometimes she didn't want to, but every man
wanted to, had to, needed to, would be crazy if he found
himself in bed with a partner who wouldn't. So Lou did, and
resented it. She hated catering to their anxiety about becoming hard, putting it in, jiggling it around, asking her if it felt
good ("No," she once said, "it feels perfectly awful,"

whereupon he lost his erection, marched out, and was never heard from again), telling her they were going to come any minute, any second, yes darling, right now, and then going ahead and coming.

So the fuck *what?* she had thought the last time she made love to a man before Vanessa. Who the fuck *cares?* Sexually men and women were on such different tracks, going in such different directions, that except for the conception of children, she often wondered what they were doing together to start with. Their coupling made no sense. It was a relief when she gave up men, a delight not to be burdened any longer by their anxieties, goals, expectations, recriminations, and soft pricks. She could concentrate on herself, totally, as she never could before. The day she joined forces with Vanessa, she felt happy, free, as though she'd just been let out of prison.

Then why was she choosing to go back to that prison? she asked herself when she finished the wine. She had no idea. Even her original motive of making Vanessa jealous was no longer valid, and yet she felt some wild impulse driving her on.

"Good luck," she said to the waiter as she paid her bill and left a large tip.

She wondered whether Peter Northrop would be at Fingerhood's wedding. She hoped so. He was the only man she'd ever met who hadn't rushed, raced, or hurried to get to the main course.

The taxi sped uptown, taking Anita and Michael to the King Croesus on Park Avenue. Instead of looking out the window at the spectacular sights (as she normally would have), Anita was remembering an incident that happened when she was nine years old and left a deep impression.

The girl who sat in front of her in school was a model student, the teacher's pet, and exceptionally pretty with delicate features and long fine hair. She also happened to be Jewish, and once when she refused to lend Anita five cents for a candy bar, Anita called her a cheap kike. The girl promptly reported it to the teacher, who asked Anita to step up front.

"Bernice told me what you called her," the teacher said sternly. "What would you think if she called *you* a fat liverwurst kraut?"

The teacher had a resonant voice and the students in the front row heard her, looked at chubby Anita, and laughed with glee. Anita reddened and tried to hold back the tears. To her mind, the teacher's hypothetical insult was far worse than the one she had leveled at Bernice. At home her parents called Jews "kikes," Italians "wops," and colored people "niggers," and Anita didn't know there was anything wrong with it. It's what those people were, it's how they were born, just as she'd been born a kraut. But she hadn't been born fat and she didn't want to be fat, so it hardly seemed fair to penalize her for something beyond her control. It seemed very mean and cruel.

The reason the incident stuck in her mind all these years was that as an adult she frequently felt ridiculed and humiliated for events beyond her control. Such as Simone taunting her about never having gotten married, or Michael laughing at the wiggly way she walked just a few minutes ago. It was the way she'd always walked, what did he mean? What did Simone mean by rubbing in her husbandless state? What did they want from her? Was she destined never to be loved (or even liked) as she was, whether it be fat, single, or seductively feminine? And if not, how come?

Anita knew that she rubbed people the wrong way, she just wished she knew why. Sometimes she didn't think it was for the reasons they said, and that hurt the most. It meant there were worse reasons, reasons too dreadful to be conveyed. Maybe it was because of those mysterious reasons that she'd never gotten married, didn't have a friend in the world (besides poor paralyzed Lucy Pickles), and felt depressed whenever she thought of the future.

"Here we are, darling," Michael announced as the taxi came to a halt. "The King Croesus in all its immodest glory."

The second Anita stepped out, she squared her shoulders, tilted her head at the most flattering angle, flung her hair back, and moistened her lips. She might kill herself tomorrow, but right now she was making an entrance at one of the most luxurious hotels in the world and there was no point in looking glum. Or as Lucy Pickles once said, "Keep your pecker up and bugger all." Good old Lucy. Anita wondered if she would ever talk again.

"Your friends must be drowning in money and no taste,"

Michael said with disdain as they made their way through the opulent lobby, which seemed to glitter with gold.

"Of course they have no taste," she replied, pretending to agree with him. "They're actors. What do you expect?"

Secretly Anita was dazzled by the rococo ceilings, crystal chandeliers, Oriental carpets, fine oil paintings, sculptured fountains, art-deco mirrors, marble columns, and fresh flowers everywhere. But catering to Michael's whims had become second nature to her; she did it automatically and he accepted it as his due. The smug beast. She let him take her too much for granted, she decided in the elevator, aware that a very dishy man was giving her the eye. His lingering gaze said that he approved of her Zandra Rhodes pink silk taffeta dress (flounced at the hem and cut daringly short), her blond shoulder-length hair (highlighted yesterday at Moulton Brown and lovingly conditioned so that it shone), her pearl choker with the teardrop ruby-and-diamond clasp (a present from Michael on their first impassioned anniversary), her silver sandals rakishly tied at the ankle (courtesy of Rayne, shoemakers to the Queen). All in all it was a very expensive, very fuck-me way to look, and a total stranger liked it.

Of course, he didn't know that underneath the finery Anita was suffering from her latest ailment, a mild vaginal yeast infection. "Yeastie beasties," her Harley Street gynecologist called the syndrome, suggesting she temporarily abstain from intercourse. Since Michael would have had a fit if he heard that one, she was doing the next best thing—sticking horrible little suppositories up there after he was asleep, and giving herself a yogurt douche every morning. Michael wondered why she'd sent the bellman out earlier for ten containers of plain yogurt, but did he wonder why a handsome well-dressed stranger couldn't keep his eyes off her? He did not. Had he himself made one comment on her appearance this evening? He had not, she fumed as they got out on the fiftieth floor and switched to a private elevator which took them to the sixty-seventh floor. Anita had never been that high in her life and felt it was the closest to heaven she would probably get, unless God relented and decided to admit kept women (maybe he would make an exception for her mother's sake).

"I hope Simone hasn't gotten too big for her britches," she said anxiously as Michael rang the bell to Triplex A. "You never know how success will affect certain people."

"Quite. A chap I went to school with discovered the cure for some obscure kind of canine disease. After that, he refused to have anything to do with his dog."

Anita stared at him. Was he serious, or was he making fun of her? Just as she was about to ask, the door to Triplex A swung open and Simone stood framed in the doorway.

"*Bonsoir, mes amis.*" She was slender, girlish, poised. "Welcome to the King Croesus and all that razzamatazz."

Anita rushed to embrace her. "Darling, you look fantastic! Not a day older than the last time we met!" As she kissed the air she tried to detect telltale signs of cosmetic surgery, but the lighting was too diffused. "I'm going to make you tell me all your wicked beauty secrets, you sly fox."

"Oh, there's nothing secretive about them. I just had everything lifted, tucked, or removed." To her dismay, Anita was more luminescent than ever. Simone had always felt fiercely jealous of her ex-roommate's beauty, and becoming an acclaimed movie star didn't seem to change those feelings. "I've got to talk to you alone," she hissed before turning her attention to the tall, handsome blue-eyed man, who was gazing at her appreciatively. "You must be Sir Michael Harding. I've heard some very nice things about you."

"Delighted," he said, kissing her hand in the most intimate, most suggestive fashion. "I'm a great admirer of yours. I saw *Charmer* three times. You were first-rate, my dear, decidedly first-rate."

"How kind of you to say so." She opened the door wider. "Please do come in. It's not much, but we call it home."

Anita gasped. The forty-foot, gray-velveted, Persian-carpeted, smoky-mirrored living room shone like a jewel in the sky. Unreachable, untouchable, unbearably beautiful. The glow from the crystal chandelier and winding gold staircase added to the room's luminosity, while far below the lights of Manhattan seemed to emphasize its celestial niche. To Anita it was something out of a dream, an Arabian Nights fantasy.

"Colin is getting dressed, he'll be down in a minute," Simone said. "Please make yourselves comfortable. What can I get you to drink?"

"Whiskey and soda would be lovely." Michael seated himself on the huge pearl-gray velvet sofa. "Anita?"

*Cyanide*, she wanted to say. "Armagnac," she said, her eyes following her hostess. Simone wore an extremely well-cut black tuxedo with satin lapels, a ruffled white dress shirt, pointed little black dancing slippers, very white foundation on her face, very pale lip rouge, fourteen tons of eye makeup, and instead of looking vulgar or cheap she looked fabulous. Dramatic. Outrageously different (a talent she'd had even before she became a movie star, Anita thought enviously). Her mauve hair was longer than in *Charmer* and more wildly tousled, more sexy. Her only jewelry was a Concord Delirium, which cost a minor fortune and was the thinnest watch in the world. Anita felt stupidly overdressed and overfrilled by comparison, but consoled herself with the thought that Simone had probably paid for the watch herself and still wasn't having multiple orgasms.

Anita remembered when Simone couldn't even have one orgasm. She was totally frigid and so misguided that she went around bragging about her dysfunction to anyone who would listen. Strangely enough, certain men were intrigued. They felt challenged to step in and try to triumph where others had failed, they wooed the little incompetent with a variety of sexual gymnastics that would have upset a more fastidious woman, but all Simone did was boast afterward about feats like getting screwed in a sink, or in the ass with an A&P hotdog, or in the normal place with a candle, and to no avail. Nothing worked until she met Steve Omaha and he made her salute him; then she started coming like crazy. Yes, to Anita's way of thinking, that was the beginning of Simone's march to success, because from there she had gone on to become a wife, mother, and finally a glamorous movie star now involved with an equally famous television star.

"Excuse me, darling," she said to Michael. "I must have a word with Simone."

She found her at the bar, which was situated in a nook between the living room and a majestic dining room, decorated in burgundy and burnished gold, an ornate candelabrum serving as the table's centerpiece. It was as though the management had spared no expense to cradle its guests in the most opulent comfort. Anita slid onto a leather-covered barstool with a solid mahogany back.

"We're alone," she said eagerly. "What's up?"

"I'm almost afraid to say this, but I think Fingerhood is marrying Beverly Northrop. Can you believe it?"

"Is that all you wanted to talk to me about?" Anita was

bitterly disappointed. "Relax, darling, you're dead wrong. Beverly *is* married. To some crumb in Wyoming. Besides, whoever the bride is, I doubt if it's anyone we know. It's probably some stupid young girl who can't see through him."

"What's there to see through?" Simone felt relieved that Fingerhood hadn't chosen Beverly as his bride. It was bad enough that she had to remember the time, fifteen years ago, when he'd chosen Beverly to replace her. "Fingerhood is handsome, successful, rich, and a marvelous lover."

And *I* could have married him if I weren't such an idiot, Anita thought. "He may be all those things, but he's never been faithful to a woman in his life. And I doubt if he'll change after marriage." She watched Simone dump tiny round ice cubes into a sterling-silver bucket. Behind her, crystal glasses, gold vermeil goblets, and the most costly wines and liquors sparkled in the indirect lighting. "Do you realize that thanks to Fingerhood's wedding, we're both here at the King Croesus? It's like a dream come true."

"What do you mean?"

"What the hell do you think I mean?" Anita said in exasperation. "Look around you, for God's sake. We're sitting in the lap of luxury, and you want to know what I mean? You're still as perverse as ever, Simone."

"Perverse and perverted."

"I don't doubt it." But Anita was in no mood to get into an argument with her ex-roommate, she was feeling too pampered for discord. "Remember how we used to eat canned chili off a card table when we shared that one-bedroom apartment in Murray Hill?"

But Simone was wondering how many women there were in the world with a cunt that never stopped. Leave it to crafty Fingerhood to find *two* of them. Leave it to Anita to be impressed by an overpriced hotel suite.

"Remember when you were in hock to every department store in New York City?" Anita nostalgically went on. "And I used to talk about having a walnut *podreuse* in my bedroom one day? You'll never guess what."

"Now you have one."

Anita didn't like her tone of voice. "Right. And you're not in hock any longer. Rima, the Bird Girl, has made good."

"Miss Norforms isn't doing so badly herself."

"Remember our bitchy old nicknames for each other?"

"I'm remembering how much time has passed since then. I'm thinking of all the dreams that *didn't* come true."

"*I* certainly can't complain," Anita said with a toss of her newly conditioned hair. "My life in London is pleasant, my needs are taken care of, Michael and I adore each other. What more could I ask?"

Simone doubted that Michael adored her (now that she'd seen them together), but it seemed too cruel to say so. She remembered when Anita had convinced herself that Jack Bailey adored her, too. Her ex-roommate's penchant for self-delusion didn't appear to have changed over the years. Maybe nothing changes, she thought in a moment of panic. She knew that what Anita wanted most in the world was marriage, and what she wanted was a man who made her feel like a femme fatale. Didn't people ever get what they really wanted?

"How about you, darling?" Anita said. "You must be more than happy with your lot in life, God knows you have everything a girl could ask for. Fame. Money. Beauty. Love. Children. Adulation. Colin McKenna. A gorgeous triplex at the King Croesus and an equally gorgeous home in California, I'm sure. You probably have a tennis court and swimming pool, as well as your own projection room so you can watch all the latest movies in peace and—"

She might have gone on indefinitely if Simone hadn't cut her off in a burst of temper. "Oh, shut up, you materialistic moron. Of course I'm not happy. Do I *look* happy? Is this the face of a happy person? How can I be happy when neither Jimmy nor Eddie gives a damn about me, and I've spent all my money at Neiman Marcus? Even my fucking career is in trouble, not to mention the fact that my clitoris is still as hidden as ever. What the hell do I have to be happy about?"

Anita was too startled and confused by this impassioned outburst to get angry. "Jimmy? Eddie?" Her voice echoed her astonishment. "What are you talking about? You're in love with Colin McKenna. You told me so yourself no more than twenty minutes ago. What's going on here?"

"I lied," Simone confessed, pouring three drinks into gold vermeil goblets, the price of which Anita didn't dare imagine. "If you want to know the truth, I can't stand the shithead. The only thing he really cares about is his silver Yamaha. I'm surprised he didn't insist on driving it to New York."

She always was a loser, Anita thought triumphantly. "You

can't *stand* America's top-rated television star? Most women would kill to have a date with him. It's just like you to be so masochistic and self-defeating. Why can't you *stand* him, may I ask?"

Simone was reluctant to admit how callous and insensitive Colin had been in bed. She was sorry now that she'd ever let him touch her. Not only did he insist upon turning on the baseball game while he made impersonal mechanical love, but when the three call girls marched in ready for action, he expected her to participate in a group scene. Simone's firm refusal evoked an ugly response from him.

"Maybe it's just as well," he said, giving her body a scathing second look. "I never was too crazy about scar tissue. What did you do—break the record at Cedars for cosmetic surgery?"

Whereupon Simone hit him in the head with her five-inch spike heel and nearly took his eye out. In retaliation, he smacked her across the room and she crashed into a chest of drawers, injuring her elbow. Bursting into tears of fury, she raced over, jumped on his back, clawed him as hard as she could with her long red fingernails, called him "a savage" and "a creep," and for good luck bit his left earlobe so deeply that blood ran. He started screaming like a banshee and threatened to kill her, so she left the room with as much dignity as she could muster, but not before she had taken his Vuitton suitcase and thrown it out the window.

"Colin isn't a gentleman," she said to Anita, stirring the drink with her finger. "He still has a call girl upstairs in the bedroom. She became hysterical after he spilled Pernod all over her dress. Now she refuses to leave until he goes to Martha's and replaces it, which he obviously can't do until tomorrow. It's a trashy red crepe cut down to the navel, and if you ask me she bought the shmatte at Alexander's, but there's no arguing with the lady."

"*A call girl*?" Anita's head was reeling, throbbing suddenly. She prayed she wasn't getting a headache. To her irritation, Michael had turned on the stereo and strains of an Italian opera filled the room. He was an opera buff, another enthusiasm they didn't share. "I never would have come over here for a friendly little orgy if I thought *a call girl* was involved. You should have warned me, Simone, I wouldn't have bothered bringing my best Swaine, Adeney, & Briggs whip."

"What whip? I don't see a whip."

"It's in Michael's pocket. It folds for travel."

"How disgusting. Who's Swaine, Adeney, and that other person?"

"Don't reveal your ignorance, darling. They're whipmakers to the Queen and the Queen Mother."

"You mean those two shleppy-looking women are into bondage? *Mon Dieu*, I never would have suspected!"

"Of course the Queen and the Queen Mother aren't into bondage, you French idiot. What a revolting idea. Leave it to you to think of something totally outrageous about the royal family. Swaine, Adeney & Briggs just happen to sell the finest whips and umbrellas in the U.K. The use to which people put them is their own business." Yes, she was definitely getting a headache and she didn't have her pills with her. "And speaking of one's own business, how can you let Colin go near *a call girl?* Don't you know about herpes and all the other STD's that are floating around these days? I'd heard that people in Beverly Hills were cut off from the rest of the world, but you're simply incredible."

"And you're a mass of weird contradictions. If you're so worried about herpes, how can you participate in an orgy?"

"Because I don't become intimately involved. I just do the whipping. I don't touch, you see. Or get touched."

"It doesn't sound like much fun to me." Simone closed her eyes and swayed to Bellini's music. "That's Maria Callas singing *Norma*. She sang it ninety-eight times in eight countries, and they booed her off the stage in bella Roma."

Anita felt put out that a Philistine like Simone had the audacity to be so well-informed. "Who told you that?"

"Jimmy. He's hooked on *Norma*. He plays it whenever he's creatively blocked. By the way, what's an STD?"

"It's a sexually transmitted disease, you ignoramus. And will you stop stirring that drink with your finger?" Anita's voice had risen shrilly. "Haven't you ever heard of germs?"

"I'd forgotten how hygienic you are. When we were roommates, you were either dusting the furniture or disinfecting the toilet. It's probably due to your Germanic background. The Third Reich was very neat and orderly, they always cleaned the ovens afterward." Simone spit into one of the drinks. "That's mine; now we won't have any trouble."

"How dare you compare me to the Third Reich? I was

born in this country and so were my parents, which is more than can be said of you. My father fought in the Second World War, he was a hero, he was decorated twice for bravery in action.''

"No shit, how many American soldiers did he take as prisoners?" Simone giggled. "This is fun, it's just like old times. You shouldn't take everything I say so seriously, I'm only joking.''

"Is that why you spit into one of those drinks and now I can't remember which it is? Because you're only joking?'' Simone hadn't lost the infuriating ability to make her feel foolish. "Don't you know that the mouth is the dirtiest, filthiest, most germ-ridden orifice in the entire human body?''

"I don't believe in the germ theory.'' Simone had to raise her voice to be heard above the bel canto ornamentation of Maria Callas. "And what's more, I never get sick.''

"You're probably walking around with microplasma this very second and don't realize it.'' It was impossible for anyone to be beautiful, rich, famous, and *healthy* too, Anita decided, utterly impossible. "Half the Western world is afflicted by microplasma. If I were you, I'd go to a gynecologist immediately. Then if he says you have it, you must ask Colin to use a condom. That's the only way to keep it at bay.''

"Colin? Who care what he uses? He can screw Peter Allen and the Rockettes with a feather up his ass, for all I give a damn. On stage at the Radio City Music Hall.'' Anita and her bourgeois notions would never cease to amuse her. "Nobody's seen a condom since the Dark Ages, leave it to you to think of it. You're so sanitary, you probably wear white gloves when you fuck. Why don't you stop being so uptight and learn to relax? Stop dwelling on all these unlikely diseases, you'll never get them anyway.''

"I have news for you, I've gotten them," Anita said jubilantly. "I have chronic active hepatitis, a lingering pain on the right side of my face, a vaginal yeast infection, an irregular menstrual period, a headache this very minute, cyclic diarrhea followed by cyclic constipation, a blood-clotting problem the origin of which is anyone's guess, and if you want to know the whole truth, I wouldn't be surprised if I needed a hysterectomy and a laporoscopic before too long.''

Simone lit a Gauloise. "You're sick, Anita.''

"You're telling *me*? I spend half my life in doctors' offices, I'm a regular fixture on Harley Street. If things go on like this, they'll erect a statue to my memory in Cavendish Square." She coughed and waved the nicotine fumes away from her face. "Will you put out that dreadful cigarette? How can you smoke? Are you crazy? Do you want to get lung cancer?"

The music swelled as Callas, as Norma, the Druid princess, hit a perfect high C, and Simone shivered a little, moved by her artistry. Thanks to Jimmy's constant replaying of the opera, she associated it with him. But now she suddenly wondered whether in years to come she would associate it with Michael Harding. She had a funny feeling that Anita's arrival with the handsome Englishman was no mere coincidence, and she doubted if Kate, her astrologer, would think so either. She intended to call Kate as soon as they all left to find out if Michael Harding was what she'd meant by "a new life." Simone's blood was racing in anticipation of Kate's reply.

"There's something that escapes me," Anita said, wondering how someone with Simone's unhealthy habits had avoided a long hospital siege. "If you don't love Colin and he's not your fiancé, then why did you fly three thousand miles to check into the King Croesus together? What's the point?"

"It has nothing to do with romance, it's strictly business." In a second Simone had explained Eddie's publicity plans to a startled Anita. Then she lit another Gauloise. "Now do you understand why I'm so jumpy? I have ten more days of togetherness with Colin McKenna to look forward to, ten more days of pretending to be in love with the world's biggest jerk. Wait until you meet him, you'll see what I mean."

"I'm dying to meet him," Anita admitted. "What's taking so long?"

"Who knows? The last time I checked, he was drinking Pernod out of the hooker's twat." She sighed philosophically. "The creeps I put up with because of my career! It's ironic when you stop and realize that I never even *wanted* a career. If I could find a nice reliable man who cared for me, I'd say good-bye to all this Hollywood hustling in one second flat and be a wife again. Happily."

Anita was astonished. "You too?"

"Why not me?" Simone said indignantly. "I'm only human."

"I thought you would agree with the feminists. They believe that in order to be truly whole, we should have a man *and* a career."

"Their beliefs leave me cold. Thanks to the feminists, women are going crazy trying to be superwomen." *Sì, sovr'essi alzai la punta*, trilled La Callas. "We're expected to balance work, a husband, and children, give charming dinner parties, knit afghans in our spare time, look smashingly turned out all the time, then on top of that be a great lay too. Who the hell has the energy? Not me. When I'm working on a movie, I'm in bed at eight, have dinner on a tray, and Vaseline on my face, I don't even want to talk to Jimmy unless it's about the movie, never mind making love to him. I'm too busy conserving my strength for the next day's shooting. Not that Jimmy is exactly ripping off my nightgown, *tu connais*."

"Undersexed?" Anita asked.

Simone nodded sadly. *"Mais oui."*

Anita debated whether that was better or worse than the position she found herself in with Michael and his cronies. The evening with Dickie Wembley came to mind once more. She could still see the welts begin to rise on Dickie's fat behind as she continued to whip him with her Whanghee riding cane (while Michael jerked off behind the gold filigreed screen). She could still remember her feeling of revulsion and shame at the thought that this was what she had been reduced to. If Simone was languishing because of too little sex, she was languishing because of too much. And yet basically they were both in the same boat. Neither of them had what she wanted most. Love. Under the circumstances, she wondered if Simone would object to her making a play for Colin, who was not only young, handsome, and talented, but Rich & Single. R&S was such a rare combination that Anita didn't think she should let this opportunity slip by, she owed it to herself (and her mother) to take advantage of it. If a woman didn't try, how was she ever to succeed?

"And what about Sir Michael?" Simone asked with a gleam in her eye. "Sexually, that is."

"He's not like your Jimmy. He's demanding, sometimes too much so."

Simone rolled her eyes and made her imbecile face. "It

sounds good to me. Is he really in love with you, Anita? Tell the truth.''

"Oh, you know how it is with married men." Vaginal yeast infections and grief on weekends, that's how. "No matter how smitten they are, their first allegiance is to their wives. At least when the bastards are single their first allegiance is to you despite the fact that some of them have a strange way of showing it.''

"I know what you mean," Simone said wistfully. "Before we got married, Steve was a little dictatorial but devoted. And afterward we had the twins, we had some good times, in retrospect even some of the bad times were good . . . he was my husband.''

"At least you were married. Look at me." A sob caught in Anita's throat. "Are we going to have problems with men for the rest of our lives, Simone? Aren't we ever going to be happy? Adored? Worshiped? Catered to? Like those women you read about whose husbands shower them with furs and jewels, surprise them with first-class tickets to exotic places, and are at their side through thick and thin?''

"I don't know what fairy tales you've been reading. Men like that don't exist.''

"I used to think they did, and I still like to think so. But I also thought I would have met one by now. In fact if anyone had told me fifteen years ago that we'd be standing here having this conversation, I would have laughed in his face.''

"Clark Gable is dead in more ways than one, but there's no point in being morbid." Simone brightened and put the three melting drinks on a gold vermeil tray. "Maybe Beverly and Lou are worse off than we are.''

"I hope so. Beverly has undoubtedly been drinking herself to death in Wyoming." Anita followed her back inside. "And Lou is a lesbian. Is that worse?''

"It sure sounds worse." *Norma* came to a heartbreaking, powerful, and sublime end. The suite was very quiet now, causing Simone to whisper. "Remember how I tried to kill myself after Fingerhood left me?''

Anita nodded sympathetically. "Remember how I *wanted* to kill myself after Jack Bailey left me? We were both so much in love, we thought the end of the world had come.''

"What did we know?''

"Nothing, absolutely nothing," Anita agreed. "The tragedies had only begun."

They hugged each other, the tray awkwardly between them,
the past weaving into the present, stretching into the future in
more ways than one. Simone stole a glance at Michael Harding across the room and decided he was the most attractive
man she had seen in a long time. What's more, she knew
from the way he kissed her hand that he wanted her. Ordinarily she would have considered him off limits, but she remembered that when she was still bereft over Fingerhood it didn't
stop Anita from plunging headlong into an affair with him.
She always resented Anita for that, it showed a certain kind
of callousness that Simone had never forgiven. Maybe she'd
been waiting all these years to pay her back.

*"Good evening, folks! Are we late?"*

To everyone's surprise, Colin McKenna came sliding down
the gold staircase, wearing the call girl's red crepe dress,
which was darkly stained in front. The girl herself was in his
arms, naked, laughing, cradling a half-empty bottle of Pernod.
They landed on the Persian carpet with a thud, only feet away
from where Sir Michael Harding was seated lighting his pipe.

"What's in there, Pops?" Colin asked, picking himself off
the floor and adjusting his deep décolletage, through which a
few curly chest hairs were visible. "Grass? Hash? Opium?"

Anita now realized why Simone had called him a jerk; he
was obviously stoned on something more ominous than Pernod.
She preferred not to think what, the drug scene being so
unhealthy, so unsanitary. Still, Colin was Rich & Single (she
reminded herself) and therefore worth salvaging. Of course it
would take a lot of work to turn this shamelessly depraved
creature into a loving, responsive partner. It would take
effort, encouragement, support, tenderness, determination,
greed, kinky sex, the patience of Job, plus an unlimited
supply of duplicity, but weren't those the very qualities she
prided herself on having in abundance? Perhaps she'd been
wasting them all these years on the wrong man. Perhaps her
mother would be proud of her yet.

"You see?" she said triumphantly to Simone, who now
spit in the other two drinks. "I knew it was a good idea to
bring that whip."

# 6

The following morning was sunny, soggy, hot, with a temperature-humidity index that promised it would be a scorcher of a day. Anita sat up in bed and cursed. The air conditioner at the Gramercy Regency had broken down in the middle of the night and her beautiful, newly conditioned hair was glued to her neck and shoulders.

She quickly showered, slipped into her Sonia Rykiel black knit shift, and was applying a shade of lipstick called Burnished Carnival when Michael opened one eye and stared at her. "What are you doing? Where are you going? What time is it?"

"Ten-thirty." She wiggled her feet into a pair of red strappy sandals with a walking heel. "I'm going uptown to get my dad a gift for Father's Day. And afterward I thought I'd buy Fingerhood and his mystery bride a wedding present."

"Sounds like a heavy schedule. Aren't you planning to have breakfast first?"

"I'm not hungry."

That one eye was still fastened upon her. "When can I expect you back?"

She stuffed her limp hair under a jaunty white straw cloche that she'd picked up at Harrods and blotted her lipstick. All things considered, she didn't look half bad. "When you see me," she replied, sailing out the door.

"Taxi?" the doorman asked.

Out of habit she gave him one of her dazzling kept-woman smiles. "No, thank you."

The heat was stifling. She had forgotten how wretched New York could be in the summer, but she didn't have far to go and she felt like stretching her legs. After she took a seat on the Madison Avenue bus, she allowed herself to remember last night's dismal culmination. . . .

Just when she and Simone had cemented their friendship with hugs, kisses, and a lot of warm feelings, Simone ignominiously betrayed her. The next time Anita turned around, there she was making a flagrant pass at Michael, beckoning to him with those flirtatious come-hither eyes. To Anita's chagrin, Michael followed her across the gray-velveted living room like a dog in heat. She could still see the two of them huddled in a dark corner, whispering and laughing, exchanging intimacies, oblivious of everyone else, lost in a world of their own. The attraction between them was clearly mutual, electric.

A sense of despair gripped her then, a sense of helplessness and futility. Was life always going to be unfair and unrelenting in its harsh punishment? And if so, *why*? What had she done to deserve betrayal by a woman who professed to be her friend and a man who professed to be her devoted lover? She felt alone, alienated. Colin McKenna and the call girl were nakedly ensconced on the love seat, fondling each other and guzzling Pernod. Anita thought of her romantic intentions toward Colin and realized that she no longer wanted to pursue them. What had seemed like a brilliant idea only a few minutes ago now struck a sour note. She didn't care if he was Rich & Single (plus all those other things she found so appealing). She couldn't think beyond the sight of Simone and Michael, their hands clasped around each other's waists. Seconds later her headache worsened, her liver began acting up, and her vaginal infection started to itch like crazy.

"My medication, Michael. I don't have it with me." She doubled over and clutched her stomach, ironically the one area that didn't hurt. "I'm sorry, but we must go back to the hotel at once."

He extricated himself from Simone and gazed at his mistress with ill-concealed fury. "Very well, my dear, if you insist."

Simone followed them to the door. "I hope you feel better, *chérie*," she said with a sly smile. "I'm sure that Michael will take devoted care of you."

Then she batted her fourteen layers of mascaraed eyes at him, flushed with triumph. Anita felt like strangling the sneaky little bitch. Was it any wonder she had no women friends, except for poor Lucy, who was married and therefore no threat? Her mother had been right when she told her never to trust an unattached female.

"I'm sorry if I ruined your evening," she said to Michael in the taxi, trying to make amends. "It was stupid of me to have forgotten my liver medication. I won't let it happen again."

"You're a bloody hypochondriac and I'm bloody well fed up with it," he said, refusing to be appeased. "You take pills for everything under the sun. The sheer proliferation of your doctor bills is a constant source of astonishment to me, inasmuch as I don't believe there's a thing wrong with you—"

"Now, just a minute!"

"Not medically wrong, at any rate. You use these scare tactics for your own twisted purposes, although God knows what those were tonight. The only thing I do know is that you wanted to go home, and you certainly have achieved your purpose, you selfish creature."

"How dare you call *me* selfish? All you ever think about is yourself and your own sick pleasure. The fact that I might have to be hospitalized for chronic active hepatitis doesn't occur to you for a second. You're too angry about being separated from that French whore to have the decency to be concerned about me or the pain I'm in. You're a snake, Michael, and so is Simone. The two of you deserve each other."

"Simone and I were merely having a quiet little chat," he coldly replied. "I don't know what you're getting so worked up about."

"A quiet little chat, my ass. You were practically in each other's pants. One more minute and you would have been." She had never spoken to him like this. "Do you think I'm blind? Must you humiliate me publicly? Don't you think I feel humiliated enough as it is, catering to you and your perverted friends? Don't you think I have feelings? What am I to you? A stupid little sex toy that you can throw away when one of the parts wears out?"

To her own astonishment she burst into tears of fury, self-pity, rage. Six years of diplomacy flew out the window as the taxi raced down Park Avenue. The hell with patience, silence, biting her lip, and making the best of things, she thought, sobbing. The hell with him and his money. The hell with it all. She was fed up with her life and fed up with him.

He could die for all she cared. She felt like dying herself; suddenly it didn't seem worth going on. For what? For whom? She was a failure, a reject, a nothing.

When she and Michael were in Lisbon a few summers ago, they'd gone to the *fado* music houses and listened to the Portuguese lament of love sung by women dressed all in black. The *fado*, their guide explained, said that nothing ever changed, that life was sad and cruel and short. At the time Anita had laughed at such cynicism; now as she remembered the haunting strains of melancholy, a dark curtain descended, blotting out reason and logic. She reached blindly for the door's handle, jerked it up, the door swung open, and she tried to throw herself out of the speeding taxi, but something held her back, pulled her in, locked the door, shook her until she understood where she was and what she had nearly done.

*"You tried to kill yourself."*

The expression on Michael's face was different from any she'd ever seen before. A moment later, she realized why: he was looking at her as if she were human.

Lou was finishing her second cup of cappucino, desperately trying to wake up. Seated at the long pine kitchen table, her hair drying from the shower, she wore a bright pink crepe-de-chine peignoir that tended to mask the lines of weariness on her face. After she came home last night she made the mistake of confronting Vanessa with the ultimatum she'd decreed earlier.

"Does our being 'through' mean that we're 'through' as business partners too?" she asked, trying to find out what Vanessa had in mind. "Do you want to dissolve the partnership? Do you want to buy me out? And what about this apartment? Who's going to keep it? Who's going to move? What's the plan?"

"You're taking this very well," Vanessa resentfully replied. "I imagined you would put up more of a fight, but maybe you're relieved it's over."

"I'm not relieved about anything." It wasn't altogether true. She was tired of Vanessa's bad moods, repeated infidelity, and endless reproaches about her lack of commitment to radical feminism. More tired than she had known. "I just wish you would be explicit."

"I haven't thought it all out yet, it's happened so suddenly."

She gazed at Lou as though asking to be told that their relationship could still be salvaged, that the final tie hadn't been cut, but Lou didn't say anything. "Give me a few days and I'll decide what I want to do."

"Take all the time you need. I hope we can continue to work together, though. Some Like It Hot is flourishing. It would be a shame if you walked out now."

"That's one of the things I love about you," Vanessa said bitterly. "You're such a romantic."

"Sorry, I didn't mean to sound so hard-nosed."

"But business is business?"

Lou could feel herself start to bristle. "If you must put words in my mouth, then yes. Is it a sin to be practical?"

"It depends on the circumstances. I find it hard to think of business now that the most important relationship of my life is about to fly out the window, but that doesn't appear to deter you one bit." She observed her lover from behind betrayed eyes. "Maybe I've been wrong about your feelings from the start, maybe you never gave a damn for me, maybe all you cared about was my contribution to Some Like It Hot. Because if you did love me, I don't see how you can take this so casually."

"Of course I loved you." Lou reddened. "I mean, I do love you but you're the one who wants to end it. You're the one who said it was over. It wasn't my idea."

"Wasn't it?" Vanessa had become furious. "Your not clarifying our relationship to Joan was your way of ending it. Your sneaky, underhanded way. I expected more of you. I expected forthrightness, decency, honesty, but you couldn't even give me that."

"So now I'm dishonest in addition to my other flaws." To Lou's irritation, Vanessa had succeeded in drawing her into the combat zone. "I'll tell you something: I'm tired of your accusations. There's so much about me that you don't approve of, and you haven't stopped beating me over the head with it for four years. I've listened, I've felt guilty, I've tried to change, but it was never enough for you. I was constantly doing something wrong, something that didn't meet your lofty standards. I was never up to par, was I?"

"Don't exaggerate," Vanessa said nervously, attacking her cuticles. "I didn't come down on you that hard."

"Sure you did, you picked on everything. My attitude

toward men, my clothes, my makeup, my jogging, even my goddamned brassiere.''

"I was only kidding about your Jogbra. Can't you take a joke?''

"The joke's on you, Vanessa.''

"What do you mean?''

"I mean you should be pleased that this very flawed, very imperfect woman won't be around to irritate you much longer. You're free to pick up all the lanky strangers who appeal to you and you'll never have to worry about getting a lecture from me when you return home. How come you're not smiling?''

Lou grabbed Liberation and retreated to her bedroom, thinking that in a love relationship the person who did the criticizing and carping was the more needy person, even though it usually appeared to be just the opposite. Vanessa needed her more than she needed Vanessa, but neither of them had realized it until now. It was Vanessa's turn to suffer, she thought, remembering all the years she had suffered over Vanessa's infidelity and incessant rebuke.

"I'm well out of this," she told Liberation, who curled up on the quilt beside her and started to purr. "I deserve better. I deserve a man.''

Who would he be? What would he look like? Where would she find him? Fingerhood's wedding still struck her as the most likely place, and she fell asleep dreaming of a handsome stranger approaching her after the bride and groom had had their first dance, holding out his arms as the music continued to play. . . . But in the middle of the night she woke with tears streaming down her cheeks and a heavy feeling of sadness in her heart. After four years of day-and-night togetherness, she and Vanessa were parting. That was the hard unvarnished truth and suddenly she wasn't sure she could face it. It wouldn't be as easy to switch partners as she wanted to believe. The phantom of a handsome stranger dwindled into the blackness, and only her suffering felt real, concrete, tangible. There was no escaping the pain that accompanied a breakup, and it didn't matter how justified or inevitable that breakup seemed to be. There was no escaping the raw anguish of love turned sour. . . .

The fact that Vanessa looked even lousier than she did this morning afforded Lou very little consolation. When she'd gone into the kitchen a little while ago, Vanessa was already there preparing a crepe batter, her face haggard, her eyes red and watery, her manner withdrawn. Lou felt like putting her arms around her and saying it was going to be all right, but she hesitated, not sure if that were true. It was a relief when the telephone rang.

"Some Like It Hot," Lou said. "Can I help you?"

"Hi, it's Sally Northrop." She sounded anxious. "Did I get you at a bad time?"

"No, not at all. In fact, I was just about to call you. Fingerhood tells me that you still haven't bought a wedding gown. Is that true?"

Sally laughed uncomfortably. "I'm afraid so. Ridiculous, isn't it?"

"Well, then, how would you like to go shopping?" She couldn't wait to get out of this tense atmosphere.

"Sure," Sally said eagerly. "Where?"

"Madison and Sixty-fourth in about an hour. The shop is called Queen Victoriana."

"This is awfully kind of you, Lou. I appreciate it. See you."

"You're going to lose that bet about Sally calling off the wedding," she couldn't resist saying to Vanessa, who was pouring batter into a crepe pan. "You should have heard her just now. She sounds exactly like a nervous, happy, anticipatory bride."

"Cocaine does that."

Lou felt like throttling her. She'd never known anyone as stubborn as Vanessa; when she got an idea in her head, nothing could dislodge it. "Cocaine does *what*?" she irritably asked.

"Changes your mood. One minute you're up, the next minute you're down. Then you're depressed, euphoric, paranoid, and in the end, schizoid, really spaced out." She flipped the crepes over with a spatula. "The public is grossly misinformed about cocaine. They think it's a harmless recreational drug like marijuana, and for some people it is. But there are plenty of other people whose lives have been ruined by it."

"Just because Sally happens to be moody is no reason to assume she's a cokehead."

"There are other clues," Vanessa smugly replied.

"Such as?"

"That story she told us at Fingerhood's penthouse about how she ran away from Radcliffe intending to become a high-fashion model, couldn't hack it, went to see Fingerhood for a secretarial job, and fell in love with him. Doesn't that strike you as strange?"

"No. Why?"

"This is New York, for heaven's sake! There are thirty million jobs available and she goes to see her mother's ex-lover for one, and you don't find anything unusual in that?"

"I suppose you're going to tell me that that's cocaine-related too."

"What I'm going to tell you is that people who do drugs are sneaky and dishonest. You can't believe what they say and you can't predict what they'll do. Or why. Sally claims she looked up Fingerhood because she didn't know anyone else in New York, but I don't buy it. I think she planned to get involved with him before she ever laid eyes on him."

"Why would she want to do that?"

"Because her mother was once in love with him and her father hates him!" Vanessa shouted.

"What are you getting so excited about?"

"You and your blockheaded stupidity. Sally is one very vindictive lady, can't you see that? Look how much she's made her parents suffer already, and imagine how much more they'll suffer when they find out about her and Fingerhood. Oh, what's the use in trying to talk to you?" Vanessa flung the crepe pan across the room and ripped off her apron. She was red with rage. "You're so attracted to her that you can't see straight."

"I'm *what*?" Lou was flabbergasted by the accusation. "That's the most idiotic thing I've ever heard you say." But at least it explained Vanessa's unjustified attack upon a girl she barely knew: she was jealous.

"You and Sally deserve each other. After you help her select a wedding gown, be sure to take her to lunch. It's a great way to start a romance, remember?"

"Vanessa, don't do this. You're only projecting your own past infidelities onto me. I have no designs on Sally. How could I? I think of her as a daughter."

"Tell it to Marabel Morgan."

"Please, Vanessa. You're behaving irrationally. Let's sit down and talk this over. It's not like you think."

"*You* sit down."

With one fierce thrust Vanessa shoved her into a chair, stalked out of the kitchen, and locked herself in her room. Like a recalcitrant child, Lou couldn't help thinking. No amount of wheedling would persuade her to open the door, and she finally gave up, realizing she had to hurry or she'd be late for her date with Sally. *She and Sally Northrop?* Was Vanessa crazy? Jealous or not, didn't she know her any better than that? Obviously not or she couldn't have jumped to such an unlikely conclusion. Being misunderstood by someone she felt so close to depressed Lou. It made her wonder what other misconceptions Vanessa harbored about her, what other distortions. Maybe we never get to know anyone even if we live with them all our lives, she thought, maybe it's impossible to fully understand another human being. Maybe that was what the endless quest for love was all about: someone to fathom our every inclination—no matter how slight, no matter how strange—and to love us in spite of it.

In the bedroom Lou chose a deep blue Norma Kamali shirtdress, nipped it at the waist with a crushed leather belt, and adorned it with lots of jet-black jewelry. A bluish-red lipstick helped bring her face to life, but her hair was still bothering her. She felt momentarily grateful for the distraction. Long, thick, and bone straight, she had let the stylist layer it yesterday so that the sides were now shorter than the back, and bangs brushed across her forehead.

"I'm not sure about this cut," she dubiously told him. "It makes my face appear less angular, which is good, but it also plays up my eyes and the lines beneath them, which is bad. Very bad."

William nodded sympathetically. "Maybe you shouldn't keep coloring your hair black. It might be time to lighten it, soften it. That would help your eyes."

"Forget it. I'm in the Elizabeth Taylor camp. I was born with black hair and I will die with black hair. I don't give a damn if it is supposed to be aging, I look lousy in any other shade."

"Then how about a body wave for fullness? It would help counteract the downward flow."

"I love your tact."

Rule of thumb was that the older a woman got, the softer

her hair color and style should be. According to the experts, shorter and lighter were more flattering than longer and darker. It sounded logical, but when Lou thought of all those middle-aged blonds with fluffy permanents and pink scalps running around New York trying to fight gravity, she winced.

"We're approaching this from the wrong angle," she decisively told William. "What I have to do is get an eye tuck."

She smiled at herself now in the hall mirror, and the lines beneath her eyes deepened. She resolved to make an appointment with a plastic surgeon (whose name she had on file) right after Fingerhood's wedding. Unfortunately, there wasn't time to do it before, which meant she would have to meet that handsome stranger when she wasn't looking her very best. She grabbed a pair of gigantic black sunglasses that covered half her face and ran out the door, cursing the aging process.

"What's it going to be today? Jogging or driving that cute pink truck?"

To her amazement, the man with the Leica was standing in front of her building, smiling, suntanned. She hadn't seen him since that time he showed up on Park Avenue when she was on her way to deliver Jean Pierre's dinner.

"You've been following me," she said, wondering if this was one of those days she should have stayed in bed. "What do you want? No, never mind. Just go away."

"I've got a better idea." His smile was ingratiating. "Why don't you join me for a cup of coffee? I'd like to talk to you." He was well-spoken, clean-shaven, neatly dressed (short-sleeved navy cotton knit polo shirt, immaculate chinos, ox-blood moccasins, bronze-buckled cowboy belt); and probably had a record for attempted rape.

"Look, I don't appreciate being surreptitiously followed by strangers," Lou said. "Now kindly let me alone."

"My name is Keith Rinehart." He reached for her hand and shook it before she could draw away. "See? Now I'm not a stranger anymore. What's your name?"

"Get lost, Keith Rinehart." But she couldn't stop staring at the hair on his wrists, bleached even blonder from the sun. "And if I find you anywhere near me again, I'm calling the cops. Don't think I'm kidding."

"Hey, I'm harmless. Honest. I just like the way you look. At least, that's all it was at first, but then when I realized that you—"

She cut him off. "So you *admit* you've been following me?"

"Sure!" Instead of appearing embarrassed or guilty like a normal person, he appeared proud of himself. "I would have caught up with you sooner than this, but I've been out of town on a photo assignment. Jamaica. Just got back late last night."

"And you couldn't wait to rush right over here this morning."

"Didn't want to waste another minute," he agreeably replied. "After I spotted you driving that delivery truck for Some Like It Hot, I knew we had a lot more in common than I ever dreamed possible. That's what I want to talk to you about."

"The only thing we have in common is that we're both standing on West End Avenue," she brusquely informed him. "And if you're not gone in one second, you'll have the police to contend with. I mean it."

"I love your new haircut," he said, waving a friendly good-bye. "It makes you look like Ali MacGraw."

"And *stay* away!"

A taxi was discharging passengers at the corner and Lou ran for it. "Sixty-fourth and Madison," she told the driver, lighting a cigarette to calm her down. A second later she was staring at herself in her compact mirror. Ali MacGraw? Actually, the new haircut did create a slight resemblance she hadn't noticed before. She snapped the compact shut, appalled by her own gullibility. Was she so desperate for a masculine compliment that she no longer cared where it came from?

"Creeps and nuts," she muttered. "The city is crawling with them."

"You say something, lady?" the cabdriver asked.

"Just talking to myself."

"You and everyone else."

The minute Anita marched out of the Gramercy Regency, Sir Michael Harding heaved a sigh of relief and picked up the bedside phone. He dialed the King Croesus.

"Simone?" he said eagerly. "How are you, darling?"

"Desolate that you had to leave so abruptly last night. Desperate to see you again. Has Anita recovered yet?"

"So much so that she's gone shopping." Just the sound of

the actress's delightfully accented voice made his heart feel
lighter and his future more hopeful. "What are you doing,
darling? I'd like to come over, if that's all right."

"Oh, would you? I've been lying awake all night thinking
of you, wondering if you would call, praying you would.
How soon can you be here?"

"Soon. Is McKenna still hanging around?"

"He's in his room sleeping it off, but don't worry about
Colin. He means nothing to me, *rien du tout*. He's strictly
business."

"That's all I wanted to know." Michael swung his legs
onto the floor. "Because I'm strictly romance."

Simone couldn't believe her ears, men never said things
like that anymore. "You are?" she asked incredulously.

"More than you realize. I have very serious designs on
you, my dear. Very serious indeed."

"You do?"

"Most decidedly."

*Travel, adventure, a new life*, Kate had predicted, and now
it looked like they were all coming true. Simone shivered
ecstatically in the pink-and-gold bedroom from which she
could see the spires of St. Patrick's Cathedral off in the
distance. She began to pray that this was not another false
lead, the way Jimmy and Eddie had turned out to be. Because
if Sir Michael Harding represented her new life she could
stop worrying about getting the lead in *Rockabye Princess*,
she could abandon those stupid publicity plans with Colin,
forget her anxieties over the twins' schooling, and last but
definitely not least, never have to concern herself again with
whether or not she could afford another sequined Bob Mackie
gown. She'd be able to afford fifty if she felt like it, a
hundred, she would tell Michael that she needed a separate
room to house her entire Bob Mackie collection (which, of
course, would be cataloged and coded with accessory numbers),
and he would give it to her happily because he loved her so
much. A faint cloud drifted across her rosy future.

"Where is your Sun?" she said into the phone.

"Excuse me?"

She enunciated carefully. "Where is your Sun?"

"He's in Gloucestershire with his mother. Why do you
ask?"

"No, no, not your child, you silly man." Kate, whom

she'd called a few minutes ago, told her to get Michael's time and date of birth, otherwise she could do nothing. "Your S-u-n. Which month were you born?"

"Oh, that astrology business. October. Why?"

"October what?" Simone asked, her heart quickening.

"The fourteenth."

"We're not only the same sign, we were both born on the same day!"

"Is that good?"

"I'm not an expert, but it sounds marvelous to me. Stupendous, in fact." It probably meant that they thought alike, felt alike, were alike. Soulmates. "What time were you born?"

He laughed. "Really, darling, you can't expect me to know something arcane like that."

"Then you'll have to write to the hospital and ask."

"But I was born at home."

"Oh, dear. Is your mother still alive? Because if so, you must call her immediately and see if she remembers. Without the time of birth, it's impossible to chart your rising sign."

"Can I wait until I return to England before I call her?"

Simone knew when she was being teased. "Forgive me for getting so carried away, but my astrologer thinks I'm ready for a new life and I was wondering if you would be part of it."

"Even without knowing my time of birth, I can assure you that I am. Now may I come over?"

She felt as though she were about to expire with happiness. At last, after so many years of frustration and discontent, things were finally starting to go her way. "Hurry, darling, hurry."

She met him at the door in a striped pink satin sleepshirt that barely covered her ass and was tantalizingly unbuttoned to the waist. He put his hands inside the shirt and pulled her to him, luxuriated in her soft pliable flesh. He could feel her nipples tense as he bent to kiss her on the neck, on the breasts, on the mouth. Her lips tasted as delicious as he knew they would.

"Oh, darling," he whispered. "I want you so terribly."

*"Vraiment?"*

"Yes, oh yes. More than you'll ever know. You can't imagine how desperately I want you."

Nobody had wanted her terribly or desperately in such a long time (except for Eddie, who wanted her for all the wrong reasons) that she was a little afraid to believe her most cherished dreams were coming true.

"I wanted to make love to you from the moment I saw you last night." He buried his face in her throat. "You're so lovely, so desirable. I've been looking for you all my life."

Simone nearly swooned. "You have?"

"Oh, yes, darling. And I knew I'd found you the minute I laid eyes on you. I'm a very lucky man to have realized my heart's desire."

No one had ever spoken to her like that before. Her head was reeling, her senses were on fire, but there was the usual sexual anxiety coursing through her, goddammit. She trembled in his arms, thinking that maybe this time she wouldn't strike out. Maybe she was finally about to be appreciated and loved as a femme fatale. Maybe all it took was a fellow Libran, the closest kind of soulmate there was, to do the appreciating.

"Why don't we go upstairs?" she suggested.

"First, take off this damned shirt."

She glanced nervously at the upper level. "What if Colin should—?"

"Bugger Colin. I'm mad to see you naked and I refuse to wait one second longer. Here, darling, let me help you."

He eased her out of the sleeves and threw the shirt on the floor, scooped her up in his arms (she was so much smaller than Anita), and proceeded to carry her up the stairs, kissing her passionately all the way.

"I feel like Scarlett O'Hara," she murmured. "You're so strong, I feel like I'm going to faint."

"I have a much more viable suggestion. Why don't you plan on fainting afterward?"

She looked into his blue eyes. "Will it be good?"

It was such a trusting, childlike question that he fell in love with her on the spot. "As good as I can make it."

"Then I'm sure it will be wonderful."

Those were the last words either of them spoke for a while. Simone surrendered to him totally and he became like a tiger: strong, wild, daring. He twisted and turned her into positions she'd never dreamed of, he pounced and bit, he recoiled and was sly, he growled and pawed, he attacked and was fierce, he did everything under the sun he could think of to keep the two of them wrapped around each other as long as humanly possible. It was a virtuoso performance, as though he'd taken his whole bag of tricks out of a trunk and shined them up just for her sake. Not to show off, the way some men might have, but to please her and make her happy. Simone was impressed, touched, moved in a way she'd never been before. She hadn't realized how badly she needed to hear a man say that he adored and worshiped her, as Michael had repeatedly been saying.

"Say it again," she implored him.

"I'm crazy about you, I can't live without you."

"Again."

"There's nothing I wouldn't do for you. There's nothing I have that isn't yours. There's nothing I wouldn't give you."

"*Again.*"

"You're my darling, my angel, my madness!"

Simone could have expired on the spot. She felt overwhelmed with love, tenderness, pain, brutality, pleasure. Not the ultimate pleasure, she thought, cursing her hidden clitoris, but more pleasure than she'd experienced since Steve Omaha made her salute him. Michael was better than Steve, kinder, fiercer, more sensitive, more depraved, better than Eddie, he was even better than Fingerhood, *zut alors!* And when exhaustion struck them both and they fell breathlessly back on the bed, she was so delirious that she didn't know what to do with herself.

"Anita will kill us," she said when she could speak.

"Bugger Anita. I'm finished with that scheming little bitch."

Simone giggled. "In that case, she'll *doubly* kill us."

"You just leave Miss Schuler to me. I'll take care of that gold-digging hypochondriac, don't worry."

To their amazement, the sound of applause suddenly greeted their ears. Simone yanked the covers over her head, while Michael sat up ramrod straight, shaken.

"I didn't know you had it in you, Pops." Colin McKenna stood on the threshold, wearing a big grin and clapping his hands enthusiastically. "Ditto for you, Frenchie, wherever you're hiding. You surprise me. How about if I join you two swingers for a little encore?"

Michael had turned a dark angry purple. "What the hell are you doing here, McKenna? How *dare* you intrude?"

"Relax, Pops. I heard the action from the hallway and couldn't resist checking it out. I've got to hand it to the two of you—that's some of the best fucking I've witnessed in years."

*"Get out of here this instant, you stupid bastard.* And don't ever set foot in this room again or I'll personally cut your balls off." Michael put a protective arm around the lump beneath the covers. "I'll have you know that this is the woman I love and from now on you'd damned well better treat her with respect. Do you understand that, you bloody savage?"

"Hey, no offense meant, Pops."

"Out!"

Colin threw up his hands in graceful surrender. "Now you see me, now you don't."

After a moment Simone fearfully emerged from the covers and looked around. "Is he gone?"

"He is, I assure you." Michael observed her with a demanding curiosity. "Kindly explain your relationship with McKenna. It seems bloody peculiar to me. What is he doing here, anyway?"

So Simone told him all about *Rockabye Princess* and Eddie's P.R. plans for her to land the lead, and how she had reluctantly agreed to them due to her near-zero bank balance. She even threw in a heart-wrenching mention about the possibility of the twins' being expelled from Le Lycée Français de Los Angeles because their mother (and sole means of support) couldn't pay their tuition. And she made sure to point out how much she disliked and disapproved of Colin, the drippy-nosed cokehead whom she would have to kiss and publicly cuddle up to or else forfeit her chances of playing the Danish princess in Sandler-Roma-Weintraub's multimillion-dollar production, scheduled to start shooting in January.

As she spun her tale of woe and maternal sacrifice in her charming lilting voice, Michael listened gravely, he listened intensely, he nodded at appropriate moments, he seemed to understand everything she had gone through and would still have to go through if she hadn't met *him*.

"You can call your agent and tell him that you won't be participating in any of those amorous stunts with McKenna," Sir Michael Harding instructed in a voice that was used to being obeyed. "Tell him that as far as you're concerned, the movie deal is off. Finished. Over. Kaput. Fini."

"It is?"

"Absolutely. Tell him that you've ceased to have any interest in appearing in *Rockabye Baby* or any other piece of cinematic claptrap he comes up with and that he can start looking around for another actress to kiss that twit McKenna at Studio 54. Do you understand?"

"It's *Rockabye Princess*," Simone said, feeling a rustle of uneasiness she could not define.

"I don't care what the bloody film is called. You tell your agent what I just told you." Having failed to put his foot down with his headstrong wife who'd sullied their beautiful home with the screeching and droppings of those dreadful birds, he was not about to make the same mistake again. Simone would know from the start who was in charge. *He* was. "And be sure to underscore the fact that due to an abrupt change in circumstances, you're no longer in dire financial straits. Is that clear, darling?"

"What's happened to my financial straits?"

"They're my concern now, you don't have anything to worry about. I intend to take very good care of you, Simone. Excellent care. The best."

"You do?"

He nodded solemnly. "What time is it in California?"

She looked at the clock, pointing to noon. "Nine in the morning. Why?"

He reached for the phone. "What's your agent's number?"

"I . . . I can't remember." She heard herself lie, strangely panicked. Michael not only professed to love and adore her, he was offering to assume monetary responsibility for her. What more could she want? This was the answer to her dreams, wasn't it? "Besides, Eddie doesn't get in until at least ten. I'll call him in a little while. Right now I can't bear to think of anyone or anything except you."

She said it so winningly that he was mollified. For the moment. While he'd fervently admired Simone's movie work before he met her, was attracted to her primarily because of it, he had no intention of letting her continue to exhibit herself half-naked for the mindless masculine masses after they were married. It simply would not do, not for a man in his station. The charms of Sir Michael Harding's wife had to be limited to Sir Michael Harding alone, and they would be. He kissed her hands, cradled her in his arms, getting used to the slightness of her small-boned body after Anita's sturdier, fleshier one. He allowed himself to feel protective of this delicate, fragile creature who had entered his life so unexpectedly and was about to have such a stunning effect upon it.

"Do you really love me?" she asked, anxious because it occurred to her that she was transferring all her hope, faith, and dreams from Jimmy (whom she hadn't even mentioned) to Michael, whom she barely knew. It was a major emotional shift. "You're not just saying it because . . .?"

"Because I made love to you?" He smiled at her feminine insecurities, adored her all the more for them. "I never say what I don't mean. Appeasement and hypocrisy aren't my game. I do love you, Simone. Very much. Please don't doubt that. Ever."

She felt warmed, the rustle of uneasiness subsiding. She snuggled closer to him. Safe. She was safe at last. "I hope you weren't disappointed when we were making love and I didn't . . . you know . . . I couldn't . . . I mean, you were wonderful but my clitoris is rather hidden so I never can . . . not through intercourse, although I realize that wasn't all we did . . . but it's a problem with me . . . and I didn't want you to think it was your fault . . . or feel bad . . . because frankly I've never been happier in my life . . . and I love you, too."

He tilted her face up. "Do you, my darling?"

*"Vraiment."*

Michael smiled at his femme fatale and kissed her mauve hair, which of course would have to be dyed back to its natural color. As soon as he returned to England, he intended to ask his cold haughty wife for a divorce and marry Simone. He would put the twins in St. Paul's, where they would get discipline *and* education, two items he felt certain they were being deprived of in the Los Angeles wasteland. As for him and Simone, they would have a good life together, a wonderful life. He could hardly wait.

"I've never been happier either," he said.

And he meant it. The fact that she had a hard time achieving orgasm was the greatest punishment he could ecstatically imagine.

*         *         *

Madison Avenue was aglow with beautiful shops, many of them bearing French, Italian, and English names. The Queen Victoriana was wedged between a fashionable men's boutique and a store that specialized in custom-made lingerie. Lou glanced around, but Sally was nowhere in sight.

"*Exquisite*," a woman murmured about the mannequin in Queen Victoriana's window.

"Yes, isn't it?" Lou agreed.

The high-necked wedding gown of delicate antique lace was appliquéd on rose silk and had seed pearls woven throughout the bodice. An ivory cameo brooch was pinned at the throat in keeping with the style of the period and the face was demurely shaded by a rose mantilla veil to which was attached one of the longest sweep trains Lou had ever seen. As a finishing touch, the mannequin held a spray of baby's breath tied with a lilac satin ribbon. The overall illusion was so brilliantly executed that she half-expected the mannequin to start walking and talking.

"Wasn't that how brides dressed when they were advised by their mothers to close their eyes, spread their legs, and think of England?" asked a cheerful voice behind her.

"Hi, Sally."

Fingerhood's future wife wore faded jeans, the same gaunt look as the other day, and diamond stud earrings that sparkled in the June sunlight.

"Are those new?" Lou asked. "They're lovely."

"They couldn't be newer. Fingerhood freaked when I refused to accept an engagement ring, so he shot over to Tiffany's and came back with these. I had to take them, he was so upset."

"What do you have against engagement rings?"

"Are you kidding?" Sally stared at her in dismay. "They're one of the most primitive and degrading of all bridal traditions. They originated in the days when men bought their wives. The betrothal ring represented the buyer's down payment, as well as his honorable intentions. I thought if anyone should know that, it's you."

"When I became engaged, I walked around with a ring the size of a rock. I was also registered at Tiffany's bridal department. What do you say to that?"

"Were you happily married?"

"Very." Remembering the woman she had been ten years

ago made Lou feel sad. Never again would she entertain that
same expectation of lifelong bliss or imagine that it could
be provided by another person. "My husband was Vanessa's
father. Didn't Fingerhood mention it?"

"No, he doesn't talk about anything these days unless it's
directly related to our wedding. He kept me up half the night,
imploring me to agree to Chicken Turban as the entrée. So I
agreed." She looked at Lou curiously. "It's none of my
business, but didn't you feel strange making it with your
stepdaughter?"

Lou was startled that Sally knew about her and Vanessa.
Fingerhood must have perceived their relationship and then
mentioned it to his fiancée. Had the two of them enjoyed a
good laugh over it? She could feel the blood rush to her face,
even as she chastised herself for continuing to be such a
hypocritical prude.

"Have I embarrassed you?" Sally was looking at her with
concern. "I didn't mean to. I'm sorry. Look, let's just drop
the subject."

Lou couldn't. To do that would be to concede her shame.
"I don't mind talking about Vanessa," she said evenly. "No,
I didn't feel strange—I assume you mean *guilty*—when I
became involved with her. Vanessa had been attracted to me
for a long time before anything happened, and when it did it
was by mutual consent. There was none of that older-woman-
seduces-younger-girl kind of silliness. Actually, Vanessa was
the more experienced one, since she'd been involved with
women before. I hadn't." Lou remembered a contributing
factor. "And in an odd way, I thought Zachary would
approve."

"Why would he approve of something like that?"

Her own answer surprised her. "He could hardly be jealous of his own daughter, could he?"

"Oh, so Vanessa was safe," Sally said shrewdly. "A man
wouldn't have been."

"I never thought of it like that. Maybe you're right."

"But Zachary was dead, Lou. How could he be jealous of
anyone?"

"When a person dies very suddenly, as Zach did, it takes a
while to realize that he's gone. His death didn't seem real to
me for a long time. I loved him very much, you see."

"So much that you became a lesbian?"

Sally's bluntness revealed an aspect of her relationship with Vanessa that she hadn't allowed herself to recognize: so long as she restricted her love life to Zachary's daughter, she was not being unfaithful to his memory. Lou shivered in spite of the heat. Was that what her attraction to Vanessa had been about? Was that *all* it had been? A way of remaining tied to Zachary? A way of remaining the innocent widow? If so, it explained why the attraction would inevitably fade as Zachary's death became ancient, accepted history. It might even explain this newly awakened desire for a man.

"Did you have a big wedding, Lou?"

"The biggest. Engraved swizzle sticks, personalized matchbooks, fountains dripping champagne, imported caviar, the works. Does that make me persona non grata in your eyes?"

"I just don't see why anyone would want to subject herself to all that hoopla. My idea was to tie the knot in City Hall, but Fingerhood wouldn't hear of it. He said that having waited forty-eight years for this day, he'd be damned if he were going to utter his vows in an assembly-line ceremony before some klutz of a civil servant." Sally curled her lip. "He said it wouldn't be romantic."

"Don't be so quick to condemn. Fingerhood and I come from the last romantic generation and we take certain rituals very seriously."

"I know you do, but *why*?"

"Because we grew up believing in true love and commitment, unlike your generation, which grew up not believing in much of anything."

"There are two sides to that. You also grew up with girdles, very little birth control, and a lot of puritanical inhibitions. By comparison, we were free and unfettered. We had the pill, pantyhose, and no taboos to speak of."

"That's actually a shame."

Sally was surprised. "A *shame*? I thought you'd be envious."

"Are you kidding? Never!" Lou nostalgically remembered all the impassioned groping in backseats of cars when she was a teenager, the thrill of doing the forbidden, the first astonished glimpse of a man's penis—purple and throbbing—the first time she rebelled against straitlaced convention and actually *did* it, the rush of excitement afterward, the exhilarating sense of danger. "You don't know what you missed by not having to wear garter belts or worry about getting pregnant every month.''

"What?"

"Dirty sex," Lou said with a wink. "I understand it doesn't exist anymore, now that nothing is off limits. Or so my daughter informs me. The way she describes it, sex these days is a nice healthy little pastime sort of like playing a few sets of tennis. Come on, let's go shopping."

After trying on five different gowns, Sally settled on white moiré taffeta and Victorian lace with a high ruffled neck, tiered sleeves and skirt, and for fun a white lace umbrella to match.

"What is Fingerhood planning to wear?" Lou asked.

"A white linen suit by Armani that he bought several weeks ago and keeps wrapped in plastic, would you believe? He's an even bigger narcissist than my father."

"Your father isn't such a narcissist. He merely takes pride in his appearance."

"The two of you were lovers, weren't you?"

Lou was caught off guard. "How did you know?"

"My mother never recovered from it. After the divorce, whenever she was in her cups she would cry and blame you for everything."

"I'm surprised to hear that. I didn't break up her marriage. In fact, Peter left me to go back to her."

"Oh, the divorce wasn't your fault. It was alcohol talking. When my mother drinks, she imagines all kinds of things, she blames everyone for her problems, she pictures herself as a helpless pitiful victim. It's very tedious. She can't handle booze and she refuses to stop."

"You haven't seen her in two years," Lou said. "Maybe she's stopped by now."

"Maybe the earth is flat."

"Are you sure you don't want to call her and let her know you're okay? Drunk or sober, she must be worried sick."

"I appreciate your concern, Lou, but I'm under enough pressure as it is without having to deal with an alcoholic mother and a homosexual father." Sally bit her lip. "You have no idea what my life was like before I left Radcliffe."

"Why don't you tell me?"

"It was sheer hell." Sally seemed to have forgotten where she was; her eyes were remote and bitter now. "I hated living at home with that creep my mother married and with her smashed out of her mind half the time. I hated going to Paris and staying with my father and his swishy boyfriend. I hated Radcliffe because it was where *they* wanted me to go. As though by sending my brother and me to the finest Eastern schools, they could somehow exonerate themselves. . . ."

Her contempt knew no bounds. For as long as she could remember, she came last in their hierachy of values. When she had problems, there was no parental figure to turn to. Beverly was either drunk or in bed with a hangover, and even before the divorce Peter Sr. was too busy pursuing a career to spend much time with his family. After the divorce, Beverly carted them off to Wyoming so she could drink in peace and seclusion, and things got worse. Much worse, in Sally's opinion. She no longer had friends and teachers to confide in in moments of crisis, she had nobody except a bunch of washed-out-looking hicks who'd never been to a city larger than Casper. When she learned that Casper boasted a population of less than fifty thousand, she laughed in their faces. Why, her old Upper East Side neighborhood was bigger than that! No wonder these kids were so naive.

"Shmuck!" she said to one boy who was extolling the virtues of Richard M. Nixon. "You don't know anything about anything."

It turned out that he didn't know what "shmuck" meant and looked at her suspiciously, as though she were speaking a foreign language. Maybe she was, at that. Maybe her crazy drunken mother had moved them all to a foreign country where she had nothing in common with anyone. From the age of ten she couldn't wait to run away, lead her own life, live in New York. It was all she thought of, planned for, dreamed of. . . .

"Here you are." A plump saleswoman handed Sally a large lavender box and smiled a studied smile. "I hope it doesn't rain on the lucky day."

As they stepped out into the bright sunlight, Lou said, "Would you like to have lunch? I'm in the mood for an omelet. How about Madame Romaine de Lyon? It's only a few blocks away."

"Okay."

Just as she took Sally's arm, she felt someone tap her on the shoulder. "*Lou?*" A gorgeous blond in a Sonia Rykiel black knit shift and jaunty white straw cloche was staring at her with incredulity. *"Lou Marron?* Is it really you, or am I dreaming?"

Lou took off her sunglasses. She recognized that voice, those china-blue eyes, the flawless complexion. *"Anita?"* she said weakly. *"Anita Schuler?"*

"None other, darling, what a fabulous coincidence!" She kissed her on the cheek. "Let me look at you."

"How did you ever recognize me?" Lou asked, stunned. "What are you doing here? How are you, Anita?"

"I've never been better, darling. I was buying antique cufflinks for my father." She indicated the men's boutique next to Queen Victoriana. "As for recognizing you, you haven't changed that drastically, you sly fox. Your hair is different, but you still have those wonderful cheekbones. If I didn't remember them from the old days, I would swear you had your face remolded."

Lou thought of her resolution to get her eyes done.

"I must be lucky, I've managed to escape the surgeon's knife so far." Anita saw no reason to mention the mini face lift she'd had last year when Michael was attending the trials at Badminton. "But wait until you get a load of Simone. She's had everything done and I mean *everything*."

"She must look wonderful."

"She does, the rotten little bitch. Well, darling, now that I've seen you, the only one still to be accounted for is Beverly. I'll bet she's a mess. Those curvy voluptuous types are attractive when they're young, but they rarely hold up well in the long run."

Lou swallowed, acutely aware of Sally's presence. "Maybe she went on a diet and trimmed down."

"Spoilsport." Anita laughed her old callous laugh that made Lou remember how much she used to dislike her. "It's one of the things we titless wonders have to be grateful for, isn't it? We never sag."

Just as Lou was wondering how they could escape before Anita discovered Sally's identity, she realized it was too late. Anita was staring at the lavender box in Sally's hand. Part of the connection had been made. It was Sally who spoke first.

"Excuse me, but were you referring to Beverly Northrop?"

"As a matter of fact, I was," Anita replied, fastening a microscopic eye on her. "Why? Do you know the lady?"

"She's my mother."

"I beg your pardon?"

"Beverly Northrop is my mother. Why do you look so surprised? Actually, her last name is Kirby now."

"Your mother?" Anita's mouth had fallen open. "Just a minute. Let me understand this. You're Fingerhood's fiancée, aren't you? I mean, that's what you and Lou were doing in Queen Victoriana—buying a wedding gown, right?"

"What if we were?"

Lou opened her mouth to introduce them, but no sound came out. Instead the sound came from Anita. Loud and shrill, it ricocheted down beautiful elegant Madison Avenue.

*"Holy shit,"* she cried, forgetting her English accent. *"That cradle-snatcher is marrying Beverly's goddamned daughter!"*

There were five hundred and twenty omelets listed on the menu at Madame Romaine de Lyon on East Sixty-first Street and the sheer proliferation of exotic combinations was driving Sally crazy.

"I can't decide between Rochambeau and Maxim," she said to Lou, who'd already decided upon Jourdan (caviar, ham, bacon, onions, mushrooms, and cheese). "Maybe I should put my hands over my eyes and point."

"Why don't you?" Lou said, distracted. She was certain she'd spotted Keith Rinehart just before they entered the restaurant. He was standing on the other side of the street, about a block away, watching them. "All the omelets here are delicious."

"I've chosen Supreme." Sally opened her eyes and read the ingredients (chestnuts, chocolate sauce). "It's a dessert omelet. I don't want that. I'll have what you're having."

"Two Jourdans," Lou said to the French waitress, wondering if she could have been mistaken. Maybe it was someone who looked like Keith Rinehart. "And two of your delicious green salads, please."

The restaurant was jammed, bustling, noisy. Sally leaned across the table. "Do you think Anita will tell my parents that I'm marrying Fingerhood even though you pleaded with her not to say anything?"

"For all the good it will probably do me. That woman is a born troublemaker." And nothing about Anita's behavior led Lou to believe she'd changed. The crazed look of triumph on her face when she discovered Sally's identity did not bode well. "What if she does tell your parents? Would it be such a tragedy? I don't understand why you're so determined to keep them in the dark right up until the last minute."

"Because they'll try to stop the wedding, if they don't murder Fingerhood first. My mother has never forgiven him for dropping her for Anita. And my father has never forgiven him for having an affair with my mother. If they find out, it will be sheer bedlam."

"No, Sally, I think they'll be so glad you're alive and well that they won't care if you married Meatloaf."

"Well, they *deserve* to suffer. If they were better parents, I'd never have run away."

If she had been a better parent, would Joan be having an affair with every steel-guitar player in the Western world?

"Now that I've met Anita Schuler, I don't understand what Fingerhood ever saw in her," Sally said. "She's so grasping and pushy, really obnoxious."

"Men look at these things differently."

"How do they look at them?"

"Through their pricks."

Sally smiled. "Isn't that a sweeping generalization?"

"It sure is and that's because it's sweepingly true. Flatter a man's sexual ego and he's your slave forever. If there's one woman who knows that, it's Anita Schuler." Lou noted Sally's troubled face. "Hey, you're not jealous, are you?"

"I suppose I am a little jealous. You see, I was a virgin when I met Fingerhood."

For some reason, that startled Lou more than if Sally had said she was a gun runner in Nairobi. She thought again of Joan and her nonending stream of lovers. Would she prefer it if Joan were a virgin?

"How come?" she asked Sally. "It can't have been for lack of opportunity."

"That's what you think. Do you know what my nickname was at Radcliffe? *Northrop Pole*."

The fact that no one had desired her sexually meant there was no one to put his arms around her and hold her close, make her feel accepted, loved. It wasn't passion she sought, so much as affection.

"I may have grown up during the sexual revolution, but thanks to my parents' influence, sex had lousy connotations for me. In my mother's case, I associated it with being drunk. And in my father's case, I associated it with with being gay." Sally reddened. "I hope I haven't offended you."

"You mean, about being gay? It's all right."

"What is it like to make love to a woman? I've always wondered."

Lou thought of the sign hanging in Vanessa's bedroom— LIB MEANS NEVER HAVING TO SAY YOU CAME—and was going to reply, "It's less pressured, more honest." But she stopped herself, remembering Sally's earlier comment. Perhaps, in her own misguided fashion, she'd used Zachary's daughter as a means of remaining true to Zachary. Perhaps she hadn't been very honest with Vanessa after all.

Seeing Lou's hesitation, Sally went on. "I guess what I'm asking is, do you *really* prefer women?"

"I used to," she heard herself say, suddenly aware that her feelings about Keith Rinehart were mixed. On the one hand, she was afraid of him; on the other hand, she was fiercely attracted to him. She wondered if he sensed it. "Now I'm not sure where my inclinations lie."

"It must be fun to be bisexual. You have so many more people to choose from."

"I never thought of it quite like that." She couldn't imagine why she found blond hair at the wrists so strangely exciting. "I'm still curious about your being a virgin when you met Fingerhood. What did he do to make you weaken?"

"He didn't have to do a damned thing. I was desperate to lose my virginity because it meant that I'd be a grown-up at last, independent of my parents, a woman in my own right."

"Is that why you're getting married? So you can feel like a grown-up?"

Sally flushed. "No. I want Fingerhood and the kind of life he can offer."

"What kind of life is that?"

She was about to leap to her own defense, then thought better of it. "I feel as though you're cross-examining me, Lou, and I don't like it. Why are you doing it?"

It was a good question. Why, indeed? Something told her that she was using Sally as a substitute for her own daughter. She and Joan had never enjoyed a close or particularly honest relationship even when Joan was young, and when she reached adulthood the gap between them widened. Joan's personal life was *so* personal that aside from periodically learning the identity of her latest lover, Lou knew almost nothing about her. At least not in the areas that counted. She had no idea where Joan's vulnerabilities lay, what her fears were, who peopled her dreams. No wonder she had lit upon Sally with such avid curiosity.

"I'm sorry," she said lamely. "I didn't mean to sound so overbearing. What you do with your life is your own business. I guess all I really wanted to know was whether you had any career plans, and if so, what they were." She gave Sally an apprehensive smile. "Am I being too pushy?"

"No. Actually, I like talking to you. I could never talk to my own mother."

"And I could never talk to my daughter."

They looked at each other, acknowledging the pain that that lack of communication had produced over the years.

"It must have been awful for you," Lou said sympathetically.

"It was," Sally agreed. "And for you, too."

Lou nodded. To her chagrin, she felt tears come to her eyes. "Joan was my only child and we were so far apart. *Always*. We got off to a bad beginning, and nothing I tried to do later on brought us any closer together. Now it's too late."

Sally reached for her hand. "Still, you must be proud of her. She's a respected musician and it couldn't have been easy to succeed in rock 'n' roll, not with all the macho discrimination that exists against women in that field. It must have taken a lot of guts on her part."

"She has guts, all right," Lou said, with pride. "She's very self-sufficient, determined, ambitious. Maybe I shouldn't be surprised—I was exactly the same at her age."

"Not me," Sally said cheerfully.

"Not you *what*?"

"I'm not ambitious at all. I'm not interested in a career, or climbing up the corporate ladder, or any of that executive stuff that's become so fashionable for women. Thanks to the efforts of people like you, I don't have to prove anything. You and your generation have very kindly done that for me." Sally fingered her diamond stud earrings. "That doesn't mean I want to feel like my husband's property. Nor does it mean I don't have a mind of my own."

"Stop me if I'm being a pain, but what about money of your own?"

"No problem. I come into a handsome trust fund in another year, so I can pretty much do what I please. I realize that my inclinations may seem frivolous to someone as career-oriented as you, but they suit me. I like to stay up late, have breakfast in bed, indulge myself. I like to make love, fool around with drugs, live voluptuously. So long as I don't hurt anyone, is there anything terrible about that?"

Lou remembered Vanessa's dire warning. "What kind of drugs?"

"Nothing serious. Just the soft stuff."

"Cocaine?"

"It's delicious for sex," Sally said with a sly smile. "If you haven't tried it, you don't know what you're missing."

It annoyed her that Vanessa had been right, it worried her. "I've heard that cocaine is much more dangerous than publicized, much more addictive."

"I don't know who told you that, but it isn't true." Sally seemed irritated by the suggestion. "Cocaine is a recreational drug. An occasional toot is like an occasional glass of wine would be for you. It's nothing to worry about, I assure you."

"Not if it's as occasional as you say."

"I would never allow myself to get hooked, I'm not that stupid." Her irritation had deepened into defensiveness. "I saw what addiction did to my mother. I would never make the same dumb mistake."

But children of addicts frequently did, Lou thought, not knowing whether to believe her. *Like mother, like daughter?* she couldn't help wondering. A close similarity seemed to apply in another area (so why not this?). Beverly had never worked and now Sally didn't want to either. She had always worked, and so had Joan, ever since she graduated from high school and formed her own rock group. Was it mere coincidence? Lou didn't think so.

"How about some white wine?" Sally seemed fidgety all of a sudden, edgy. "Do you see the waitress? They're never around when you need them. I don't know why that is."

"She's taking someone else's order."

Sally looked as though she were about to jump out of her skin. "Why the hell isn't she taking ours?"

But after the wine and omelets, she calmed down and Lou didn't think any more about it. Lou was enjoying herself, inasmuch as she rarely went out to lunch these days. *It's a great way to start a romance,* Vanessa had said earlier, mistaken about her feelings for Sally. Poor Vanessa. She must have been remembering that fateful meal at Victor's, a Cuban restaurant on Columbus Avenue, where their own romance was launched. Lou had nearly forgotten that long-ago tryst. It took place a few weeks after Zachary's funeral; the bereavement period was over and both women were coexisting in the large apartment, trying to ignore their attraction for each other. Finally Lou decided that something had to be done and she suggested lunch—to celebrate.

"What are we celebrating?" Vanessa wanted to know.

"At the risk of sounding crass, the fact that we're alive."

It was the first time Vanessa had smiled since her father's death. "Sounds good to me."

They ordered an enormous meal of arroz con pollo with all the trimmings and a bottle of champagne. It was a dismally cold day in February, Lou recalled, and the sidewalk outside the glassed-in restaurant was packed with icy snow.

"To Zachary, wherever he is," she said, raising her glass. "I know he'd approve."

Vanessa looked at her guardedly. "Approve of what?"

"That you and I are going to be such good friends."

"Nothing more?"

"That depends."

"On what?"

"On how you feel."

Vanessa was still hedging her bets. "How do *you* feel?"

Lou took her hand. "I think you know."

Relief flooded Vanessa's face. She laughed nervously, gratefully. "I was afraid those desires were one-sided. I didn't think you were interested."

"I'm interested," Lou said, sounding much more confident than she felt. Inside, her heart was pounding and she knew she would drink too much champagne to quiet the sound. "But you'll have to bear with me. I'm new at this."

Vanessa's eyes were filled with admiration and the barest hint of envy. "You may be new, but you're sure as hell cool. . . ."

Sally broke into her thoughts. "There's something I've been meaning to ask you, Lou. Would you be my matron of honor? It would mean an awful lot to me."

She had caught Lou off guard. "I'm flattered. We barely know each other. But how will I explain it to your mother?"

"What does she have to do with it? It's not as though the two of you were friends. You were rivals for my father's love."

"That was a long time ago and it has no bearing on the matter." As a mother herself, she dreaded seeing another mother get hurt, and Beverly was sure to be devastated when she found out that Sally had taken her into her confidence. "She's in New York, you know."

Sally nodded. "Fingerhood told me that she and my father are staying at the old apartment." She was speaking quickly now, jaggedly. "My father may not come to the wedding."

Lou felt sharply disappointed. "Why not?"

"He never forgave Fingerhood for having that affair with my mother, and naturally, he doesn't know about me." Sally fumbled for a cigarette, dropped it, cursed, struck three matches before she was able to light one with trembling hands. "On the other hand, my father is wildly unpredictable so there's no telling *what* he'll do."

Lou couldn't imagine why she was so nervous. "Are you all right?"

"Sure. Fine. Terrific." She looked like she was about to jump out of her own skin. "It's just this goddamned wedding, so many arrangements to make. So? Will you be my matron of honor even if my mother attacks you in a drunken rage and my father tries to put the make on the best man?" She ran the words all together, as though she had a train to catch.

"When you ask me like that, how can I refuse? By the way, who's the best man going to be?"

"A photographer friend of Fingerhood's. A guy named Keith Rinehart," Sally replied, and suddenly made a dash for the ladies' room.

Beverly was just about to make herself a sandwich and then go over to the Burlington Book Shop, when the telephone rang.

"Hello, Beverly?"

"Yes?"

"This is Anita Schuler. Remember me?"

"Of course, dear. How are you? How nice to hear from you after so long. Are you in New York for the wedding?"

"Just got in yesterday. Look, I know this is short notice, but could we have lunch?"

"You mean *now*?"

"There's something I want to talk to you about. In fact, I took the liberty of calling Lutèce and making a reservation for two."

Beverly was wearing baggy pants and one of Peter's old shirts. "I'm not exactly dressed for Lutèce."

"So change."

She hesitated. It had occurred to her in the middle of the night, when she couldn't sleep, that it might be a nice gesture to send Dwight a copy of Henry Kissinger's new book, *Years of Upheaval*. Not only did Dwight consider hardcover books an unaffordable luxury, but he was especially fond of memoirs written by and about international figures. From time to time he told her that he used to dream of interviewing someone like Kissinger and writing such a book himself. Whenever she asked why he didn't do it, he would shrug and call himself a newspaper hack, not "a real writer." Despite her repeated attempts at encouragement, he continued to deprecate his own potential, and she often wondered whether his refusal to even take a stab at his secret dream didn't account for a lot of his hostility and bitterness.

"Could we make it tomorrow, or later this week?" she asked Anita. After buying the book, she planned to see a racy French movie that was playing nearby and would never be shown in Wyoming. "I'm kind of busy today."

"Too busy to find out where your daughter is?"

Beverly thought she had heard wrong. "Excuse me?"

"Your daughter, Sally. I know where she is."

Beverly's hand gripped the receiver so hard that her knuckles turned white. "Is she all right? Has something happened to her? Is she in trouble? Tell me!"

"I'll see you at Lutèce in twenty minutes."

The line went dead. Beverly was trembling, shaking, she had to sit down. The apartment felt ominously silent with the cleaning woman gone and Peter at Bloomingdale's to see about his franchising deal. Across the room, their old liquor cabinet glistened in the clear June sunlight. It seemed to Beverly that there was one of everything: Scotch, bourbon, vodka, gin, sherry, rum, white wine, red wine, rosé, sweet vermouth, dry vermouth, Campari, Drambuie, Pernod, Calvados, Armagnac, Kahlua, Courvoisier, champagne.

Her mouth felt dry and her stomach was twisted into knots. *Dare she?* She had abstained for two years and paid her penance, hadn't she? She deserved a drink after all this time, didn't she? Her old dissuasive trick of telling herself that a drink would not bring Sally back didn't help now. Not in the frantic condition she was in, not with her mind imagining the worst. Maybe Sally was dead. Maybe that was what Anita meant by knowing where she was: the morgue.

She wished she could get in touch with Peter at Bloomingdale's, but she had no idea which department he was in. If only she could talk to him, she might be able to calm down. The liquor cabinet drew her like a magnet. It even contained her favorite brand of Scotch, Cutty Sark, goddammit. A second later she broke open the seal and poured herself a stiff drink, finished it in two swallows, and poured another. The Scotch tasted even more delicious than she remembered. How could she have ever given it up?

"Fiftieth between Second and Third,"she told the cabdriver, minutes later. "And hurry, please."

She was high from the Scotch and sweating. The pleasant air conditioning of the apartment made her forget what a lousy combination alcohol and hot weather were. Even her underarms were soaked, her best green silk dress probably ruined, but what did she care? The only thing she cared about was hearing what Anita had to say for herself. How could she sadistically keep her in suspense like this? Beverly wondered as the taxi came to a halt in front of a nondescript brownstone that housed one of the city's most prestigious restaurants.

"Miss Schuler is upstairs," the distinguished maître d' said. "Would you kindly follow me?"

Beverly had never dined at Lutèce when she lived in New York, at least not that she could remember. Of course she was often too drunk to remember where the hell she had dined, or with whom, and frequently Peter used to have to remind her. That she was back in New York and on her way to being drunk again was a thought she irritably pushed aside. The upstairs dining room was bright, quiet, sedate, the tables set far apart with a rose on each one, the atmosphere more of a private club than a restaurant. Beverly spotted Anita immediately. She hadn't lost that too-bright, too-eager smile. Too bad.

"Darling, you look divine!" Anita patted the banquette and kissed her on the cheek. To her dismay, Beverly *did* look divine, wrinkle-free, firm. Yes, she was still a wildly attractive redhead with the kind of curves Anita would have died for. She graciously tried to ignore the redolent smell of Scotch. "I'm sorry we couldn't get a table in the garden, but we're lucky to have gotten a reservation at all on such short notice."

Dismissing her, Beverly turned to the maître d' before he could vanish. "I'd like a double Cutty Sark and soda," she said. Soda was good, it made the alcohol enter the bloodstream faster. It couldn't be fast enough for her. "Right away, please."

He nodded at her sound of quiet authority and disappeared.

"I was hoping you'd share some of this lovely wine with me, it's so refreshing in this beastly weather." Anita touched a bottle with a French label, cooling in an ice bucket. She wondered why maître d's were never as properly respectful to *her*. "Then I was going to suggest their Timbales d'Escargots a la Chablisienne to start. It's a specialty of the house, darling."

"Anita, what do you know about Sally?"

"I see that we don't believe in the little pleasantries of life, do we? You might say hello first. It has been fifteen years."

"Hello," Beverly snapped. "Now, where's my daughter?"

Anita felt rebuffed, her attempts at civility rudely ignored. Beverly was treating her like some kind of a servant or underling whose only function was to supply the lady of the manor with the information she requested—and be damned quick about it. A sharp stab of anger and hopelessness shot through her. She had imagined that after all those years of improving her social graces in England, she would finally manage to rise above her humble origins and be accepted as an equal by someone of Beverly's status. Apparently she was mistaken.

"I'll tell you where Sally is in a moment," she said, forcing back the tears, trying to regain her pride. "Actually, I had hoped you'd be a little more relaxed when you heard the news. If you don't mind my saying so, you seem awfully tense."

Beverly felt her heart sink. "Is the news that bad?"

Anita considered the question objectively. "That depends what you mean by 'bad.' Sally isn't sick, hurt, dead, incapacitated, or victimized by one of those terrible cults. She isn't a prostitute, or on drugs, she isn't—"

"*Where the hell is she?*"

Diners at the elegant restaurant paused to see who was responsible for the resonant outburst. The maître d' closed his eyes in prayer. Waiters froze. Anita's tears dried. So! Even Beverly Fields Northrop Kirby, with her impeccable credentials, wasn't above creating a public scene. It made her seem more human, more vulnerable, less the pillar of good taste and lofty standards that Anita used to resent (and envy) so much. She realized that she had a fifteen-year-old grudge against Beverly and it didn't result from anything Beverly had ever done to her, it resulted from what she *was*: rich, well-educated, and married straight out of Wellesley to rich Peter Northrop, by whom she'd had two picture-perfect children.

Beverly's life was the life Anita always wanted for herself and was never able to achieve. Beverly's ladylike airs were the airs that Anita had tried her best to cultivate, but was never sure if she succeeded. Beverly's breasts were the size and shape that Anita had wished her own breasts to be, lots of luck. And as if all that weren't discouraging enough, Fingerhood once confided that Beverly was a fabulous fuck. Since he made the admission shortly after they began their own affair, she felt the sharp slap of insult.

"If Beverly was so great," she said to him, "then how come you threw her over?"

"She drank too much."

"You mean, if she didn't drink, you would still be with her?"

"No, sweetheart, it was more than that. I wanted to be with you."

"Then why are you telling me about Beverly's sexual superiority? Why are you comparing us? Are you trying to hurt me?"

"I'm sorry, sweetheart. I didn't mean to imply she was superior. I was just thinking that if you could move your ass a little more, instead of lying so still . . ." He trailed off, embarrassed.

Anita flushed. "The way Beverly moved *her* ass, I suppose?"

"Forget it, sweetheart. I love you exactly the way you are. I should never have mentioned it."

It galled Anita that Beverly was not only a lady but an uninhibited lay, as well. It didn't seem fair that the other woman should be so blessed, it didn't seem right. After that Anita became a lot more energetic in bed, yet it failed to change anything. Nobody wanted to marry her, nobody wanted to have picture-perfect children with her. Maybe if she had Beverly's breasts, she used to think late at night, maybe if she'd gone to Wellesley, maybe if she came from a rich and distinguished family . . .

"Look, Beverly, I know you're anxious," she said now. "And I sympathize with your plight—really, I do—but I'd like to tell you about Sally in my own way. All I'm trying to do is lessen the severity of the shock. It's a rather sordid story, I regret to say."

Beverly swallowed. "Sordid?"

Had she used too strong a word? Anita wasn't sure. If the situation were reversed and Sally were *her* daughter, she would consider the relationship with Fingerhood sordid as hell. She couldn't imagine that Beverly would view it in any other light, but perhaps Anita felt more possessive about her ex-lover than Beverly did.

"Maybe 'sordid' is overstating the case a bit," she confessed, not wishing to upset Beverly still further. "Maybe 'distasteful' would be more appropriate. Or possibly 'disheartening.' It might be best to let you decide that."

Fortunately, Beverly's drink arrived at that moment. She asked the waiter for another, then emptied the contents of her glass. She was furious with Anita for having provoked her into losing her temper seconds ago. She was not in the habit of shouting in restaurants (or anywhere else, for that matter), she was not in the habit of forgetting her manners. She tried not to forget them now as she kept her voice steady, low, controlled.

"Perhaps you don't understand, Anita. I haven't seen or heard from Sally in two years. Nothing can be worse than leaving me in this agonizing suspense, so whatever it is that's happened to her . . ." Beverly leaned over and hissed in her face, ". . . *just say it, goddammit.*"

Anita was sorry she had arranged this luncheon appointment. There was something unhinged about Beverly. She seemed far closer to the edge than Anita could have ever anticipated, and she felt afraid that if she told her about Sally and Fingerhood, she would push her over that edge.

"Maybe we should wait for the waiter to come back with your drink," she nervously suggested.

Beverly's eyes were blazing now. "I've had enough of your evasions, you stupid, sadistic bitch. Apparently words don't impress you. Maybe actions will." She grabbed Anita's wrist with one hand and dug her nails into it with the other. Her nails weren't very long, but they were hard and sharp.

"What are you doing?" A cry of pain escaped Anita's lips. "You're hurting me. Let go of me!"

Beverly dug deeper until she saw blood. "I'll kill you if you don't tell me where Sally is this instant."

"She's living with Fingerhood. She's going to marry him."

Beverly felt as though someone had conked her over the head with a crowbar. *"What?"*

"That's who the dear boy is marrying. Your long-lost daughter." She spoke with indignation now. "I was trying to do you a favor by warning you about the wedding, and instead of a polite 'thank-you,' what do I get for my efforts but a bleeding and possibly infected hand?"

Anita's hand was released. She regarded it with great concern, dabbed water on it, realized that what she needed was a germicide, but she hesitated to abandon Beverly. The blood had drained from her face and she seemed to be in shock.

*"Fingerhood?"* Beverly's voice sounded weak, wispy. Her anger was gone, replaced by dazed incredulity. "You can't be serious, Anita. I can't believe it."

"Believe it."

"But how did Sally meet him? How long have they been together? Oh, God! How can this be happening?"

"How the hell should I know?" Anita dipped the napkin into Beverly's glass of Scotch and squeezed it on her wrist. It stung. So did Beverly's obvious lack of concern for her. They might never have been friends, but they were old acquaintances and surely she had the right to expect better treatment than this. "You've become an Indian living in that godforsaken state. No wonder Sally ran away and is marrying Dr. Sex. What girl in her right mind wouldn't try to escape from a crazy Apache mother? If I get blood poisoning, I'm sending you the doctor bill. I just want you to know that in advance. I have no intention of paying for this outrage myself."

Beverly didn't appear to hear her. "I spoke to Fingerhood only this morning. Why didn't he tell me about Sally then? Why has he put me through hell for the past two years? We used to be friends, lovers, we used to care for each other." She shook her head in numb confusion. "I don't understand. Did he invite me to the wedding as some sort of cruel joke? Has he become a sadist, too?"

"I can't believe you would have the nerve to dig those claws into me and then imply that *I'm* a sadist." Anita wrapped a napkin around her wrist to stop the bleeding, she waved off the waiter's concerned gesture in an attempt to maintain a dignified appearance. "My blood-clotting factor isn't up to par and I'm prone to hemorrhaging, but do you care? No. You're on the warpath. I used to think you were such a lady, so proper and elegant, I used to admire you and envy you. Now I see that you're only an Apache at heart."

It felt good to topple Beverly from her throne at last. "No wonder you can't drink like a normal person, everyone knows that Indians have no tolerance for alcohol. I'm surprised you're not wearing feathers in your hair and dancing around a tepee with the rest of your bloodthirsty tribe."

"How did you find out about Sally and Fingerhood?" Beverly asked, unmoved by Anita's denouncement. "Who told you? How long have you known?"

That Beverly didn't have the decency to be hurt by her insults was the last straw. It was as though her opinions and feelings were of no consequence. "Aren't you even going to apologize for what you did to my wrist? Aren't you going to be gracious enough to say you're sorry? Didn't they teach you any manners at all those fancy schools you went to?"

Beverly took a deep breath. "I'm sorry, Anita, but you're pushing me beyond my limits by evading my questions. *Please.* How do you know all this? Tell me. I beg you."

Anita liked being begged. It made her feel important, it helped compensate for having grown up on the wrong side of the tracks with parents who still spoke in a foreign accent.

"Nobody told me, as it happens. I ran into Lou and Sally only a little while ago. They were shopping for a wedding gown . . . and thick as thieves, I might add."

"Lou *Marron?*"

"Yes, only her last name is different now. Otherwise she's still the same snotty New York fashion plate, too thin as usual. Men don't appreciate skin and bones, you know." She gave Beverly's voluptuous body another envious once-over. "Of course you know. You're smarter than Lou on that score."

"Lou and Sally?" Beverly's head was reeling. Was she the last one to discover the identity of Fingerhood's bride? She felt like an utter fool. "How does Sally know Lou?"

"Beats me. But I must admit I was astonished to learn that Fingerhood is marrying such a young girl. I mean, he's forty-eight and has screwed everything that walks—not that I don't adore the dear man . . . still, facts are facts—and she's only a baby. You must be heartbroken and I can't say that I blame you. I told Lou I thought it was disgusting, but all she seemed to care about was that I didn't mention it to you. She pleaded with me to keep quiet, as though I could be so *hypocritical*." She emphasized the word in an attempt to prove her good intentions. "I even asked Lou what the big deal was in deceiving you about your own flesh and blood, and then the truth emerged."

"What truth?"

Anita realized she had put her foot in it. She tried to think of a way out, but couldn't. If she evaded the question, Beverly was liable to have another bout of hysteria, and God knew which part of her anatomy she would attack next.

"*What truth?*" Beverly repeated, more sharply now.

"Sally was the one who didn't want you to know. Lou was merely going along with her wishes." A desperate smile glued itself to Anita's mouth as she rushed on, hoping to distract Beverly from the implications of her daughter's duplicity. "Frankly, I've never trusted Lou. She was indirectly responsible for giving me crabs years ago, even if she did get them from your husband. Excuse me, darling. *Ex*-husband. I understand that Peter has become a pouf and you're now married to a cowboy. Are they as sexy and macho as they're cracked up to be?"

"He's not a cowboy, he's a newspaper editor."

"Really? Fingerhood must have been pulling my leg. Well, cowboy or not, I hope you've roped him into attending the wedding. I'm involved with the most divine Englishman, if I do say so myself. I can't wait for you to meet him."

Beverly motioned to the waiter for another Cutty Sark, then drained what was left in her glass. Swallow, gulp, keep it down, all the booze, all the old bitterness she once felt upon learning that Peter had gone gay, all the new bitterness upon learning that even at this stage Sally didn't want her mother to find her, all the irritation of having to listen to Anita Schuler babble on. And on.

"Michael—Sir Michael Harding—has been keeping me in a state of what I can only call exquisite pampered luxury," Anita informed her. "If you ever come to London, you must be sure to stay with me. I have a delightful guest room decorated in the most flattering peach tones, with a canopied bed that I picked up at Sotheby's. It's to die over, as they say. We can have lunch at the Savoy Grill, tea at the Ritz, go shopping on Bond Street in between. I'm sure that after living in the boondocks of Wyoming, you would enjoy a taste of English elegance, wouldn't you?"

"If you're trying to make me feel better, I appreciate it but it's not working. I'm beyond English elegance, Anita. I'm beyond everything at the moment."

"Cheer up, darling! The idea of becoming Fingerhood's mother-in-law is unsettling, I agree, but there is a bright side to this picture and that's what we must look at." She patted Beverly solicitously on the shoulder. "It isn't as bad as you think. Sally could be a lot worse off than she is. You read those hair-raising stories about runaway girls heading for the Minnesota Strip around Times Square and straight into the arms of those ugly, greedy black pimps. And we all know what they become reduced to after that, don't we?"

"Anita, could we please change the subject?"

"Forgive me. Pimps and prostitution don't make for the most pleasant lunchtime chatter, do they?" she asked agreeably. "Okay, there's the medicinal angle to consider."

"Anita, I wish you wouldn't."

"Wouldn't *what?*" She laughed, hoping to dispel Beverly's gloom. "Try to show you how lucky you are, after all is said and done? I mean, Sally could have contacted herpes or AIDS by now—or any one of a number of venereal diseases that have been sweeping this Sodom and Gomorrah of a city—but she hasn't, thank God. Naturally we have no idea what she was doing before she teamed up with Fingerhood. Still, I'm sure you'll worm it out of her. Or maybe you'd rather not know.'' Anita pondered the best course. ''If I were in your shoes, I'd let bygones be bygones. What's the point in asking for trouble? Sometimes ignorance really *is* bliss—that's what I've learned over the years.''

Beverly's nerves felt raw, jangled. ''Not ignorance, Anita. *Silence.*''

''Am I talking too much? I'm only trying to make you see that Sally's situation could be a hell of a lot more grim. At least she's engaged to be married, and that's not something to sneer at in this cynical day and age, let me assure you. So why not count your blessings instead of dwelling upon the fact that she's engaged to one of the most fickle, lecherous, philandering studs either of us has ever met in our lives? People have been known to change, haven't they? And hopefully Fingerhood will do just that after he's married and realizes what a lucky bastard he is to have landed a sweet young girl like your daughter.'' Anita's eyes suddenly widened in horror. ''Oh, my God. No, Beverly, don't!''

But it was too late, as everyone at Lutèce observed, to their amazement. Beverly's nerves has snapped. She took the bottle of wine out of its bucket and unflinchingly poured it over Anita's jaunty white straw cloche from Harrods. Nearly twenty ounces of dry white French wine dripped down Anita Schuler's face, hair, and Sonia Rykiel black knit shift. For a moment she couldn't speak. She was too dumbfounded. Her jaw dropped and her eyes filled with humiliation. Someone in the room laughed, a tinkling sound of derision. She wished she were dead, invisible, she wondered how she would be able to leave Lutèce while maintaining a shred of her precious dignity. All of her old resentment surfaced. She wanted to kill Beverly.

''I hate you,'' she hissed under her breath. ''I've always hated you, you rich, fat, arrogant, big-boobed, drunken bitch. You have the manners of an Apache Indian and the mentality of—''

She didn't get to finish the sentence because Beverly pulled the white straw cloche down over her mouth, then sailed coolly out of the room. The maître d' followed her to the door, alarmed.

''Madam did not like the wine?''

7

After Anita left Lutèce in a cloud of shame, averting her head and pretending there was something in her eye, she walked uptown to Bloomingdale's. Slowly, seethingly, trying to simmer down from Beverly's gross insult.

And the hot unrelenting New York sun helped. It dried her wet hair and baked her anger into tractable submission, so that by the time she arrived at shoppers' paradise she felt almost human again. Before attempting to select a wedding gift for the odd couple, she stopped at a telephone booth and called Michael. Perhaps she'd been too hard on him that morning, too punitive and bitchy. It was a stance she could ill afford, and no one knew that better than calculating Anita.

"Mr. Harding doesn't answer," the switchboard operator at the Gramercy Regency said. "Would you like to leave a message?"

"For your information, it happens to be *Sir* Michael Harding," Anita snippily replied in her *faux* English accent. "And the message is that I'll be home by five at the latest."

"Thank you, Princess Diana."

As Anita took the escalator to Bloomingdale's sixth floor, she wondered where Michael was. Probably out attending to business, trying to sell his plane with the laminar flow wing. That he might be with Simone never occurred to her; she had already convinced herself that their flirtation was transitory and meaningless. Last night's hysteria had long since dissolved and she regretted having bared her insecurities by trying to jump out of their speeding taxi. What folly! Michael was not a man who appreciated seeing anyone's insecurities on parade, he was far too stiff-upper-lip English for displays of naked emotion. Cool self-confidence was what he appreciated, being in command at all times and in all contingencies. She would have to remember that, at least until she found a replacement for him—a task she stealthily decided to undertake as of right now. It wouldn't be easy digging up someone handsome, rich, successful, and fascinating, but she sure as hell was going to try.

She reflexively looked at the man standing one step ahead of her on the escalator, his body arched sideways as though for admiration by all the women farther down the line. He was attractive, well-dressed in an impeccably tailored gray silk suit and crimson-striped tie. Somehow, he seemed vaguely familiar.

"Do you know which floor the gift shop is on?" she asked him, with one of her most captivating smiles.

His eyes were steely, his voice cold. "The seventh, I believe."

"You're wrong, it's the sixth."

His arrogant jawline barely moved. "If you knew, why did you ask?"

"To talk to you."

"How baroque," he said, turning his back.

Her mistake. He undoubtedly had a boyfriend waiting in his East Fifties apartment, exquisitely furnished with Bloomie's best. Anita sighed and wondered whether men were worth all the trouble. Michael's behavior last night proved that he didn't give two hoots for her—she'd been kidding herself that he planned to make her his wife one day. His wife was his wife and would stay his wife, bird problems, sex problems, incompatibility problems, and whatever other problems the two of them had, until the day they died and were buried in the Harding mausoleum, side by side.

Besides, as she had learned during her long stretch in London, the English did not divorce as readily as the impatient and optimistic Americans. They tended to stick it out, try to make the best of a rotten relationship, suffer. God forbid any of them should be happy. Even Lucy Pickles, who used to be more joyous than most of her countrymen, had once admitted that happiness was a quality the English did not actively seek. When Anita asked why not, Lucy said:

"Because it would make us feel too guilty. We're a nation steeped in self-denial."

Anita stepped off the escalator and walked briskly to the gift department, silently giving thanks that she was born an American and would always be an American no matter how many years she lived elsewhere. Her never-say-die attitude was part of her heritage and she felt grateful for it. Within minutes, she was debating the merits of:

1. A pair of tall silver swirl goblets, versus
2. A graceful glass vase handcrafted in Czechoslovakia.

"Either one would make a lovely gift," the saleswoman said, noting her expensive clothes. "You have excellent taste, madam."

That was more like it, that was the way the switchboard operator at the Gramercy Regency should have sounded: subservient and humble, as befitting her station in life. American or not, Anita liked to be groveled to just as she had to grovel to Michael when the occasion demanded it.

"I think I'll take both," she said, suddenly feeling expansive with his money. "One as a gift and one for myself."

"What a charming idea, madam."

She would give the vase to the mismatched Fingerhoods and tonight she and Michael would drink some lovely vintage champers out of the goblets. Yes, they would make up, make love, make light of yesterday's silly events, and all would go back to the way it was. At least, on the surface. It was essential that Michael have no idea she planned to replace him, but that shouldn't be difficult to manage, she shrewdly realized. He was so filled with his own inflated self-importance that the idea would never cross his mind.

"Would you like to put a card in the gift package?" the saleswoman asked, standing at a respectful distance.

"Indeed, I would."

She wrote: *To Sally & Fingerhood: May all your dreams come true.*

Then she paid for both purchases with good old American cash and looked at the time. To her surprise, it was only a little past three. There was no point in rushing back to the Gramercy Regency if Michael were out, but where to go? When the saleswoman handed her the smartly wrapped package, her destination became clear. Fingerhood's apartment, of course. She would personally deliver the charming vase and then ask the silly, sneaky, feebleminded asshole if he didn't feel ridiculous marrying a sweet young thing like Sally Northrop, who probably worshiped the ground he walked on and whose mother should drink Cutty Sark until it came out of her nose.

"Ears, eyes, cunt, and belly button," Anita amended, vowing never to forgive Beverly for having humiliated her at Lutèce.

"Michael has the Sun and Venus in his *fourth* house," Kate was patiently telling Simone. "Whereas you have the Sun and Venus in your *tenth* house. That's the problem."

"I don't understand." Simone anxiously shifted the receiver to her other hand, wondering if it had been a mistake to call her astrologer in Los Angeles. "I can never remember which house is what. What does it mean?"

"It means that if you marry this man, he'll expect you to stay home and be domestic and you won't want to."

Bingo. She wished that Kate weren't always so damned accurate. Her ability to zero in on the crux of a problem never ceased to amaze, mystify, and infuriate Simone, who often felt that these uncanny deductions had less to do with astrology than with sheer witchcraft. She once told that to Kate, and to her surprise, Kate didn't argue the point.

"The fourth house pertains to the *home,* while the tenth house pertains to *careers.* So even though both you and Michael are technically Libras, the emphasis in your priorities is altogether different," Kate explained in a sympathetic voice. "It's too bad, because otherwise you seem quite well suited. You would probably enjoy the same kind of things, the same people, be on the same general wavelength except when it comes to this important conflict between career and home."

Simone snuggled under the covers in the pink-and-gold master bedroom at the King Croesus, trying in vain to get warm. The central air conditioning which had felt so pleasant only a few minutes ago when she and Michael were making love now felt like a polar ice cap. As soon as she hung up, she would adjust the thermostat.

"I'm beginning to wish I hadn't forced Michael to call his mother for his time of birth," she said. "I was probably better off being in the dark."

"Don't talk rubbish, Libra. The aspects would be the same whether you knew about them or not. At least now you realize what you're up against."

Simone groaned. "The question is, what can I do about it?"

"'Pray that Mother was wrong about his time of birth. Parents often are, I've discovered.''

Simone's spirits were rapidly plummeting. "What are you saying? That if she's right, Michael and I don't stand a chance to be happy?''

"I wouldn't go quite that far. I'd say that it would be a very difficult and tense relationship, one that you'd have a hard time adjusting to.''

"Why do these things happen to me, Kate?''

"What things?''

"Why do I pick men I can't find happiness and fulfillment with?''

"You have an afflicted Venus.''

She wished she could blithely disregard Kate's warning, but Michael's insistence that she cancel her publicity plans with Colin and forget about *Rockabye Princess* (which he absentmindedly kept referring to as *Rockabye Baby)* attested to the fact that he expected her to be a hausfrau after they were married. He had nearly said as much. The strange part was that until actually faced with the decision, Simone assumed she would like nothing better. Only yesterday she'd told Anita how happy she'd be to give up her career if the right man came along, but now that he had, she wasn't ready to do any such thing. Why the hell not?

"My ambivalence doesn't make sense,'' she complained to Kate. "I never even thought of being an actress until Jimmy pushed me into it, it never once crossed my mind. I've been morbidly unambitious all my life, so why should I suddenly care whether I get the lead in *Rockabye Princess?* Hollywood is a cesspool, the people are monsters, making movies is a bore and a grind, it's a horrible way to live. I hate it. And Michael is offering me a beautiful alternative.''

She could see it already. "I'd be Lady Harding, a woman of style, leisure, and impeccable taste. They'd photograph me in my Edwardian living room for *Harper's & Queen*. I'd learn how to ride, hunt, pour tea. We'd have a box at Ascot, a town house in London, we'd holiday in the Scottish isles, servants would wait on me hand and foot, my husband would adore me. I might even have more children.'' She didn't know whether to laugh or cry; it wasn't as fanciful as it sounded. "What's wrong with me, Kate?''

"Jupiter.''

*Fuck astrology,* Simone thought. Everyone in his right mind knew it was nothing but hocus-pocus. She herself had never been convinced of its validity, and the only reason she continued to consult Kate was that in the past Kate's predictions usually agreed with what she wanted to hear. When they didn't, she tried to dismiss them—as she was trying now—resentful that she'd ever been gullible enough to put stock in the flaky zodiac.

"What does Jupiter have to do with my craziness?" she asked, figuring that it couldn't hurt to hear.

"I would hardly call it craziness. You're responding to a very strong celestial pull. Up until five years ago when Jimmy supposedly 'pushed' you into acting, you didn't have any major transits in your house of career. Then Jupiter arrived on the scene, camouflaged as Jimmy, and you became ambitious." Kate made it sound so self-evident. "You're still ambitious, you just haven't gotten used to the feeling. It's too new and unfamiliar."

"You can say that again," Simone pouted. "I don't recognize myself anymore. I want to go back to the way I used to be when I didn't have a care in the world, when I was glad to be a housewife, when all I longed for was a man's undivided love."

"There's no going back, Libra, not in this case. Jupiter will be around for many years, and then Mars trines your Sun, giving you the energy to put your ambitions into effect." The astrologer chuckled. "You might as well resign yourself. One way or another, you'll be career-happy for a long time to come."

"But I'm *not* happy. I'm miserable, confused, mixed up. I don't know what to do! Don't you understand anything?"

"Shouting at me won't alter the course of the planets. I don't invent these things. I only describe them."

Simone pummeled the mattress. She was fit to be tied. All her life she'd envisioned herself as a simple earthy creature whose primary aim was to be taken seriously as a femme fatale. When Jimmy failed to accommodate her, she began looking around for a man who would. That seemed only logical. What didn't seem logical (despite Kate's mumbo jumbo) was now that she'd found him, she was wavering.

*Fool!* she cried inwardly. What's wrong with you? Greedy creature, how much more can you ask for?

Because in addition to Michael's other sterling qualities, he finally told her that she had a cunt that never stopped. The fact that she had to press him to make that statement didn't matter, not when she considered all the other men she'd pressed too. They just laughed at her, whereas Michael confirmed what she'd been longing to hear for years. The last time she badgered Jimmy to make that simple statement, he said: "A cunt that never stops? Hmmmmm. Sounds pretty tiring to me. Why don't you send it to Club Med for a two-week vacation in Tahiti?"

A hideous thought now occurred to Simone. "You aren't suggesting I go back to Jimmy, are you?" she asked Kate. "Because even if I'm foolish enough not to marry Michael, I'm moving out of the house in Malibu. I've had enough sexual rejection there to last me two lifetimes, and don't tell me I'm being silly."

"I'm not telling you to do anything with anyone," Kate calmly replied. "You should know by now that that isn't my style. I'm only interpreting your progressed chart. Whatever decision you make is yours and yours alone. Good luck, Libra."

After Simone hung up, she felt like screaming in frustration but was afraid to alarm Michael. He had never seen her throw one of her temper tantrums and was liable to think that she'd gone berserk. Still, she had to find a way of dispelling the anger and annoyance that Kate had evoked within her. If only she could smash something, if only there were a beach outside her door to run along, if only she had compliant Hilda to shout at. That gave her an idea, and in another minute she picked up the phone again and was talking to Hilda in Malibu. The initial formalities over with, she let go with a bloodcurdling shriek that made the housekeeper gasp in confusion.

"What is wrong, Miss Simone? Has something happened to you? *Jag förstär inte.* Have you been attacked?"

Simone was in the middle of a second wordless shriek when the door to the bathroom opened and Michael emerged, still wet from his shower.

"Darling," he said with an uneasy laugh, "what, in heaven's name, is all the commotion about?"

She stared at him. He was so handsome, so desirable, so wonderful, and he loved her. How could she even *consider* giving him up? Was she crazy? Let Kate ruin someone else's life with her gibberish about Jupiter and major transits. Simone wasn't listening—except to her heart. She said a hasty good-bye to Hilda (who had lapsed into Swedish hysteria) and turned to Michael with a reassuring smile.

"It's just my way of safeguarding our future, *chéri*."

*"Where is Sally? What have you done with her? I demand to see my daughter immediately."*

Beverly had marched past the arrogant Sutton Place doorman (who tried, in vain, to announce her), past a helpless Jeeves (whose on-board computer system wasn't programmed to deal with imperious ladies), past Miguel (who began shrieking in rhyme at the top of his lungs), past the paranoid patient in Fingerhood's sanctum sanctorum (who tried to attack her, thinking she was her ex-husband's voluptuous new wife), and now faced the man responsible for two years of the worst anguish she'd ever endured. The flutter of surprise on his face was quickly covered up by a professional veneer of composure, but he didn't fool her. Guilt was written all over him.

"Cat got your tongue?" she icily demanded. "Do you want me to tear this place apart? Is that what I have to do in order to see my own daughter?"

From behind his cluttered desk Fingerhood offered a nervous smile, thinking that the years had been astonishingly kind to her. How the hell did she manage to look so good, considering all the booze she stashed away? Probably by having the constitution of an ox, like a lot of drunks. He suspected she was half-smashed this very minute, despite her regal manner.

"As you can see, Beverly, I'm in the middle of a session." He tried to sound casual, matter-of-fact. "Why don't you have a seat in the waiting room and I'll be with you as soon as I'm finished?"

"You'll be with me right now, you scheming bastard."

In one carefully premeditated move of her hand, she swept everything off the desk and onto the floor. Pencils, pens, Scotch tape, paper clips, a staple gun, tape recorder, an appointment book, address book, reference books on sexual dysfunction, correspondence, a box of Kleenex, an electric clock, a pipe, pipe cleaners, matches, ashtray, and an almost full cup of black coffee landed on the thick beige carpet, the coffee swirling into a garish design.

"And to think my husband left me for a nut like you," the patient cried, grabbing her purse and running out the door.

"Wait!" Fingerhood called after her. But to his chagrin, she was gone. "Do you realize what you've done?" he asked Beverly. "This happened to be a very strategic session, we were just getting to the crux of her genital fantasies. Speak of rotten timing! That was a deeply disturbed woman you drove out of here."

"Look who's talking about disturbed," she said with contempt. A hemp hammock in one corner of the office made her wonder if that was where he taught them all "The Fingerhood Position." "I'll ask you one more time before I tear those drapes off the window. *Where is my daughter?*"

Fingerhood had known this day would come, but he still wasn't prepared for it. Two years of rationalization as to why it was all right to keep Sally's parents in the dark now dissolved into waves of self-rebuke. He should never have gone along with Sally's wishes, but he was afraid that if he defied her he would lose her. *Coward*, he thought again.

"I know that Sally is living with you, so don't try to deny it," Beverly went on in the same icy tone. "Now, go get her or I won't be responsible for my actions. I mean it, Fingerhood. I'll kill you."

He didn't doubt it for a second. One of the reasons he liked Sally was that she had a cool, tranquil nature. Thanks to years of his mother's ranting and raving, he went out of his way to avoid combative females in his personal life. That must be why he treated so many of them professionally, he realized with a flash of unsettling insight. It was a form of oedipal penance.

"I'm afraid that Sally isn't here just now," he said, extending his hand to Beverly in a gesture of goodwill after she'd refused a kiss on the cheek. "Why don't we go inside and discuss this in more hospitable surroundings?"

"You monster." She pulled her hand away as though it would get contaminated. "We were lovers once. Friends, too, I thought. You've been trained to help people, not traumatize them. How could you have done this to me?"

"Beverly, I'm truly sorry. I wanted to tell you that Sally and I were together, but she wouldn't hear of it. And there wasn't any budging her, God knows I tried." He finally managed to lead her down the corridor into the oyster-beige-

and-tan living room, hoping that its peaceful ambience would dispel her drunken rage. Now that he'd stood close to her, he could smell the Scotch. "I can't help wondering something. Who finally spilled the beans about me and Sally?"

She sank into the sofa. "And I can't help wondering what I have to do around here to get a drink."

"*Mink, fink, shrinks are kinky people,*" Miguel cried. "*I deserve a diamond pinky ring for putting up with one.*"

"Not now, Miguel," Fingerhood said, disturbed by Beverly's request. "Don't you think you've had enough?" he asked her.

"Scotch. Large. Neat. And no lectures, please. You're in no position to give any." She was trying to imagine Sally living here in luxury, while she sat in Wyoming fearing nameless catastrophes. "As for who spilled the beans, it was that bigmouth, Anita Schuler."

Fingerhood was stumped. "How the hell did Anita find out?"

"Probably through black magic, although she claims she ran into Sally and Lou shopping for a wedding gown. What is my daughter doing gallivanting around town with that woman? How well do they know each other?"

"They're not bosom buddies, if that's what you mean. They met here in the apartment shortly after I hired Lou to cater the wedding." Noting the startled look on Beverly's face, he added, "I guess I should explain. Lou runs one of New York's most successful catering companies. Why are you staring at me like that?"

"I don't like Lou, in case you've forgotten."

"How come?" Fingerhood felt indebted to Lou for having arranged the shopping expedition with Sally. At least his future wife wouldn't be walking down the aisle in her blue jeans, as he'd feared. "Don't tell me you're still harking back to that old animosity of yours. I can't believe it. Lou's affair with Peter took place years ago, it's ancient history."

"To you, maybe. Not to me."

"I don't understand."

"I thought you were a psychologist," she scoffed. "*No wife ever forgives the other woman.* Don't you know that?"

Fingerhood didn't. He would never know women, not really; that was part of the fascination in treating them. He kept learning more and more about them all the time.

"I don't believe that women like Lou, who try to break up other women's marriages, *should* be forgiven," Beverly added. "In my opinion, society has become too easygoing in its attitude toward home-wreckers."

The truth was that just as Anita admired and envied Beverly, Beverly had always secretly envied and admired Lou. Lou was thin, chic, enterprising, and totally self-made. She'd been born with no money, no family connections, no nothing, and it hadn't stopped her from succeeding first as a topflight reporter for that most influential of all fashion papers, *The Rag,* and now as head of her own catering business. How did she do it? Where did she get the drive?

Up until the time Beverly moved to Wyoming and took a job at the Williams Art Museum, she had never worked a day in her life. She never had to. For that matter, she still didn't have to. The museum was a way to keep busy, a way not to think about Sally's disappearance or Dwight's drunken abuse. She didn't work for the money because she didn't need the money. She was independently wealthy. Maybe if she'd been born in less fortunate circumstances she would have become a self-starter like Lou, a career woman who wasn't above seducing other women's husbands and getting them to fall in love with her. Remembering Lou's treachery revived her old feeling of bitterness. Thinking of Lou with Sally solidified it.

"What happened to my drink?" she asked Fingerhood.

"Beverly, I really don't think—"

She firmly cut him off. "Don't patronize me with your speeches about alcohol abuse, I'm hardly in the mood. This has been quite a day. First Anita and now Lou." Something suddenly occurred to her. "God, but I'm slow. You've invited all of us to your wedding, haven't you? All your ex-flames. Does that mean you've invited Simone too?"

He nodded.

"That's the first bright note in this entire dreadful conversation. I can't wait to see her again." A slow smile spread over Beverly's face, softening her features and reminding Fingerhood of why he had once been so attracted to her. "I always liked Simone. Remember how she and Anita used to fight and bitch at each other? What a duo. Simone was the only one of us who could make Anita shut that big mouth of hers. I'd hate to tell you what I had to do to shut it earlier at Lutèce."

Fingerhood didn't want to hear. As he went for her drink, he realized that what had seemed like a stroke of inspiration weeks ago might very well turn into a horror show. He'd hoped for a friendly and joyous reunion, a nostalgic trip down memory lane, but he hadn't realized how many old hostilities and gripes still existed among Simone, Beverly, Anita, and Lou. Of all the women he'd cared for in his long playboy career, those four had meant more to him than the others, they'd touched him the most deeply, remained engraved in his memory throughout the years in ways that time could never erase. He grew sentimental just thinking about them. Simone, the charming romantic incompetent. Beverly, the sensuous suburban matron. Anita, the dazzling blond with marriage on her mind. Lou, the one with career advancement (and little else) on hers.

He could see them all in the act of love as though it were yesterday, especially Anita, who'd evoked the strongest response from him—maybe because he was never able to tame her. She remained stubbornly in love with that weirdo airplane pilot, Jack Bailey, who knocked her up and didn't seem to care that Fingerhood was the Good Samaritan who accompanied her to San Juan for the abortion. Fingerhood had been glad to go, he'd been concerned. He could still taste the banana daiquiris they'd celebrated with in her sultry hotel room after it was all over. He could still remember how lovely and brave she was and how much he desired her.

He sighed inaudibly, acknowledging defeat at last. The fact was that he never stood a chance with Anita, not really, she was the only one of the bunch who walked out on him. At the time, he pretended that *he* decided to end it, predictably switching his attentions to Lou, but he couldn't fool himself. The shoe had been on the other foot. Anita moved to Chicago quite suddenly, and he never saw her again.

He poured a shot of Scotch over ice (against his better judgment) and wondered what Anita looked like these days. Was she still beautiful? Still sexy? As he handed the Scotch to Beverly, he nearly asked, but then thought better of it. He couldn't bear to listen to another slur against the tantalizingly evasive blond. Then he realized something; it had been a long time, she was probably fat and sloppy by now, her hair might even be gray. The idea depressed him more than he would have believed possible.

"You're too damned experienced for Sally," Beverly said, her face hardening again, all signs of softness now gone. "You're too old, too fickle, too cynical. Wait until Peter hears about this. Considering how much he loves his daughter, he'll probably try to strangle you." She held out her empty glass. "No ice this time."

Yes, Peter Northrop would be difficult to handle, Fingerhood reflected, wishing the son of a bitch had stayed in Paris with his faggy lover. Their confrontation was bound to be unpleasant at best, downright vicious at worst. Yet Fingerhood didn't feel entirely disheartened. That he had made love to two generations of Northrop women appealed to him on some deep tribal, patriarchal level. He could easily imagine why Peter would want to strangle him: he had violated his women, usurped his authority, proven himself top dog. Fingerhood couldn't resist a smirk of masculine triumph.

"I'm sure that I can deal with Peter when the time comes," he said, returning with Beverly's second drink and noting her expression of distrust. "As for your own threats and accusations, they serve no purpose at all. So how about burying the hatchet, letting bygones be bygones, and wishing Sally and me luck? I'd like that a lot, Beverly."

"I'll bet you would," she replied with a glacial sneer. "But I find it impossible to accede to your wishes when all I see ahead is unhappiness—if not downright misery—for my daughter."

Fingerhood decided to try his standard approach. "Are *you* unhappy, Bev? Are *you* miserable? I notice that you've come to New York without your husband."

She flushed, thinking of her bruises and how she'd gotten them. "Unfortunately, Dwight couldn't get away. He's a very busy man, he runs our hometown newspaper almost single-handed. But why bring Dwight into this discussion? What does he have to do with it?"

Of course she was unhappy, most women were, Fingerhood had discovered. "I mention him because I suspect you're projecting your own disappointment in marriage upon Sally. Am I right?"

"No, doctor, you're dead wrong," she said, gulping down more Scotch. "For your information, I love my husband. I miss him. I wish he were here this instant, maybe he could help me deal with the shock of all this."

What a hypocrite she was. She hadn't even called Dwight to say that Sally was safe (if betrothal to Fingerhood could be called "safe"). The truth was that she felt afraid to call, afraid he might still be drunk, angry, unrepentant. In the note she left, she hadn't specified where she was going, and that probably made him drink all the more. Even so, how could she berate him when she was smashed out of her mind herself? He would hear her slurred words of reproach and accuse the pot of calling the kettle black. Was she unhappy? Was she miserable? Was the rain wet? She reflexively straightened, trying to maintain her outward composure. She refused to let Fingerhood guess how drunk she was or how muddled she felt. She had to sober up, she *would* sober up. Actually she didn't want another drink. She wanted to put her glass down that minute and ask him for a cup of coffee, but she didn't. Some demon insisted that she drink Cutty Sark until there wasn't a drop left in the bottle and she felt helpless to counteract that demon's wish. She felt utterly overpowered by it.

So she sat on Fingerhood's beige sofa and drank, even though the Scotch tasted like poison now and her stomach cried for mercy. She hated herself for being weak, but she didn't know how to be strong. It was as though the bottle had taken her strength, anger, frustration, her fury at Fingerhood, and in return given her nothing except a numb, passive curiosity about her runaway daughter.

"How does Sally look?" she asked Fingerhood, who looked too good to be true for forty-eight. Peter looked good. So did Dwight, despite his alcoholic excesses. What did men have that made them age so well? She recently read that shaving helped keep them young because it sloughed off the dead facial skin. "Do you really love her, Fingerhood?" To her dismay, a huge reservoir of tears surged up within her. "I can't believe that my baby is going to be a married woman in less than a week. It doesn't seem possible. It seems like only yesterday that she was ten years old."

She started crying then, but it was as much for herself as for Sally. It was for her inability to put down the glass and not pick it up again.

Sally was slowly walking back to Sutton Place after an argument with Lou in the ladies' room of Madame Romaine de Lyon. She felt bitterly disappointed in Lou, who turned out to be nowhere near as hip as she'd imagined.

"Jesus Christ, I don't believe my eyes," Lou exclaimed, charging into the ladies' room as though a lynch mob were after her, and staring at Sally with horror. "What's the matter, Miss Duplicity? Couldn't you wait until you got home?"

Sally calmly held one nostril closed and sniffed with the other. "Why should I wait?"

"Because it might prove that you weren't hooked."

"Don't talk to me as if I were a street junkie."

"If the shoe fits, you know what to do with it."

"It's only a little cocaine, Lou. I don't know what you're getting so hysterical about."

"Dope is dope and that's what I am for having believed your story about it being an occasional habit." Lou hated being lied to. "Now I see why you were so jumpy and nervous inside. You needed another fix."

"Don't be melodramatic. I didn't need anything, I wanted a lift. These wedding preparations are enough to depress a saint." She put the vial and coke spoon back in her purse. "Why are you spying on me, anyway? What business is it of yours?"

"I came in here to ask you about Keith Rinehart, not to spy. Oh, forget it." Lou had arrived at a decision. "I'm going to call your mother and tell her everything. You might as well know."

You can't trust any of them, Sally thought, feeling the coke clear the cobwebs away. "Would it make any difference if I asked you not to?"

"No."

"Then why warn me?"

"I believe in playing fair."

"Fair?" Sally let out a hoot of derisive laughter. "That's a hot one. No wonder my father left you to go back to my mother. She may be a lush, but at least she's not a sanctimonious do-gooder like you."

"That's the first nice thing I've heard you say about her. Maybe there's hope for you yet."

Lou walked out, feeling as though everything that could possibly happen in one day had already happened: the blowup with Vanessa, the run-in with Keith Rinehart, the encounter with Anita, and now this. The hot summer air hit her like a furnace blast. Then she saw him waiting on the sidewalk.

"Where's Sally?" Keith Rinehart asked eagerly. "I didn't realize the two of you knew each other. Boy, that's terrific. Talk about small worlds."

"Go away. I'm not in the mood for you."

She looked around for a telephone, wishing she had thought to make the call in the restaurant. There was none in sight and she began walking toward Park. So did he.

"Can't we talk a minute?" he asked. "We seem to have a few friends in common. Look, I know Sally. I know her fiancé. I even know her fiancé's mother, the venerable Mrs. Fingerhood. She's wearing ice-green chiffon to the wedding, I helped her pick it out. Would a total stranger know something like that?"

A taxi was waiting for a red light and Lou jumped in. To her astonishment, he jumped in beside her. "Where are we going?" he asked with a friendly smile.

"This man isn't with me," she informed the driver. "Will you please tell him to get out?"

The driver wearily turned around. "Okay, buddy. You heard the lady."

"That's no lady, that's my wife," Keith Rinehart said with a straight face. "Seriously, driver, we're married. She's angry because I object to her working and I'm angry because we have two kids and she's never home. I'll give you an example of how bad it is: I had to make a lunch date today to talk to my own wife. Is that fair? I blame it all on those crazy libbers. What do you think, driver?"

"I'm not getting in the middle of this." The driver stepped on the gas. "Where does everyone want to go?"

"Lex and Eighty-fourth," Lou said, incensed with the two of them. Men. Was this what she wished to get involved with again?

The taxi took off.

"What's on Lex and Eighty-fourth?" Keith Rinehart asked.

Lou looked out the window.

"Oh, I get it. You're going to give me the cold shoulder. Would it help if I said that I've never done anything like this before? I swear it. When I spotted you jogging that first time, I just flipped." He sounded surprised himself. "It must be chemistry."

"Try insanity."

"I assume you've been invited to the wedding, whatever your name is. I'll bet it's Deidre. I've always wanted to say, 'I love you, Deidre.' It sounds so romantic." He observed her stony face. "No luck, hmmmm? Okay, how well do you know Sally? What kind of gown did she buy? Come on, Deidre, give me a break."

Lou lit a cigarette. She was still reeling from the shock of finding Sally with her nose in a coke spoon. How well did she know her? That was a laugh! It was Vanessa who'd been right about her all along, dammit. She thought of what Vanessa said about people who did drugs. *They're sneaky and dishonest, you can't believe what they say and you can't predict what they'll do.* It made her wonder whether Sally really loved Fingerhood or if she was marrying him for less noble motives, as Vanessa had implied. Did Fingerhood use cocaine too? Had he introduced Sally to it? Lou's head was swimming with questions, doubts, self-recriminations for being such a naive and trusting jerk.

"I'll pay," Keith Rinehart said when they pulled up to Eighty-fourth Street.

Lou got out and slammed the door. "Keep the cab. You're going no further with me."

"Try to make it home for dinner, Deidre," he called after her. "The kids miss their mommy."

She walked straight to the building where Beverly and Peter used to live, as though it were yesterday. Someone coming out held the lobby door open and she went in without announcing herself. Memory was an amazing thing, she thought, ringing the bell to the Northrops' apartment. To her surprise, a masculine voice answered.

"Who is it?"

"Lou Marron," she said, using her maiden name.

Peter Northrop, in an impeccably tailored gray silk suit and crimson striped tie, opened the door. For a moment neither of them could speak. Fifteen years flew out the window and they were lovers again in the late sixties, utterly enamored of each other.

"Lou, what on earth are you doing here?"

"I came to talk to Beverly."

She extended her hand, but he kissed her on the cheek. She

had been his last heterosexual affair and he felt warmly toward her. "You look wonderful," he said.

*He's really gay,* she thought, disappointed that the stories about him and Georges Sorrel told the entire truth.

*She's not really gay,* he thought, relieved that the stories about her and Vanessa Greenspan told only a partial truth.

"Come in." He opened the door wider. "Beverly isn't home, but I'm sure she'll be back soon. You seem upset. Is something wrong?"

Lou entered. "You might say that."

The one and only time she had been here before was the occasion of Sally's fifth birthday party when Peter, separated from Beverly, insisted that she come and meet his daughter. Sally wore a dainty flowered summer dress with matching underpants and was delighted to see her father, if not his female companion. Beverly watched them from the sidelines.

"I know who you are," Sally had said to Lou. "You're the lady who writes about brassieres and girdles for my daddy's newspaper. I think you should write about baking contests instead."

And they all laughed but none more bitterly than Lou, who was then lingerie editor of *The Rag* and yearning for advancement, responsibility, money, prestige, a place in the international fashion scene. Like the place that Peter was gaining access to more rapidly than she. Yes, before becoming lovers they were professional rivals and Lou hated him with a passion that verged on lunacy. That should have given her a clue to something, she often thought later on, when she fell insanely in love with him. Passion was passion.

"You and Sally look more alike than ever," she now said, dropping the first bomb.

His jaw fell. His legendary sophistication deserted him. "You've *seen* her?"

"Yes. Can I have a drink?" Suddenly she needed one. The expression on his face was so terrible. "Cognac, please. Neat."

"Of course. Sit down." Moving swiftly to the liquor cabinet, he spotted the half-empty bottle of Cutty Sark. It was Georges's favorite brand of Scotch, which was the only reason he bothered to stock it. But Georges wasn't with him this trip, Georges was in Paris. What the hell? Then it hit him. "Oh, Christ."

"What is it?" Lou asked.

He showed her the Cutty Sark bottle. "She must be drinking again."

"Beverly?" Lou recalled Sally's acid comments about her mother's continuing addiction. "Do you mean to say that she'd stopped?"

"For two years." He felt terribly disappointed. "We were talking about it only last night. I was so proud of her. I wonder what could have happened. She was in a perfectly fine mood when I left this morning."

It didn't take Lou long to figure it out. "I think Anita Schuler is what happened."

Peter turned his elegant head in recognition. "Why does that name sound so irritatingly familiar?"

Fingerhood had given up trying to monitor Beverly's drinking (it struck him as an impossible, not to mention thankless, task) and decided to join her in getting quietly plastered. They were talking about how he and Sally had met when a feminine voice called out from the hallway.

"Is anyone home?" Then there was a thud, the sound of tumbling objects, and an indignant shriek. "Why are all these packages piled up like an obstacle course? Don't you believe in putting your wedding presents away, Fingerhood, wherever you are? I nearly broke my neck, not to mention this gorgeous vase I bought you. Oh, damn! I've split a fingernail."

"Anita," Beverly groaned. "I don't believe it, not twice in one day. What is she doing here?"

"I have no idea."

"You didn't invite her over?"

"Hell, no."

Secretly he was delighted that she'd come. He stood, praying he would not be too disappointed once he got a good look at her. Take it easy, he told himself, but it didn't help. His palms were sweating and he suddenly felt light-headed, yet his voice sounded thick.

"Anita?"

She was dusting herself off in the hallway. "Here I am, darling." She thrust a Bloomingdale's gift box at him with an impish smile. "That's for you and your nubile bride, Fingerhood. I met her today despite all the pains you've taken to keep her identity a secret, you silly sly thing. Give me a kiss and maybe I'll forgive you.''

To his relief, she was still as beautiful as he remembered, perhaps even more so. Pleasure spread through him. He'd forgotten how creamy her skin was, how piercingly blue her eyes, how delectable that mane of pure blond hair cascading over slightly plump shoulders. No wonder he'd fallen under her spell the first time they met. Anita Schuler seemed to have been manufactured for masculine consumption right down to the tips of her toenails, coyly painted pink. It was a color he always associated with her, he realized, feeling himself get hard. He wanted to fuck her on the spot. Instead he kissed her on the cheek, thanked her for the vase, and inhaled her tantalizing fragrance. Sally never wore scent, she claimed it was too much of a cocktease. Being so fragrantly youthful, she was able to get away without resorting to feminine wiles. Anita had never tried to; she resorted to them all shamelessly. Yes, she was a born courtesan, Fingerhood thought with approval, wishing there were more of them around. They made the world a happier place.

"Did my robot let you in?" he asked, wondering where Jeeves was. In the kitchen, perhaps, recharging his batteries.

"No, darling, I let myself in. The door was open and I wasn't looking, that's why I nearly broke my leg on these stupid packages of yours." She kicked the pile of them, scattered all over the polished parquet floor. "Aren't you worried about security? Robbery? I understand New York is devastatingly crime-ridden nowadays."

The only thing worrying Fingerhood at the moment was whether she had seen the bulge in his pants. He willed it to go away, but it seemed to have a mind of its own. *That's more than you have,* his superego admonished him.

"You look as sexy as ever, you Dracula, you." Anita wrinkled her adorable nose, posed, flirted, made it obvious that she found him attractive. "It must be all that young blood you're getting off on. Tell the truth, Fingerhood, are young girls like Sally everything they're cracked up to be? I've been told that although they screw like rabbits, they're not very imaginative. That must be a bit hard on you, darling. As I recall, you had quite a lively imagination yourself."

"So did you. I'm thinking of the time you greeted me wearing a cowboy hat and boots, then tried to lasso me."

"I'm flattered you remember."

Aside from the hat and boots, she'd had nothing else on. "How could I possibly forget?"

She had shifted her weight so that one of her hips now jutted toward him suggestively. Her eyes held his gaze and wouldn't let go. "You still know the right things to say to a woman, darling. It's a rare skill."

Fingerhood felt crazed with lust. If Beverly weren't in the next room, he would have ripped off Anita's sexy black dress and screwed her right there on the floor. Let Jeeves figure out what to make of that. She was the first woman he'd encountered since becoming involved with Sally who had that effect on him. Not that he hadn't cheated on Sally a couple of times at the beginning, but that was more out of habit than uncontrollable desire. With Anita, his desire was so strong that it seemed to stick in his throat and quicken all his senses. Standing only inches away, he could taste her aromatic skin and feel how her soft golden hair would tickle his bare chest. His erection throbbed and it was all he could do to keep from reaching out and grabbing her in a fierce embrace, and to hell with Beverly in the living room. Then he realized that Sally would probably be back any minute, dammit. What a stupid bind to be in. He looked away, trying to pull himself together.

"Jeeves!" he called out. "Where are you? Come here immediately and do something with these packages. You never should have let them pile up like this."

He picked one up out of curiosity and noticed that it was addressed to him, not to him and Sally. He opened it and found a Father's Day card inside. It read:

> To my daddy:
> Even though you don't know who I am, I know who you are. My mommy used to love you very much. Do you remember her? Her name is Gladys and you met her in the summer of 1979 out in Westhampton. She would love to hear from you. So would I.
>
> Your son,
> Mark

He frowned and tore the card in pieces. Because of all the wedding excitement, he'd forgotten about Father's Day and wished once more that women would stop playing these dumb practical jokes on him. They weren't the least bit funny and this year the number seemed to have multiplied. He poked at the package to see what it contained. A brown knit necktie. He held it up for Anita's appraisal.

"Ugh," she said, making a face. "Aside from the fact that it's perfectly hideous, it's a strange choice for a wedding present. Who sent it?"

"Someone with a ghoulish sense of humor."

For the life of him, he couldn't remember having met a girl named Gladys that summer and he very much doubted that if he did he was the father of her child. Assuming there *was* a child. One of the things Fingerhood prided himself on was being meticulous about contraception. He always checked to make sure that the woman was protected, and in the odd case where she wasn't, he took appropriate precautions himself. No little bastards for him, he used to think, wondering why other men were foolish enough to get trapped like that.

"Why so glum all of a sudden?" Anita asked.

He was remembering their trip to San Juan all over again. There was something he'd never told her at the time: had she wanted to keep Jack Bailey's baby, he would have married her. He wondered now why he never even suggested it. Probably because, in those days, he was so busy trying to uphold his reputation as New York's most swinging bachelor. He shook his head. What a jerk he had been.

When Sally let herself into the apartment, the first voice she heard was her mother's. Lou hadn't wasted a second calling her, she thought, angry all over again. Why didn't people learn to mind their own business? She debated sneaking out, then decided to face the music and get it over with.

"Hello, everyone." To her surprise, Beverly wasn't flanked by Lou but by that horrible Anita Schuler. Seated between them was Fingerhood, refilling three glasses with champagne and reminiscing about the past. *He's made love to all of us,* Sally realized, afraid to imagine which one he'd liked best. He always said it was her, but did he mean it? The possibility that he might have preferred Beverly was unbearable. "I guess the cat is out of the bag, Mother."

"Oh, my darling."

Beverly moved toward her in a flurry of slow motion. Now that the big moment had come, her feet were like lead and all the reprimanding speeches she'd rehearsed so many times evaporated on the spot. Gratitude was all she felt, thankfulness that her child was alive, safe, well. She wasn't aware that tears were streaming down her cheeks or that her eyes were shining with joy as she grasped Sally to her bosom and kissed her soft dark hair, felt the unfamiliar thinness of her, the faint but distinct thrust of resistance.

"Let me look at you." Beverly stood back, but held on to Sally's hand. "You've lost weight. You've grown up. You've become a woman. Oh, Sally, I missed you so much, worried about you so often. Dear God, why did you do it?"

"Please, Mother, not now."

"You're so thin, darling. Is something wrong? Haven't you been eating? You're not anorexic, are you?"

"Don't be silly, Mother. I just lost my baby fat, that's all."

Beverly surveyed her daughter's reedlike body with suspicion. "It looks to me like you've lost a lot more than that. I hope you're not on one of those crazy reducing diets that seem to have swept the country for reasons I'll never understand. It's unhealthy to be too thin, you know."

"Let's talk about this later. Okay, Mother?"

Beverly nodded, barely able to believe that her precious offspring was standing before her after such a long separation. There were so many times when she feared she would never lay eyes on her again. "Whatever you say, darling." Tears glistened in her eyes.

Instead of feeling sympathetic, Sally felt contemptuous. Couldn't she at least have *tried* to stay sober for this reunion which obviously meant so much to her, or was that asking the impossible? Sally remembered all the years she hadn't dared bring other girls home after school because she was afraid they would encounter her drunken, disheveled mother and be shocked. As a result she'd grown up without any close female friends, a loss that she suffered keenly and blamed Beverly for. If only Lou hadn't turned out to be such a traitor just when they were getting along so well, she thought with bitterness. Confiding in Lou had been effortless and gratifying at first, it was exactly the kind of exchange she'd always wanted to have with Beverly and could never achieve. Then came that hideous ladies'-room encounter.

"Where's Lou?" she said curiously. "I thought for sure she'd be with you."

"Lou?" To keep others from guessing how muddled she

became when she drank, Beverly had developed a habit of stalling until the situation clarified itself. "Should Lou be with me?"

"She said she was going to call you."

"That's strange."

"You mean she *didn't?*"

"No. Of course, I've been out most of the day."

Sally was elated, but confused. If Lou hadn't made good her threat, then Beverly didn't know about the cocaine. But if Lou hadn't called . . .

"You can thank *me* for telling your mother where you've been hiding out," Anita said with a satisfied smirk. "I take full credit for this touching family reunion, although why I bothered to intercede is quite beyond me. Nobody has been gracious enough to thank me. All I've received for my efforts has been a clawed hand and a bottle of wine poured over my head."

Beverly turned to her with disdain. "Don't push your luck, Anita. The day's not over yet."

"Oh, oh, the Apache's on the warpath again."

"Knock off the Indian references, would you? I heard enough at lunch."

"I'm surprised you even remember lunch. Considering how much you've had to drink, it's a miracle you can remember your own name, Beverly."

"Don't patronize me, you self-serving idiot."

Anita smiled glacially. "Have another drink, darling. You don't want to run short of your quota, do you? What have you accelerated to? A fifth a day? Two fifths?"

"Anita, I warn you—!"

"I love to see you get angry. Your face turns such an interesting shade of purple. Did you know that your lipstick was smeared?"

Sally had no idea why they were being so antagonistic. All she could think of was that this confrontation with her mother wasn't going to be a nightmare after all, thanks to Lou, who'd obviously held her tongue about the cocaine. It meant the worst her mother could accuse her of was a grievous lack of judgment for deciding to marry Fingerhood. And yet Beverly didn't even seem about to do that. She was much less angry than Sally had feared, or was it the booze that rendered her so mellow at the moment? When she sobered up, there was no telling how she would behave or what histrionics she would resort to to get her to change her mind about the wedding. Once, many years ago, she had happily given Sally permission to sleep over at a classmate's house that night. Then a few hours later when the booze wore off, she screamed her disapproval of slumber parties except on weekends, accused Sally of not respecting her wishes, and flatly refused to let her go. It was the kind of unpredictable seesaw behavior that had driven Sally crazy for as long as she could remember.

"I must call your father and tell him that you're no longer among the missing, but frankly, I'm dreading it," Beverly said, unsteadily holding out her glass for more champagne. That she had spilled some of it down the front of her green silk dress was a fact she seemed blithely unaware of. "Peter will go through the roof when he learns about you and Fingerhood. I nearly went through the roof myself when I first got here—ask your future husband, darling—but after mulling it over, I concluded that things could be a lot worse."

Sally doubted if her mother had "mulled" anything over. Instead she had gotten bombed and less judgmental, more sentimental, more forgiving. "How could they be worse, Mother?"

"The way I see it, you could be marrying someone twice your age whom we *don't* know. At least in this case we're dealing with a familiar commodity." She tapped Fingerhood's shoulder as he grudgingly filled her glass. "Don't be so stingy with the bubbly. This is my daughter's future happiness I'm drinking to."

"You'd drink to a dead horse," Anita muttered.

"Will you kindly shut up?"

"No, I will not. Your drinking is abominable, and so are your manners. How dare you refer to this handsome, rich, desirable man as 'a familiar commodity'? You make him sound like a bag of dried lima beans." She let her gaze wander appreciatively over Fingerhood's tall, attractive frame. "In my opinion, Sally is damned lucky to have hooked him. I should be so lucky, I'm not ashamed to say. And as I remember, Beverly dear, there once was a time when you wouldn't have minded hooking him yourself."

"I didn't realize that women still 'hooked' men," Beverly snapped. "How quaint of you, Anita. Apparently you've never overcome that medieval matrimonial mentality of yours and you persist in falsely attributing it to every woman you run across. As for my marrying Fingerhood, there never was any question of that. If you recall, I already had a husband.''

"Oh, yes, Peter, the pouf." The humiliation of never having been married herself was more than Anita could sanely bear. "It makes me wonder what really goes on beneath that voluptuous facade of yours. Do you like them gay, darling? Is it, shall we say, less *tiring* for you? Or perhaps it gives you the time to do what you prefer—namely guzzle yourself into oblivion.''

"How dare you talk about my parents that way?" Sally said, leaping to their defense. "You're nothing but a vicious hostile bitch. I can't imagine what Fingerhood ever saw in you.''

"Why don't you ask him sometime?"

"I wouldn't lower myself."

"I think you're afraid of what his answer might be."

Fingerhood tried to intercede, but Sally waved him off. "And *I* think you're jealous," she said to Anita.

"Of you?" Anita laughed her patronizing little laugh. "Don't be asinine."

"Of course she's jealous," Beverly said to her daughter as though they were alone in the room. "It has to do with her crazed inability to find a husband. Why that should continue to upset her so deeply—considering all the progress made by the feminists in recent years—I'm sure I don't know, but I can't figure out another reason for her vile remarks.''

"Don't exhaust yourself trying," Anita replied, angrier than ever now that Beverly had pinpointed her Achilles' heel—and in Fingerhood's presence at that. "Your brain, unfortunately, isn't as big as your tits.''

Beverly gave her a withering look. "Isn't it too bad yours is?''

"Ladies, ladies." Fingerhood was laughing despite himself. "I thought women were sticking together these days, not taking nasty swipes at each other. What's going on? This is supposed to be a happy occasion.''

"You could have fooled me," Anita said morosely, reviewing her husbandless state and wondering when her luck would change. Maybe sooner than anyone dreamed, if luck could be given a healthy shove. That was exactly what she'd tried to do today. After the encounter with Lou and Sally on Madison

Avenue, she impulsively went into Queen Victoriana and
bought the knockout gown in the window. It was being
altered this very minute for a perfect fit. She looked stunning
in it, radiant, even that imperious saleswoman agreed. The
rose mantilla veil was absurdly flattering to her peaches-and-
cream complexion, and while the sweep train wasn't as long
as Princess Diana's, it did measure an impressive sixteen feet
(the same length as Marie Osmond's train, according to
*People* magazine). The saleswoman told her she could pick it up
at the end of the week, but the question was: *when could she
legitimately wear it?* Aware of Fingerhood's lingering gaze,
she found herself starting to fantasize about him. If only he
weren't engaged to Sally Northrop. If only he were free and
unencumbered. If only she hadn't walked out on him fifteen
years ago.

Unknown to Anita, Fingerhood was fantasizing about her
with equal regret. If only she weren't hooked up with that
titled Englishman. If only he hadn't let her get away fifteen
years ago. If only he weren't being married in less than a
week. He stopped, appalled by these disloyal ideas. What
was happening to him? Had he gone berserk? When it came
to the big issues in life, he prided himself on making cool
cerebral decisions. And that was what his decision to marry
Sally had been. Now, all of a sudden, he was at the mercy of
a lustful priapic force that he didn't know how to deal with; it
was driving him insane. He tried to assure himself that the
desire to fuck Anita and the desire to marry Sally were not
mutually exclusive, not by a long shot. What the hell? Why
should they be? *C'est la guerre.* Both urges could exist
harmoniously within the same man and it wouldn't be the end
of the world, right? Other men had coped with this duality of
nature which, in his more rational moments, Fingerhood
would have said was part and parcel of the normal schizoid
masculine temperament. Unfortunately, he didn't feel rational
right now, he felt conflicted and emotionally torn. Before he
could delve into his subconscious for a quick therapy session,
the doorbell rang and a recharged Jeeves entered the room.

"One, I've had a nervous breakdown in the kitchen,"
Jeeves said with a whimpering croak. "And two, Keith Rinehart is in the foyer."

"Well, show him in, dammit." Robots that cost eight
thousand dollars weren't supposed to have nervous break-

downs any more than prospective bridegrooms were supposed to have the hots for ex-girlfriends. "What are you waiting for, you dummy?"

"That's no way to talk to an emotionally exhausted person. Why do you think I cracked up to start with? Rush, hurry, quick, not a second to lose. It's enough to make anyone flip his lid."

*"Rid, bid, are we having squid for dinner?"* Miguel was circling the group, flapping his feathers. *"Winner, sinner, inner thighs are sexy!"*

Fingerhood found himself thinking about Anita's thighs, not Sally's. He remembered them as being soft and pink and utterly delectable, like every other part of her. He wished they were wrapped around him that very minute.

"Who's Keith Rinehart?" Anita asked, snapping out of her gloom at the mention of a masculine name.

"A top-notch photographer and Fingerhood's best man," Sally replied, wondering what Lou had wanted to ask her about him. She didn't realize they were acquainted. Noting the expression of interest on Anita's face, she added, "Yes, he's single—divorced, actually, but he's not your type. Forget it, Anita, Keith goes for brunettes."

Anita tossed her beleaguered hair. "I can't imagine why."

"As a matter of fact, Sally is right." Fingerhood resented her show of interest, it made him feel overpoweringly jealous. The thought of her in bed with another man was too cruel to contemplate. He had to get hold of himself, he thought sternly; this obsession was becoming ridiculous. "I've known Keith for years and I've never once seen him with a woman who didn't have dark hair."

"Maybe he doesn't know what he's missing," Anita said with a wink. When Keith Rinehart materialized, she gave him a practiced once-over: *cute face, terrific bod, no dough.* He probably didn't make much money, and if he did, he spent it. In her experience, that's the way photographers were—devil-may-care. She wanted someone solid, someone like Fingerhood, a doctor, distinguished, respected by society, important to society.

Once upon a time she had dreamed of becoming a doctor herself. It wasn't a very serious dream, more of a whimsy really. Still, illness had always fascinated her and she wasn't squeamish, like some women she knew who couldn't bear the sight of blood. She might have made a damned good G.P., conscientious and caring and all that. She could see herself paying house calls dressed in a conservative (but snappy) navy-blue suit, carrying the little black satchel that G.P.'s carried. Instead, she'd gone straight from high school to airline training school and that had been that. Her parents were so proud the first time she came home wearing her navy-blue uniform and carrying a smart black suitcase.

"I've been trained to save people's lives in an emergency," she told them, happily filled with her own self-importance. "Being a stewardess is a little like being a nurse at thirty thousand feet."

"Just make sure that if you save someone, he's rich and single," her mother said, kissing her on the cheek. "A professional man."

"What are you worrying about?" Her father chuckled. "A beautiful girl like that? She'll make us grandparents before we're fifty."

They were in their mid-sixties now and still waiting, she thought, feeling inadequate and guilty all over again. . . .

"I've fallen in love," Keith Rinehart impulsively announced to the entire room, unable to contain himself any longer. "Problem is, I don't know her name, but you do, Sally. You were having lunch with her today. Tell me. Who is she?"

Sally was startled, pleased, confused. "You're in love with Lou? I didn't realize you'd ever met her."

"I haven't, at least not officially. Lou *what?*"

"Marron," Beverly said dully.

Sally corrected her. "It's Greenspan now," she told Keith. "Lou got married."

The life went out of him. "The woman of my dreams is married?"

"But then her husband died."

The life came back. "So she's a widow?"

"That's right." Lou wasn't so bad after all, Sally decided; she had kept her mouth shut. "Quite a lonely widow, I'd say."

"Lonely?" Anita hooted. "From what I heard, she's a dike and living with her late husband's daughter." Being a widow beat being single. *Anything* beat being single. "She doesn't sound very lonely to me."

"Don't pay any attention to her," Sally implored Keith.

She had a hunch that he and Lou would make a terrific couple. "Lou was distraught after her husband died and she turned to Vanessa for friendship. Then they started Some Like It Hot and it turned into a pleasant working relationship."

"Sure it did," Anita scoffed. "And I'm Eva Perón."

Miguel began singing the only song he knew, "Don't Cry for Me, Argentina," happy not to have to rhyme every goddamned word for a change.

"I don't care if she did have a lesbian fling," Keith valiantly declared. "At least she'll know how her own body functions, which is more than I can say for a lot of women. But what intrigues me most is that she owns Some Like It Hot. The lady and I have more in common than she realizes." Up until now he thought she just drove the delivery truck. He rubbed his hands together in joyful anticipation. "I can't wait to make my Shrimp Timbales for her."

"Keith is a gourmet cook and has always wanted to start his own catering business," Fingerhood explained to the others, relieved that the object of his friend's affection was not the seductive Anita. "I should have thought of introducing you to Lou before this. How did you get to know her?"

"I *don't* know her. I've been following her around New York for weeks, but she won't speak to me. She thinks I'm a mad rapist or something. Can't say that I blame her. Still, I *was* desperate. That's one gorgeous-looking female."

"You see?" Sally whispered to Anita. "I told you he went for brunettes."

"He could go for zebras. He's not my type."

"Why not? He's a man, isn't he?"

Anita didn't deign to explain that Keith Rinehart failed to qualify (he might be Single, but he wasn't Rich). She was too busy trying to figure out what Fingerhood saw in the snotty, sarcastic Northrop women. Something that, perhaps, she as a woman couldn't see. Maybe they were so high-class that they came in French, she thought, suddenly remembering Simone's flirtation with Michael last night. She didn't have to ask herself what Michael had seen in Simone; it was obvious. Simone was a sexually adventurous piece of goods, she would try anything. A horrible thought crossed Anita's mind. What if she'd tried Michael today?

"Can I make a phone call?" she asked Fingerhood.

"Use the extension in the bedroom. You'll have more privacy."

"If I don't call Michael at least three times a day, he becomes insanely jealous," she said coyly. "You know how possessive men are when they're in love."

"Invite him over." Fingerhood had a morbid urge to meet the English son of a bitch. "It looks like this little party isn't going to break up for quite a while."

"I just realized who's missing," Beverly observed. "Simone. I'm dying to see her again. Does anyone know where she is?"

"At the King Croesus," Anita said, praying that Michael wasn't with her.

"Someone else is missing," Keith Rinehart murmured. "The woman of my dreams."

Moments later, just as Beverly was starting to forgive Lou and feel less threatened by her (hadn't Peter himself said she'd become a lesbian?), Lou walked in looking stunning. She was accompanied by a very angry Peter Northrop. They made an exquisite couple, Beverly realized, feeling the past rear its hurtful head again.

8

While Beverly was busy yearning to see Simone, Simone was yearning to see her children. She missed them more than she would have dreamed possible.

"I want you to send them to New York on the next plane," she instructed Jimmy, whom she'd called right after Michael left for Cartier's. "I've fallen in love and I want the twins to meet him."

At the other end of the line Jimmy Newton felt exasperated, frustrated, lonely. Not only had the studio insisted upon a tenth rewrite of *Rockabye Princess* (thanks to the mass popularity of Princess Diana, they wanted additional scenes showing *his* princess at home in the palace), not only had he lost his shirt in Gardena for three nights running, not only was he miserable without Colin or Simone, but now she was trying to take the twins away from him. He would go crazy alone in that house. Hilda and Harold kept to their quarters, they were no company at all.

"Writing is the most solitary profession in the world," he said, trying to reason with her long distance. "I can't do it living by myself, it's inhuman. Besides, the twins still have another week of school."

"Just tell the headmistress that their mother needs them in New York and she needs them immediately. Are you listening to me, Jimmy? I want them here tomorrow at the latest."

He sighed wearily. "Who are you in love with, kiddo?"

"That's what I adore: passion, jealousy, inflamed senses." How had she lived with this unromantic man for five years? He and Michael were like night and day. "I'm in love with an Englishman named Michael Harding and he's in love with me. He's asked me to marry him."

*"Marry him?"* This was another matter. "What does he do for a living? Who is he? I mean, where will you live?"

245

"In England, of course. He's an airplane manufacturer. Have you ever heard of Harding Aerospace? Well, Michael owns it."

"How the hell can you make movies living in England?" Jimmy slumped into his typewriter chair. "And don't tell me you're planning to commute."

"What I'm planning to do, you silly man, is retire. I'm through making movies."

This was the worst news yet, she had to be joking. "What about *Rockabye Princess?* What about your publicity plans with Colin? What about your career?" He wanted to say, "What about me?" but restrained himself.

"That's all over. I never wanted a career, it was your idea. "I'm going to be a full-time housewife and mother, and what's more, I'm looking forward to it. No more getting up at five in the morning to drive to the studio, no more worrying about every new line on my face, no more exercises to save my gluteus medius, no more punishment. Hooray!" He had remained ominously silent. "Aren't you going to wish me luck, Jimmy? Aren't you happy for me?"

"I feel like I'm listening to funeral arrangements. What time does the hearse arrive?

"I don't know what you mean."

"What I mean, dummy, is that you're making the biggest mistake of your life. You weren't cut out to be a full-time housewife and mother. You're an actress, remember?"

"Not really. I've never studied acting, I've never cared about it. My success is just a fluke."

"That's bullshit," he said heatedly. "Some of our biggest stars never took a lesson in their lives. Marilyn Monroe hit it big *before* she went East to study with Strasberg. Besides, Marilyn had something that can't be taught, and so do you."

"What's that?"

"The camera likes you. Correction. *Loves* you. When you're on screen, the audience can't look at anyone else. It's a gift, don't throw it away."

"The camera didn't love me so much on my last movie," she reminded him, touched nonetheless by his heartfelt words. Was she really that good? She couldn't believe it. To her mind, people like Jane Fonda and Diane Keaton were the true actresses because they knew their craft; she was a lucky amateur.

"Everyone bombs from time to time, it's par for the course," Jimmy assured her. "Do you want me to list the stinkers that people like Joan Crawford and Bette Davis appeared in at the height of their fame? Some of those movies were so lousy they make your last one look like Academy Award time, but did Joan and Bette walk out? No, they made other movies, better movies, terrific movies, and so will you."

"They couldn't walk out. They had studio contracts. I don't."

Why was she being so unreasonable? In the past, she'd always deferred to him. What was happening? "Look, I was talking to Eddie only yesterday and he thinks you have an excellent chance of playing the Danish princess provided you and Colin get going on this P.R. scheme. So how about it? Postpone your wedding plans at least until you wrap *Rockabye Princess*. If this airplane guy loves you, he'll wait."

"Why does it matter so much to you? You don't love me—at least not the way Michael does. Not enough to marry me."

He was too honest to say that he did, but he was too honest to say that he didn't. Since she'd been gone, he was trying to sort out his confused feelings. "It matters because I don't like to see talent wasted. It's too rare and precious a commodity."

"That's sweet, but it doesn't change anything. Ask Hilda to pack two suitcases and get airplane reservations for the twins. Then call me back and give me the flight info. I'm counting on you, Jimmy."

"And I'm counting on you to star in *Rockabye Princess* and make it a hit." That she could sail out of his life like this was unthinkable, unbearable, ridiculous. He missed her already. "You're walking away from one of the greatest roles you'll ever be offered. Actresses kill for roles like this."

"Let them. I'll be in Gloucestershire tending to my garden. Of course, we have to wait until Michael's divorce comes through," she made the mistake of adding. "But that won't take long, he's calling his solicitor today."

"Why didn't you tell me the son of a bitch is still married?" Jimmy laughed. She had obviously fallen for a smooth-talking limey, poor kid. "I'll put the twins on a plane if you insist, but don't back out of *Rockabye Princess* until you see a ring on your third finger, left hand. Trust me. I'm a man and I know what I'm saying.''

"Oh, really? Well, I'm a woman and I know what I'm doing." Taking Michael away from Anita vied with being nominated for an Oscar any day in the week. "Anita is going to kill me. She wanted to marry Michael herself.''

"What does this guy have that makes everyone so eager to march down the aisle with him?''

Simone giggled. "Not much. He's just handsome, rich, loving, tender, warm, and a sensational lover. I can't wait to see Anita's face when she hears the news.''

"I thought this woman was a friend of yours.''

"Of course she's a friend, *vieux schnock*. It wouldn't be any fun otherwise!''

Jimmy found himself listening to a dial tone. Damn. He'd forgotten to mention that the studio had optioned *The Fingerhood Position*—it was in *The Reporter* that morning. And he had an appointment that afternoon with the head of production to see about getting the screenplay assignment. He would pick up a copy of Fingerhood's book and figure out how to tailor it for Simone's unique talent. Then if she lost *Rockabye Princess*, she would have a good shot at this one. He refused to believe that she would abandon her career for some sexy fly-by-night Englishman; he wouldn't let her do it. She was his creation, his masterpiece, his necessity. The realization that he needed her so much infuriated him. He kicked the desk, threw his typewriter against the wall, and punched the sofa. It didn't help.

He turned on the stereo. *Norma* flooded the room with its full range of emotions: hatred, rage, jealousy, fear, despair, and ultimately self-sacrifice. Jimmy was beginning to understand why he played Bellini's opera so often: because up until now he had identified with Norma, the sacrificial victim. But no more. He was tired of losing at cards, at love (or whatever it was that he felt for Simone). The time had come to fight for what he wanted. No way was he going to let that crazy French broad walk out of his life, at least not without one hell of a struggle.

"I'd like to make a reservation for three to New York,'' he told TWA a few minutes later. "Two children and one adult. Tomorrow morning.''

\*      \*      \*

As Anita hurried back to the Gramercy Regency, she felt relieved that this day (surely one of the worst of her life) was about to have a happy ending. It couldn't have started off on a more wretched note.

First came the startling discovery that a tall skinny flat-chested girl had conquered the unconquerable Fingerhood, then Beverly poured a bottle of wine over her head, Sally called her a vicious bitch, Keith Rinehart preferred diky brunettes to beautiful blonds, and as the last straw Peter Northrop turned out to have been the snotty man on Bloomingdale's elevator. When he recognized her at Fingerhood's, he raised an eyebrow and said, "I hope you didn't have any trouble finding the gift shop." The pain on the right side of Anita's face which had steadily been growing worse would have disintegrated into agony then and there, had it not been for the fact that she'd just spoken to darling Michael and he had a present for her.

"What kind of present?" she asked.

"Your favorite, darling."

Her heart quickened. "Jewelry?"

"Cartier's best.'

Not only did the facial pain disappear, but her vaginal yeast infection (which seventeen containers of plain yogurt had not yet cured) suddenly stopped itching. "I'll be home in a jiffy," she told him.

Fingerhood was the only one sorry to see her leave. Peter and Sally were deep in argument over her wedding plans, Lou and Keith were in the throes of becoming acquainted, and Beverly was getting drunker by the minute. Fingerhood walked Anita to the door.

"Try to come back with Michael," he urged her, looking forsaken. "I'm planning to send out for Chinese food in a little while."

"I'll see. I'll call you."

He took her hand. "I hope you're not too upset by some of those nasty remarks that Sally and Beverly made about you. They're just jealous."

"They are?" she coyly said, knowing he was right.

"Count on it. You're so gorgeous, what woman *wouldn't* be jealous?"

"Thank you, Fingerhood." She surprised the two of them by kissing him smack on the mouth, and unless she was dreaming, he had a hard-on. She pressed against him a second longer than she had to, reveling in this homage to her desirability. "You seem to be the only person who's on my side. I can't tell you how much that means to me."

"How much?"

She opened her arms wide, like a little girl. "A great big bunch much."

"If I weren't marrying Sally . . ."

There was a misty faraway look in his eyes, but she was out the door before he could finish the sentence. She couldn't wait to see Michael. When she walked into the Gramercy Regency, the first thing that caught her eye was his umbrella. Strong, sturdy, menacingly black, it stood in a corner neatly furled, twice as large as its American counterpart. Even though she'd told him that it almost never rained in New York in June, he insisted on packing it anyway. Now she felt glad he had. The umbrella was a comforting reminder of a life shared back in London, a life that suddenly seemed very dear to her.

"Is that you darling?" Michael called out.

She found him pacing the living room and ran straight into his arms. He encircled her awkwardly, still holding the distinctive Cartier's gift box.

"I'm sorry we quarreled last night," she said, kissing him with even more warmth than she had kissed Fingerhood. "Where have you been all day? I called and called."

"That's one of the things I want to talk to you about, but first let me give you this." He held out the small box, praying it would help turn an ugly situation into a slightly less ugly one. He had no illusions about getting off the hook scot-free. "I hope you like it."

"Oh, darling, you didn't have to!" She laughed tremulously as she undid the ribbon. "But I'm delighted that you did."

Snuggled against the dark velvet interior was a necklace, glittering, dazzling. She gasped. It was one of Cartier's famous sapphire-and-diamond link-motif designs, originated by Louis Cartier himself back in the early twenties (if there was one thing Anita Schuler knew, it was the history of precious gems), and easily worth about fifteen thousand smackeroos.

"I'm speechless," she said, feeling tears come to her eyes.

He must love her more than she realized. "I just don't know how to thank you, darling. It's more than I deserve."

He smiled weakly. "Nonsense."

"It is, darling, truly it is. I'm overwhelmed." She covered his face with kisses.

Damn her. She was making this even harder for him than it had to be. Maybe he shouldn't have bought the bloody necklace. No, he'd done the right thing. She would be able to turn to it for consolation later on when she found herself alone.

"Here, let me put it on you." He took it from its box and fastened it around her soft, smooth neck. "There. Now, don't you look super?"

She ran to the mirror and admired herself, tears of joy streaming down her cheeks. "Oh, Michael!" The diamonds against the yellow gold were the most beautiful sight she had ever seen and the blue of the sapphire brought out the blue of her eyes. "It's utterly magnificent. I don't know what else to say."

"Don't say another word. Let me do the talking."

Something about his tone alerted her immediately. Her hand dropped from her throat and her heart began to flutter. "What is it?" She sat down in the most comfortable chair, as though sensing that she would need its support. "I'm listening."

He continued to pace. "It's about Simone." He looked out the window at Gramercy Park, his back toward her, his voice firm and clear. "I don't exactly know how to put this, but we've fallen in love."

For the first time in her life, Anita was genuinely beyond words. She merely stared at him. And sat. And slowly began to finger the gold-and-diamond necklace for solace. It had looked so warm and shining a second ago, but now it felt cold and hard, as cold and hard as the statement he'd just made. She couldn't absorb that statement, it was too shattering. As he went on talking, explaining, elaborating, she realized what it all meant: the end of her safe, protected world. It meant no more house on Cheyne Walk, no more charge accounts at Bond Street shops, no more winter holidays on the Algarve, no more indolent mornings in bed, no more teas at the Ritz, no more being a lady of leisure. It meant having to find a job, a man, a new life.

Anita wished her mother were here, she wanted to sob on her breast. Her mother would know what to say and do to help ease this knife-sharp pain, the worst of which was yet to come (she remembered that from the Jack Bailey disaster). Maybe her mother would be able to explain what she had done wrong or, better yet, what that cunt Simone had done right. If nothing else, her mother would love her unconditionally the way no man ever had.

"Aren't you going to say anything?" Michael had turned around to face her. This silence was worse than any amount of insults, accusations, or temper tantrums could possibly be. He laughed nervously. "Aren't you going to throw something? Call me terrible names? Threaten an expensive lawsuit?"

Anita felt too immobilized to move, she could barely think. At the moment, only one thing interested her. "How did it happen?"

"The details aren't important. What's important is that it *did* happen. Very suddenly, I might add, very unexpectedly. We didn't plan this. Simone and I were both caught off guard."

"I'll bet." The scheming Frenchwoman must have urged him to call her today as soon as the coast was clear, which Anita had obligingly made possible by going shopping. This was the reward for being a dutiful daughter and conscientious wedding guest. "I assume you've already slept with the little nymphomaniac."

"*Really, darling.*" He was indignant.

"Did you, or didn't you?"

"You certainly can't expect me to answer that inappropriate question."

"Never mind, your shit-faced expression says it all." The thought of him dashing over to the King Croesus the minute she was out the door made her see red. "So you've screwed her and fallen in love with her all in one day, less than a day. You deserve a medal for supersonic cheating, Michael. I'm too much of a lady to say what *she* deserves, but I would like to know what she has."

"Has?"

"As in sexual wiles. What is it about Simone that you find so irresistible? I'm curious."

"I'm afraid I can't satisfy your curiosity. That's something a gentleman doesn't discuss."

"A gentleman? Is that how you see yourself? What a joke." As she got to her feet, every medical symptom she'd ever known returned with a vengeance. The pain on the right side of her face was back, a headache pounded in her skull, her vaginal yeast infection began to itch, her liver started acting up in the form of nausea and sudden indigestion, and she could have sworn that her period, which wasn't due for another week, was about to strike. "You're an insensitive, uncaring, two-timing creep—three-timing, if you count your wife. Did you really think you could appease me with this good-bye necklace? Am I worth so little to you that you imagined a piece of jewelry could buy me off? Is this all I mean to you after six devoted years?"

"I thought it would show that you mean quite a lot," he replied as diplomatically as possible. "This happens to be a very costly piece of jewelry and I want you to have it as a measure of my deep respect and affection."

"I don't want your *respect and affection*, you fucking animal. I want your *love*, your *devotion*, I want to be your wife!"

"Oh, dear." This was turning out to be even more messy than he'd anticipated. "I'm afraid Simone is going to be my wife. I've asked her to marry me, you see."

Anita didn't know which part of her anatomy to grab first; everything was screaming for attention. "You did *what?*"

"I've proposed marriage to Simone."

"But you *are* married. To Lady Philippa." One hand pressed the pain in her temple, one attended to her liver—if only she were an octopus. "Or have you forgotten?"

"I'm getting a divorce. I've already been in touch with my solicitor. As soon as it comes through, Simone and I will be wed."

Why didn't she pass out? Why didn't she drop dead of shock? "You can't be serious."

"I am. I assure you."

Anita could see that Dr. Smythe-Kitson was right. She had better have that hideous laporoscopic and get it over with or her liver condition would never be cured. The image of a long shiny needle plunged into her bare abdomen made her feel faint. She swayed, wondering how to sanely cope with Michael's bombshell. Maybe there was no sane way. In the last few minutes she'd been trying to tell herself that as bad as his infatuation with Simone was, it didn't necessarily mean curtains as she'd imagined at first. Love didn't mean curtains either, especially not when it happened in such a tumultuous manner as this. Sometimes passions like his and Simone's flared and subsided with equal rapidity, but marriage? That wasn't just curtains, that was the definitive good-bye to everything she ever dreamed of for herself. Respectability. Security. Her head held high. The commitment of love. She choked back the sobs, realizing that she'd lost it all to that French bitch, who was probably gloating in triumph this very minute.

"You know that Simone is living with someone, don't you?" She suspected that nothing could help her cause now, yet she felt unable to capitulate. Some force drove her on. "He's a movie director, quite famous actually. I thought it was a serious relationship."

"On the contrary, it's been over for a long time. No problem there." Michael seemed immensely pleased by the lack of complications. "Simone is flying her children in tomorrow to meet me. Then when I wind up my business here, we're all off to the Continent for a bit of a holiday."

"How jolly."

He missed her sarcasm. "We'll be just in time for the Spoleto festival. They're doing *La Colombe*, I believe."

"And when you return to the U.K.?" Anita could definitely feel the onset of her period now. One week early meant a heavy flow due to her blood-clotting problems, cramps, pain, chills, agony, misery. "Will you install Simone in a London flat until your divorce becomes final?"

"No, we're going to live together. I thought it would be best for the twins' sake if they got used to my being around permanently." He smiled with obvious satisfaction. "Like a proper dad, you might say."

"And what about your own children?" If, God forbid, she should need a liver operation, there would be her blood-clotting problem to take into consideration. Dr. Smythe-Kitson had been afraid all along that surgery could prove dangerous. "Won't you miss them?"

"They're teenagers, away at school. I'll see them as often as I see them now," he said offhandedly. "Besides, they'll be in university soon, then married, parents themselves before long. There's no point in trying to cling to one's offspring, is there?"

And all this time she assumed he was waiting for them to grow up before he left home. She should have known better.

When lust struck, men ceased being paternal and became animal. *Beast*, she fumed, wishing she would stop itching, burning, hurting, aching, bleeding.

"It sounds as though you've worked everything out," she tersely observed. "And in such a short time, too."

"There's nothing like being organized." He was pleased to see her finally behaving in a civilized fashion. That necklace must have done the trick. "As for yourself, darling, I don't want you to worry about the hotel bill or any other bill, for that matter. I'll take care of everything. In fact, should you wish to stay in New York longer than we originally planned, please be my guest."

It was an unfortunate choice of words. *"Guest?"* she said sardonically.

"You know what I mean, darling, don't quibble."

"Right. How very gauche of me. How very unsporting."

"I don't like the look in your eye. Where are you going?"

"Not far, Michael."

She overcame her pain-itch-ache-burn-bleed long enough to grab his sturdy black umbrella, hit him over the head with it, and knock him out cold.

"What I should do is knock you flat on your ass," Peter Northrop said to Fingerhood, facing him after his talk with Sally. "I can't believe that a man in your position—a doctor, a psychologist, a person whose profession is to help others—could have deliberately harmed so many people in his personal life. And I'm not only talking about Beverly and myself, I'm talking about Sally as well. Don't think you're doing her any favors by marrying her. Christ, just the idea makes my blood run cold."

"What is it that bothers you?" Fingerhood said calmly, wishing Anita hadn't left. He couldn't get his mind off her. "My age? My reputation? The fact that I once had an affair with your wife?"

"Don't push your luck, buddy." Peter involuntarily clenched his fists. "Everything about you bothers me. I admit that I didn't like or trust you years ago, but I wouldn't let an old animosity carry over to the present if you hadn't once more proven yourself unworthy of trust. Well? What do you have to say in your own self-defense?"

"Only what I'm sure Sally has already said to you. That

we're both sorry others had to be hurt—and you'll note the operative word is 'both.' If you're going to talk about trust, you'd better apply it to Sally as well. It wasn't my decision not to tell you where she was, it was hers. I merely complied with her wishes.''

"You had no right to comply. She's a child, she didn't know any better. But you did, goddammit, and you still kept your mouth shut. It was your responsibility to have notified us, can't you see that?''

"What interests me is what *you* can't see. Sally is no longer a child. She's twenty, a woman, a grown-up. You talk about her as if she were Little Red Riding Hood and I were the big bad wolf.''

"I wish it were that innocent, which brings me to my next point. Why the hell did you ask her to marry you? Why couldn't you have gone on as you were? What's the big rush in legalizing your relationship?''

"That's a new twist. Usually it's the parent who pushes for respectability, whereas you're suggesting the exact opposite. Besides, I'd hardly say that Sally and I were *rushing* to get married, not when you consider how long we've been together. I thought you'd be pleased that I want to make an honest woman out of her.''

"You thought wrong, buddy. Without legal ties, she'd be free to leave as soon as she comes to her senses and sees the kind of man you really are. But once she becomes your wife she'll be trapped, doomed, miserable. Like every other woman you've given the business to. Especially if there are kids involved." To Peter's irritation, Fingerhood appeared unperturbed and unruffled by his charges. "I don't know what you're up to, but I can't believe that you love Sally. I'll never believe it.''

Fingerhood was beginning to have doubts himself, inasmuch as he kept getting an erection every time he thought of Anita. "But I do love Sally," he insisted as much for her father's sake as to convince himself. "Why else would I have proposed? What would be my motive?''

Peter shook his head. "The guy without a motive—that's the one who scares the shit out of me." The image of this aging reprobate fucking his daughter was obscene. "What kind of life can you offer her? She deserves someone younger, less jaded, someone who hasn't screwed everything on two feet and will probably continue to do so, marriage or no marriage. Do you think that Sally's mother and I brought her up with every advantage in the world so she could throw herself away on a crumb like you?''

"Stop it, Daddy." Sally inserted herself between the two men. "You're behaving like an inquisitor. Fingerhood and I both said we were sorry. Now, why can't you let bygones be bygones? Please, Daddy, for my sake. I love him.''

Peter felt torn. On the one hand, Sally was old enough to do as she wished; on the other hand, she was still his little girl. When she was very young, he used to push her on a swing he'd set up on their back lawn and she would squeal, "Higher, Daddy, faster!'' But no matter how high or fast he pushed, it was never enough—she always wanted the unattainable. She still did, as far as Peter was concerned. Not for one second did he think that Fingerhood would be faithful to her, and fidelity was surely one of Sally's primary requirements. He had never known a woman to whom it wasn't.

"I didn't realize you had such a low opinion of me,'' Fingerhood said to him. Fathers who had been the most unfaithful themselves were always the most suspicious of other men; he saw it often in therapy. "And obviously it's because you assume I'm the same person I was fifteen years ago. But the fact is, I've changed. I've improved, if I do say so myself. I've matured, if you will. Why can't you give me the benefit of the doubt?''

"Don't bullshit *me*, buddy.''

"Don't call me buddy.''

"I'm sure as hell not going to call you son-in-law, because I'd choke on the words.''

"Daddy, you're being uncivilized.'' To Sally's mind they were like a couple of wild animals fighting over territorial rights (she was the territory). "I don't want to hear another disparaging word. What I want is for you to give me away next Saturday. Will you do that?''

Peter eyed Fingerhood with mounting suspicion and dislike. How could he give her away to this philanderer who once tried to steal his wife and was now stealing his daughter? In all good faith, how could he pretend to condone this unhealthy liaison, which was going to prove disastrous for Sally? How could he live with himself if he did? What he remembered most vividly about his own wedding was the moment Beverly's father relinquished her hand so she could place it in his for the onset of the ceremonial vows. Watching his beautiful young bride being transferred from one protective man to another signified a very masculine rite of passage for Peter Northrop. He would burn in hell before he transferred Sally to Fingerhood.

"I can't do it," he told her. "It's out of the question."

Her lower lip trembled. "Daddy!"

"I'm sorry, but it goes against my deepest principles."

"How dare you talk about principles?" She was hurt, humiliated by his refusal. "You're living with someone half your age and he's a man to boot. In addition to that, everyone in the fashion world knows about your extracurricular affairs. They're legion. You should be pleased that I asked you to give me away, you should be *grateful*. A lot of daughters wouldn't be so understanding."

Peter stiffened. "I didn't realize that I needed your stamp of approval to carry on with my chosen life-style. The next time I hop into bed with someone, I'll be sure to call and ask for your permission."

Fingerhood put a conciliatory hand on his shoulder. "I wish you'd reconsider, Peter. It would mean a lot to both of us."

"Take your hand off me." His anger lay coiled within him like a rattler. "I have no use for you, you bastard. I never did and I refuse to turn into a hypocrite by pretending I do now. If you want to marry my daughter, you'll have to do it without my participation or good wishes. Good-bye."

"Daddy!"

But he was gone. Sally couldn't believe it. She felt like sobbing, screaming. For two years she had tried to pretend that she didn't have a father, at least not the specific father she did have (Parisian-depraved). Then when she saw Peter come into the apartment a little while ago, she forgave him everything. He seemed so sure of himself, so suavely pulled together. How could he be doing anything wrong? Her old childlike awe of him returned (she used to liken him to Cary Grant) and she felt as though *she* were the one in the wrong. To rectify that, she asked him to walk down the aisle with her on the most important day of her life and he flatly, indignantly refused. Now it was like not having a father all over again, only this time for real. She turned anxiously to

Fingerhood and he took her in his arms, held her close, as across the room Beverly poured more champagne, only dimly aware of her ex-husband's departure.

"How could he be so cruel?" Sally asked Fingerhood. "I thought my mother was the one we'd have trouble with. I thought my father was sophisticated and worldly enough to understand, forgive. Instead, it's the other way around."

"The horniest men are the last ones to let go of their daughters."

Sally hadn't considered that. "They are?"

He nodded. "If you'd been a son, he'd be clapping you on the back this very minute and applauding your sexuality. But no father wants to think of his daughter getting fucked, it puts him in a real emotional bind. And a father like Peter, who's done more than his share of fucking, certainly doesn't want to think of it. He remembers how badly he's used women in the past, so he assumes you're going to be used the same way. Whenever I have a patient who tells me that her dad is morbidly strict and suspicious of her boyfriends, it turns out he's a promiscuous, lascivious son of a bitch. Even if only in fantasy. It never fails."

"I feel so rejected," Sally said, clinging to him. "By insulting and demeaning you, he was insulting and demeaning *me*. Couldn't he see that?"

"I doubt it. He thought he was protecting you from being hurt by a bastard like himself. What a man like Peter never seems to grasp is that his daughter might have chosen someone who's different from him, nicer, better, not such a shit. Sometimes years pass before men like Peter are able to acknowledge this fact. Sometimes they only forgive the sons-in-law when children arrive, because then their little girl turns into a little mother."

"You mean, her sexuality becomes blurred?"

"Yes, in her father's eyes. And believe me, it's a big relief to him. It's a weird fact of life, but every father goes to his grave secretly convinced that his daughter is a virgin—even if she's been married eighteen times and has screwed every man in sight." Fingerhood kissed her on the forehead. "Try not to be too hard on him. He's only acting true to form."

Sally was confused. "You sound sympathetic."

"I am."

He couldn't pretend not to be. The blunt truth was that

despite all his psychological insights and explanations, Peter Northrop happened to be right up to a point and both men knew it. If Fingerhood were in his shoes, he wouldn't have given Sally away either. He, too, would have stormed out and tried to bring her to her senses. Not that Sally seemed about to be swayed by his abrupt departure. The fact that she sided with her future husband rather than her father was an indication of faith, not perspicacity, Fingerhood reflected, feeling insanely jealous whenever he thought of Anita in bed with that damned Englishman. He wondered if he could get her in bed himself before she went back to London. There wasn't much time, he would have to work fast. And stealthily. A bitter smile curled his lips. Peter Northrop was no fool; still, he didn't know the whole story behind his daughter's wedding plans. Peter's outrage was not misdirected so much as it was misinformed. . . .

Fingerhood had been startled when Sally called him out of the clear blue nearly two years ago.

"Beverly Northrop's daughter?" he said. "Christ, the last time I saw you, you were five years old. How are you? What are you doing these days? Where are you?"

"I'm in New York looking for a secretarial job and I thought I'd take a chance and try you."

"I don't have a secretary," he confessed. "My practice doesn't warrant one. But why don't you drop by this afternoon and we can talk. How's your mother, by the way?"

"She's just fine," Sally coolly replied. "See you."

He was pleasantly surprised when a tall, slender dark-haired girl walked into his office a few hours later. She looked nothing like Beverly; instead, she seemed to have inherited Peter's features and coloring. No one would call her beautiful, Fingerhood thought (she was too sharp and angular for that), yet there was something intriguing about her eyes and the way she used them to flirt with him. Had her behavior not been so obviously seductive, he would have restrained his impulses and treated her like a Dutch uncle. Still, there was no mistaking her intentions.

Fingerhood felt flattered. He had just broken up with a girl almost ten years older than Sally, who said that she found him "sweet, but a bit too settled for me." By "settled," he knew she meant "old," and as he watched her go, he wondered whether time's long hand had finally come to rest on his shoulder. He was forty-six then and starting to restrict his intake of salt, meat, liquor, and saturated fats. Two colleagues of his had suffered heart attacks in recent months, and to his horror, he was beginning to feel the dread rustle of middle age. Sally couldn't have appeared at a more opportune moment. Her young girl's guilelessness left no doubt in his mind that she found him not merely attractive, but wildly desirable.

They were in bed within an hour of her arrival. The fact that she was a virgin appealed to him tremendously, once he recovered from the shock of it. He liked being *numero uno,* it made him feel important and virile again. She moved in with him the next day. That she adored him seemed apparent from the start, and he gratefully returned her affection, thinking this was what the doctor should have ordered: a sensuous, eager, *fresh* young girl.

It wasn't until many months later that he learned she had walked out of Radcliffe without telling anyone where she was going, or that neither of her parents had a clue as to her whereabouts. Appalled, he reached for the phone, but she stopped him. She said that if he called her parents, she would leave him and he would never find her. Then she burst into tears and begged him not to call them, saying it would be a wasted gesture inasmuch as Beverly had become a hopeless drunk, her stepfather was a callous violent boor, and Peter was too preoccupied with his young male lover to have time for her. The picture she elaborately conjured up of the three of them was a grim and unpleasant one and Fingerhood didn't suspect that it wasn't the whole picture. Perhaps he didn't want to believe she was deceiving him, he often thought later on when the truth emerged. He was too satisfied having his ego stroked and his middle-age fears erased to want to imagine that the girl who'd entered his life so unexpectedly and fortuitously was an accomplished liar and drug addict.

It took him even longer to catch on to her coke habit than it did to learn that she'd left her parents cruelly in the dark. Because Fingerhood sometimes used cocaine himself (the way he sometimes drank a glass of wine), he was accustomed to having the stuff around and didn't think much of it when Sally joined him for an occasional snort. What he didn't know was that she was snorting behind his back with increasing frequency. He only discovered it when their sex life started to go to pieces. Alerted to the fact that something was terribly wrong, he asked himself what it could be. Unable to come up with a reasonable answer, he then asked Sally who accused him of having an overactive shrink's imagination. She insisted she was merely going through "a phase." Fingerhood waited for the phase to pass, and when it didn't, his patience wore thin.

Because the sex had been so fantastic, he'd come to depend on her free-wheeling eroticism more than he realized; he'd come to need her easy and natural sensuality as badly as he needed air to breathe, and suddenly it wasn't there. First she began having problems achieving orgasm, then she began avoiding intimacy altogether. The few times he did manage to cajole her into bed proved dismal and unrewarding, with her lying there like a corpse. Fingerhood couldn't understand it. Her old touching desire to please and be pleased was gone. He had never seen such a dramatic reversal.

In addition, she was losing weight, becoming nervous, fidgety, irritable. Even so, the truth didn't dawn on him. Like most people who didn't have an addictive personality themselves, he failed to suspect addiction until openly confronted with it. Then one day, quite by accident, he caught her with her nose in a coke spoon and the truth spilled out. She first tried cocaine when she was modeling and heard other models say it was great for weight control and the release of sexual inhibitions. Afterward, she found that she needed more and more of the stuff just to get through the day and keep from going to pieces. One of the models became her connection and she paid for her habit by selling off pieces of jewelry that her father had given her for her birthdays over the years.

"Just a minute," Fingerhood said, trying to make sense of her wavering explanation. "You couldn't possibly have been worried about your weight when you started this craziness— you're reed thin—and neither could you have been worried about sexual inhibitions. I've never seen anyone as free in bed as you."

"You have cocaine to thank for that."

He was astonished. "You mean all that passion and excitement wasn't *natural?*"

"Why do you think I was a virgin when we met?"

"Because you were waiting for the right man." Even as he

said it he saw how absurdly self-flattering the concept was. "It never occurred to me there could be another reason."

"Well, there was," she defiantly replied. "Fear. I was scared stiff."

"I wouldn't have guessed." He shook his head. "You seemed so sure of yourself right from the start . . . the way you flirted with me that first afternoon . . . the deliberate way you came on . . . ."

"I was stoned out of my mind."

He felt like a fool. "I had no idea."

"I know."

She seemed proud that she'd tricked him, which made him realize what a sneaky business drugs were, so much easier to conceal than drinking for instance. And a drug like cocaine was especially easy because its effects were so subtle to the unsuspicious eye. When he asked her if she knew what made her afraid to begin with, she unhesitatingly blamed her parents. With a sexpot for a mother and a swinger for a father, she claimed she'd grown up terrified of being considered inadequate, unexciting. The fact that she had come of age at the height of the sexual revolution only magnified her fears because of peer pressure to participate, experiment. All around her, her classmates were jumping into bed with strangers as casually as they were popping the pill and pretending to be blasé about enjoying sex for its own sake rather than as an adjunct of love. When Sally found she couldn't do that, she felt abnormal and retreated from sex even more. If she never tried it, no one on campus would learn what a washout she was.

She left Radcliffe because she knew that she wouldn't be able to lose her hated virginity there. She needed a more anonymous atmosphere, a more experienced man than the college boys who teased her and called her "Northrop Pole." When she came to New York it wasn't that she wanted to be a model, so much as she wanted to *look* like one—glamorous and sophisticated. But the modeling arena quickly turned sour for her, for two reasons:

1. She didn't have what it took, professionally;
2. Most of the men she met there were gay.

It was then that she decided to contact Fingerhood. She had heard her parents talk about him for years as an infamous, notorious stud. If anyone could help her bridge the gap to womanhood, she felt that he could. A few toots of cocaine, and she dredged up the courage to call him.

Fingerhood listened to her story with growing concern, and when it was over he hugged and kissed her, chastised her for having held out on him so long, assured her that everything was going to be all right. She must go for treatment, and after she was weaned of cocaine, they would work on their sexual problems—assuming that any still existed. He explained that while cocaine was an aphrodisiac at first, it could also boomerang and make the user sexually uninterested. And that was what had obviously happened in her case. To his amazement, Sally flatly refused professional help. The more he insisted that it was the only solution, the more stubborn and resistant she became. By then she was snorting all around the clock and Fingerhood was at his wits' end. Finally he threatened to call her parents unless she agreed to go for drug rehabilitation at once.

She tried to make a pact with him. "After we're married, I'll go then."

He was mildly surprised. "I didn't realize you wanted to get married."

"Doesn't every woman?"

"Maybe. It's just that you never mentioned it before. Are you serious about the treatment part? You'll go?"

She nodded gravely. "Yes, after we're married. I need something to hold on to: a husband, a sense of security. I can't face it otherwise."

So he proposed. Aside from the fact that he loved her, he felt it was the least he could do. Although he didn't get her started on coke, he felt responsible because he didn't actively discourage her. He wished to hell he had, but how could he have guessed that she wouldn't be able to handle it normally (like him, for instance)? How could he have predicted that she would turn into an addict (like her mother)?

"I'm getting hungry," Beverly said across the room, slurring her words. "What are we going to do about dinner? Does anyone have a suggestion?"

Sally whispered to Fingerhood. "Excuse me. I'll be back in a second."

He knew where she was going. Off to the bathroom for more coke. He saw Lou watch her go and thought he detected an expression of concern on her face, but maybe he was imagining it. Sally never told anyone about her dependency problems, she was too ashamed. Fingerhood wondered if she wasn't most ashamed of having ended up like her mother. Different drug, same addiction.

"How about if I order Chinese food?" he said to the others, as he heard someone enter the apartment. A familiar French-accented voice told him it was Simone, whom he had not yet laid eyes on. "I know a Hunan place that makes the best General Tso chicken in town."

Beverly collapsed into a fit of laughter. "Tso what are you waiting for?" she asked.

A moment later Simone walked in and triumphantly announced her forthcoming marriage to Sir Michael Harding of Gloucestershire, England.

Lou knocked on the bathroom door. "Sally? It's me."

"Can't a person even pee in peace?"

"Sure, if that's what you're doing."

Sally turned on the faucet. "That's what I'm doing." She tapped some of the fine white powder into her coke spoon and inhaled deeply. Instant relief, just like the commercials for those nasal decongestants—only in this case it hadn't been her nose that was stuffed, it was her brain. She put the paraphernalia away, flushed the toilet, and unlocked the door. "See?" she said to Lou, feeling revived and unassailable once more. "Perfectly innocent."

"I hope so. I didn't tell Peter about your little habit." Oddly, it was Lou who appeared furtive and guilty. "I thought he had enough to cope with, learning about Fingerhood and the wedding."

"And you didn't tell Beverly, either. Thanks. I appreciate it."

Lou hated the position she found herself in. She could still see the look of shocked disbelief on Peter's face when she said that Sally was not only living with Fingerhood but was going to marry him. It was the same look she had once seen on the face of a terminally ill cat before she turned it over to the ASPCA for extinction. Watching Peter Northrop painfully try to maintain his equilibrium, she felt that she couldn't assault him with news of his daughter's drug habit. It would have to wait.

"Don't thank me," she said to Sally. "I haven't dropped

this matter, I've merely postponed it. As soon as Beverly sobers up, I'm going to speak to her and Peter together.''

"Is that what you came running in here to tell me? And I thought it was only *good* news that traveled fast.''

Lou had been admiring a Raphael Soyer nude that hung over the medicine chest. It was a small, exquisite watercolor of a woman with long dark hair sprawled on a bed. In the pink bathroom light, the woman looked rosy and glowing, as though she were eagerly awaiting her lover.

"I don't blame you for being angry,'' she said to Sally, thinking that she resembled the woman in the painting. "If I were in your shoes, I'd be angry too. But I'm not in your shoes, that's what you have to understand.''

"I don't have to do anything. You seem to be managing quite well on your own. How come you haven't mentioned telling Fingerhood? After all, he is going to be my husband. Doesn't he have a right to know my deep, dark secret?''

"I'm sure he already does.'' That was one of the things bothering Lou. "Why hasn't he dealt with it by now?''

"Maybe he can't. Maybe my parents won't be able to, either. They have no jurisdiction over me, remember? What do you hope to gain by upsetting them more than they already are?''

"I was only thinking of your welfare.''

"How noble of you. I suppose you expect me to be grateful.''

"Not particularly.''

"What a relief!'' Sally replied with exaggerated sarcasm. "I can't tell you how much better that makes me feel!''

"You think I'm meddling, don't you?''

"You said it.''

Lou felt like a hypocrite for having barged in where she wasn't wanted. She wondered if she was using Sally's problems as a convenient excuse to run away from Keith Rinehart, whose attentions had started to panic her. Ever since she got to the penthouse, he'd glued himself to her in the most all-consuming manner. Although she wiggled uncomfortably beneath his gaze, her previous opinion began to change. She saw that he was intelligent, sensitive, witty, and mad for her. That she could be the object of so intense a desire amazed her. It scared her, too. She hadn't been with a man in such a long time that she felt certain she wouldn't know how to behave when the opportunity presented itself. The fact that that opportunity didn't seem very far off only made her more nervous. *It's like riding a bicycle*, people always said, *you never forget*. Lou wasn't sure. Right now she found it virtually impossible to believe that she'd ever opened her legs to receive a man, let alone had the slightest notion of what to do afterward. For the last five years she hadn't needed that knowledge (she was too busy taking lessons in radical feminism). What if it were lost to her forever?

"Why is everyone becoming so moral all of a sudden?" Sally demanded. "First my father and now you. The next thing I know, Beverly will say she's giving up booze."

"For your information, she did give it up. For two whole years."

Sally was jolted. "I've never known her to give it up for two whole days. When did she start drinking again?"

"Apparently right after she found out about your wedding plans."

"Are you implying it's *my* fault she fell off the wagon?"

"I'd certainly say you had something to do with it."

"I did not." To Sally's mind, the accusation was grossly unfair. "My mother is a drunk, that's why she started drinking again. How dare you blame me?"

Sally felt boxed in by disapproval, censure. Whichever way she turned, someone was against her, attempting to change her, improve her, cure her. Even her future husband. She shivered at the thought of going to one of those places where they detoxified you, educated you, lectured you, supposedly "rehabilitated" you, then sent you back into the same chaotic world and expected you to survive without drugs. Were they crazy? Was she for agreeing to go? Still, she had made a deal: *marriage for drug surrender*.

In retrospect, it didn't seem like a very fair deal. How could any man—even one as wonderful as Fingerhood—take the place of drugs? It was impossible. She wondered if Beverly thought along those lines when she turned to the comfort of Scotch after a depressing run-in with one of her husbands, children, life. It was the first time she had compared herself to her mother, and the emotional proximity felt strange (cokeheads sneered at drunks). And yet despite her reluctance to identify, she could see one obvious similarity. Scotch, like cocaine, was a sure thing. You knew for certain what you were getting when you sipped or sniffed. You knew for certain what the end result would be: pleasure.

With people, you never knew. They could trick you, betray you, leave you, dishonor you, cause you infinite pain. Who, in her right mind, wouldn't choose pleasure over pain? Happiness over misery? The fact that most of the human race chose to go it alone, without a crutch of some kind, impressed the hell out of Sally. They must be braver than she, more willing to gamble with their happiness. She had seen so little of that precious commodity in her twenty years that she was zealous of its safekeeping, afraid that if she didn't squeeze it tight she would be left with nothing.

"I shouldn't have blamed you for your mother's relapse, it wasn't fair," Lou apologized, leaning against the bathroom door. "I didn't come in here to talk about your mother, anyway. It's you I want to talk about."

Beneath the rush of the drug, Sally suddenly felt tired. "What's left to say?"

"Just that I hope you'll do something about your habit. It's not too late, you know."

"What isn't it too late for?" Sally couldn't stop thinking that deal time lurked just around the corner. "To kick drugs or cancel my wedding plans?"

Lou registered sharp surprise. "I didn't realize the latter was even under discussion."

"It isn't. I don't know what I'm saying. Don't pay any attention to me." She was frantically trying to hide her panic. *Marriage for drug surrender.* She didn't want Lou to guess the nature of the trade-off. "I must have those prewedding jitters. They say that all brides get them sooner or later."

"Yes, of course, I understand." She wondered what Sally wasn't telling her. She wondered whether to go back to Keith's apartment later on. He had asked her to, but should she? What if it were an unqualified disaster? What if she'd lost the knack for making love to a man? She didn't want to have to face that unflattering possibility, the thought of it staggered her. "I understand," she said again.

"You don't understand a goddamned thing," Sally lashed out. With longer hair Lou could have been the nude in the Raphael Soyer painting, serenely awaiting her lover, not a flicker of trepidation on her face. "How *could* you understand?

When all is said and done, you're just as self-assured as my mother."

"Self-assured?" Lou was confused by her outburst. "How? In what way?"

"When it comes to sex, neither one of you knows the meaning of fear. It's always been a picnic for you, hasn't it?"

The irony of the charge reduced Lou to bitter laughter.

"What's so funny?" Sally demanded.

"The terrible knack we have for deceiving each other."

Keith Rinehart's apartment was small, plant-filled, and cheerful. Except for a solitary black-and-white photograph hanging on the living-room wall: a reproduction of seamy Parisian nightlife by Brassai, the page torn out of a magazine and tacked carefully above a chrome-and-leather chair.

"To keep me modest," he said to Lou by way of explanation. "Would you like a drink?"

Not after all that champagne and no Hunan food, she wouldn't, shouldn't. "Yes, thanks." They had left Fingerhood's penthouse just as he was calling the restaurant and frantically beckoning them to stay. Although she would have liked to talk to Simone, she had decided to go home with Keith before she lost her nerve. She could talk to Simone tomorrow. "I think a gin and tonic would be a nice idea."

She didn't want to get bombed, but she didn't want to be totally sober either. She was too nervous for that. The Norma Kamali shirtdress felt like wool against her hot tingly skin and she could hardly wait to step out of it. On the other hand, she couldn't imagine stepping out of it and facing *him*. All she had on underneath was a pair of skimpy lace panties. Things might be a lot worse, she told herself. She could have failed to shave her legs yesterday, she could have pendulous breasts, she could be hiding a multitude of hip sins beneath the dress's full skirt. But she hadn't, didn't, wasn't. While her hips weren't quite as slim as she would have liked, they would do.

Lou remembered reading that, in bed, women worried most about their bodies and men about their performance. It sounded logical. Had she worried about her body the first time with Vanessa? She couldn't remember, Vanessa was a million years ago. He placed the ice-cold glass in her hand just in time. One more second and she would have chickened out.

"Cheers," she said with a brave smile.

"*Salud.*"

They stood like idiots, drinking, no one daring to make the first move. He felt too awed by her and she felt too virginal.

"Maybe I shouldn't have come here," she ventured. "It might have been better if we waited."

"Why?"

It was one of the things she liked about him and detested. He was so infuriatingly direct, the way he'd followed her all over New York without knowing her name, the way he jumped into that taxi and made up that absurd story about them being married. "Why?" she repeated, trying to think of an answer. "Well, sometimes it's not smart to rush into things."

"We aren't rushing," he pointed out. "We're taking our time. We're drinking, talking. Do you feel that I'm rushing you?"

"Yes, sort of. But I feel as though I'm rushing me, also." Or was the blond hair on his wrists doing that? "And I don't want to. I really want to slow down."

"It's called anxiety. We all have it."

"You're not anxious. At least you don't seem to be. You seem very direct and self-confident."

"Thank you, but that's not altogether accurate. I may be direct, but I'd hardly say I was self-confident."

"You could have fooled me."

"Obviously I *have* fooled you," he said with a smile. "People put on their masks to face the world, but underneath, we're all scared."

"You too?"

"Sure. Everyone. Aren't you scared?"

"More than you'll ever know." She was trembling inside; tiny involuntary waves of fear had gained control of her body. "It's beginnings. They're so nerve-racking."

"The way to look at it is to ask yourself what's the worst thing that can happen. Then it doesn't seem so awful."

"You're wrong. It seems worse."

"Why is that?"

"Because the worst would be that you didn't like me."

Had she actually admitted that? The trembling grew more violent. She wondered if it showed, if he could sense it.

*"Not like you?"* His tone reflected incredulity that such a response would be possible. "You must be joking. How could I possibly not like you? I'm crazy about you."

"You are?"

"Mad. Overwhelmed. Cuckoo."

Again she admired his directness. "And you're not embarrassed to tell me that?"

"Why should I be embarrassed? It's true and, hopefully, it's flattering." He put his glass down and kissed her—of all places—on the nose. "I'm glad I followed you for weeks, but I'm even more glad that we finally met through mutual friends. Of course it makes me mad as hell to realize that Fingerhood has known you all these years and never once mentioned you to me. What a waste of precious time."

"He didn't want us to leave before," Lou mused. "Did you notice? He seemed almost frantic."

"He was, but it had nothing to do with us. I suspect he has cold feet about getting married."

"Really? That's very interesting." Sally appeared to have cold feet too. "Did he say that?"

"He didn't have to. It was pretty obvious."

It hadn't been obvious to Lou. "What do you think is bothering him?"

A locker-room grin spread over Keith's face. "Anita Schuler."

"What? You're kidding. I don't believe it. You think Fingerhood is interested in *Anita?*"

" 'Interested' isn't a word I would choose," he replied, with an insinuating chuckle. "I think he'd like to fuck her brains out. Didn't you see the way he couldn't keep his eyes off her? He was mentally undressing her, and then some."

"Anita left shortly after I got there, so I didn't see much of anything. Are you sure about this?"

"I'm positive. But if you don't mind, I'd rather not talk about Fingerhood's problems right now."

Lou was horrified. Maybe Sally knew that Fingerhood desired Anita, maybe that explained her prewedding jitters. Poor thing. "I may be dense," she said to Keith, "but I don't understand why Fingerhood would prefer that trashy Anita to someone as nice as Sally."

He shrugged. "I guess he finds Anita more fuckable."

Lou saw purple. "Is that all men can think of? Doesn't anything else matter to you? Do you all have one-track, centerfold minds?" She felt furiously disappointed in him; he was just like the rest. "And you wonder why women are fed up. You wonder what you've done to antagonize and alienate us. Jesus, it's a miracle that women are still *talking* to men!"

"Hey, calm down." He grabbed her arm and stopped her from leaving. "Be reasonable. We were discussing Fingerhood, if you recall, not me."

"That's what you think," she said, pulling her arm away. "The only reason you asked me to come here is because you wanted to make love to me."

"And what did you want?"

"Women always want more than that."

"You're awfully smug, you know. What makes you think that men don't?"

"Because of the way you're acting right now."

He was coming closer. She could feel his breath on her neck, see his lips zero in on her hot skin and paste themselves there. It was a very sensuous feeling, very unrelenting and single-minded. Just like him, she thought, irritated and gratified all at once. Part of her felt like walking out and never seeing him again, but another part refused to budge. She admired him for standing up to her and yet she hated him for it. Even if she disagreed with him about everything for the rest of her life, she wouldn't be able to dismiss him with a glance of contempt. He was that most menacing of sparring partners—an equal—she thought as his hand traveled down the front of her dress and grabbed her right through Norma Kamali's skirt, just went and grabbed her cunt, just like that. Most men would have gone underneath and tried for naked flesh, but there was something more exciting about it this way, something more depraved. Maybe that explained his penchant for Brassaï's seaminess. Maybe it explained her own (Brassaï happened to be her favorite photographer). The image of Keith's blond wrist hair pressed against her dark pubic hair was a powerful aphrodisiac.

Lou hadn't experienced blunt crude sex in a long time, not since Peter Northrop. . . . Carnal scenes and images came tumbling forward from her memory bank, startling her by their hard-edged explicitness. It was going to be like that with him. Very blunt, very carnal, but with tenderness afterward, not during. She preferred it that way, herself. How nice that they'd found each other out of all those millions of people who opted for interspersed tenderness and a barrage of words. To Lou, sex was a kind of ballet and didn't require words. In fact, too many of them turned her right off. Once she found herself in bed with a new acquaintance who babbled incessantly about everything: what they were doing and what he would like to do, what he would like *her* to do, what he had done with other women and what they had done to him, what his ex-wife liked sexually and what she didn't like, why some women were so difficult to please and why some were so easy, why some bodies were so wonderful and some were so awful, and so on. He talked so much that she finally pretended to faint. Right in the middle of everything. He shook her until she opened one bleary eye.

"What's the matter?" he said, white as a sheet. "Don't you feel well?"

"No, I need a doctor."

"I *am* a doctor. What's wrong? Where does it hurt?"

She pointed to her ears. "There."

"I don't get it. Your ears hurt. How come?"

"Because some bigmouthed son of a bitch I know won't shut up."

"Really?" He turned his head, listened for sounds. "I don't hear a thing. Are you sure you're not imagining it?"

She had no idea why she thought of that now. Probably so she wouldn't have to think about what Keith was doing or what she was feeling. He had taken his hand away from her skirt and put it around her torso, both hands, he was kissing her on the lips, pulling her close, insisting, demanding, sinking into her deeper and deeper, while she—wet, limp, slightly crazy—swayed against him and kept murmuring, "No. No. No. No. No. No. No. No. No. No. No. *No!*"

"Yes."

His teeth ground into hers; it felt good, animalistic. He could bite her to death if he wanted and she wouldn't make a move to stop him. She would just let herself be devoured, inch by willing inch. What an odd thought. How unlike her. How very peculiar. Who was this man, anyway? What was he doing to her? She pulled back and stared at him, incredulous at what was happening.

"I don't know you," she said, bewildered by her desires. "You're a stranger."

"That's true. So what?"

"So you're a stranger and I'm frightened."

"I'm frightened too. After all, you're a stranger to me. There's only one way to stop being strangers, isn't there?"

"Yes," she lied, thinking of the men with whom she'd remained strangers afterward. Sadness engulfed her. "I'm afraid so."

"Don't be afraid. Help me. Be optimistic."

"Deep down, I am optimistic. It's just that the anxiety is on the surface, pushing the good feelings away."

"Don't let it. Push back."

"I will. I'll start right now. I don't approve of that anxiety. It's never helped me overcome anything, it's only hindered me." And meanwhile, she was kissing *him*, devouring *him* inch by willing inch. "You're beginning to feel a lot less strange."

"So are you."

"Good."

"No. Wonderful."

She came up for air. "Why did you follow me all around New York?"

"Because I wanted to get into your pants, Deidre. Why do you think?"

"Don't be so goddamned honest," she laughed.

"Okay. Because I liked your brain."

"Or so sarcastic."

"Because I liked the color of your delivery truck?"

"Or so patronizing."

"Because I liked *you*?"

"What did you like about me?"

"The fact that you're going to be crazy about my Shrimp Timbales."

"Are you putting me on? That's what you liked about me?"

"It's a compliment. They happen to be very unusual timbales—I add grated zucchini to the mix—but not everyone appreciates the subtle flavor. I'm sure you will, though."

"Don't bank on it. I not only know zilch about cooking, but my tastes are strictly meat and potatoes. My partner handles the cooking end, I'm sales."

"So you balance each other?"

"Yes." She wondered what he was getting at. "Fingerhood said you were a gourmet cook. Have you always been interested in cooking?"

"As far back as I can remember. At one time I even considered doing it professionally. You're not looking for a sous chef by any chance, are you?"

"Not on a permanent basis. Vanessa hires them as the need arises." She was starting to get an uncomfortable feeling. "I thought your field was photography."

"That's how I pay the rent, but my ambitions in that area have slowly faded. Cooking a good meal has begun to feel a hell of a lot more gratifying than taking a good picture." He brushed a wisp of hair out of her eyes. "I love black hair and brown eyes, they're so Mediterranean."

"I'm sorry to disappoint you, but there's no Mediterranean blood coursing through these veins."

"Sure, there is. Somewhere way back—farther back than your family remembers—you had beautiful Mediterranean ancestors who lived beside the sea."

It was a lovely thought. She shivered. "Do you really think so?"

"I'm positive of it, Deidre."

Then he proceeded to make blunt, carnal, wordless love to her.

# 9

The following morning Simone drove to JFK with Colin in a rented limo, his Vuitton suitcases (minus the one she'd thrown out the window at the King Croesus) piled into the trunk. She was meeting the twins' plane, due in at eleven, and Colin was taking a flight to Phoenix at approximately the same time. When she told him that she didn't want to pursue their publicity plans inasmuch as she was ending her career, he called the studio and said he was ready to start shooting *Arizona Pete* again.

"What made you decide to give up your career?" he now asked her.

"I've fallen in love and am moving to England."

"No kidding. What about *Rockabye Princess?*"

"You'll just have to stick your tongue down some other actress's throat during the love scenes. Sorry about that, Colin."

"Did I hear you say *England*? I was there once on location. Jesus! Why would anyone want to live in *England*?" He made it sound like a third-world country. "It rains constantly."

"When you're happy and fulfilled, a little rain doesn't matter."

She expected him to jeer at that, but to her surprise he seemed sympathetic. "I'm beginning to agree with you. I used to be content dividing my time between Phoenix and L.A., I thought I had the best of both worlds. But lately it's all begun to go stale."

She couldn't believe her ears. He actually sounded human. "What do you think is missing, Colin?"

"I've been giving that a lot of thought." He tapped his head. "Love, sweet love is the missing ingredient. Yessiree, age must be catching up fast. Staying out late and tooling around the Southwest on my Yamaha—much as I dig it—

isn't enough anymore. The Malibu scene isn't enough. I need a steady chick.''

"You must meet zillions of them all the time. What's the problem?''

"They're all *actresses*," he said with disdain. "Self-centered. Temperamental. They want the whole fucking world to revolve around them.''

"And you want it to revolve around *Arizona Pete*?''

"Damned right! Where I come from in Shawnee, Oklahoma, women cater to their men. It's the natural order of things. That reminds me. How is Jimmy taking being jilted? And what did Eddie say about your retirement? He must be plenty pissed, you've made a lot of dough for him the last few years.''

"I can handle Jimmy." Simone smiled to herself. "As for Eddie, I haven't told him yet.''

She was enjoying this interim period before she broke the news of her bombshell engagement to Edwin Lee Drake. After years of being dependent upon him for work, money, security (and recently, a solar-powered orgasm), she relished never having to rely upon him again. For anything. That she would soon be forced to rely upon Michael was so unsettling a thought that she pushed it right out of her mind. The possibility that she wasn't ending her dependency upon one man, but merely transferring it to another man, wasn't something she cared to think about at the moment. They stopped for a light on the Long Island Expressway.

"Yeah, sure, you're welcome, anytime," Colin said, signing his name on a piece of paper extended to him by a female passenger in the next car. The passenger didn't see Simone, who was huddled in a corner of the limousine trying to adjust to her new noncelebrity status. "Aren't you going to miss this sort of thing?" Colin asked her. "People wanting your autograph and all that. It kind of gets to you, after a while.''

"You mean it gets to *you*." She stifled the twinge of jealousy she felt and contemplated taking up croquet. "I can live very happily without the adulation.''

"I wonder. I've heard it's addictive and I believe it.'' Then he set his ten-thousand-dollar black-and-gold Submariner Rolex back three hours and winked at her. "What was all that screaming and yelling in the middle of the night? I didn't know you liked noisy sex, Frenchie.''

"It had nothing to do with sex."

"Really?" He was grinning, unconvinced. "What did it have to do with?"

"Jealousy. Rivalry. Insanity."

She and Michael had been sound asleep when a creaking door awakened her. The room was pitch black and she was too frightened to turn on the bedside lamp. Pulling the covers up around her neck, she tremulously called out, "Is anyone there?"

"Yes," came a familiar voice. "Me."

Simone's heart began beating again. "Anita?"

"That's right, Jezebel."

"It's three o'clock in the morning. What are you doing here?"

The response was bitter. "As if you don't know."

"But I don't," she said in the darkness.

"You're in bed with the man I love, you stole him away from me, you're going to marry him, and you have the nerve to say you don't know?"

"That's no reason to scare the wits out of me like this. How did you get in here? What do you want? Michael said you hit him over the head with an umbrella and then left him lying there for dead. Have you gone crazy?"

Just as she reached for the lamp switch, the overhead chandelier light flicked on, bathing the room in an unnatural yellow glow. Simone gasped. Anita stood framed next to the door. She wore peach satin lounging pajamas, high-heeled mules with peach marabou trim, a glittering gold-diamond-and-sapphire necklace, and was holding a small black pistol in her hand, aimed directly at her.

"Why is that gun pointed at me?" Simone asked, frantically wishing that Michael would stop snoring and wake up. "What are you doing with a gun, anyway?"

"Planning to shoot you."

"That's not very funny."

"I'm glad you agree."

Simone swallowed hard. Strangely enough, Anita didn't look insane. Her hair was artfully lacquered, her eyes deftly made up, her shade of lipstick painstakingly chosen, she'd even thought to wear a padded brassiere for her wacko mission. The outline of her breasts, Simone knew from memory, was not the outline of her breasts.

"Why are you staring at my chest?" Anita asked. "Is one higher than the other?"

"No, they're both the same inflated size. You don't need a padded brassiere, what you need is a padded cell. No normal person would come barging in here like this, frightening innocent people half to death. You should be arrested."

"You call yourself innocent? That's a good one! You're so self-deluded, you probably believe it, too. Well, let me tell you something, Miss Marseillaise of 1903, I've been sick as a dog at my fleabag of a hotel while you've been here in this golden palace enjoying yourself with Michael and laughing at me behind my back. And I refuse to take it one minute longer."

"Sick is right," Simone muttered.

Anita waved the gun at her. "One more crack like that and you'll be pushing up daisies sooner than you think. Yes, I'm sick, but not the way you mean. I'm physically frail, delicate. I've been under a liver specialist's care in London for the last few years. I might need a laporoscopic before very long, maybe even a hysterectomy, not that I came over here to complain or kvetch about my health problems."

"Do you have another word for it?"

"I'm warning you, Simone."

"Then why *did* you come here?"

"To inform you that, sick or not, I don't intend to keel over like an invalid and let you take Michael away from me. Not on your life. He's mine and I plan to keep him."

"How? By shooting me?"

"Can you think of a better way?"

Actually, Simone couldn't, and it made her realize that instead of taunting this deranged woman, she should be trying to placate her. "No one's been laughing at you, Anita, you have it all wrong. Michael and I are extremely concerned about your state of mind. Hitting someone over the head with an umbrella and now threatening to kill me aren't hallmarks of a well-balanced person." She attempted a brave smile. "Is that gun really loaded?"

"Do you want to play Russian roulette and find out?"

"No, thanks, I saw *The Deer Hunter*. But you know, if you shoot me you'll go to prison—maybe for life." She raised her voice in the hope of arousing Michael, but his snores persisted with rhythmic regularity. "You'll have to wear one of those awful gray uniforms, and you look lousy in gray. Only redheads can get away with that color. Then you'll gain weight because prison food is all starch, and on top of everything else, your roots will grow in. You'll look like shit, Anita, so I would think this over very carefully if I were you."

"I have thought it over." She reflexively touched her shining glory. "I'm beyond vanity. Why should I care about my appearance when the man I adore has cast me aside like an old stick? What do I have to look forward to? I'm thirty-nine years old and without prospects."

"Forty. You're a year older than I am."

"You have to remind me, don't you? Even at a time like this when your life is in danger, you can't resist pointing out that I'm a year older, can you? That's one of the reasons I'm going to kill you, Simone. Because you're so infuriatingly arrogant. You think you know everything, you've always made fun of me even in the old days when you couldn't come and didn't have a pot to pee in. And now that you're rolling in dough, fame, motherhood, orgasms, you take delight in rubbing it in."

"That's not true," Simone said frantically. "My orgasms stink, sometimes I don't even have any. You shouldn't envy me on that score. You see, I have this hidden clitoris—"

"I'm not interested in your fucking clitoris. You're about to get married for the second time, while I haven't had the courtesy of being asked once. And as though that weren't insulting enough, you're marrying the man I love, worship, adore, and financially depend on. Did you honestly think I would take this lying down? Because if so, *you're* the one who's flipped her lid, not me." She put her finger on the trigger. "Get ready to meet your maker, you sneaky little bitch."

"Oh, my God. No, don't do it, Anita. I beg you. Remember what good friends we were when we shared that flat in Murray Hill? Remember how you used to call me 'Rima, the Bird Girl'? Now I have an eight-year-old daughter named Rima. Do you want to leave her motherless at such a young age? I have a son too, a darling little boy. I named him after *The Little Prince.* Please, Anita, if you can't think of me, think of them."

"It's too late to appeal to my good nature."

Was this really how it was going to end? Simone couldn't believe it. She had always expected to die peacefully in her sleep, an old woman, like Coco Chanel. She felt desperate.

"I'll give you money, Anita." The fact that she didn't have any was beside the point. "I'll transfer all my assets over to you, if you let me live."

"You will?"

Simone nodded eagerly. "Yes, yes. You can have everything."

Anita took her finger off the trigger. "It's a tempting thought, but how do I know you're telling the truth?"

"I swear it. On my word of honor."

"You don't have any honor."

"If you just put that gun away, I'll write my intentions down on a piece of paper. Then tomorrow we'll take it to a lawyer and it will be as binding as a promissory note."

"How much are you worth?"

"One hundred thousand dollars." Simone named the first sum that popped into her mind. Maybe it wasn't enough. "Plus I'll give you all my jewels, furs, and the house in Malibu."

"Is it in the Colony?"

"Smack in the middle. Goldie Hawn is on one side of me and Burt Reynolds is on the other. It's extremely valuable property. If you wanted to, you could sell it and make a fortune. Or you could keep it and live in the lap of luxury. Either way, you can't lose."

"You're lying."

Simone trembled. "What do you mean?"

"You don't have any money, you fuck-up. You told me so yourself the first night I came over here with Michael. Remember?"

Trembling had turned into shaking. "I don't know what you're talking about."

Anita put her finger back on the trigger and aimed the gun at Simone's heart. She stood only inches away. "I was busy envying you your wonderful good fortune, when you admitted that not only were you miserable but that you'd spent your last dime at I. Magnin's. What do you have to say to that?"

"It was Neiman Marcus," Simone croaked.

"That does it." Anita turned a dark angry color. "That's the last goddamned straw."

"No!" Simone screamed at the top of her lungs.

"*Au revoir*, darling. *Auf Wiedersehen* in heaven, or wherever liars and cheaters end up. Toodle-oo."

Just as Anita pressed the trigger, Michael sat up in bed. A thin jet of water flew through the air, missed Simone, and hit him smack in the eye.

"What the hell is going on around here?" he asked, squinting furiously, as Anita pressed the trigger of the water pistol again, and again, and again.

The minute Simone saw the twins enter the airline terminal, her heart stuck in her throat. This was motherhood, she thought, feeling everything melt inside her. They looked so much taller than she remembered. To her astonishment, Jimmy stood beside them, looking shorter and younger, as if he were the child and they the parents.

"What are *you* doing here?" she asked as she hugged and kissed the twins, whose faces were grimy from the trip.

"That's what I love—a warm welcome." He wore a Hawaiian shirt, loose gray pants, dirty sneakers, and needed a shave. No one would have guessed that he was a brilliant and innovative movie director, a bona fide *auteur* of the first rank. They would have guessed he was an unemployed pretzel salesman. "I'm here to talk some sense into you, but I didn't expect to find you mingling with the lowly masses. I expected a chauffeur or flunky to meet us. What gives with the democratic touch, kiddo?"

"I wish you'd stop calling me kiddo, just as I wish you'd stop thinking of me as an aristocratic movie star." The fact that she looked like one in a sexy Galanos floral silk jacquard chemise, red kid pumps on a stiletto bronze heel, her lavender hair tumbling over her shoulders Hollywood style, and her face obscured by Mikli's enormous black sunglasses, didn't seem to cross Simone's mind. "That movie-star business is in the past. Besides, why shouldn't I meet my own children if I want to? Where are their suitcases?"

"We have to go to Baggage Claim. We can talk on the way."

"If it's about *Rockabye Princess*, forget it. I told you, I'm getting out of the rat race before it's too late."

"Too late for what?" he asked as they joined the crowd heading in the direction of the arrows.

"For love. Romance. Marriage. A real life." The twins clung to her, one on either side, and she had to talk to Jimmy across them. "By the way, you just missed Colin. His plane was taking off as yours was landing."

"I know." Colin had called him yesterday to say that Simone wasn't kidding around with this marriage obsession of hers. "I don't understand what you mean by 'a real life.' What do you think we had at Malibu? Wasn't that *real* enough for you?"

"Don't be perverse, Jimmy. You know perfectly well what I'm talking about."

"The hell I do."

Nobody could exasperate her like Jimmy Newton. She forced a smile for a teenage boy who asked her to autograph his football and then told her she was his favorite actress.

"You see?" Jimmy said when the kid moved off. "You'll be missed."

"Maybe, but it's not enough. I want to be happy. I think I deserve some plain old-fashioned marital happiness after all the crap I've been through with you and Steve Omaha. And I damned well intend to get it."

"Listen, you self-deluded bubblehead, you'll never be happy married to that Englishman or any other man who expects you to throw away a brilliant career. Don't you understand anything?" They had stopped walking and angrily faced each other, nose to nose. If he exasperated Simone, she drove him crazy with her mindless whims. "What you're planning to do is downright suicidal and I won't let you go through with it."

"How do you intend to stop me?"

"I have a card up my sleeve."

"And a rock in your head. Stop meddling in my business, Jimmy."

"It's my business, too. I discovered you, which means I have a stake in your future."

"Is it true, Mommy? Are you going to marry an Englishman?" Rima's lower lip trembled. "Why didn't you tell us?"

"I was planning to, darling, but Jimmy beat me to it." She gave him a furious look. "You mustn't be upset, darling.

We're all going to live in London and visit Buckingham Palace a lot. Won't that be fun?''

Prince's good spirits faded and Rima began to cry. ''I don't want to live in London, Mommy. I want to live in Malibu where all my friends are.''

Simone kissed her. ''You'll make new friends in London.''

''No, I won't.'' Rima was sobbing now. ''Why can't you marry Jimmy instead? Then we wouldn't have to move anywhere.''

''The kid has a point,'' Jimmy said.

''You shut up,'' Simone hissed at him. She managed to calm her daughter down and the four of them started walking again. ''This was all I needed after last night's fireworks—a pair of traumatized twins on my hands. Thanks a lot, Jimmy.''

''They're not traumatized, you know how kids are. *What* fireworks?''

''For openers, Anita Schuler pretended to shoot me in the middle of the night but it turned out to be a water pistol, so nobody was hurt. Then Michael had to get out of bed, take her back to her hotel, and feed her tranquilizers until she was able to doze off. But just when he thought she was asleep, she ran to the window, screamed that she couldn't stand the pain any longer, ripped off her nightgown, and tried to jump. In desperation, he called Fingerhood, who came over and agreed to stay with her. I didn't get to sleep until five A.M.''

''Mommy, what does 'traumatized' mean?'' Prince asked.

''Deeply disturbed. You weren't supposed to hear that.''

''Mommy, I'm not traumatized,'' Rima said. ''I'm hungry. Can I have a candy bar?''

''No.''

'Why not?''

Simone stopped to give autographs to a group of gardening-club women on tour from Ohio. ''Because candy is bad for you,'' she told her daughter. She heard one of the women say: *''Next to my prize dracaenas, I'll value this the most.''*

''What's good for me?'' Rima persisted.

''English food.''

''What's in English food, Mommy?''

''Englishmen,'' Jimmy replied. ''Cut up in tiny pieces and boiled in beer. That's what you're going to eat if your mother marries Mr. Harding.''

Rima giggled. "Is Mr. Harding nice, Mommy? Is he as nice as Daddy?"

"Yes," Simone said.

"As nice as Jimmy?"

"Nicer, but not nearly as entertaining." Jimmy had stuck his hands in his ears and was wiggling them furiously, much to the twins' delight. Even Simone had to smile, he looked so ridiculous. Knowing how much he hated to fly, she was surprised he'd come. Did he honestly believe she was a talented actress with a career worth saving? Did he care for her more than his actions indicated? She winked at him. "Where are you staying in New York, sailor?"

"With you. Where else?"

"Like hell you are. It's out of the question. Michael has moved in."

"So what? That's personal. This is business. All I want is a chance to talk to you."

"What do you think we've been doing on this mile-long trek?" Her feet hurt, her throat was parched, there was no air conditioning, and she felt hot, sticky, irritable. "Are you sure there *is* a Baggage Claim? Maybe it's a plot by the KGB to get us all to Russia."

"Mommy, do they have Disneyland in Russia?" Rima asked.

"No, darling, they most certainly do not."

"What do they have in Russia that I'd like, Mommy?"

"Nothing."

Rima pouted. "Then I don't want to go."

"Me neither," Prince said.

Simone hugged them both. "That's good because we're not going to Russia. We're going to a large beautiful hotel in the heart of Manhattan."

"Is Jimmy going with us?" Prince asked.

"Maybe," Simone said, noting the hopeful look on her son's face.

"I could stay in Colin's old room," Jimmy suggested.

"Sure you could, but how am I supposed to explain your presence to Michael?"

Jimmy decided to pull out his ace in the hole. "You just tell him that the studio has asked me to write a screenplay of *The Fingerhood Position* and I have to work with you on the lead. Character development and all that jazz."

"What are you talking about?"

"You." He beamed. "I think you'd be perfect for the lead, and what's more, Eddie thinks so too. So does the studio!" This would deflate her ill-timed wedding plans, but good. "I discussed it with the executive producer only yesterday and he said that the part is made to order for your specific talents."

"But the lead in the book is *a hammock*."

"Forget the book. In the movie, it will be a lovely lost suburban housewife who's been married for fifteen years and hasn't had an orgasm." A man in a wheelchair distracted Simone by holding out an envelope for her to sign. "Then the housewife goes to a sex therapist, who suggests that she and her husband practice transcendental lovemaking in a hammock. They do, she has the Big O, and their marriage is saved. I can see Chevy Chase as the therapist and Dustin Hoffman as the frantic husband. Well?" he asked eagerly. "What do you think?"

"Mommy, what does 'transcendental' mean?" Prince asked.

"Let me alone." Simone had always wanted to play opposite Dustin Hoffman (who didn't?), he was her idea of terrific. So was Chevy Chase. "I think it sounds very promising, Jimmy, but you'll have to find another actress. I'm not interested."

He was stunned. He expected her to leap at the opportunity and thank him for helping to make it possible. He expected her to be grateful; instead, she didn't give a damn. He couldn't believe her indifference. She was really serious about marrying this Englishman and giving up her career!

"If that's the way you feel, Simone, I'll never mention *The Fingerhood Position* again." He would have to think of another approach, another deterrent to her suicidal plans, but he needed time. "Can I stay in Colin's room, even if we don't have business to discuss any longer? Come on, you said it was a large suite."

"Mommy, what's a 'Fingerhood position'?" Rima asked.

"Don't bother me, darling."

"I'll keep the twins out of your hair whenever you want to be alone with England's gift to the Colonies," Jimmy said. "That's fair, isn't it?"

The prospect of having a built-in baby-sitter whom she could trust (and the twins adored) was tempting, but dare she risk it? Michael was bound to be outraged when he discovered her five-year relationship with Jimmy. "If you're not going to badger me about *The Fingerhood Position*, why remain in New York at all?" she asked him.

"I have business here, people to see. Fingerhood, among others. The studio asked me to clear certain technicalities with him regarding the screenplay. Actually, I'm anxious to meet the guy. From your description, he sounds like quite a character. Has he changed much?"

"Hardly at all. It's almost sinister."

Simone had stayed for the Hunan dinner last evening, relieved to find that even though Fingerhood was just as handsome as ever, he no longer appealed to her. She wondered why. Was it because of her involvement with Michael, or had time finally worked its magic?

"You mean it's all over between Anita and that Harding guy?" Fingerhood asked after she impulsively announced her wedding plans. He seemed astonished, thrilled. "I can't believe it."

"Believe it. I stole him right out from under Anita's nose. In fact, at this moment he's telling her the news. Why do you look so pleased?"

"I'm pleased for *you*." He tried to stop smiling, but only partially succeeded. "I feel sorry as hell for poor Anita. She seemed convinced of his undying devotion."

"*Tant pis*. Maybe this will teach her never to take a man for granted."

"Maybe," Fingerhood said, his smile widening. . . .

Rima now pulled at her dress. "Mommy, why don't you tell me what a 'Fingerhood position' is?"

"Because it doesn't concern you, darling."

"Does it concern Prince?"

"No."

"Does it concern Daddy?"

"It does not."

"Who does it concern besides Jimmy?"

Simone wanted to scream, but no one would have heard her. They'd arrived at the madhouse known as Baggage Claim. Unfortunately, everyone else seemed to have arrived at the same time and was pushing and shoving toward the revolving luggage tier. Jimmy managed to find a space for the four of them in between a pair of weight lifters in white undershirts and a man with a wooden leg. They squashed themselves in and proceeded to watch the parade of suitcases, cosmetic cases, attaché cases, totes, overnight bags, duffel bags, garment bags, cartons, bicycles, baby strollers, and one mysteriously wrapped octagonal package going round and round.

The sight of them reminded Simone of other, less prestigious days when she was broke and without prospects and had to appear at places like Baggage Claim by herself, unaided and unabetted. How had she handled it without going crazy? The overheated, confined area was sheer bedlam. Someone pushed her in the back and someone else stepped on her toe. She squealed in pain, but nobody apologized. In his zeal to get to his luggage, one of the weight lifters elbowed her out of the way. She reached down to rub her toe, and her brand-new silk Dior stockings ripped. When she straightened up, something in her lower back snapped. She was too angry with Jimmy to think about the spasm of pain that shot through her. She felt like killing him for having put her in this stupid, undignified position.

"Why didn't you bring carry-on luggage?" she cried. "Don't you know how to travel with finesse? What are you—a peasant? Because that's the way you dress, that's the way you act: no class, no style, no consideration." Another burst of pain caught her in the same place. "Oh, how I hate you!"

Jimmy chuckled. "One of your charms is that you've never learned how to channel your anger. You're pissed off because deep down you'd like to do *The Fingerhood Position*, but at the same time you'd like to marry Harding and take up gardening. You're in a bind and you resent it, so you yell at me about being a peasant."

"*I wasn't yelling, I was complaining*," Simone shouted. "I'm a star! I'm not used to standing at Baggage Claim with all these assholes, being pushed and hustled around. I'm used to people taking care of things like this for me. When I make a movie and the weather is cold, somebody warms my pantyhose. When it's hot, they fan my face. When it's wet, they dry me off. And when it's too dry, they turn on a humidifier." Was she going to give up all those luxuries? They had never seemed especially important to her until now. "I'm used to being waited on, catered to, coddled, babied, shielded from unpleasantness, irritation, and all the stupid, boring, mindless inconveniences of life, goddammit to hell!"

"You tell him, lady," the man with the wooden leg said.

"Mind your own fucking business," she informed him.

"Mommy, can I have an ice-cream soda?" Rima asked, leaning against her.

Simone pushed her away. "No, you cannot."

"Can I have a Coca-Cola?"

"Shut up."

"Ask your mother if you can have English food," Jimmy said with a smile. "See if she still thinks it's so good for you."

Fingerhood was patiently spoon-feeding Anita a late breakfast when she clamped her mouth shut.

"Come on," he coaxed, tapping the teaspoon against her lips. "Have some more soft-boiled egg."

They were seated across from each other at the round dining table in her hotel suite overlooking the park. Outside it was hot again, fiercely sunny, the sky an unmarred blue. Fingerhood shivered in Michael Harding's terry robe that was too short for him, the air conditioning at the Gramercy Regency having been fixed to freezing. It amazed him how delectable Anita looked, despite last night's tense ordeal. What he didn't know was that while he slept she had showered, set her hair, redone her makeup, and changed into a baby-pink Charmeuse caftan slit to the knee. She might be rejected, suicidal, half out of her skull, and bleeding menstrually like a stuck pig, but she still took pride in her appearance, she thought with a burst of feminine satisfaction. Or as her mother crudely, but wisely used to say, "If you're going to cover your rear end, you might as well do it in style."

"I hate soft-boiled eggs," she said to Fingerhood with a beguiling pout. "They make me gag."

"You need your strength." He tried to wedge the spoon in. "You've had a rough time and you haven't eaten for hours."

Not since that terrible lunch with Beverly at Lutèce. Was that only yesterday? Anita felt as though months had gone by, so much had happened. As for dinner last night, she'd been far too distressed to eat. When Michael recovered from the umbrella blow to his head, he stormed out cursing and vowing never to speak to her again. She ran after him in a frenzied attempt to apologize for her behavior and got as far as the elevator, at which point he looked at her with such unmistakable venom that she ran right back to the suite and burst into tears of despair. She was alone, miserable, confused. *What was going to happen to her? Who would look after her? Who would care?* When the answers to these questions didn't seem forthcoming, she changed into a sexy summer knit and made her way down to the bar, hoping to find a sympathetic soul and forget her troubles for a while. A man in a Perry Ellis suit began flirting with her (or so she thought), but when she flirted back he took a water pistol out of his pocket and gleefully squirted her on the chin.

"You look exactly like my ex-wife," he snarled. "That's the witch who cost me a cool three hundred thou in exchange for my freedom. Here's what I think of the two of you."

And he squirted her again, this time smack in the right eye. Just before he was thrown out, he tossed the water pistol to Anita, telling her to get rid of "the murder weapon" at the first opportunity. Dejected all over again, she put it in her purse and tried drinking herself into oblivion, forgetting that she had no capacity for hard liquor. She never did. Two and a half martinis later, she returned to the suite violently ill, threw up, passed out. When she awakened it was the middle of the night and Michael had not come home. That was when she became hysterical, changed into peach lounging pajamas, and decided to pay him and Simone a little visit, taking "the murder weapon" with her. If nothing else, she could scare the shit out of the two of them.

"Okay, maybe one bite more," she now said to Fingerhood, allowing the teaspoon to enter.

"That's a good girl." He looked down at the tray that room service had sent up and broke a few bacon slices in half, as though for a child. "We're going to eat our bacon, aren't we?"

She nodded and closed her eyes. He sounded strangely like her mother, who used to wheedle her into cleaning her plate, when she was growing up in Cleveland, Ohio. And because Anita's father was a pork butcher, bacon was one food with which she'd enjoyed a long and nostalgic relationship.

"I like bacon," she said to him, unconsciously lapsing into a childish voice. "Provided it's not greasy."

"I'll blot it with the napkin. Okay, here we go. Open wide."

Anita obligingly opened. Maybe Simone had done her a favor by luring Michael to his destruction. Maybe last night's misery would turn out to have a silver lining. Maybe her mother was right when she said that ultimately everything happened for the best. Fingerhood was here with her, wasn't he? And no one could accuse her of going after him or trying to steal him away from Sally, since it was Michael himself who'd summoned him with a desperate SOS phone call after she tried to jump out the window. The night before, it had been a speeding taxi, and now a window, she remembered thinking as Michael dragged her back in and accused her of being insane.

But as soon as Fingerhood arrived, she knew that everything would be all right, he would *make* it all right. In accordance with his mysterious healing powers, her suicidal tendencies dissolved, she simmered down and gradually began to weep. He sat beside her in bed and held her close for hours, letting her cry on his shoulder, letting her get it all out of her system—all the pain and agony of the last six years. He didn't say a word, he didn't have to. His being there for her was more important than any words could possibly have been, and when she talked herself out and her eyelids felt droopy, he tucked her in and said he would sit there until she drifted off.

"You won't leave after I'm asleep, will you?" she anxiously asked.

"Not if you don't want me to. I'll call Sally and explain."

"I don't want you to."

He smiled reassuringly. "Then I'll stay."

The first thing she saw when she opened her eyes this morning was Fingerhood asleep on the chintz-covered chaise. He was gently snoring, needed a shave, and no one had ever looked so dear. Anita gazed at him with gratitude and remembered how he'd gone to Puerto Rico with her those many years ago when abortions were illegal in New York. It seemed that he had always been her savior, protector, her guardian of mercy.

"How do you take your coffee?" he now asked. "Cream? Sugar?"

"Black, thank you."

He gave her the cup, his hand brushing across hers. "Feel better?"

"Much." His touch made her tremble. "I can't believe I went to the King Croesus last night, pretended to shoot Simone, tried to jump out of the window. Maybe Michael is right and I am crazy. You're a psychologist. Do you think I'm crazy?"

"Of course not. You didn't have a real gun and I doubt if you really tried to jump. I think you just wanted to scare Michael, which was a pretty normal reaction, considering what he did to you. You poor darling. No, you're not crazy."

"Thank you, that means a lot to me." Unlike many other people, Fingerhood never thought of her as a nut or a bitch. Quite the contrary, she suddenly realized. His attitude showed that he saw her as a gentle fragile flower, to be protected from harm. A tea rose, perhaps. Or a violet. "It's nice to know that someone believes in me."

"You bet I believe in you. You're a courageous and wonderful woman. It's just too bad that others don't know the real you."

Anita thought it was too bad also. She liked herself a lot more when she was with Fingerhood. She felt better about herself with him. On the whole, her impulses were kinder and more generous.

"I wonder if Simone and Michael will actually get married," she mused, hoping they both rotted in hell for the grief they'd caused her. There were some people who didn't *deserve* kind impulses, she hastily decided.

"Do you think you could handle it if they did get married?" he asked solicitously.

"I'm not sure. I'm still shocked by the suddenness and sneakiness of their relationship. I'm still appalled that they could have behaved in such a tawdry fashion, but I pray that I can find it in my heart to wish them well if they go ahead with their plans."

He looked at her with pride. "That's my brave girl."

"I'm trying to be strong," she said with a sigh. "But it's not easy."

How about trying to be practical? she asked herself, remembering the wedding gown she'd foolishly bought yesterday at Queen Victoriana. Maybe it wasn't too late to return the damned thing. Maybe if she called right away, they would take the gown back and give her cash. It was a brilliant idea (particularly since she had paid for it with Michael's money), but she would have to wait until Fingerhood left. She didn't want him to find out what a silly romantic dreamer she was for buying that gown to start with.

"Drink your coffee," he said, lifting the cover off a gorgeous creamy strawberry cheesecake. "Look what I ordered for dessert."

"It's my favorite. You won't have to feed that to me."

"Too bad." There was a twinkle in his eye. "I was beginning to enjoy myself."

"So was I. What I meant was that you won't have to feed it to me because I can't eat it. My hips, you know."

"What's wrong with them?" Fingerhood admired their luscious shape through the clinging caftan. "They look sensational to me."

"Michael thinks they're too big."

"But you're not with Michael any longer."

"That's true." She would probably have to readjust her values, standards, wardrobe; it seemed to happen every time she changed men. Shortly after meeting Jack Bailey, she shoved all her pastel clothes to the back of the closet and bought new ones in bright primary colors because those were the colors Jack liked. With Michael, she never wore anything sporty or tailored, since he only liked sensuous feminine things. She wondered what Fingerhood liked other than hippy women. Yet Sally wasn't hippy, she was straight as a stick. "Shouldn't you call your fiancée?" she asked, trying to impress him with her thoughtful selfless nature. "She must be wondering what's happened to you."

"It's okay, I spoke to her last night after you fell asleep. She said that Beverly was staying over, so I'm sure they're busy talking their heads off this morning and don't miss me in the least."

Anita felt pleased that he was in no hurry to rush home. She wanted to keep him a little while longer. "You'll be an old married man soon. How does it feel, Fingerhood?"

"Nerve-racking," he admitted. "Frankly, I never thought this day would come."

That was an encouraging sign. "Why not?"

"I just never saw myself getting married."

"Until you met Sally?" she prompted him.

"Right."

"What made you change your mind? True love?"

"Yeah." He seemed uncomfortable. "Something like that."
She pressed on. "Are you and Sally planning to have children?"

"We haven't discussed it, but I guess we will. If she wants to."

"Don't *you* want to?" She couldn't figure out what was making him so uneasy.

"Sure, except I'm getting kind of old for kids."

"So am I, yet I don't think I could stand it if someone told me I would never be a mother. My greatest ambition is to have children."

Outside, a nursemaid was wheeling an infant in a shiny old-fashioned baby carriage. Anita tried to imagine where they lived and what the child's mother was like. She could see herself married to Fingerhood with children, a boy and a girl. The girl would be her favorite, even though she would go out of her way to hide it. She would dress her in exquisite lacy clothes and pamper her shamelessly. Her daughter would have her blond hair and Fingerhood's large dark eyes and people would comment on the exotic combination. The picture was so clear and distinct that she felt as if she were looking at a movie of her future life. Then she realized that the only other man she'd wanted to have children with was Jack Bailey; not once did the thought cross her mind with Michael, despite all their years together.

"I'm sure you'll get married someday and have kids," Fingerhood said to her. "You'd make a wonderful mother. I've always thought so."

"You did?"

"Yes." He nodded unhappily. "When are you going back to London?"

"After the wedding."

It was a dismal prospect. Even if Michael should let her keep the house on Cheyne Walk, she couldn't go on living there. For one thing, it held too many memories. For another, she would have to find a job and she sure as hell didn't intend to work in London, where female employees were treated like dogs. The prospect of looking for work after all those lazy mornings in bed struck terror in Anita's heart. Maybe the airline would take her back, she thought bleakly, wondering which city to live in. Chicago would remind her of Jack Bailey. New York would remind her of Fingerhood. San Francisco had too many gays. Los Angeles was too competitive. Phoenix would dry her skin out. Minneapolis was too cold. Miami was too hot. Maybe Atlanta, the South, where men were supposed to be men and chivalry still reigned.

"*You mean you're staying for my wedding?*" Fingerhood cried.

"Of course I'm staying. Why do you look so surprised?"

"I thought you'd go back to London on the next plane."

"And give Simone the satisfaction of knowing she'd driven me away? Never."

"You have guts, Anita." His eyes were filled with admiration. "I didn't realize how much."

Neither did she until now. Her life was a shambles for the umpteenth time, her health was a disaster area, she was forty years old and didn't know where she was going or how she was going to live, but she'd be damned if she would slink away like a thief in the night. Simone was the one who had stolen Michael. Let *her* do the slinking.

"I was in love with you fifteen years ago," Fingerhood suddenly blurted out. "Did you know that?"

She couldn't believe her ears. "No, I had no idea. Why didn't you say something?"

"I was embarrassed. You were so hung up on Smiling Jack that half the time you didn't realize I was alive."

"That's silly. We had an affair, remember?"

"Sure. You used to call me 'Jack' without being aware of it."

"I did? I'm sorry. You should have told me how you felt."

"Would it have made a difference?"

"Maybe. Probably. Absolutely."

Why did she always fall in love with the wrong man? Jack had betrayed her (just like Michael), and before her own wedding day at that. She thought of the different course her life might have taken had he not suffered that heart attack, had they gotten married as planned. Maybe they would be divorced by now, but she couldn't believe she would feel this miserable or this abandoned. At least she would have had the semblance of a normal family life, even if only for a while: a husband, a home, children, sharing the good and the bad.

Instead what she had at the moment was a big fat nothing. If Michael had never left Lady Philippa, never asked her to marry him, Anita could have understood. What she could not understand or forgive was his leaving her for Simone.

"I think I'm still a little in love with you," Fingerhood said, looking at her with hopeful eyes. "Maybe more than a little."

"Do you know what you're saying?" Anita's heart quickened. Could he possibly mean it? "You're getting married in less than a week."

"One thing has nothing to do with the other."

"Wait just a minute," she said sharply. "If you imagine you're going to have one last fling with me before you march off into the sunset with Sally, you're sadly mistaken. Nothing doing. Forget it, Fingerhood."

*One last fling.* How final it sounded, like a door closing on his future. The barren image startled him. Was that how he envisioned life with Sally? As the end?

"That wasn't what I meant," he quickly said, afraid of offending her, losing her. "You must know that I'd never try to take advantage of you, please don't think that. It's just that I've been going out of my mind ever since you walked into my apartment yesterday afternoon. I can't stop fantasizing about you, desiring you, I even dreamed about you last night. It's crazy, but I can't control myself. I'm obsessed with you, Anita."

His words brought that blonde-haired, brown-eyed little girl back into focus again. This time Anita saw her climbing up on Fingerhood's lap, laughing. He was laughing back, tickling his daughter.

"I'm pretty obsessed with you, too," she said.

He blinked in astonishment. "You *are*?"

"Yes. And maybe more than obsessed."

"What do you mean?" he croaked.

"I mean, I'm in love with you, Fingerhood."

For a moment he couldn't speak. "Really?" he finally managed to say.

"Really and truly."

"Why didn't you tell me?"

"For the same reason you didn't tell me fifteen years ago. I was embarrassed. Don't forget, you'd already committed yourself to Sally."

"Sally, yes, she has been an obstacle." To his surprise, he was using the past tense. "Wait a minute. Are you serious, Anita? Do you mean it? You're not kidding, are you?"

"I wouldn't kid about something so important," she said with a beguiling, lingering smile. "I've probably always loved you, but was too stupid to realize it."

"Jesus, that's wonderful! Fabulous! Spectacular! I'm the happiest man alive!" He leaped out of the chair, then slowly slunk back into it. "I just thought of something. How can I marry Sally, feeling the way I do? It wouldn't be fair to her or to me."

"It wouldn't be fair to me, either."

"You're right," he said in an awed tone. "You're absolutely right."

"You bet I am." Anita was sick to death of being taken advantage of, cheated on, thrown over for other women. "The question is, what are you going to do about it?"

"*Do?*" he weakly asked.

"You just admitted that marrying Sally would be a disservice to the three of us. So what I want to know is, how do you intend to rectify matters?"

"I'm not sure. Give me a chance to think." The possibility that he might have to call off his long-awaited nuptials was just beginning to dawn on Fingerhood. It made his head swim with confusion, excitement, dread. How could he weasel out, considering the pact that he and Sally had made? If he dumped her now, she might never be free of drugs. "All the wedding preparations have been taken care of," he miserably told Anita. "We've hired a minister, asked people to stand up for us, Lou's daughter has agreed to provide the music, my mother is so happy she hasn't stopped crying for a week."

"You can't marry Sally to please your mother."

"I'm aware of that." His eyes met hers head-on. "But I still find it hard to believe that you love me. You're not just feeling grateful because of the way I came over here last night, are you? If that's what it is, you only have to tell me and I'd understand. Sometimes people confuse gratitude with love."

"Silly man."

She dragged him to his feet, flung her arms around him, and pressed her body to his. She wasn't wearing a stitch beneath the pink silk caftan and she knew he could feel it.

She pressed more forcefully, then kissed him on the mouth with all the fiery passion that had been building up ever since she realized she stood a chance with him. This was one man who wouldn't get away!

"I adore you," she said when they drew apart. "I'm mad about you. When you touch me, I go to pieces."

"You do?"

"Yes, I can feel myself get all mushy inside."

"You can?"

"Oh yes, it feels so good." She nuzzled his neck. "Mmmmmmmm, that's nice, delicious. *You're* nice. I want so much to please you."

Fingerhood's lust knew no bounds. Sally hadn't wanted to please him in months, he'd forgotten what pleasure was. Aware of Anita's belly rubbing against him, he became dizzy, crazed, hard as a rock. He had to pull himself together, he thought, he had to be logical. Was Sally's cocaine habit his responsibility? In a way, yes. But what about his responsibility to himself? What about *his* happiness, not to mention Anita's?

"We've told Some Like It Hot to serve Chicken Turban for the main course," he mumbled, feeling his erection turn to stone. "Vanessa plans to bake a spectacular five-tiered cake, Simone's children are going to act as flower girl and ring-bearer, Sally has bought a wedding gown . . ."

He droned on, but Anita had stopped listening. His unexpected reference to Simone clinched it. It was now or never, she decided, pressing her soft, seductive, semiclad body against him with renewed determination.

"I bought a wedding gown too," she whispered, nibbling his earlobe.

Beverly had opened her eyes at dawn and found herself in an unfamiliar bedroom, wearing an unfamiliar nightgown, feeling sick. Cursed with a throbbing headache, an acid stomach, a galloping heartbeat, and partial amnesia, she knew that something terrible had happened, but *what*?

As she sat up in bed, it came back to her. After two years of painstaking sobriety, she'd fallen off the wagon with a thud. She would have liked to place the blame on all the unsettling things that happened yesterday: that terrible lunch with Anita, learning about Sally and Fingerhood's wedding plans, seeing Lou and Peter come marching in together, arm in arm. But she knew better. She started drinking again because she was a drunk. Her first reaction was one of infinite regret; her second reaction was to stagger into Fingerhood's living room for a hair of the dog. To her relief, he had an abundant supply of Cutty Sark. She found a glass and poured. By the time Sally awakened hours later, Beverly had drunk herself out of the shakes into a semblance of normalcy, gotten dressed in yesterday's clothes, and was reading the New York *Times*.

"Mother, there's something I have to talk to you about." Sally rubbed the sleep from her eyes, feeling drained. She'd spent the night having ominous dreams about her wedding and at one point woke herself up screaming. Fortunately, Fingerhood wasn't there to hear her. "I don't know how much you remember, but you passed out in the middle of dinner and I had to put you to bed in the guest room."

"That was sweet of you, darling. I hope I wasn't too much trouble." She's going to berate me for my drinking, Beverly thought, mortified. "I'm not used to champagne, it must have gone to my head."

"It's not the champagne I want to talk to you about. It's the bruises on your body. I couldn't help seeing them when I undressed you, and frankly, I was shocked. They're dreadful. Where did you get them? What happened?"

Beverly felt trapped, conflicted, confused. To say that Dwight was responsible for pummeling her black and blue was not an admission she felt ready to make, at least not to Sally, who looked like a little girl in her short summer nightgown, her face devoid of makeup. And yet to think of another culprit was beyond her mental capacities at the moment.

"Darling, could we discuss this some other time?" she suggested with an appeasing smile. "It's such a lovely morning. I don't see any reason to spoil it by talking about unpleasant things, do you?"

"But, Mother, someone obviously did this to you. Those bruises didn't get there by themselves." Sally was outraged, indignant, exactly what Beverly knew she herself should be and wasn't. "It was Dwight, wasn't it?"

Beverly hedged, wishing her hangover would go away, wishing Sally had not undressed her, wishing her second husband was not a brute. "Not exactly," she replied.

"What do you mean? Either Dwight did this to you or he didn't. Which is it?"

"It's not so simple."

"But it is, Mother. Either Dwight beat the shit out of you or some other man did." Her eyes filled with horror. "You weren't attacked when you drove cross-country, were you?"

Beverly was tempted to lie and say that it had been a stranger, a madman, a lunatic who forced her car off the road in the middle of nowhere and made her submit to unmentionable acts. The reason she felt tempted was that she would then be considered an innocent victim, whereas if she told the truth, there'd be no denying her complicity. *It's not my fault, I'm not to blame!* The words ran hollow in her ears. She knew that it was partly her fault, if not at the start, then certainly afterward, for having let the assault continue unchecked and unchallenged. Even worse than that, even more shameful was that she felt like crawling back to Dwight and pretending nothing was wrong. She wanted to believe her husband did not have a serious problem, because if he didn't, then she didn't.

"Mother, aren't you going to say anything? I'm waiting for an answer."

Beverly wondered why their roles had become reversed. Why was Sally acting like the mother and why was she feeling like the child? She wished she could have a drink to tide her over this, just one, but she had done Sally enough harm with her drinking and endless evasions about everything under the sun. Maybe if she were truthful for once in her life, Sally would be truthful with her. There was so much she still didn't understand about her daughter's disappearance.

"No, I wasn't raped and I wasn't attacked by a stranger," she said. "It was Dwight."

"Oh, Mother!"

"You must let me explain, darling. It's not the way you think. You mustn't jump to all sorts of unfair conclusions."

"How can you say that?" Fear and disillusionment shone in Sally's eyes, as though some basic belief of hers had been shattered forever. "Why are you trying to protect him after what he did to you? Why haven't you had him arrested? How can you live with someone like that?" She shuddered. "Is that why you came to New York alone? Because you're running away from Dwight? Oh Mother, how awful."

"I'm not running away, I'm merely putting some breathing space between us." Beverly was afraid she might have gone too far and misgauged Sally's ability to handle this. "We both need to be alone and get things in perspective. Then, when I return to Wyoming, we intend to seek professional help and work this problem out."

Sally's mouth fell open. *"You mean you're going back to him?"*

"Why are you so shocked? Of course I'm going back. He's my husband."

"I don't believe this." Sally shook her head in denial. "I can't believe I'm hearing this. It's not possible."

Despite herself, Beverly laughed. "Why not? What do you expect me to do? Run away because my marriage isn't one hundred percent perfect? File for divorce? Find another man? Become a lesbian? Join a convent?"

"I don't see what's so unfeasible about getting a divorce or looking for another man. In fact, I should think you'd have already taken steps in those directions. Don't you want to get out of this mess? Aren't you appalled by it?"

"Certainly I'm appalled, but you overlook one very important fact. I happen to be in love with Dwight."

Sally measured her carefully. "Even after all he's done to you?"

"Even after that. Haven't you ever heard of loving someone in spite of his faults?"

"Sure, but there are limits."

"That's right, and each person must draw her own."

"So what you're saying is that Dwight beating you up is still within your limits of acceptability."

"In a manner of speaking, yes. But only because I believe that in time he'll overcome his problem. If I didn't believe that, I would leave him right now."

Sally went to the kitchen and came back with two cups of coffee, one of which she gave to Beverly in the same way that for years Beverly had given her cereal and orange juice: no questions asked.

"I don't understand you, Mother, but then, I never have." The anger had drained out of her and was replaced by a quiet bewilderment. "I don't understand why you drink, why you're unhappy, why you divorced Daddy, why you make excuses for Dwight. Is the sex that sensational?"

"Really, Sally."

"Really *what*? Don't act so demure, Mother. You've always been a hot number, this is no time to start denying it."

The cup shook in Beverly's hand. Sex was a subject that she and Sally hardly ever discussed, and then only in the most vague and general manner. "I'm not trying to deny anything, although I find your description of me rather flamboyant. How did we get sidetracked onto sex, anyway?"

"We didn't. I brought it up, I think it's relevant. Ever since I was a child, I saw the way men used to stare at you, the look they'd get in their eyes when you came into a room. Daddy too, and later Dwight. I didn't know what it meant at first, but it fascinated me. When I got older and figured it out, it continued to fascinate me, but by then I'd become jealous. I felt inadequate compared to you. I didn't know how to compete."

"Compete?" They were in dangerous waters. "Why would you want to compete sexually with your own mother?"

"Maybe what I'm saying is that I didn't see how I could measure up to your standards. You were beautiful, voluptuous, seductive. Whereas I was tall, scrawny, and flat-chested. I hated that. I wanted to look like you. Instead, I looked like Daddy's side of the family, which seems to work just great for men, but not for women. You can't imagine how ugly I felt, how inferior. I used to wonder if a man would ever find me attractive, but I didn't see how he could."

Beverly leaned back against Fingerhood's sofa, wishing that Peter were here to help her with this. Sally's anguish was like a burning recrimination. What did I do wrong? she asked herself. What should I have done differently?

"Darling, you were never ugly," she said. "I don't know where you got that image of yourself, but it's totally inaccurate. You were always a pretty child."

"I got it from having a sex bomb for a mother."

The phrase caught Beverly off guard. *A sex bomb*. How extraordinary that that was how her daughter should perceive her. How ironic and ludicrous. If she had been the sex bomb of Sally's fantasy, Dwight would never have turned violent. If she hadn't resisted his advances for two years, she would not be black and blue this minute. Some sex bomb. She remembered being jealous of her own mother, who resembled Elizabeth Taylor. When she was growing up in Salt Lake

City she used to cry because she knew she would never have her mother's green eyes, black hair, or devastating attraction for men. Like Sally, she imagined her mother as leading the kind of wild erotic life she could never hope to emulate, and it made her feel miserable, also curious. She would often stare at her mother, trying to fathom what she was like in the act of love. Had Sally done that with her? Probably. Beverly shook her head, dismayed by the unreality of both their illusions. In later years she discovered that her mother had been celibate for a long time, thanks to having discovered Jesus Christ and the joys of puritanical living. What irony.

"Do you know the real reason I ran away from college?" Sally was saying, caught up in her own web of confession. "Because I needed to prove I was desirable. None of the boys on campus thought so, but I pretended they were too young for their opinions to matter. I figured if I became a high-fashion model, no one would ever question my sexiness again. And in the world of modeling, there's almost no such thing as being too tall, too thin, or too flat-chested. It seemed made to order for me, but even there I didn't have what it took." She had lied to Fingerhood about why she gave it up, too embarrassed to reveal the true reason. "They said I tensed up in front of the camera and that my smile wasn't grabby enough. What they meant was, I couldn't sell sex."

"Oh, darling, I'm so sorry."

"That's why I called Fingerhood. By then I was desperate to have a man find me desirable, and not just any man, but one who'd been around and whose opinion counted for something. I planned to have an affair with him before I ever laid eyes on him. I planned to get him to fall in love with me if it was the last thing I ever did. I planned to prove that I could be as good in bed as you, maybe better. And I succeeded." She faced Beverly defiantly, guiltily, needily. "What do you think of that, Mother?"

"I think I've failed you terribly. I wish I could go back and do it all over again, so that you needn't have suffered so much pain." She smoothed Sally's hair, the way she used to when she was a child. "I wish I had been a better mother, but I did the best I could."

"Then you're not angry at me?" Sally was surprised.

"How could I be angry? You grew up feeling inadequate,

which means that I didn't help you gain the confidence you needed. If anyone has the right to be angry, it's you.''

"I was for a long time. I remember a jade-green nightgown of yours, it had spaghetti straps and an empire bodice. Once I came home from school early and you were still in bed, doing your nails, wearing that gown, your hair falling over your naked shoulders. And I thought: *that's my beautiful sexy mother, whom I'll never be like*. I carried that picture of you around for years. It sounds ridiculous, doesn't it?''

"No, sweetheart, it sounds poignant. It goes to show how little we know about each other's feelings, even those of our own children. But that's all in the past. You're an attractive woman now in your own right and you're about to be married. So maybe this story has a happy ending after all.''

"I hope so,'' Sally said, without conviction.

"I admit I was upset when I found out about you and Fingerhood, but now that I've seen you together, I think it will be a good marriage.'' She wanted to give her as much belated support as she could. "By the way, where is your future husband? Still asleep?''

Sally explained about his having been called to the Gramercy Regency in the middle of the night to pacify Anita. "She was in pretty bad shape, so he stayed over to keep an eye on her.''

"And you didn't object?''

"Why should I?''

"Oh, darling, how can you be so innocent and trusting? Don't you know what a manipulative, scheming, man-hungry bitch Anita is? How could you let Fingerhood go there by himself? You should have gone with him and protected your interests.''

"That's the difference between your generation and mine. You tend to think of other women as the enemy, whereas I think of them as the ally. I admit I don't like Anita, but I do feel sorry for her. Finding out that Michael left her for Simone must have been a real kick in the head.''

"*Michael left her for Simone?*''

"That's right, you missed all the excitement.'' Beverly had been passed out cold in the guest room, she realized. "Michael Harding has fallen in love with Simone and asked her to marry him. How do you like that for an interesting development?'' To her surprise, Beverly began to laugh so hard that

Sally didn't think she was ever going to stop. "Why do you consider that so funny, Mother?"

"Funny?" Beverly managed to say between gasps. "I consider it hilarious. The idea of Anita being left high and dry fills me with glee, and I'm not ashamed to admit it. But if I were you, I'd get Fingerhood out of her clutches fast. Otherwise, you might never see him again."

"Don't be silly, Mother. I trust him. He would never do anything like that. He's very protective of me."

"You're lucky."

Beverly wished that Dwight were protective of her, nurturing and caring. Instead he only seemed to care about his own lack of achievement, it gnawed at him constantly, making him feel like a failure. He once told Beverly that no matter what he accomplished, he would still be stuck with a poor background, inferior schooling, and parents that never had the social graces she'd grown up with. She couldn't understand why it should matter so much at this late date, and he couldn't understand her lack of sympathy. "My rich bitch of a wife" was how he referred to her after he'd had one too many bourbons and a bad day at the *Herald*. Was he upset by the disappearance of his rich bitch of a wife? Beverly wondered. What if he were relieved that she'd walked out and left him in peace? What if he were indifferent? The thought stung.

"Mother, were you nervous before you married Daddy?"

"Yes, and before I married Dwight, too." Beverly berated herself for thinking of her own problems at a time when Sally needed guidance and advice. Yet with one divorce behind her and a second marriage in trouble, who was she to hand out words of wisdom? "All brides are nervous, darling. It comes with the territory, as they say."

"Actually, I'm more than nervous. I'm scared stiff."

"You'd be a damned fool if you weren't. You're about to make a lifelong commitment. But believe me, you'll be fine as soon as you're standing at the altar repeating your vows. That's when all the nerves and apprehension disappear, your self-confidence returns, and you know that you've made the right choice."

"What if I haven't?"

"What do you mean?"

"I mean, what if my marrying Fingerhood is a terrible mistake?"

"Why would it be a mistake?"

"It's hard to explain."

"Try."

Sally shook her head. "I can't."

"I don't understand. You love him, don't you?"

"Yes, but—"

"But *what*, darling?"

Her mother's adamant refusal to leave Dwight came to mind. Beverly loved him enough to stay in the marriage through the proverbial thick and thin. Sally knew she would never love Fingerhood that way. The only reason she wanted to marry him was that in a moment of weakness she had thought that with his support she could kick drugs. But how could she tell that to her mother? For years she'd criticized, denigrated, and complained about Beverly's addiction to alcohol. How could she now admit that she was an addict too?

"I just can't explain," she said.

Beverly gazed at her daughter, trying to fathom whether this was the usual prewedding jitters or whether something she didn't know about had plunged Sally into a state of alarm. "How can I help you if you don't tell me what's bothering you?"

"No one can help me."

People always exaggerated their problems, Beverly thought, knowing she did it too. Dwight was undoubtedly devastated by her unexplained departure. He must have called all her friends and the police by now, blaming himself for having driven her away. He might even be feeling suicidal. The image consoled her immensely.

"Is it really as bad as all that?" she asked Sally.

"It's worse."

"How? Talk to me."

"Talking won't do any good."

She should never have made that pact with Fingerhood. *Marriage for drug surrender.* She'd been stupid to think she could go through with it, she'd been naive and unrealistic. Detoxified and rehabilitated, she would be forced to face herself without a crutch of any kind, and the prospect was horrifying. She still had memories of the passionate woman she'd been for a little while, the one who aroused Fingerhood to fever pitch and made him forget all other women as he held her in his arms and whispered how important she was to him. That feeling of closeness went beyond the physical, it was a bonding of souls on the deepest, most intimate level. She wanted, *needed* that intimacy once more. The fact that cocaine had failed her as an aphrodisiac didn't make her lose faith in the drug, quite the opposite. She stubbornly clung to its imputed powers of pleasure-enhancement, feeling that if it had worked before it could work again. It had to work. It was all that stood between her idealized image of herself and the skinny, frightened, unloved girl who haunted her dreams and made her scream in her sleep.

"Are you afraid that Fingerhood will be unfaithful after you're married?" Beverly asked. "Is that why you're upset?"

"I'm upset because . . ." The thought of being hospitalized for cocaine addiction had reduced her to panic. She wanted a toot right now, twenty toots. She wanted to feel good, elated, in control. She didn't want all that gorgeous self-assurance taken away from her. She would die without it. "I'm upset because—"

"Because *what*?" Beverly was looking at her with alarm. "Tell me."

"I can't talk." Sally felt like a fish floundering on the shore, caught, trapped. Her pulse was racing and she was suffocating. "I can't breathe."

"Easy, darling, it's going to be all right." Beverly took her hands, rubbed them, warmed them. "You're hyperventilating. It feels worse than it is. Just speak slowly, calmly. Tell me what's wrong."

The words rushed out of her like an express train. "I don't love Fingerhood enough to go through with the wedding."

Then she fell into her mother's arms, gasping for air.

When Lou arrived home after spending the night with Keith, her skin was glowing in a way it hadn't glowed for years. She observed herself carefully in the lobby mirror while waiting for the elevator, and even in that lousy lighting, she looked radiant. The way she felt was another matter: both exhilarated and guilt-ridden, she dreaded the initial confrontation with Vanessa.

"I'm back," she said, trying to act casual and thinking of the many times Vanessa had stayed out all night. "What's happening?"

"Jean Pierre called. He wants us to do a big Fourth of July buffet dinner." Vanessa was putting breasts of chicken into the food processor, adding egg whites, heavy cream, seasonings. "And Liberation won't eat her breakfast."

Lou sat down on one of the pine chairs flanking the kitchen table, aware of a wet, sticky, achy sensation deep inside her. *Use it or you'll lose it,* the sex manuals threatened. Well, she had used it after a four-year hiatus and now felt like she'd just gotten laid for the first time. It was such an extraordinary sensation that it took all of her willpower to focus on more mundane matters. "If Liberation won't eat her breakfast, you must have given her something she doesn't like. What was it?"

"Tunafish."

"*People* tunafish? You know she doesn't eat that, it happens to be bad for cats. Why didn't you give her regular cat food?"

Vanessa turned off the processor and emptied its contents into four ring molds, then began reloading with more of the same. She still hadn't looked Lou in the eye. "Because there isn't any cat food."

"That's impossible." Lou went to the cupboard and moved canisters of whole-wheat pastry flour aside, reaching back on the shelf to produce several cans of Chopped Platter. "What do you call this?"

"I call it cat food and I also call it magic," Vanessa said above the sound of the motor. She appeared even younger than usual in an oversized shirt and cut-off denim shorts, her long hair held back with a frayed pink ribbon. "How was I to know where you hide these things? What am I, a mind reader?"

Liberation chose that moment to crawl out from under the long pine table and emit a bloodcurdling yowl. Lou picked her up and kissed her soft fur. "Don't cry, little girl. Your aunt isn't very bright sometimes, but I'm going to give you your breakfast now." She opened the can and placed the cat's dish in its regular corner.

"That's right," Vanessa said dourly. "Blame me for everything."

"What else have I blamed you for?"

"Never mind."

"If you have something to say, say it."

"I don't have anything to say."

"Good." She watched Vanessa fill four more ring molds with the chicken mixture. "What's that? It looks yummy."

"If you'd been home when Fingerhood called last night, you would know. This is Turban of Chicken for his god-damned wedding."

"So you do have something to say. Look, Vanessa, I could remind you of all the times *you* weren't home when far more urgent matters were at stake, but why quibble? I'm willing to forgive and forget. How about extending me the same courtesy?"

"In a pig's eye. Have you been up since six this morning trying to figure out how to make Chopped Liver Swans for fifty guests?"

"Since when did the Swans get into the act?"

"Since Fingerhood asked me to forget the Striped Bass in Aspic with Cucumber Mousse, and substitute the Swans as a favor to his mother. She wants them with *gribinitz*, yet."

"What's *gribinitz*?"

"Only the heart and soul of Jewish cooking. They're crack-lings made from chicken skin, fat, and onions. And I'll have you know that aside from the Swans taking forever to prepare, they can't be frozen either. Merely stored in the fridge, taking up tons of space."

"Stop complaining and get a couple of sous chefs to help out." Lou chuckled at the image of serious young cooks with *nouvelle cuisine* aspirations making Chopped Liver Swans. "What did you tell Jean Pierre?"

"That you would call him back."

"I will. In a little while."

"Too drained to take care of business?" Vanessa asked snidely. "It must have been quite a night."

"It was."

She poured herself a cup of coffee, relieved that Keith hadn't tried to make love to her again this morning. Aside from her distaste for A.M. sex, she was so exhausted that she wouldn't have been able to respond. She'd forgotten how energetic it could be with a man. To her surprise, he turned out to be a wickedly good lover. To her double surprise, he said the same about her.

"How did you think I'd be?" she asked, playing one of her favorite games.

"Cool. A little detached. Definitely on guard."

"And?"

"And you weren't."

"Stop teasing. How was I?"

They were sitting up in bed smoking the cliched after-sex cigarette and eating praline ice cream laced with cognac. When she'd kissed him a second ago, his mouth was a lovely combination of praline, cognac, tobacco, and lingering desire.

"You were intense, passionate, and very feminine," he said.

"What do you mean by feminine?"

"Melting."

"It sounds like a pot of chocolate."

"Receptive, welcoming." He searched for a more accurate word. "Hot."

"I was hot?"

"I thought I'd get scorched. Don't you believe me? You look skeptical. It's a compliment, you know."

"I'm just surprised. I was afraid I might not be able to respond."

He took her empty ice-cream dish and placed it with his on the end table. "Why were you afraid of that?"

"I haven't been with a man in a long time."

"But you've been with somebody."

She stared at him. "How did you know?"

"Yesterday at Fingerhood's, before you arrived, that flashy blond said you've been living with your business partner. It's true, isn't it?"

"Yes." Lou watched the ember of her cigarette die in Keith Rinehart's ashtray from the Palace Hotel in Madrid. She was pleased that he'd found Anita flashy, displeased by what he'd learned. "Vanessa and I have been together for four years. Does it bother you?"

"You mean, that she's a woman? No, not that part. What bothers me is that you're involved with someone else. I'm jealous, Deidre. I want you to be involved with me."

She realized that whenever he called her "Deidre," something serious was at stake. She longed to put his anxieties at rest by saying that she and Vanessa were about to break up and therefore she was a free agent. Still, it wouldn't be fair. Within the last twenty-four hours Vanessa's anger might have subsided, causing her to change her mind about leaving. If that should happen, Lou wanted them to be able to talk things over and not feel hindered by the pressure of another commitment.

"I *am* involved with you," she said. "I won't say any more than that right now because my situation at home is confused."

"See if you can unconfuse it. Vanessa is occupying the role I'd like for myself."

"She is?"

He nodded decisively. "I want to be your lover and I want to be your partner."

"Partner? In Some Like It Hot?"

"Sure. Don't you think we'd make a great team?"

"I hadn't considered it." His forthrightness disarmed her. "I don't know what to tell you."

"You mean you might decide to stay with her?"

"It's possible."

"I'm sorry to hear that, Deidre. I was hoping you would fall into my arms, vowing to get rid of all other entanglements." He smiled in a self-deprecating way. "Obviously, I overrate myself."

"No, what you overrate is everyone else's ability to move as quickly as you." She didn't want to lose him. She wanted to keep him dangling until the coast was clear. "I find you very appealing, very charming, but you're asking an awful lot of me. We've just met."

"What you're saying is, you don't trust me."

"Should I?"

"Sure. I trust you."

"You don't have as much at stake. Some Like It Hot is one of the most successful catering companies in New York. Do you blame me if I'm somewhat paranoid about being used because of it?"

"Not at all."

She held his gaze. "You're angry."

"Disappointed." He swung his legs onto the floor. "How about some cognac? No ice cream this time."

"I think that's a good idea."

"Booze has its place," he agreed. "Right now it can help blot out this damned irresolution, which I'm having trouble dealing with. I'm a very impatient person. A very neat one, too. I like my relationships all nice and tidy, no loose ends.

It's a defect I keep intending to correct, but so far I haven't had much luck.''

That he was a man who made his own luck seemed obvious to Lou. Had he charmed her, flattered her, and seduced her only so that she would get rid of Vanessa and make him a partner? Were any of his feelings for her genuine? Or was she being conned right down the line by a smooth-talking hustler?

"One cognac for you and one for me." He placed the glass in her hand. "Here's to our future, Deidre, which I hope will be clear sailing."

"I'll drink to that."

Despite her fears and reservations, he would probably be nice to have as a partner. Smart, imaginative, enterprising. Maybe the business could use some new blood; in the last year it had been coasting along on past success. She could redecorate Vanessa's room for him, get rid of that sign—LIB MEANS NEVER HAVING TO SAY YOU CAME—and rename the cat Clint Eastwood. There was only one problem: how could she be sure what he was after—her love or the company's profits?

"What are you thinking?" he asked. He'd gotten back in bed but was lying on top of the covers now, unclothed, his long tanned legs flexed at the knees, blond hair glistening in the dim bedroom light. "Are you thinking nice thoughts?"

She put her arms around him and smelled a tangy aftershave, which he must have just put on. He didn't miss a trick. Had he brushed his teeth, too? She kissed him lightly on the lips. Yes, minty fresh.

"Why don't you tell me about yourself?" she said. "Aside from the fact that you're a gourmet chef, terrific lover, and like to follow strange women around New York, I don't know much about you."

"What would you like to know?"

"Why don't you start by telling me where you were born?"

"Okay."

Lou leaned back against his shoulder, sipped her cognac, and waited for him to assure her that he was more than just a smooth-talking hustler. . . .

"If you're agreeable, I'm willing to let you buy me out," Vanessa declared, starting to shell pistachio nuts. "I've been told that two hundred thou is a fair price. You can pay it to

me over eight years—in twenty-five-thousand-dollar install-
ments. At ten percent interest. How does that grab you?"

"Buy you out? I didn't realize we had reached that stage of
negotiations. Are you sure this is what you want?"

"Quite sure. I don't care to be your partner anymore, and
I'm offering you what I think is a fair deal." The mound of
shelled nuts grew higher. "I discussed it with our lawyer this
morning, and those are the terms he suggested. If you don't
believe me, call him yourself."

"I believe you. I'm just surprised by how fast you've
worked. But if I buy you out, what will you do?"

"Go to Paris and study at Cordon Bleu. It's something I've
wanted to tackle for a long time, and this strikes me as the
perfect opportunity. I thought I'd leave next month."

"So soon? I mean, it almost *is* next month. This is the end
of June."

"I know."

How could she walk away so easily, seemingly so painlessly?
That she wanted Vanessa to go was beside the point. Lou
hated the feeling of being discarded in this blithe a manner.
"It's an awfully sudden decision," she pointed out. "Maybe
you should give it more thought."

"That's all I've been doing for the last twenty-four hours,
and the conclusion I've reached is that I can't go on being
your partner without also being your lover. Since there's no
point in pursuing the latter, I'm pulling out altogether."

"Why isn't there any point in pursuing it?"

"Because you're ashamed of our relationship, as proven by
the fact that you won't even tell your own daughter about it."
The mound of shelled pistachio nuts had grown to an alarm-
ing height and Vanessa started to dice prosciutto. "Plus
you've been unfaithful."

"What about all the times you were unfaithful?"

"Those were one-night stands. They didn't mean anything."

"How do you know this doesn't mean anything either?"

"Because I saw how attracted you were to Sally, remember?
I saw it!" Vanessa whirled around, giving full vent to her
anger at last. "You went shopping with her yesterday, you
went to lunch with her, and you went to bed with her. Since
you're not a casual person, I can only conclude this is a
serious piece of business on your part. I don't profess to
understand why you chose who you chose, but I sure recog-

nize the choice for what it is: betrayal. And I'm not interested in hanging around trying to compete with a confused kid like Sally Northrop, okay?''

"*Sally Northrop?*"

"Don't play dumb."

"You think I went to bed with *Sally Northrop*?"

"I suppose you're going to sit there and deny it."

At first Lou was stunned. Then laughter began pouring out of her with such force that the cat raced from the kitchen, yowling. "Come back, Clint Eastwood. You're missing the best part."

"Why are you calling Liberation 'Clint Eastwood'?" Vanessa asked. "Why are you laughing? What the hell's the matter with you?"

"I can't help it. It strikes me so funny." She wiped the tears from her eyes. "In your wildest dreams, how could you possibly imagine I was with *Sally Northrop*? Honestly, Vanessa, grow up."

"Are you pretending you weren't with her?"

"Of course I wasn't, you fool. Where did you get such a harebrained idea? *Sally Northrop*?" She had to control another attack of hysteria. "I can't believe that's what you seriously thought."

A shade of doubt glimmered in Vanessa's eyes. "Don't tell me you picked up a stranger, Lou."

"Okay, I won't tell you that."

"And don't tell me you slept over at Joan's."

"I won't tell you that, either."

"Then where were you?" Vanessa was sprinkling shelled pistachio nuts and diced prosciutto over the chicken mixture in eight ring molds. "At an all-night movie?"

Lou thought of the times she'd wondered where Vanessa had been. It was gratifying to have the shoe on the other foot for a change. "No, I was in bed with a man."

Vanessa's reaction could not have been more shocked and disbelieving than if Lou had said she was in bed with Yasir Arafat. "You're lying," she replied. "You're just saying that to hurt me, to get back at me for my own infidelities. It won't work, Lou. I know you're making this up."

Lou lit a cigarette, pleased that Keith smoked too. Non-smokers like Vanessa were forever giving her a hard time. "Why would I do that?"

"Because you're pissed off that I'm pulling out of Some Like It Hot. You don't know where you're going to get another cook, let alone another built-in lover. If I were in your place, I'd probably say something equally vicious." Vanessa covered the shelled nuts and prosciutto with more of the chicken mixture. "I guess I should be flattered that you're upset enough to want to hurt me."

"I'm not upset. I'm relieved."

"Good try, Lou, but you can't fool me."

"I'm not trying to fool you. I'm trying to say that you're wrong about Sally, wrong about my feelings, wrong about everything."

Vanessa covered the ring molds with aluminum foil, put them in pans of hot water, and placed them in the oven. "If I'm wrong, why don't you enlighten me?" she smugly said. "Tell me where you were last night."

"I don't think you'd like to know."

"Why not? Do you imagine I'll go to pieces? You overestimate yourself, Lou." She began to melt butter in a saucepan for Watercress Sauce. "Come on, let's hear it. I promise not to faint."

"Just remember this was your idea."

"I'll bear that in mind," Vanessa replied with a patronizing smile.

"Okay, I spent the night with a man named Keith Rinehart who is not only slightly crazy about me, but who happens to be a gourmet cook. He has diplomas from La Varenne and—are you ready for this?—Madeleine Kammen's school in Annecy, not to mention Cordon Bleu. To say that he would leap at the chance of becoming my partner is an understatement. It would be more accurate to say that he is *dying* to become professionally involved with Some Like It Hot."

She was gratified to watch the smugness fade from Vanessa's face and total horror engulf it. "Keith was interested in Some Like It Hot before we ever met, and as I've already said, he's more than interested in me. He seems to be smitten, despite our short acquaintance. So you see, Vanessa, I'm not at all worried about replacing you either as a partner or as a lover. Is there anything else you'd like to know? Otherwise, I'm going to sleep. It's been a long night."

Vanessa picked up the saucepan with the Watercress Sauce and hurled it against the far kitchen wall, where it hit one of her copper *au gratins* with a resounding bang. A dark green liquid dribbled down the sparkling white wall. Then she ripped off her apron, hands trembling, eyes blazing.

"I always knew you weren't serious about your radical feminism, but I never thought you'd sink so low as to jump into bed with the enemy. Never! It just goes to prove what a hypocritical, two-faced, middle-class, conventional jerk you really are. I'm ashamed that I was ever involved with you. I'm ashamed to say I know you. I hope that you and this Keith Rinehart idiot find happiness in the missionary position, or will it be doggie style? You being the dog, of course. I hope the two of you go jogging together, you in your Jogbra and he in his Jogstrap. Just do me a favor, Lou. When you discover what a sexist oppressor he is, don't come crawling back to me and say that you've rediscovered radical feminism and want to pick up where we left off, because I won't give you the time of day. Is that clear?"

"Perfectly."

"Good!"

"There's just one more thing, Vanessa."

"What's that?"

Lou smiled sweetly. "Fuck radical feminism."

# III

# *THE WEDDING*

# 10

Two days later, everyone knew that Sally and Fingerhood had called off their wedding and that he was marrying Anita instead. The reaction to this bombshell varied immensely.

Beverly burst into tears—first of relief and then of regret when she learned the reason why. Peter went out and bought a shotgun with which to kill Fingerhood, whom he was convinced had gotten his daughter hooked on cocaine. Lou repeated her theory that men saw everything through their pricks. Joan asked her if Mink & Sable still had to play at the wedding (Lou said, "Hell no!"). Vanessa stuck her tongue out at Lou and jeered, "I told you Sally would never marry that creep." Keith tried unsuccessfully to get a refund at Barney's on his best man's suit, then informed Anita that he was standing up for Fingerhood whether she liked him or not. Sir Michael Harding sang "God Save the Queen" with such enthusiasm that the switchboard at the King Croesus told him he was disturbing the peace. Simone sang the "Marseillaise" with equal enthusiasm. Rima and Prince asked her whether the change in brides had anything to do with *The Fingerhood Position* (Simone stopped singing long enough to say, "Maybe"). Mrs. Fingerhood fainted dead away, although not before remarking, "My son, the doctor, may have rocks in his head, but at least he's not a *fagele*." Dwight Kirby, whom Beverly had finally called, said, "Wedding? What wedding?"

"It was supposed to have been Sally's," Beverly explained to her husband in Wyoming. "But at the last minute she bowed out, so Fingerhood is marrying someone else."

"Sally? You mean she's turned up? Why didn't you tell me immediately? I sweated through those two years same as you, Bev. I had a right to be told."

"I know you did, Dwight, and I'm sorry about the delay. It's just that I needed time to think."

"Think about *what*?"

"Us. Your drinking. My drinking. Your other problem." She couldn't say "abusiveness" with Peter sitting across the room. "Our marriage and where it's going."

"What do you mean, *your* drinking? You don't drink anymore."

"I started again when Anita wouldn't tell me where Sally was."

"Who the hell is Anita?"

"The woman Fingerhood is now marrying."

"I can't keep up with all of this," he muttered. "Is Sally all right? None of the things that we dreaded might happen to her have happened, have they?"

"No, none of those things."

When it came to drugs, heroin was what they'd feared. They hadn't known enough about the widespread popularity of cocaine at the time. Beverly now felt that she should have been better informed. Was she living in the Dark Ages? With her eyes open at last, she found that literature about cocaine was everywhere. The more she read, the more guilty she became that her only daughter had turned to a drug which was described as immensely dangerous, life-threatening, and seductively fashionable. Somehow, she felt that she should have been able to prevent it.

"Where are you staying?" Dwight pressed on. "Even your brother has no idea. I've been out of my mind this past week, worrying about where you were, how you were, whether you were even alive. I don't think I could survive another week without being able to get in touch with you. Give me the name of your hotel."

"I'm not at a hotel. I'm at my old apartment."

"You don't have an old apartment. You told me that you gave it up years ago and your ex-husband kept it."

"Technically, that's right." Why was he making such a fuss? "I'm staying at Peter's apartment."

"And where's Peter?"

"He's sitting right here, reading *The Rag*. Any other questions?"

"Jesus Christ, I've had our neighbors and the Wyoming police force combing the state for you. Eunice and the Women's

Support Group have formed an all-female posse. I was ready to call in the FBI, CIA, and NOW, and all this time you've been shacked up with that faggot you used to be married to, and you have the nerve to act blasé about it!''

"I am not shacked up with anyone," she said evenly. "I just happen to dislike hotels."

"Say no more, Beverly. The next words I hear from you are going to be spoken to me in person. I'm getting on a plane for New York and I don't care if the *Herald* goes down the fucking tubes. I'll see you tomorrow."

"Are you sober?"

"I'm not only sober, I've just come back from my fourth AA meeting. You wouldn't believe the horror stories I've heard this past week. They'd curl your hair. Now, what's that address?"

As she gave it to him, her thoughts went to Sally. If Sally weren't addicted, Beverly knew that she would be whole-heartedly congratulating Dwight on these first steps to rid himself of addiction. The fact that he'd gone to AA surprised her; it was a move she never thought he would voluntarily make. It proved he was serious about wanting to change. She felt glad for him, happy, proud, but her joy remained soured by her daughter's unresolved plight.

"I love you, Beverly," he said. "I didn't realize how much until you were gone. I didn't realize the hell I've put you through, either. But we can talk about that when I get there."

"I love you, too." After hanging up, she turned to Peter. "Dwight just made me realize that I can't drink, not ever again. And I have to get help to make sure I don't. I can't afford not to."

"Because of your marriage?"

"Because of *me*. Sally and I have the same problem, just a different drug. She has to clean up her act for herself, and so do I."

As soon as Sally had called off the wedding, she moved out of Fingerhood's penthouse and into her father's apartment. Her parents had been discussing treatment centers for her for the last couple of days, with Peter insisting that he wanted only the best for his daughter. He'd spoken at length to the Drug Abuse people and then made several hushed follow-up calls.

"It sounds as though Alena Lodge in Blairstown, New Jersey, is it," he finally announced with a triumphant flourish. "It's expensive, exclusive, carefully run, and they even dress for dinner."

"All she wears are blue jeans and a T-shirt," Beverly reminded him.

"So she'll buy a new wardrobe to get detoxed and rehabilitated."

"Stop talking about me as though I weren't here," Sally objected. "It makes me feel like a child again: helpless, incompetent, at both your mercies. I hate it."

"I'm sorry, daughter dear, but since I'm paying for this little excursion of yours, you *are* at my mercy," Peter replied. "I spoke to the manager at Alena Lodge. They can take you a week from today. How does that grab you?"

"The only good thing about it is that I'll be here for the wedding."

"You mean you want to go?" Beverly was surprised.

"Sure. I could use a good laugh before I freak out with withdrawal symptoms while I'm dressing for dinner in Blairstown, New Jersey—wherever the hell that is."

"I have a hunch it won't be as bad as you think," Beverly said, trying to give her courage. "Cocaine withdrawal is supposed to be a breeze compared to most other drugs, you know."

Peter consulted his notes. "They say that you'll need a minimum of one month hospitalization, maybe more, Sally. And antidepressants afterward, if they're medically indicated. It depends on how much of that crap you've been shoving up your nose the past two years."

"Don't be angry at me, Daddy. I feel rotten enough as it is."

"I'm not angry. I'm merely giving you the facts, as they were given to me."

Sally shrugged her bony shoulders, resigned. "If that's how long I need, then that's how long I need. I don't like it, but what can I do?"

"Absolutely nothing, young lady. And remember, no snorting between now and the time you check yourself in."

"I'll tell you what." Beverly was determined to help ease Sally's predicament. "I won't drink if you won't snort. We'll be each other's watchdogs. How about it?"

"Why not?" Sally said, without too much conviction. "Where are you going for your detox?"

"Nowhere near as elegant as the Alena Lodge. Only Smithers." She had been making phone calls also. "They have a one-month program for alcoholics and they can take me the day after you go in." Actually, they could have taken her right away but she wanted to be with Sally to the end.

"Hey, that's great," Sally said, showing the first signs of enthusiasm. "We can attend the wedding together. You too, Daddy. The three of us. Please?"

Beverly and Peter looked at each other. Sally was their child and she was asking them for a favor. Behind her eager facade, they both knew she was terrified and needed their support.

"All right, I'll do it for your sake," Peter relented. "I'll overcome my dismal opinion of Dr. Fingerfuck and his peroxide bride to attend what I'm sure will be the year's most vulgar and trashy affair."

Sally giggled. "Don't be such a snob, Daddy."

"I can't help it, it's the way I was born."

"In that case, I'll do it too," Beverly agreed. "If nothing else, Dwight should get a kick out of it."

"*Dwight*?" Sally said. "You mean he's coming to New York?"

"First thing tomorrow. So it won't be the three of us, it will be the four of us."

"You can be my date," Peter said to Sally, knowing how much she disliked her stepfather. "But you must buy something truly spectacular to wear or I won't be caught dead with you. Snob, remember?"

"I'll go to Bendel's today."

"I'll go with you." Beverly tried to sound jaunty, despite the fact that she was heartbroken over the ordeal Sally faced. Her own seemed minor by comparison. "It's settled, then. First we'll go to Bendel's, then we'll go to the wedding, and then we'll go get ourselves straightened out."

Peter gazed at the two women in his life, his eyes misty. "I'm sorry this has happened to two such terrific ladies. I know it's not my fault, but I can't help wishing it were me rather than either one of you. I'd change places with you in a second."

Sally patted his hand. "That's sweet, Daddy."

Unlike Peter, Beverly could not rid herself of the conviction that what had happened to Sally *was* her fault. If only she hadn't been drinking all those years. If only she'd been a more responsible parent. She suddenly prayed that Dwight would cancel his trip to New York. As much as she longed to see him, she felt that she didn't have the energy or inclination to deal with him and his problems. She was too busy being a mother to think of being a wife again.

"I have my work cut out for me today," Simone informed Michael over breakfast at the King Croesus. "Now that Anita has asked me to be her matron of honor, it means shopping, shopping, and more shopping."

"Sorry to hear that, darling. Shopping is a beastly business." Michael was buried in the London *Times*. "Hate it myself, avoid it as much as possible."

"That's typically masculine. I love it. I'm going to Bendel's for my gown and to Altman's for the twins' outfits. I just hope I can find what I want on such short notice."

"The twins?"

"Didn't I tell you? Anita has asked Rima to be her flower girl, and Prince her ring-bearer."

"It sounds as though she's planning quite an elaborate affair."

"Why shouldn't she?" Simone scoffed. "She's only waited forty years to become a wife. I still can't believe that she got Fingerhood to propose, although my mother used to say that there was a cover for every pot."

Michael mumbled something about maternal wisdom, but Simone could tell that he was only half-listening to her. At times she felt convinced that the only essential difference among all the men she'd known was the newspapers they read. She added more cream to her coffee, thankful that Jimmy had taken *Variety* upstairs to his room, where he was having breakfast with the twins. To her surprise, she had encountered no resistance in getting Michael to accept Jimmy as their guest. At first she tried to lie about their relationship. Instead of admitting that Jimmy was the man she'd been living with in California, she pretended he was an old Hollywood associate who needed a place to stay. Michael wasn't fooled.

"You're the famous screenwriter-director, aren't you?" he

said pleasantly. "Anita told me all about you and Simone. Welcome. This should be a most enjoyable little ménage."

"What did he mean by 'ménage'?" Jimmy asked her later. "Something fishy is going on with that guy."

"Maybe he was just trying to be hospitable."

"I hope that's all it is."

"What else could it be?"

"Threesomes."

Remembering Jimmy's appalling disinterest in sex, Simone crossed her eyes, sucked in her lips, and made her imbecile face. "If that's Michael's game, he sure made a mistake choosing *you.* . . ."

Michael looked up briefly from the *Times*'s stock quotations. "I think it's marvelous that you're able to forgive her, darling."

Simone had forgotten what they were talking about. "Forgive who?"

"Anita, of course. And consented to be her matron of honor after all the nasty things she's said and done to you. You have my highest admiration."

"Thank you, sweetheart."

Simone basked in the flattery, even though it was grossly misplaced. Michael didn't understand her strange love-hate relationship with Anita. He didn't understand that after all was said and done—all the bitter words, deeds, and craziness, like Anita scaring the wits out of her with that water pistol, then the next day sending Simone a wedding invitation that read, "Small tits triumph in the end," to which Simone replied, "I didn't realize that Fingerhood liked your tits in his end"—she *wanted* to be the bitch's matron of honor. She wouldn't have missed it for the world. She equally wanted the twins to be Anita's attendants, but not until Anita apologized for her uncivilized behavior. It came as no surprise when Anita did just that.

"Look, Simone, I know you must hate my guts by now, but I want to make amends. I wasn't myself when Michael threw me over for you. I said and did a lot of things I'm deeply ashamed of." She had dropped by the King Croesus yesterday and dragged Simone down to the Gold Doughnut, on the lower level, for her little atonement speech. "I was a crazy lady when I lost Michael—I'll be the first to admit it—but I'm sane now and I want us to be friends again. I've always liked you, despite our past contretemps. What do you say? Forgive me, darling?''

''Why should I?''

''Because I have a little proposition to make and I'm not too proud to say that I'm making it on my hands and knees, so to speak. It has to do with you, the twins, and my wedding. Before you turn me down, Simone, try to bear in mind how much your cooperation would mean to me and Fingerhood.''

''How much?''

''A great deal. I'm at your mercy, darling.''

''It's about time,'' Simone said with a grin. ''What color gown do you think I should wear? I've been considering French blue, which only happens to be one of the most yummy shades in the rainbow. In addition, there's always violet, tea-rose pink, not to mention ecru. But I think I'd look *un peu* washed out in the latter, don't you agree?''

''Wait just a minute! Hold your fucking horses! I haven't told you what the proposition is.''

''You don't have to, *stupide*. I'm a zillion steps ahead of you, as usual. Now, stop interrupting. French blue is a cross between blue and lavender, it has no yellow in it, which is why it's so flattering to me. Frankly, I look like shit in yellow.''

''Of course you do,'' Anita said with her old imperious Lana Turner air. ''Only blonds can wear yellow, you needn't explain something so obvious. But before you get carried away with this whimsical notion of French blue, let me give you my suggestions for the matron of honor's gown.''

''Why should I listen to your suggestions? I'm the one who would have to appear before fifty guests in an unsuitable color.''

''Who said it would be unsuitable? Do you think I'm dumb enough to ruin my own wedding? I want you to look absolutely gorgeous, darling, which is why I've decided on the palest, most delicate shade of apricot. Silk, naturally. Perhaps something with a dropped waistline.''

''Are you out of your mind?'' Simone was so outraged that the coffee cup shook in her hands. ''Apricot is orange, no matter how you slice it. And orange doesn't have any pink tones in it, which means that it would age me at least ten years!''

"So you'd look sixty," Anita said with a sly smile.

"Ten years older is *fifty*, shmuck!"

"What are you getting so excited about? I was only kidding. What happened to your legendary sense of humor?"

"I don't find anything *amusant* in looking ten years older than I have to. And as I recall from the night you pretended to shoot me, you're pretty uptight yourself when it comes to age. You tried to lie by one lousy year, so don't criticize me for wanting to shine on your wedding day."

"I want you to shine too. You haven't been listening, Simone. I said 'the palest, most delicate shade of apricot.' That makes it an entirely different color from the one you've conjured up in your demented brain."

"My brain is not demented and you're the one who isn't listening. I don't give a shit how pale or delicate you say it is. Apricot is apricot and it doesn't have one tiny itsy bitsy touch of pink in it. Not one, you self-serving manipulator. Not one!"

"Stop screaming," Anita said between clenched teeth. "The apricot I'm thinking of has pink in it."

"Then it isn't apricot."

"Yes, it is."

"Isn't."

"Cunt!"

"Bitch!"

Two waitresses at the Gold Doughnut exchanged amused glances.

"How can you be so impossible?" Anita demanded. "It's my wedding, remember? I don't think it's too presumptuous of me to have a say about what my own matron of honor wears."

"You can say whatever you like, but I know why you'd like me to choose a gown with a dropped waistline. Don't imagine that you're putting anything over on yours truly."

"Only Einstein could have done that. Okay, *why*? If you're so smart."

"Because it would make my breasts appear nonexistent, that style always does. Do you think I'm a moron?"

"What I think is that I must be a saint for having put up with you all these years. You're the most arrogant, stubborn, willful creature I've ever met. When you get an idea in that birdbrain of yours, even a tank couldn't dislodge it."

"I'd rather be willful than end up resembling an ironing board, while you come waltzing down the aisle in an empire concoction with your tits shoved up to your nose and wearing a padded brassiere to boot."

"For your information, my gown is not empire and I've thrown away all my padded bras. Fingerhood told me he likes my breasts *au naturel*. What's more, the reason I suggested a dropped waistline was so that you'd be cool and comfortable. Don't forget, that terrace will have been baking in the sun all morning. What do you have to say to that, you vain and frivolous woman?"

"You call *me* vain?" Simone laughed so hard that her false eyelashes nearly fell off. "That's a joke. I still remember when you used to bathe your breasts in ice-cold water in the bathroom sink, so they'd get larger. Hydrotherapy. Wasn't that what you called it?"

"At least I didn't get fucked in the bathroom sink, like you once did at a party. I seem to recall your saying that you were too horny to wait another second."

"You've always been jealous of my earthiness, haven't you?"

"What's there to be jealous of? You'd screw a snake."

"It's better than marrying one."

"Oh, really?" Anita shot back. "Then why have you agreed to be Michael's wife?"

"Jealous jealous jealous!"

"Depraved depraved depraved!"

It was just like old times.

Simone and the twins were in a taxi.

"Mommy, what's a flower girl?" Rima asked.

"A little girl, like you, who strews flowers as she walks down the aisle before the bride."

"Why?"

"Why what?"

"Why does the flower girl do that, Mommy?"

"To make the wedding procession look pretty."

"What kind of flowers?"

"Any kind the bride decides to buy. At this time of year, there'll be a large selection."

"I only want to strew violets. They're my favorite."

"You'll damn well strew what you damn well get," Simone replied as they arrived at B. Altman's.

"Mommy, what does 'strew' mean?" Prince asked.

"To throw or sprinkle."

"Then why did you say 'strew'?"

"Because it's a more appropriate word."

"Mommy, what does 'appropriate' mean?"

"Shut up."

Simone had decided to outfit the twins first and get that task out of the way, so she could then concentrate on herself. B. Altman's was pleasantly quiet and tranquil, with the counters situated far enough apart for her to breathe without bumping into another shopper. They took the escalator to the children's department on the second floor.

"Mommy, can I buy a purple dress—the same color as your hair?" Rima asked.

"My hair is mauve, not purple."

"What's the difference?"

"Purple is vulgar."

"Is that why you're wearing that funny brown wig?"

"I'm wearing a wig so nobody recognizes and pesters me."

The fact that nobody had upset Simone more than she cared to admit; she was used to strangers asking for her autograph and gushing all over her. The only times she became annoyed was when they chose unlikely moments to show their admiration. Like the afternoon she'd been in the ladies' room at Neiman Marcus, in Beverly Hills, and a woman pushed a piece of paper under the wall separating Simone's cubicle from hers and said, "Make it out to Janet, would you?"

"I don't want to be a ring-bearer," Prince said, looking dubiously at the racks of boys' clothing. "I want to be a baseball player."

"You can be both," Simone told him. "Ring-bearers make the best baseball players in the world. Ask anyone."

"Why do I have to carry the ring, Mommy?"

"Because the bride and groom can't get married without it."

"Why can't the groom carry it?"

"Because it isn't the custom."

"Why not, Mommy?"

An hour later, the project was completed. She had purchased layers of frilly white Valenciennes lace for Rima, white lace knee-hi's, and an arc-en-ciel wreath to wear over her long fine hair. For Prince she'd chosen a navy linen knicker-and-vest outfit with a shirred Russian-style shirt that struck the right note between elegance and comfort. It seemed obscene to try to make an eight-year-old boy resemble a little man in jacket and tie. Anita had promised to buy the ring-bearer's pillow herself, relieving Simone of the obligation. While the purchases were being wrapped, she called Jimmy and told him to get down there pronto. To her relief, he was waiting outside the store when they emerged.

"I appreciate this," she said. "I'll be home when I finish at Bendel's."

"You've interrupted genius at work. Wait until you read the part I've written for you in *The Fingerhood Position.*" He smacked his lips. "You're going to change your mind about marrying Rex Harrison, believe you me, kiddo."

"Don't hold your breath."

Then she handed him the packages, kissed the twins goodbye, and realized that she treated Jimmy more like a husband than she did Michael. She couldn't imagine being quite so familiar with Michael. Intimate, yes, but that was different. That was sex, and sex wasn't everyday life. Simone had too practical a Gallic nature to delude herself that what happened in the bedroom was any kind of barometer for what happened in the rest of the house. During her most passionate years with Steve Omaha, he continued to enrage her with his habit of leaving clothes scattered on the floor, draped over lampshades, hanging from the backs of chairs. He never picked up *anything.* No matter how much he had pleased her in bed the night before, she couldn't forgive him his defiant sloppiness the next morning. Once she threatened to leave because of it. She said that he treated her like a maid; he didn't deny it. If she'd had the money, she might very well have left, but financial dependency kept her from walking out the door. Especially after the twins came.

"Make sure they eat a proper lunch," she said to Jimmy (trying to imagine saying it to Michael). "No chili dogs, please."

"Is pizza a proper lunch?" Rima asked.

"It most certainly is not."

"Is Big Mac a proper lunch?"

"Only if you want to grow up fat."

"I want to grow up and look like you, Mommy. But without the purple hair."

"Mauve."

"Is Kentucky Fried Chicken a proper lunch?"

Simone gritted her teeth, waved good-bye, and got into a taxi. When the twins were older, she would remind them of all the years they spent driving her crazy with improbable questions, and the terrible part was that they wouldn't believe her—not until they had children of their own and found themselves on the other side of the fence.

"Fifty-seventh and Fifth," she told the driver.

It was so long since she'd gone shopping in New York that she had forgotten how sharply the stores differed. If Altman's was sedate chintz, then Bendel's was elegant skinny. This was no place for size twelves, not even for size eights. Size threes, that was where Bendel's was at. Size threes with narrow shoulders, anorexic impulses, and healthy bank accounts. She bought a wedge of Stilton for Michael on the luscious ground floor and then got into the elevator, which oozed with expensive scent. Her nose distinguished Joy and Opium before she stepped off and headed for the bridal shop.

"Okay, we're in agreement," Anita had finally said after they stopped arguing about the matron-of-honor gown. "You'll try for pinky-apricot, but if you have no luck and there's French blue in a flattering style, so be it. No matter what you wear, I'm sure you'll look beautiful."

"You should get married more often, it does wonders for your disposition. Still, I wouldn't want to outshine the bride."

"Don't worry, darling, you won't. When you see my gown, you'll plotz."

"What color is it? You still haven't told me."

"Skin color."

Simone observed her friend's lush peaches-and-cream complexion with envy. Her own skin was a pale, uneven shade of yellowish-gray and relied heavily upon Pan-Cake makeup to give it a smooth texture. "Your wedding gown is avocado and iodine?"

"For once I'm not going to let you bait me," Anita said with a smile. "I feel too happy. I still can't believe I'm getting married."

"You and Fingerhood should have tied the knot years ago." The more Simone thought about it, the more she realized that theirs was a match made in medical heaven: Anita, the hypochondriac, marrying Dr. Kronkeit himself. "Maybe now you'll find out how misplaced your jealousy has been all these years."

"What jealousy?"

"The kind you've harbored for every woman who's ever had a husband, even if he was Jack the Ripper. Maybe you'll finally see that marriage isn't all candlelight and romance."

"What do *you* think it is?"

"Damned hard work."

"You don't sound too eager to try it again. What's the matter? Are some of Michael's more outrageous inclinations starting to get to you?"

"I don't know what you mean."

"Come, come, darling. Don't tell me he hasn't yet initiated you into his favorite indoor sport."

"Which sport is that? Squash?"

"No. Threesomes."

She remembered her conversation with Jimmy. So he'd been right. And yet Michael hadn't tried to include Jimmy in any of their nocturnal adventures. Why not?

"The third party will be someone Michael went to Eton and/or Cambridge with," Anita gleefully declared, watching her face for a reaction. "You'll be expected to do the honors. The *sexual* honors, I should say. How come you don't look more shocked?"

"Sorry to disappoint you, Anita, but I'm French and these little bedroom games don't throw me the way they would a puritan like you." So that explained Michael's disinterest in Jimmy: no Eton and/or Cambridge connection. "Also, you don't know Michael as well as you think. With his kind of upper-class background, he might expect his girlfriend to participate in an orgy, but never his wife. And that's what I'm going to be, so I fail to see how the information of yours applies to me at all."

Anita was disappointed that her little ploy hadn't worked. "Even if your analysis is correct, how will you feel when you discover that he's participating in threesomes on the sly? Won't it bother you? Won't you be jealous?"

"Certainly not. There's no point in becoming hysterical

just because your husband has a special itch and occasionally needs to get it scratched.''

Beaten at her own game by a better player, Anita could only add, ''With an attitude like that, you might make a go of it after all.''

''I intend to.''

Simone was trying to think positively about her second matrimonial venture; she didn't want it to end as dismally as her first. Lately she'd been reevaluating the Steve Omaha fiasco and wondering where it really went wrong. For years she had held the feminists to blame, yet no one forced her to listen to their views. She listened because she liked what she heard. Then when Steve objected to her attempts at independence and took a walk, she absolved herself of all responsibility and pointed an accusing finger at Ms. Steinem, Friedan, Millett, et al.

But the fact was that she never tried to get Steve back. What she did instead was go around badmouthing him and the young cocktail waitress he left her for. Although she didn't care to admit it (preferring to remain the injured party), she secretly used to wonder whether she would have taken him back if he'd come, whether she *wanted* him back. In certain ways, she had passed him by. During the course of their ten-year marriage she'd grown up and didn't know it until her husband replaced her with a carbon copy of her old nubile, complacent, submissive self.

Then she met Jimmy, became a movie star, got used to being waited on and catered to, and realized how nice it was, how luxurious. No wonder men had wives. She didn't think it was a coincidence that the girl Steve picked was a waitress—his choice seemed in keeping with his rigidly enforced role as the household's lord and master. Simone doubted if she could ever live with a lord and master again. It was too demeaning, too boring, too unfair. Did that mean she couldn't live with Michael? Englishmen were notorious for being lord and master, as proven by his insistence that she give up her career. Why did *she* have to make all the sacrifices? Why was it always *the woman*?

As she strolled past the Fancy (Bendel's very fancy dresses at very fancy prices) she spotted a familiar redhead dressed in a jade-green suit. Beverly's large breasts swelled above the jacket's V neckline in a way that used to stop masculine traffic—before men became brainwashed into pretending they didn't notice tits any longer. Next to her Sally looked like a tall drink of water. Simone wondered what Fingerhood had ever seen in her other than extreme youth. Maybe that was enough. Maybe, like Steve Omaha, he wanted the kind of adulation that only a very young girl (or a courtesan like Anita) could bestow.

"Sally, you wouldn't dare!" Beverly exclaimed. They were arguing about a spectacular creation by Zandra Rhodes: black silk chiffon with a handscreen print worn over a black jersey shift.

"Wouldn't I?" Sally said.

Simone was surprised by how jaunty she looked. No one would have pegged her as a girl whose ex-fiancé had found another bride only hours after their breakup.

"Black at an afternoon wedding in June?" Beverly was appalled. "Are you mad? It's the most inappropriate color I can imagine. Everyone will think that Fingerhood threw you over for Anita and in retaliation you're being spiteful and mean."

"But he didn't throw me over, Mother. We threw each other over. Besides, I don't care what people think."

So it was mutual. What a stroke of luck for Anita, who'd been around to take advantage of the opportunity. "If I didn't have to be the matron of honor, I'd wear the dress myself," Simone piped up. "It looks sexy as hell."

Sally smiled at her shyly, impressed with her star status. "Thank you, Simone. I'm glad that someone is on my side. I wish you could convince my mother."

"Well, she can't," Beverly said, turning to Simone with surprise. "What's this about you being Anita's matron of honor? I can't believe she would ask you, after you stole Michael right out from under her nose."

"Believe it. She hated me at first, but now that she's got Fingerhood, all is forgiven."

"And you've got Sir Michael Harding." Sally seemed impressed by his title. "You must be thrilled at the prospect of going to live in London. It sounds so exciting."

Simone thought of the lead in *The Fingerhood Position* that Jimmy was writing just for her. She thought of how nice it would be to win another Academy Award nomination. "It *is* exciting," she staunchly replied. "I can hardly wait." She poked the exotic black dress. "Why don't you try it on, so we can see how it looks?"

"You're encouraging her," Beverly wailed.

Simone winked at Sally. "I know. Isn't it sinful of me?"

"Beautiful," Lou said to her reflection.

She stood before the bedroom's full-length mirror, admiring the way she looked in her favorite Oscar de la Renta. Now that she didn't have to worry about being matron of honor, she didn't have to worry about buying a special gown for the wedding. Instead she would wear this white sequined jacket edged with gold sequins, white silk crepe trousers, and navy silk organza tank top, which struck her as ideal for a June day. If it got too hot, she could simply remove the jacket.

"Accessories," she reminded herself.

A pair of gold strappy high-heeled sandals, two ropes of fake pearls, and a crushed gold belt did it. As she tightened the belt, she heard a familiar mocking voice.

"That's not even catering to the enemy." Vanessa stood in the open doorway. "That's more like groveling at their feet."

"If you object, I must be doing something right." She whirled around to watch the trousers flare. "What are you planning to wear to the big event? Your denim overalls?"

"I'm not planning to wear anything. I'm not going."

Lou stopped in mid-whirl. "How come?"

"Because I'm quitting as of now."

*"Quitting?"*

"Leaving. Departing. Walking out."

"You can't do that! Vanessa, you promised!"

"Sue me."

"Oh, Jesus."

She drew Vanessa into the room and sat her down on the chaise. While their personal relationship had been strained the last couple of days, they'd managed to affect a satisfactory if monosyllabic work relationship. Vanessa's departure date for Paris was a month away and she agreed to fulfill her culinary obligations for the wedding, provided Lou kept Keith out of the kitchen. Having upheld her part of the bargain, Lou was stunned by this latest development.

"You can't quit now," she said anxiously. "There's still

tons of work to be done. You haven't baked the cake, made the vegetable side dish, or finished the cheese straws.''

"Not to mention the shrimp and crab éclairs or the spinach-stuffed phyllo.''

"Then how can you quit? What are you thinking of? What's wrong?''

"The blushing bride is what's wrong. She just called to say that she wants to change the entire menu.''

Lou felt the blood drain out of her face. "I don't believe it.''

"Believe it. Everything that Sally and Fingerhood had decided on, Anita has decided against. And I mean *everything*. From the appetizer to the goddamned cake.'' Vanessa was livid. "I explained that we'd long since started cooking, baking, and freezing, but that brainless blond doesn't care. She said that if she doesn't get what she wants from us, she'll hire another caterer.''

"Two days before the wedding?''

"That's what she said.''

"But that's ridiculous. No respectable caterer would do it on such short notice.''

"I tried to explain that, but her highness didn't seem to be listening. She was too busy stipulating every last detail of her new menu—which sucks, I might add. Do you know what she plans to serve as an entrée?'' Vanessa's voice had risen shrilly. "Bavarian Three-Meat Goulash!''

"I'm not a cook, I don't understand. What's the matter with it?''

"It's a winter dish. You serve something like that when it's five degrees outside, not on a June day in Manhattan. People will be sweating like pigs. To accompany this atrocity, she suggested German noodles and a tacky coleslaw recipe that's been in her family for three hundred years and sounds it.'' Vanessa tore agitatedly at her cuticles. "Here's the last straw: she vetoed the traditional tiered wedding cake that I was going to bake for Sally. In her words, it's too *ordinary*.''

"What does she want instead?''

"A mammoth Sacher Torte. What is this woman, anyway? A neo-Nazi?''

"Calm down, Vanessa. It's not as bad as it seems.''

"It's worse.''

"No, it isn't.'' Lou had been doing some mental mathematics. "I discovered a long time ago that there's a solution to everything."

"Then what's the solution to this? Because if you think you'll get her to change her mind, forget it. I spent twenty minutes listening to her ranting and raving, and a steamroller wouldn't make a dent in her brain."

"How did you leave things?"

"Frankly, I got so mad that I hung up." She regarded Lou with suspicion. "If you plan to go along with this crazy scheme, you can count me out. I've just finished making eight huge Chopped Liver Swans with *gribinitz*—one Swan per table—and I'll be damned if I'm starting all over again with eight *Schweinsulzes*."

"What's that?"

"Her father's favorite. Jellied Pork Loaf."

Despite the seriousness of the problem, Lou couldn't help laughing. "Anita's parents must be thrilled now that the old maid is finally getting married. Her father is a pork butcher in Cleveland, you know."

"He could be Hermann Hesse in Spandau, for all I care. You make *Schweinsulze* with pigs' feet, ugh. I looked it up in the German cookbook while we were on the phone. It's a disgusting dish."

"Are you positive she won't consider the Swans?"

"Would Hitler consider Gefilte Fish?"

"What did you tell her?"

"Well, as I was looking through the German cookbook, I saw a recipe for *Schlemmerschnitte*, which is like Oysters Rockefeller compared to what she had in mind and it's also a cinch to make. So before hanging up, I suggested it as a compromise. Guess what? No luck."

Lou giggled. "*Schlemmerschnitte*?"

"What's so funny? That's ground steak and caviar piled on slices of toast. I don't know why you find this so hilarious. I don't find anything the least bit amusing about German cuisine. No wonder they lost the Second World War. Their army must have had acute indigestion."

Vanessa's lack of humor had always bothered Lou. The outrageous didn't tickle Vanessa, it irritated her. And for a long time Lou tried to pretend that it didn't matter because there were other compensations, other redeeming qualities. But she soon realized that the gap in their sense of humor was indicative of a much wider and more serious gap: they saw the world through entirely different sets of eyes, values, judgments. People who laughed at the same follies were bound by a tie that was closer than tears. Keith would have laughed at *Schlemmerschnitte*.

"What are you going to do?" Vanessa got up from the chaise. "Pull out of this dumb deal altogether, take Finger-hood's deposit, and call it a day?"

"Not on your life."

"You're not going to accede to that woman's demands, are you? Lou, you wouldn't!"

"Before you jump to conclusions, tell me one thing about this new menu. Is it very difficult to prepare?"

"You mean, could we get it done in time for the wedding if we were insane enough to tackle it?"

"That's what I mean."

"You're not thinking logically. You're making a big mistake. We'd lose our shirts on the deal."

"You didn't answer my question."

"Sure we could get it done, if we hired a couple of sous chefs and worked around the clock. But that isn't my point. What the hell are we supposed to do with the eight Chopped Liver Swans in our refrigerator? Not to mention the fifty Turbans of Chicken in our freezer?"

"Charge them to Fingerhood as planned, then resell them to another customer."

"What if nobody wants them? How long do you think we can keep them here?"

"You seem to have forgotten about Jean Pierre's July Fourth blowout."

"That's right. He always leaves the menu selection up to us." Vanessa pondered this possibility. "But Jean Pierre is such a snob. Do you think he'd sit still for Chopped Liver Swans with *gribinitz*?"

"Vanessa, do you seriously imagine that someone born John Miller in Fargo, North Dakota, knows a *gribinitz* from a white truffle?"

"Maybe you're right. And if we can unload Sally's meal on Jean Pierre, it would mean a double profit for us."

"More than that."

Vanessa blinked. "Go on."

"It's quite simple, really. The only way I'll agree to a new

menu at this late date is if Fingerhood pays for every cent of
the old one and then gives me twice what I'd normally charge
to serve Anita's Teutonic dinner.''

"That's a *triple* profit," Vanessa said, awed.

"Don't we deserve it for all our hard work and good-
natured cooperation?''

A small smile curled Vanessa's lips. "I'm going to miss
you, Lou. You may be an oppressed female in your personal
life, but you sure are one hell of a tough businesswoman. I
wonder if Fingerhood will go for it.''

Lou pulled the crushed gold belt tighter and admired her
waistline. "What choice does the poor bastard have?''

She still hadn't decided what to do about Keith.

Anita Marthe Schuler, soon to be Fingerhood, was seated
in the Sutton Place living room drinking iced tea with Sweet
'n Low and making a list. She had titled the list

  EMERGENCY!
     1. If Lou doesn't call back in thirty minutes, call
        every caterer in Manhattan and offer to double
        their fee;
     2. Take Fingerhood shopping for new wedding suit;
     3. Make plane arrangements for parents, then get guest
        room ready;
     4. Check with Simone to see what color gown
        she bought and if the twins are properly
        outfitted;
     5. Tell Mrs. Fingerhood about Chopped Liver Swans;
     6. Convince Fingerhood to disinvite *all Northrops* to
        wedding;
     7. Hire new band;
     8. Buy gifts for Fingerhood, Simone, Rima, Prince;
     9. Make sure that Fingerhood has musicians' and
        minister's fee;
    10. Make sure he has purchased a gift for Keith, a
        bridal bouquet, corsages for both our mothers,
        boutonnieres for men, and (hint, hint) a gift for
        his beloved bride;
    11. Talk to Fingerhood again about honeymoon!!!

Anita shook her head in despair. How would they ever
manage it? There wasn't enough time. Other than having

gotten their blood tests, marriage license, and matching gold wedding bands, she and Fingerhood were pitifully unprepared. She had considered pushing up the date another week, but superstition prevailed. If she delayed the wedding, something told her it would never take place at all.

"I must be practical," she murmured, thinking of how Jack Bailey had dropped dead on her days before she was to become his wife. "I must remember my priorities."

So what if the food turned out to be mediocre, Mink & Sable played "Here Comes the Bride" in hard rock (because she couldn't find a decent band at the last minute), the Northrops arrived en masse, Fingerhood's mother kvetched because there were no Chopped Liver Swans, Simone walked down the aisle in French blue, they were married by a Unitarian minister instead of a Lutheran one, and honeymooned right here in the penthouse? When all was said and done, did it matter that much? Not if she kept her goal clearly in mind. *To get married*. That was the goal, and everything else had to be viewed accordingly.

Anita felt fortified. Grabbing the Yellow Pages and her address book, she got on the phone to caterers, musicians, airlines, florists, the King Croesus, personalized shopping services, Mrs. Fingerhood, and her confused parents in Cleveland. She had booked them on a United flight tomorrow afternoon, which would give them twenty-four hours to catch their breath before the wedding ceremony began. They had taken the news of her sudden engagement fairly well, meaning they were in such a state of shock when she told them about it two days ago that this was the first time either of them could speak coherently.

"You are sure you know what you're doing?" her father asked in the guttural accent he'd never lost. "You do not marry this *Herr Doktor* out of necessity?"

"I'm not pregnant, Father, if that's what you mean. What an idea. What kind of daughter do you think you've raised?"

"One of virtue, I pray. Despite the godless times we live in."

"I'm filled with virtue, Father, you should know that." She wondered what he thought she was up to during that long stretch with Sir Michael Pervert Harding. "Now wish me luck and let me talk to Mother."

*"Gluckwunsch, mein Kind."*

"You're not supposed to say 'congratulations' to the bride," she gently reprimanded him. "It sounds as though you're congratulating me on having trapped a husband."

"*Und* that's not what you have done?"

It was no use arguing with her stubborn provincial father, who'd devoted his entire life to selling pork chops, knockwurst, and pigs' knuckles to a staunchly German clientele. He hadn't changed his ideas in sixty-odd years, and never would. Her mother was just as hopeless, although her English was better.

"I've been thinking about your future husband's last name," her mother said with a note of suspicion. "It isn't Jewish, by any chance, is it?"

Anita had expected the question and was prepared. "It most certainly is Jewish, which means that I don't want to hear any anti-Semitic remarks out of you or Pop. Do you understand? And while you're staying at our apartment, make sure he doesn't sing you-know-what in the shower."

"What?"

"Don't play dumb, Mother."

"You don't want your father to sing 'The Star-Spangled Banner' when he bathes?"

"You know that's not what I'm talking about. Of course I don't mean 'The Star-Spangled Banner.' Why would I object to our national anthem?"

"How should I know? Maybe because your future husband is one of those long-haired Communists."

"Fingerhood a Communist?" Anita chuckled, wondering how much he had paid for this sumptuous penthouse with its wraparound landscaped terrace, eighteen floors above the bustle of Manhattan. Probably more than her father would earn in a lifetime of center-cut pork chops. "When you see where we live, you'll understand what a farfetched notion that is. Robert Fingerhood happens to be a famous psychologist and sex counselor. He's written a best-selling book that's going to be made into a major motion picture. He's rich, clean-shaven, a bona fide capitalist."

"He wrote a book?" Her mother sounded impressed for the first time. "What book?"

Anita hesitated, then threw caution to the winds. "*The Fingerhood Position.*"

"*Gott in Himmel! Schweinhund!* That's who my only child is marrying? The man who wrote that filthy, dirty, disgusting piece of trash? I pray to God your father never finds out, it would kill him.''

"For your information, Mother, *The Fingerhood Position* happens to be a very respectable book. It's a self-help manual for achieving lasting satisfaction and happiness in marriage.''

"Don't lie to me, *Tochter*. It has illustrations with all those . . . those . . . I can't bring myself to say it. All those positions. I know because Berthe Hauschild showed it to me. Her daughter-in-law, the Ukrainian belly dancer, left it lying around.'' Mrs. Schuler made a clucking sound of disapproval. "You're marrying *that* Fingerhood and you have the nerve to worry about what your poor father sings in the shower? For shame, *Tochter*, for shame!''

"Just tell him to forget he ever knew 'Deutschland Uber Alles,' '' Anita whispered into the receiver. "See you tomorrow. And don't forget to pack your wedding clothes.''

She was worried about their clothes, despite the fact that her mother swore she'd bought a perfectly respectable peach polyester gown at Halle's and that her father's old navy-blue worsted was in excellent condition. Why polyester? Anita thought. Why couldn't her father have splurged on a new suit? Why didn't her parents have any style? It was no use torturing herself, she decided, as the telephone rang.

"Sweetheart,'' Mrs. Fingerhood purred. "I'm sorry I couldn't talk when you called before. The seamstress was here, pinning me.''

At least she didn't have to worry about her future mother-in-law's gown, which was ice-green chiffon with a detachable capelet. Jewish women of Mrs. Fingerhood's generation knew the score when it came to making themselves look good. She only wished that her mother, who was forty pounds over-weight and leaned toward floral housedresses, had more of a knack in that department.

"What was the seamstress pinning?'' she politely asked.

"My capelet. I want it to have more of a sleeve effect to hide my upper arms.'' A sigh of resignation came across the telephone wires. "When you get to be my age, you'll be hiding your upper arms too. So what did you want to talk to me about?''

"The Chopped Liver Swans.''

"Yes, sweetheart? What about them?''

"There aren't going to be any.''

"No Swans?" Mrs. Fingerhood thought a moment. "So maybe there'll be Chopped Liver Ducks."

"No Ducks either, Mrs. Fingerhood. I'm sorry, but there won't be any chopped liver. Period."

There was a long, uncomfortable pause. "What kind of wedding can you have with no chopped liver? Frankly, I'm confused. Sally gave me her word—excuse me, sweetheart, I realize you don't like to be reminded of your predecessor— but she specifically promised that the caterer would serve Chopped Liver Swans for the appetizer. I even said that if it was too much trouble, she could forget the *gribinitz*. I'm not a fussy demanding person, sweetheart. Ask my son if you don't believe me."

"I believe you, Mrs. Fingerhood. It's just that I don't want to trouble your son with the menu. He has enough things to take care of, as it is."

"So you're taking care of the menu?"

"Yes. That's right."

"I'll put it to you this way, sweetheart. My husband is dead, may he rest in peace. The Swans were supposed to be a kind of gesture to the groom's one surviving parent. A token of esteem, if you get my drift. Now do you understand?"

"I understand, Mrs. Fingerhood, but I'm afraid they're out of the question."

"Call me Edith."

"I'm afraid they're out of the question, Edith. You see, I've already canceled Sally's entire menu and there's no way I can ask a new caterer to start making Chopped Liver Swans in less than forty-eight hours. Besides, I thought I'd serve *Schweinsulze* instead."

"*Schwein* . . . ?" She couldn't pronounce it. "What's that, sweetheart?"

"Jellied Pork Loaves."

"*Oi gevalt!*" Mrs. Fingerhood shrieked. "It's a *shandah* for the neighbors. It's bad enough that my son is marrying a *shiksa*, but to find out at this late date that he's planning to serve *hozerai* is more than I'm emotionally equipped to deal with."

"What's *hozerai*?"

"Pig food."

"Now, just a minute, Edith!"

"Call me Mrs. Fingerhood."

"My father happens to be a pork butcher and I don't think he'd appreciate that description of the first-class meat he's been selling for the last forty years. So if I were you, I'd temper my remarks when I met him."

"I'll be sure to do that. Now I must go lie down." Mrs. Fingerhood's voice had become faint. "I'm not feeling too well."

"That's too bad. Is there anything I can do?"

"Thank you, sweetheart. You've done enough."

"It must be all the wedding excitement," Anita said solicitously. "To tell the truth, I'm a little bushed myself."

"Not too bushed to cancel the Chopped Liver Swans," Mrs. Fingerhood said, hanging up.

On location outside of Phoenix, TV cameramen were shooting a motorcycle-car chase on Interstate 17 for a crucial scene of *Arizona Pete*, when a strange thing happened. In fact, the event was so unusual and so unprecedented in the annals of television history that it would be spoken about for years to come.

The famous silver Yamaha (with the ARIZ PETE license plate) being driven by the series' star, Colin McKenna, was chasing a dark Mustang being driven by his prime suspect in a recent series of brutal murders. Because the murder victims were all innocent senior citizens who'd moved to the Sun Belt to live out their days in the warm desert climate, their deaths aroused bitter fury in Arizona Pete (Green Beret veteran, private eye, and moral crusader), who intended to see that justice was done. Colin had always performed his own stunts and today was no exception.

The director told him to register fierce determination mingled with glinty rage as he pursued the alleged killer. Colin nodded, a dreamy faraway look in his eyes. He'd been snorting, boozing, and staying up late, making his concentration practically nil. At the moment he was thinking of Jimmy Newton and how much he missed him.

The director continued. When the Mustang made a sudden diagonal slash across the highway—nearly colliding with oncoming traffic and then reversing direction—it was Colin's cue to follow suit. He was supposed to accelerate, bear down on his suspect, sideswipe him off the road, drag him out of the car, restrain himself from breaking his jaw, and engage in a rapid cross-examination that would infallibly establish the man's guilt. Did Colin understand? Again he nodded in the same dreamy way.

It had been a long hot day and everyone—actors and crew alike—were eager to wind up the scene and return to their air-conditioned hotel suites. A few of the regulars remarked that Colin seemed more spaced out than usual, but no one thought much of it.

"Remember you hate this guy for what he did to those poor retired suckers," the director added as the makeup man dabbed at Colin's shiny nose and the wardrobe woman adjusted his crash helmet. "You're going to nab this bastard if it's the last thing you do."

"I hear you, Pops."

"Action!"

The vehicles took their places on the roped-off highway and the sequence began, but within seconds it was clear that something had gone terribly wrong. Colin did not drive diagonally across the highway, as he was supposed to. He did not accelerate. He did not register glinty rage. Nor did he attempt to chase the suspect. Instead, to everyone's astonishment, he grinned, gave the camera his finger, and kept driving north on Interstate 17 until his silver Yamaha was lost in a blur of desert dust.

All attempts to catch up to him proved fruitless and production was temporarily suspended on one of the most popular series of the past two seasons, while newspapers, radio, and TV asked the same plaintive question: "HAS ANYBODY SEEN ARIZONA PETE?"

Anita spent the next hour getting the guest room ready for her parents with fresh linens, towels, Kleenex, a thermos on the bedside table, an electric clock on the bureau, and two vases of freshly cut flowers. Then she told Jeeves to disinfect the adjoining bathroom (with Pine Sol) and clean it (with Fantastik) until it sparkled and shone.

"Where should I disinfect?" the robot asked. "I've never done this before."

"*Never disinfected?*" She tried not to think what this meant about her future husband; the implications were too ominous. "You disinfect everywhere, the entire room. And don't overlook the area behind the toilet. That's where germs get trapped the most.''

"If you say so, madam."

"I most certainly do.'' She handed him the cleaning agents. "Get going."

"Yes, madam."

How could Fingerhood never have disinfected? she wondered as she slipped into her own bathroom to check the Anyday panty-liner she'd put on that morning. Her period seemed to have mysteriously stopped after only two days, but there was no telling when it might return—or with how much force. A fast examination now revealed that it was still absent, but she changed the liner nonetheless. It never hurt to be fresh and dainty, and Anyday was a marvelous brand, much thicker and more absorbent than the English Minima. Anita didn't know how she had lived before the advent of panty-liners, they were a true godsend to discriminating women like herself. She then returned to the living room and managed to get Simone on the phone.

"What kind of gown did you buy?" she asked, in no mood to waste time. "Describe it to me, please."

"It's made of the sheerest cotton voile and has a handkerchief skirt trimmed in Chantilly lace, with a darling flounced underskirt. You'll love it, Anita. I plan to wear matching satin slippers."

"I notice you haven't mentioned the color."

"Oh, it's French blue," Simone said breezily. "But before you blow your stack, I'm accessorizing it with an apricot cummerbund. Which it didn't come with, I might add. I spent hours looking for that precise color because I know how keen you are on apricot."

What the bitch meant was that she'd be preceding her down the aisle in French blue after all, with only a smidgen of apricot at her waist. Oh, well, it could be worse. At least Simone was vaguely trying to cooperate, unlike Lou, Mrs. Fingerhood, or that dopey robot, who seemed determined to try her patience. She planned to get rid of Jeeves right after the wedding and hire some decent help. A staff of three was what she had in mind: housekeeper, cook, and cleaning person. Maybe the housekeeper could live in and serve them breakfast in bed, like Nancy Walker used to do for Rock Hudson and Susan St. James on that wonderful old TV series, *McMillan and Wife*.

"What will the twins be wearing?" she asked Simone, making half a check next to number four on her EMERGENCY! list.

"Don't worry about Rima and Prince, they're going to look adorable. But there is someone whose attire you might not be too crazy about."

"Who is that?" Anita tried to think of her enemies. "Beverly?"

"No. Sally. I ran into her at Bendel's. Brace yourself." Simone couldn't help smiling. "Her dress is by Zandra Rhodes."

"Oh, shit." The last thing she needed was to be upstaged at her own wedding. "What is it like, Simone? I want the absolute truth."

"The truth is, it's black."

*"Black?"*

"You said you wanted the truth."

"Sally is wearing *black* to my wedding? I can't believe it. Are you serious?"

"Of course. You don't think I'd make up something like this, do you?"

"You bet I do. I know how perverse you are. Is it really *black*?"

"As the ace of spades."

"Hold on a second." Anita ran out onto the terrace and screamed at the top of her lungs: *"Fuck, shit, screw! I hate Sally Northrop!"* Then she picked up the receiver and coolly said, "If she wants to show up looking like a ghoul, I guess I can't do anything about it."

"That's the spirit. Why should you care if the dress is provocative as sin, sexy as hell, and hugs her cute ass like there's no tomorrow?"

"Provocative? Sexy? How sexy?" Last night she dreamed that Fingerhood said he couldn't marry her because he still loved Sally. "Are you trying to unnerve me forty-eight hours before my wedding?"

*"Moi?"*

"You're the one who relayed this unsettling news."

"I did it for your own sake. Just like you told me about Michael and threesomes for my sake. Forewarned is forearmed, remember?'' Maybe this would teach Anita to keep her big mouth shut. "Anyhow, why should you care what Sally Northrop wears? She's not the one who's hooked New York's most eligible bachelor. You did. And your ass is cuter than hers, even if no one will be able to see it.''

"Thank you, darling. I'm sure you mean that as a compliment.'' Footsteps could be heard coming down the corridor that separated the apartment's living quarters from Fingerhood's office. "I must go, Simone. Talk to you later.''

"Did you hear about Colin McKenna disappearing into thin air? It was just on the radio.''

"*Later*, I said.'' She turned and smiled brightly at her future husband. "You look tired, sweetheart. Tough morning?''

Fingerhood grunted. He had just completed an intense session with a famous Broadway actress who hadn't had an orgasm since her husband ran off with the stage manager, and he felt both exhausted and overstimulated. There was only one sure antidote to his condition: sex. To his annoyance, Anita suddenly waved a list in front of his eyes.

"The first thing we must do is dash to Barney's and get you something decent to be married in,'' she said, having made asterisks next to the items that pertained to him. "There's a limo waiting downstairs and we'll use your mother's seamstress for the alterations. I got her to agree, despite our argument over the Chopped Liver Swans.''

"What the hell are you babbling about?''

"Nothing, darling.'' She kissed him tenderly on the cheek. "Forget I ever mentioned Chopped Liver Swans.''

"That won't be hard.''

She picked up the lizard purse that Michael had given her after an especially grueling night with Dickie Wembley and the spring tree saddles. "Come on. Let's go.''

"Go? Go where?''

Poor thing, he was exhausted from all those nonorgasmic patients of his. She would have to learn to be patient. "I just told you, darling. To Barney's.''

He looked at her in alarm. "That's *downtown*.''

"I know. Why do you think I hired a limo? Aren't you proud of me for being so efficient and practical?''

"Practical and efficient aren't what interest me at the moment.'' He was pleased to see her looking gorgeous as usual, in a striped silk overblouse with bright blue trousers that outlined her curvy ass. He grabbed it. "Hot and sensuous are what interest me."

She deftly pulled away. "They interest me too, darling, but we *are* getting married on Saturday and you need a new suit."

Fingerhood felt frustrated. Aside from his itch, he was in no mood for this hustle-bustle craziness, partially because the famous Broadway actress (whom he'd had a yen for for years) suggested he join her in her hammock and ethically he couldn't; partially because he wasn't sure he liked Jimmy Newton's shmaltzy concept for the screenplay of *The Fingerhood Position*, which he felt distorted the serious tone of the book; and partially because he still couldn't believe he was getting married. And to Anita Schuler instead of Sally Northrop. It wasn't that he didn't love Anita. It was that he'd switched brides so suddenly, he hadn't quite adjusted to the upheaval.

"What's wrong with my white linen suit?" he peevishly asked. "It's by Armani and it's brand new."

"It doesn't do you justice, darling. It doesn't make you look as handsome as you really are." The real reason she objected to it was that Sally had okayed it. "Now, let's get going. We'll discuss the other stuff in the limo."

"What other stuff?"

Anita stashed the EMERGENCY! list in her purse and took her future husband's arm. "Let's get all comfy first, then we can talk." She wondered what he would say when she told him that she'd made reservations for two at Jamaica's most luxurious seaside hotel. If he objected, she would cry and divulge her long-cherished fantasy of a Caribbean honeymoon. She would beg and wheedle if necessary. He was probably so brainwashed by years of his mother's begging and wheedling that he had no defenses left. She could thank Mrs. Fingerhood for that, if nothing else.

"Who the hell wants to talk?" he said, sidling up close behind her as he followed her out the door. He pressed his body smack against hers, feeling the shape of her generous hips. It was a wonderful feeling. "This is what I want to do."

She turned around and frowned. "Really, Robert. There's a time and place for everything."

"You're so right." He leered. "This is the time and this is the place."

*"In the hallway? Waiting for the elevator?"*

"Why not? We have the only apartment on the floor. We needn't worry about being disturbed. Haven't you ever wanted to get laid in a hallway?"

"Not that I can remember." She laughed, trying to make light of it. "It looks awfully uncomfortable."

"Let's lie down and try it," he suggested, grasping her hand.

She pulled loose just as the elevator arrived in the nick of time. Men! The world could be rocked by a nuclear blast and the entire masculine population would be thinking about getting laid one more time before they went to meet their maker.

"We'll do it later, when we come back," she promised, trying to show her good intentions by putting her arms around his neck. He immediately got a hard-on. "Control yourself, darling."

"We'll do it in the limo, or I'm not going." He was all worked up from listening to the famous Broadway actress describe her multitudinous attempts at achieving orgasm with some of the brightest names in the entertainment world, then slyly suggesting that he might have it all over them. "I assume the windows are blacked out."

"I don't know." She didn't like the way this was heading. "I didn't make any special requests. I was in too much of a rush."

He grabbed her in a passionate embrace as the elevator reached the lobby floor. "I want to fuck you senseless, Anita, and I have no intention of waiting."

"But I don't have my diaphragm in."

"How come you're not on the pill like everyone else?"

"Because it makes me bloat too much. Besides, it's not recommended to anyone who suffers from a blood-clotting problem." To her relief, the limousine had clear windows. "You wouldn't want me to get pregnant so soon, would you?" Then she saw that it had discreet gray curtains that could be slid shut.

"No, pregnant isn't a good idea," Fingerhood agreed as he followed her into the air-conditioned leather interior. "We'll have to do something else in that case, won't we?"

"Barney's" she nervously told the driver. "Seventh Avenue and Seventeenth Street. And *hurry*."

Fingerhood decisively pushed a button and a smoky glass

partition rolled up, separating them from the driver. Then he pulled the curtains shut and unzipped his fly.

"The suit I have in mind for you is called 'The Southampton,' " Anita said, trying to ignore his penis, which loomed large, throbbing, purple-veined. Fortunately there was a small television set next to the well-stocked bar. She turned it on low. "It consists of navy trousers and vest, a white jacket trimmed in navy, navy polka-dot bow tie, and wing-collared shirt. I saw an illustration of it in *Today's Bride*." The TV set revealed two doctors gravely discussing a patient's hematoma on *The Guiding Light*.

"Who wants to wear a vest this time of year?" Fingerhood stretched out on the seat, a smile of anticipation on his moist lips. "Sounds too damned hot for me."

"Oh no, not at all," she hastened to reassure him. " 'The Southampton' is made of the lightest-weight silk-and-cotton blend on the market today. In fact, the photograph in *Today's Bride* was of a garden wedding in June, and the caption said that—"

"Later, Anita." He pushed her head down.

She coyly resisted, raising her head a fraction of an inch and remembering that he never disinfected. "The salesman told me on the phone that 'The Southampton' was specifically designed for summer wear and that they've never had a complaint from a customer yet." On the soap opera, one of the doctors had walked off camera and a pretty young nurse was now talking to the remaining doctor about a personal matter. It was clear from the subtext that their relationship transcended the professional. "I'm sure that when you try the suit on at Barney's, you'll agree the salesman was right."

"I said, *later*."

"You horny bastard, you."

Fingerhood wasn't smiling now. "Yes, I am."

"I've never seen a forty-eight-year-old man with your incredible sex drive." The limousine stopped short for a red light and she nearly fell off the seat. "Aren't you ever afraid you might overdo it?"

"The only thing I'm afraid of is that if you don't stop stalling, I'm going to come all over this brand-new leather upholstery."

She sighed in desperation, positioned herself so that she could see the TV screen, mentally reviewed her EMERGENCY!

list, decided that maybe she'd better not discuss the Jamaican hotel when she got through, but tell him about the gifts he had to buy, the Northrops he had to disinvite, the band she still hadn't hired, the fact that Some Like It Hot would be catering their wedding at the most outrageous fee she'd ever heard in her life, and suggest in no uncertain terms that he shut up and pay it, since she couldn't find another decent caterer on such short notice, and besides, that switch hitter, Lou Marron Greenspan, had deigned to start the bridal dinner with *Schweinsulze*, which was bound to make Fingerhood's future father-in-law absolutely ecstatic. And then with her brain sufficiently distracted, Anita began to suck.

"As the saying goes, 'Nobody promised me a rose garden,' " the pretty nurse lamented on *The Guiding Light*.

# 11

The day before the wedding was one of exceptional activity, with the following events taking place:

• Colin McKenna, who was still missing, had made the front pages of the newspapers across the country and was the target of a nationwide manhunt;

• Sandler-Roma-Weintraub Studios, who produced *Arizona Pete*, were offering a huge reward to anyone who had information as to the star's whereabouts, while at the same time initiating a multimillion-dollar lawsuit against him for breach of contract;

• Eddie Drake flew in from Los Angeles, hot on the heels of his elusive client, who reliable sources assured him was somewhere in the metropolitan area;

• Simone received a phone call from Eddie, telling her that although the lead in *Rockabye Princess* had been rewritten for Diana Ross, she stood an excellent chance of getting *The Fingerhood Position* if she didn't abandon her career now;

• Simone replied that she was hiding Colin McKenna under her bed and when Eddie walked through the door, minutes later, he was greeted by a barrage of gold vermeil goblets aimed directly at his head;

• Michael Harding left for England after receiving an emergency phone call from the family doctor, saying that Lady Philippa had been severely bitten by one of her toucans;

• Jimmy took advantage of his absence by asking Simone to ditch the Englishman and marry him, whereupon he received the same gold-vermeil-goblet treatment for the Diana Ross treachery and was called a string of vile names;

• The twins asked Simone whether "a two-timing motherfucker" was better or worse than "a Fingerhood position";

• Dwight Kirby moved Beverly out of her ex-husband's

apartment and into the Gramercy Regency, where Colin had just registered disguised as a middle-aged Frenchman;

• Sally insisted on going along to make sure that Beverly didn't drink;

• Peter Northrop Jr. drove down from Harvard to attend his sister's wedding, only to learn that she was no longer the bride;

• Anita frantically offered Lou a five-hundred-dollar fee if she would whip the penthouse into shape by the next day, and Lou accepted;

• Reverend Freshwater, of the First Unitarian Church, told a miffed Anita that it wasn't necessary to have a dress rehearsal that afternoon, since the processional was so small;

• Anita's parents arrived looking like they'd just gotten off a ship from the old country, and she rushed them to Macy's to try to repair the damage;

• In Macy's Big City Woman Shop, where she was persuading her mother to buy an expensive silk dress, Anita felt the return of her period, a savage clobbering of her old facial pain, and a liver attack that left her in a weakened condition;

• Vanessa and three sous chefs from a particularly militant branch of the feminist movement, SUCK (Society to Undermine Cock as King), alternated around-the-clock cooking and baking for the Fingerhood wedding, and justified their endeavors by vowing to donate all wages to the revolutionary efforts of SUCK;

• Fingerhood spent a rotten morning with his mother's seamstress nearsightedly pinning and jabbing him, then with the famous Broadway actress hysterically accusing him of having unethical designs on her. He was so unnerved by both experiences that when Simone stopped by for dress rehearsal, he fucked her on top of his desk, saying it would help them both relax;

• Mrs. Fingerhood called her son to ask if he knew what he was getting himself into, to which he replied, "Probably not, but I know what I'm getting out of" (meaning Simone);

• In response to his mother's next question ("What are your in-laws like?"), Fingerhood said, "The Third Reich";

• Mrs. Fingerhood begged Some Like It Hot to substitute Stuffed Derma for *Schweinsulze* "on humanitarian grounds," and was told by a militant feminist: "The only humanitarian movement to concern yourself with is the Sisterhood, so join SUCK today";

• While Simone was detained in Fingerhood's office, the twins wandered into the kitchen and ate four bowls of whipped cream intended for the wedding cake;

• Lou and Keith spent the entire day clearing Fingerhood's living room of as much furniture as possible; arranging eight dining tables with place cards, two champagne fountains, hors d'oeuvres stations, and a sideboard of wedding gifts (mostly addressed to Fingerhood and Sally); making space for Mink & Sable to perform in, making sure that all kitchen appliances were in good working order, that the bathrooms were replenished with toilet tissue, Kleenex, soap, and guest towels, that scented candles and floral displays were everywhere; setting up folding chairs on the terrace where the ceremony was to be performed, stringing Japanese lanterns, rearranging a trio of potted palms to create an arbor for Reverend Freshwater to stand in front of, and laying in a cache of striped beach umbrellas in case (God forbid!) it rained;

• Upon returning from Macy's, Anita found the penthouse looking so shipshape that she ignored a hastily departing Simone who said she'd come over for dress rehearsal;

• Lou called out that Simone really meant "fuck rehearsal";

• Anita had to be put to bed and given a tranquilizer by a solicitous Fingerhood, who assured her that Lou was mistaken;

• Anita's father sang *"Deutschland Uber Alles"* in the shower, despite repeated warnings by both his wife and daughter;

• Afraid that he was marrying into a family of Nazis, Fingerhood proceeded to get blind drunk, wandered out to the terrace, crashed into the trio of rearranged palm trees, and bloodied his nose;

• Trying to escape all the commotion, Miguel flew into the guest bedroom where Mrs. Schuler was taking a nap and hid in the closet;

• A little while later, Mrs. Schuler opened the closet door to admire her new silk dress and found a large blue parrot shitting on its bodice;

• All of Jeeves's lights flashed on at the same time as Mrs. Schuler ran screaming from the bedroom and was intercepted by: Fingerhood pressing a cotton ball to his bloody nose, Fingerhood's mother, who'd arrived unannounced, and Mr. Schuler in an SS uniform.

# 12

On the day of her wedding, Anita awakened at dawn. Fearfully. Apprehensively. The weather report had predicted clear sunny weather, but who believed weather reports? With a prayer in her heart, she opened her eyes and peeked out. Thank God. The sky was blue, the sun was rising in the east, all was well with the world.

Then she noticed the pale green floral wallpaper and darker green decor of the room. *Where the hell was she?* She sat up in the hard, narrow, monklike bed—so different from the huge, soft, sybaritic bed she'd been sharing with Fingerhood—and tried to remember how she'd gotten here. Something about yesterday did not want to be unearthed, it fought her for oblivion, she fought back and won. She almost wished she hadn't. . . .

"Did you or didn't you screw Simone?" she had asked Fingerhood when she groggily awakened from the tranquilizer he'd given her. It was close to midnight, but she couldn't go back to sleep until she heard his firm denial. "And if you didn't, then why did Lou make that nasty crack about 'fuck rehearsal'?"

"Probably because she's gone off the deep end, like everyone else connected with this wedding." Fingerhood turned over beside her, his tone one of petulance and frustration. He couldn't stand to see his home in disarray and disruption. When familiar objects were not in their familiar places, he felt as though the world were coming to an end. "You're lucky you've been in dreamland and missed the floor show. I sure wish my mother had missed it. She fainted dead away, I had to revive her with coffee and brandy."

Anita felt miffed. If anyone deserved to be in a bad mood, *she* did. How dare he adopt this long-suffering attitude, when all he'd done was stay home, treat a few nonorgasmic patients, screw Simone, and minister to his mother, who'd probably fainted to gain sympathy over the Chopped Liver Swan issue? Then she saw his bandaged nose.

"How did you get that?"

"I ran into a couple of potted palms, but that's the least of it." He touched the gauze pad gingerly; it was dry, meaning the blood had caked at last. He was furious with Lou for moving those potted palms without his permission and then ratting on him to his future wife. "Anita, why didn't you ever tell me that your father used to be with the SS?"

"The SS? Where did you get such an absurd idea?"

"From the uniform he was prancing around in earlier."

"I'm sorry if Daddy frightened you." She laughed joylessly, her mind still grappling with the image of him and Simone banging their brains out while she was trapped in Macy's Big City Woman Shop. "The uniform was from a little-theater production he once starred in. Daddy played an SS officer who turned against the Führer and in the end got shot for his treachery." The play had been sponsored by the German-American League, all revenues going to help support a local orphanage. "It was Daddy's first and last acting role and the poor dear has never quite recovered from the thrill of applause. You must forgive him. He only wears the uniform if he's had a little too much schnapps and is feeling nostalgic."

"For what? The Gestapo?"

"Don't be mean, darling. For his short-lived acting career. It was the highlight of his life."

"He should have said so," Fingerhood peevishly replied. "My mother had relatives in Auschwitz."

"I didn't know. I'm sorry. What was your mother doing here so late? I hope she didn't come over to badger you about the Chopped Liver Swans."

"No, she'd just gotten through badgering Some Like It Hot. Not about Swans, though, Mom has progressed to Stuffed Derma." Fingerhood wished he were on a ship going to Zanzibar. "Unfortunately, when she called Some Like It Hot, she got one of Vanessa's feminist weirdos on the phone. That's when the trouble began."

"What trouble?"

"The weirdo not only told my mother there would be no substitutions for *Schweinsulze*, but strongly urged her to join their organization, SUCK."

Would this terrible day never end? "SUCK?"

"Society to Undermine Cock as King, as the weirdo painstakingly explained before my poor mother could hang up. Mom was shocked, mortified, she hasn't heard language like that in her life. So she came dashing over here to ask what kind of animals are cooking our wedding dinner and why they think she's their sister. Then she ran into your father in his SS uniform."

Fingerhood sighed the sigh of a man who didn't expect to regain his strength. "I can't take much more, Anita. I've had it with deranged parents, seamstresses jabbing at my ankles, furniture in all the wrong places, wedding gifts arriving every other minute, people traipsing in and out like it was the IRT, Reverend Freshwater telling me that the text from *The Fingerhood Position* was unsuitable for a wedding service. I informed him that either he'd read page 352 or we'd find ourselves another minister."

"You did *what*?"

"Relax. He said he'd do it, provided he could translate the passage into Spanish."

"Spanish?" Anita was appalled. "Are you sure he didn't mean Latin?"

"Quite sure. Reverend Freshwater's real name happens to be Carlos Aguafresca. He may have rejected the Catholic faith and the Holy Trinity in favor of a single god and the Unitarian way of life, but he sure likes to spout the old *español*. He recently married two gays in an all-Spanish service, even though they were both WASPs. He claims it brought a note of romance to the occasion." Fingerhood's nose felt as though it were going to start bleeding all over again. "Someone should have warned me what was involved in arranging a small, informal home wedding."

"And if they had?"

"Nothing. Forget it."

"I don't want to forget it. What were you going to say?"

"Look, I'm tired and on edge. Anything I say now, I'll only regret in the morning. So why don't we change the subject, or better yet, go back to sleep?"

Reason told her that he was right, but indignation prevailed. *He* was the one who'd cheated on her with Simone, and *he* was acting like the injured party! "You were going to say that if someone had warned you how unnerving it was to get married, you wouldn't have proposed to me in the first place. Isn't that true?''

"Don't put words in my mouth.''

"Then tell me what you were going to say.''

"I've forgotten by now.''

"You're avoiding the issue, which means I'm right.''

"No, you aren't. What it means is that I would have proposed anyway, but I would have prepared myself for this crazy home circus.''

"Were you so unprepared that you needed a fast fuck to relieve your tension? Is that what you're implying? Because I can tell you about tension. You want tension? Try to deal with musicians who have three guitar players but no organist, with caterers who charge outrageous fees to argue about your menu selection, with a minister who says you don't need dress rehearsal—although now that I know he wants to conduct half the service in Spanish, I'm not surprised—with parents looking like they just got off a cattle ship from Bavaria, with your mother-in-law hounding you about Chopped Liver Swans, with your matron of honor buying the color dress *she* likes, with Sally Northrop threatening to show up in black, with your fiancé making you go down on him just because you want him to get married in a decent suit, then go to Macy's Big City Woman Shop in the middle of the afternoon with size-fifty-two tanks draining all the oxygen in the room, blocking your path, stepping on your toes, and asking whether a garment big enough for an elephant looks slenderizing on you. *That's* tension!''

"There's no need to shout.''

"Isn't there? And in the midst of all that, I got my period again, I had a liver attack, and my old facial pain returned with a bang. Okay, I can live with those. What I can't live with is to come home, drained and exhausted, to be informed by Lou that you'd been screwing Simone. I was so humiliated, I wanted to die.''

"Calm down and listen to me.'' He tried to grasp her by the shoulders, but she pulled away. "I tell you for the last time that I did not screw your best friend. How can you consider me capable of such an act? What kind of man do you think I am?''

"She's not my best friend. She's an unethical, back-stabbing, self-centered nymphomaniac.''

Anita felt perilously close to tears. Why couldn't she find a fiancé who was faithful? What was there about her that made them cheat? Maybe if her breasts were larger, if her hips weren't spreading, if she weren't forty goddamned years old. Then she remembered that Simone was only thirty-nine. It wasn't fair. He might have had the decency to cheat on her with one of those empty-eyed, gum-chewing, ear-plugged roller-skaters who whizzed around the streets of New York showing girlish thighs in skimpy shorts. A young skating zombie wouldn't count.

"If you weren't screwing Simone, what the hell was she doing here? I called her hotel this morning and left a message that dress rehearsal had been canceled."

"Apparently she never received it. She even brought the twins because they're in the ceremony, too."

"She brought the twins to try to cover up her real reason for coming: *you*."

"It's no use." Frazzled, he longed for Sally's quiet passivity. It had just occurred to him that he was marrying a combative woman like his mother after all. Secretly, he always knew he would. "You'd rather believe a bitchy person like Lou than your future husband. Very well." He made a motion indicating that the subject was closed. "In that case, I'd appreciate your spending the night in the other room. Maybe by morning you'll come to your senses and realize that you owe me an apology. I hope so. I wouldn't want to start off married life on a note of mutual distrust."

"Mutual?" She leaped out of the huge, soft, sybaritic bed and indignantly wrapped herself in a blanket. "Why should you distrust *me*?"

"Because you've just demonstrated what a highly suspicious mind you have. And since people tend to judge others by their own actions, I wonder what I'm getting myself into. Does this mean I'm committing myself to a woman whose integrity I can't rely on, whose word I can't believe, and whose honesty I must continually question?"

Anita knew when she had been outmaneuvered. If she wanted to marry him tomorrow afternoon, she had better retreat and pretend she was wrong about Simone. What good would it do to go on insisting that she (and Lou) were right? She thought of the old adage: *I'd rather be right than president.* It had never appealed to her less than it did at that moment.

She would much rather be wrong as Mrs. Robert Fingerhood than right as an unwanted, unloved, unmarried woman.

"Maybe I did jump to a hasty and unfair conclusion," she said in a warmer tone of voice. "But it's only because love makes me insanely jealous. Deep down, I know that you wouldn't betray me." She blinked back tears of genuine remorse; if she lost him now, she'd kill herself. "Can you forgive me, darling?"

"We're both under a great deal of stress, don't give it another thought. In years to come, we'll laugh about this little misunderstanding." Off the hook, he observed her with renewed interest. "Why don't you get rid of that silly blanket and come back to bed? I'm starting to miss you."

She knew that tone of voice by now. "Sorry, sweetheart, but I have my period."

"So what?"

"So we shouldn't."

"Shouldn't what?" He reached over and playfully tried to grab her leg, thinking she was being coy. She withdrew. "What shouldn't we do?"

"Shouldn't make love when I have my period."

"Are you kidding?" Had she been this squeamish fifteen years ago? He couldn't recall. "Menstruation is a natural female function, it's not intended to interfere with sexual relations. Besides, periods don't bother me in the least."

She was horrified. "They don't?"

"Not at all. I'm a doctor, remember?"

She envisioned him trying to stick it into her with all that blood either clotting or coursing around. Ugh! "You mean you would actually make love to me *now*?"

"Sure. People do it all the time."

Still stunned from learning that he didn't disinfect, she couldn't hope to absorb this latest unsanitary practice all at once. The current AIDS scare was uppermost in her mind. She tried to remain calm by remembering that the disease usually affected the four H's: homosexuals, Haitians, hemophiliacs, and heroin addicts. Although Fingerhood did not fall into any of these categories, changes were going to be made around here in the personal-hygiene department, *big* changes. Meanwhile, there was no point in rocking the boat. She dredged up her most conciliatory manner.

"Darling, you know how much I love you and how close I

want to be to you, but I was thinking that aside from my period, it might be best if I slept in the other room. Sort of as a gesture to old-fashioned wedding etiquette. Please don't laugh at me, but there is the solemnity of the night before to consider."

He smiled at this quaint girlish notion. "Your parents might prefer it too."

"I'm certain they would." The understatement of the century. Her father had been giving her dark looks ever since he arrived and her mother had trustingly asked which of the bedrooms was hers. "The small one with the narrow bed," Anita replied like a dutiful daughter. "I'd like one last virginal night before I start my new life as Mrs. Robert Fingerhood, happiest woman in the world."

His smile grew broader. "I'm sure that can be arranged."

"You don't mind?"

"I mind passionately, but if it's what you want, you're entitled." He felt flattered that she would wish to save herself for his exclusive legal consumption after tomorrow. "You won't be having too many virginal nights from here on in, will you?"

That was what she was beginning to be afraid of, but better not let him know it. "I hope I don't, sweetheart. I wouldn't like that at all."

His sovereignty restored, Fingerhood could afford to dispense regal favors. "Get thee to a nunnery," he said, slapping her affectionately on the ass. . . .

From her window of exile, Anita now looked across the river to Roosevelt Island, where a sentry of trees shone in the thin morning sun. How straight and proud they appeared, how unbending, how inspiring. It seemed to her that she'd spent her life bending (so as not to break), compromising, telling endless little white lies, like the lie she told Fingerhood about believing in his fidelity. She knew that he'd fucked Simone, but she went on record as pretending she didn't. She would continue to go on record pretending all sorts of things she realized to be false until the day she died. It wasn't that she especially liked to lie; she would have preferred to tell the truth—it was so much less complicated—but the truth wasn't always feasible or sensible. The truth had to be occasionally stretched to accommodate human needs.

Anita sighed, yawned, opened her eyes wider. People were

flawed and imperfect, they floundered around doing the best they could, then covered their tracks when they behaved ignobly. Fingerhood had lied too, by pretending he didn't make love to Simone. He lied to keep from hurting her, just as she lied to keep from hurting him. It saddened her to know that this was the way things were, it was how grown-ups operated, it was what made the machinery of the world keep turning. People told little white lies in order to protect each other's feelings, vulnerabilities, vanities. In the end, it was known as good manners. People were not trees.

This struck Anita as such a profound insight that she wondered if she could persuade Reverend Freshwater to incorporate it into the wedding ceremony. Remembering that his real name was Carlos Aguafresca, she decided against it. There was no point in adding to the poor man's burdens. He would have his hands full trying to translate *The Fingerhood Position* into Spanish.

When Simone opened her eyes, the first thing she saw was huge cartoon figures of Popeye and Olive Oil fighting with each other in brilliant blinding color. She thought she was dreaming until the twins came into focus. They sat on her bedroom floor, shrieking, giggling, and pummeling the carpet whenever television mirth became too much for them.

"I hope Olive Oil knocks him out!" Rima squealed.

"I hate Olive Oil!" Prince replied, jumping up and down.

"And I hate inconsiderate children who intrude on their mother's privacy." Simone sat up and flopped against the tufted satin headboard. "What's wrong with the TV set in your room, may I ask?"

"It broke down after *Captain Kangaroo*," Prince said.

"What's wrong with the set in the living room?"

"It wiggles."

"What's wrong with the set in Jimmy's room? No, don't tell me. He's writing and doesn't want to be disturbed. Either that or he's sleeping and doesn't want to be disturbed."

"He's not doing any of those things, Mommy. Jimmy went out a few minutes ago."

"Out? It's only ten after eight. Where did he go?" The twins had no idea. How strange, Simone thought, considering the fact that he rarely went anywhere until after his morning stint at the typewriter. "Okay, what I want you children to do is hightail it downstairs, drink your orange juice, eat your Crispy Wheats 'n Raisins, and watch Popeye in the living room. Now, scram.''

"We don't eat Crispy Wheats 'n Raisins anymore," Rima said. "We've switched to Grapenut Flakes."

"Then go eat your Grapenut Flakes."

Rima hooted with laughter. "We can't, Mommy. There isn't any in the refrigerator!"

Simone observed her daughter with a mixture of crazed fury and sly admiration. "I suppose you think it's funny to trick me like that. Well, I don't think it's so funny. A flower girl who tricks the matron of honor has to pay a penance. Do you want to know what the penance is?"

"No, Mommy!" Rima giggled.

"The penance is to take the ring-bearer downstairs, call room service, order two big bowls of Grapenut Flakes with sliced bananas and milk, and let me the hell alone. Now, get going."

The twins reluctantly stood up.

"Is there a penance for ring-bearers too?" Rima asked.

"That's not fair," Prince protested. "I didn't do anything. Besides, I hate Grapenut Flakes. They stick in my teeth."

"Use a toothpick, darling."

"What if I can't find one?"

"Use your toothbrush."

"But I'll be in the kitchen, Mommy."

"Use your little finger."

"Hilda says that's vulgar."

None of the books she'd ever read about motherhood had prepared her for this. None. *"Fuck Hilda!"* she screamed. *"You're driving me crazy! Use your fist! Use your nose! What do I care? Stop torturing me!"*

Prince looked at her gravely. "You said a bad word, Mommy."

"Tough shit."

"You said another one," Rima pointed out. "Mommy, are you going to marry Mr. Harding?"

"Yes, after you and your brother go downstairs. We plan to be wed in a secret ceremony right here in the closet."

"You can't do that, Mommy." Rima was smiling again. "Mr. Harding went back to England."

"That's what *you* think." Simone looked out the window

at the clear sunny sky and thought of how relieved Anita must feel. Her own wedding day had been marred by buckets of rain, a grumpy bridegroom, and nervous diarrhea. She would have bet anything that Anita didn't have diarrhea. Joy and happiness were what Anita had, and who could blame her? She was finally seeing the fulfillment of all her dreams (although thirteen years ago Simone had thought so too). "For your information, Mr. Harding never left New York. At this very moment he's hiding in my closet with Reverend Freshwater, who's going to make us man and wife."

Rima hopped up and down with joy. "Can he make you man, wife, and children?"

"No, darling. Children don't get married, only the principals."

"What's a 'principal,' Mommy?"

"If you start that *merde*, I'm going to scream," Simone cautioned her daughter.

"Mommy, why did you say *merde*, when you really meant *shit*?"

Simone threw back her head and let out a long wordless piercing howl. Did other children ask as many questions as the twins? She doubted it. Something told her she'd been cursed by abnormally inquisitive offspring. *Why me, God? Why was I singled out?* At home in Malibu, she never realized how stifling and maddening it must be to operate as a full-time mother. There she had Hilda and Harold to field the twins' curiosity, plus her own acting career for diversion. What would she have in England as the wife of Sir Michael Harding? An English couple, but no career. Was it enough? She reminded herself that when she was married to Steve Omaha and working at CheapSkates, she'd managed quite nicely with a high-school girl in the afternoons. Yes, but the twins were younger then and so was she. They hadn't yet reached the obsessive question stage and she hadn't yet been spoiled by a taste of success, fame, independence.

The telephone rang. It was Michael.

"Darling, how are you?" he asked. "I didn't wake you, did I?"

"No, the twins beat you to it." He'd been gone for less than twenty-four hours and already his voice sounded strange, foreign, unreal. It conjured up those tinkling Noël Coward plays filled with make-believe people doing make-believe things in a make-believe world. "How was your flight? How is Lady Philippa? How is England?"

"Super, darling, truly super. In response to all queries." Unlike her, he was jubilant. "What rot, though, bringing me home because of a bloody toucan bite. You should see the woman! One day after plastic surgery and she's fit as the proverbial fiddle. In better shape than I am, I daresay." His laughter was edged with acidity. "At least she was until I asked for a divorce."

*He had done it.* Simone felt acutely panicked. "What happened then?"

"She called me a snake—a boa constrictor, to be exact. Claimed that I've choked the life and vitality out of her. Then she suggested that I pack my bags and vacate the premises." He chuckled. "Rather what I had in mind myself, ey?"

The panic was getting worse, not better. "Does that mean you're going down to London as planned?"

"First thing in the morning. Have you booked your flight to Los Angeles yet?"

"Not exactly."

"What do you mean, darling? Either you booked it or you didn't."

Simone hesitated. They had agreed that immediately after Fingerhood's wedding, she would return to Malibu, get her affairs in order, and ship everything to the Grosvenor House. Michael thought it would be jolly good fun to take a large suite at the fashionable Mayfair hotel while he shopped around for a flat. And at the time he made the suggestion, so did she. That was only yesterday, Simone realized with a jolt.

"I didn't call the airline because Rima isn't feeling well." Her face clenched up, as it did whenever she had to tell a lie. "I'm afraid she might not be well enough to travel tomorrow, so I thought I'd wait and see."

"Bloody bad luck, darling. Nothing serious, I trust?"

"Oh, no. You know how children with nervous stomachs are." Rima's stomach was made of solid cast iron. "It's probably just the excitement over being a flower girl, but I want to be on the safe side."

"Right you are." He smacked his lips. "Well, I guess that's it for now. Next time I see you will be in London, darling. I can hardly wait."

"Neither can I. I'll call as soon as I know my arrival time."

"I love you, darling."

Her face clenched even tighter. "I love you, too."

Laying down the receiver, she caught a glimpse of her matron-of-honor gown hanging in the closet. In only a few more hours she would be walking down the aisle, smiling and outwardly serene, despite the uncertainty that beat in her heart. She envied Anita her neat secure future. Anita might be a lot of things (greedy, bitchy, dumb, shrewd), but she wasn't ambivalent.

"I can have a neat secure future with Michael," Simone said out loud. "If only . . ."

Last night, Jimmy had let her read the first sixty pages of his screenplay, and to her surprise, she found the female lead wildly sympathetic, appealing. In fact, she had never before identified so closely with a character as she did the frustrated suburban housewife of Jimmy's invention. They shared many of the same problems—sexual anxiety, emotional suffocation, an uncertain tomorrow—and Simone knew she could play her convincingly. The part was made to order for her.

"What do you think?" Jimmy asked. "You could really sink your teeth into this, couldn't you?"

"And if I said yes, what would happen?" She was remembering Diana Ross and the *Rockabye Princess* treachery. "At the last minute, you'd end up rewriting the part for another actress."

He put his hand over his heart. "On my word of honor, I wouldn't."

"Forget it. One, I'm getting married. And two, it isn't even your decision. It's the studio's."

"The studio likes you for the frustrated housewife. They told me so."

"They liked me for *Rockabye Princess*, too. Until they stopped liking me."

"Hey, there are no guarantees, kiddo. You know that. Not with anything."

There were no guarantees that she and Michael would make a go of it. No guarantees at all. *Career versus marriage, marriage versus career.* Why couldn't she have both? Goddammit, it wasn't fair. She needed both, one to balance the other. Marriage to get her through the madness of movie-

naking, and movie-making to get her through the madness of
narriage. No wonder men didn't seem to fall apart as readily
as women: they rarely put all their eggs in one basket, as she
was being forced to do.

Seconds later, she was on the phone to room service. "One
chocolate milkshake, double thick. And one slice of chocolate cake, please."

She felt like a naughty child because she hadn't ordered a
sensible, nutritious, high-protein breakfast. The feeling of
naughtiness was an old one, a familiar one, and usually a
most enjoyable one, but now it failed to satisfy. Screwing
Fingerhood on top of his desk yesterday had failed to satisfy,
too. Why had she done it? Even Fingerhood was surprised
when she agreed.

"You *will*?" He couldn't believe his good luck.

"Sure." She tried to act nonchalant, carefree. "Why not?"

What appealed to her about the invitation was its spontaneity,
its desktop nuttiness. Desire had not even entered into it.
When she asked him why the desk (and not the floor, or one
of the bedrooms), he replied, "This desk is too damned
respectable, it needs a proper christening." That seemed
logical to Simone, who remembered that she hadn't done
anything outrageous in a long time. Was she getting middle-
aged and stodgy? Was she losing her quest for adventure?
Disturbed by the possibility, she got out of her clothes in
three seconds flat.

Fingerhood followed her lead. Foreplay was held to a bare
minimum and then he was on top of her, in her, in and out of
her, and in her again. As she watched him thrashing away with
his eyes half-closed and his face contorted by lust, Simone
felt bold and free and rebellious. *Hey, world, look at me!
Aren't I the naughty little girl?* Afterward she felt ashamed
and chagrined. What had possessed her? What had she
accomplished? She'd betrayed both Anita and Michael for the
sake of a fast fuck with a man she no longer cared about.
Quickly putting on her clothes, she made a dash for the door.
Fingerhood ran after her, mumbling something about celebrating with champagne, but she waved him off.

"I don't feel like celebrating. I feel like repenting."

"Was it that bad for you?"

"Don't be an asshole. I'm not talking about the sexual
mechanics. You haven't lost your touch, Fingerhood."

"Then what are you repenting for?"

She thought of her poor innocent children. Didn't they deserve a more self-respecting mother? "For behaving like a retarded cheerleader. . . ."

Rima was tugging at her shoulder now. "Mommy, someone is ringing the doorbell downstairs. Should I answer it?"

Simone patted her daughter's soft fine hair, inhaled her sweet scent. It constantly amazed her that she'd produced this child and then her brother, fraternal twins, with whom she'd been in labor for eighteen terrible hours. She remembered the doctor stitching her up afterward. An episiotomy, it was called. He hadn't knocked her out enough and she groggily told him that she could feel the stitches. She would never forget that sensation of exposing her most private self to a total stranger, doctor or not. It served to bring her back to her most primitive roots. So this was what life was all about—literally being torn open to release the next generation. It made everything else pale by comparison.

"I'll answer the door," she told Rima, putting on a satin-ribbed peignoir that matched her nightgown. "It must be room service."

It wasn't room service. It was a highly distraught Beverly.

"Sally has disappeared again." Beverly stood on the threshold, looking like a wounded animal. "She's not with you, by any chance, is she?"

"No. Come in."

"Oh, Mommy!" the twins wailed in unison when she told them to turn off the TV set and go watch *Meatballs & Spaghetti* in her bedroom. "Make up your mind!"

Beverly's gaze followed them up the stairs. "They're adorable, Simone. So was Sally at that age, but I wonder if I would go through it all over again, knowing what I now know."

"Have kids, you mean?"

Beverly nodded. "You do your best, but in the long run it's a crapshoot. There's no guarantee how they'll turn out. Then you torture yourself that you *didn't* do your best, that maybe you should never have become a parent, that you don't have what it takes. Then you look at your other child and he's fine, so you wonder whether it's something in the genes, and not their upbringing or environment. . . ." Her voice trailed off aimlessly.

"Would you like some coffee? Tea? Breakfast?"

"No, nothing, thanks. I couldn't." She sank into the gray velvet sofa with a sigh. "It's so strange to be reliving an old nightmare, it's so unreal."

"Why don't you tell me what happened?"

"Sally had lunch with Dwight and me at the Gramercy Regency coffee shop yesterday afternoon. We were going shopping afterward for a wedding present and we left her there, finishing cherry-vanilla ice cream." Beverly's voice trembled. "That was the last time we saw her."

"When did you realize she was missing?"

"Just a little while ago. She had a dinner date with her brother last evening, so I didn't bother calling. But when she failed to answer the phone this morning, I thought it was strange. I asked the management to open the door. Her bed hadn't been slept in and Peter Jr. said she never showed up for dinner." Beverly looked as though she'd aged ten years. "I can't go through this hell all over again. I'm frantic with worry. I don't know what to do. I was hoping against hope that maybe she came over here to see you. She seemed to take to you that day at Bendel's."

"Have you notified the police?"

"Yes, but she hasn't been gone long enough for them to issue a missing-persons report. I didn't tell you this before, but Sally has a drug problem. I'm afraid she might have run into someone who offered her cocaine. If that happened, God knows what trouble she's in. Oddly enough, she was scheduled to enter a rehabilitation clinic in less than a week. Now this setback."

"What about Fingerhood? He might have an idea where she is."

"He doesn't. I called him before coming over here. He said that Sally probably ran away because she couldn't face going for treatment."

"Didn't she agree to go?"

"Yes, but I guess she didn't mean it. Fingerhood feels that Peter and I might have unwittingly pushed her too hard in that direction, without realizing it was a decision she had to make for herself. You see, he tried to push her too and her reaction was to cancel the wedding." She caught Simone's look of surprise. "Don't jump to conclusions. As I understand it, Fingerhood was *relieved*. I don't think he wanted to marry her in the first place. I think he was just trying to be noble and help her overcome this terrible problem. Do you know why Sally started using cocaine?''

She didn't wait for Simone's reply. ''To lose weight and to enjoy sex! I tell you, Simone, the pressure on girls of Sally's generation is much worse than anything we had to contend with. When we were growing up, the times were still pretty puritanical as far as sex went. And if a girl was a size ten, she was considered acceptable. Today ten is a goddamned tank and everyone feels compelled to have multiple orgasms.'' Beverly's voice broke. ''Poor Sally. She couldn't cope.''

Simone put her arms around her old friend. ''I have an idea. Maybe she'll turn up at the wedding. She sure seemed eager to sock it to Anita in that brazen black dress.''

''That means she'd have to come back to the Gramercy Regency to change. The dress is still hanging in her closet.'' Beverly's eyes begged for confirmation. ''Do you honestly believe there's a chance she might do that?''

''Only if Fingerhood is mistaken.''

''What do you mean?''

''Maybe she didn't run away because she feared going for treatment. Maybe she met someone at the Gramercy Regency coffee shop after you and Dwight left. You know how hotels are. All sorts of attractive men are forever passing through, and if Sally is as sexually oriented as you say, she might have gone off with one of them.''

''And be shacked up with him this very minute,'' Beverly mused.

''Right. In which case her disappearance would have less to do with drugs and more to do with romance.''

Wouldn't that be ironic? Beverly thought. Romance was what she'd been busily denying herself ever since Dwight got to New York. Last night he tried to make love to her and she pulled away, not because she didn't desire him (suddenly, she did all over again) but because she felt it wouldn't be right.

''What's the matter?'' he asked.

''I don't know, darling.'' She held him close. ''I just don't know.''

But she did know. She could not stop fretting about Sally's drug problem. She could not stop blaming herself, depriving herself. She mumbled something about being tired from the move into the Gramercy Regency, then turned over and stared listlessly into the dark night. . . .

She stood up. "I should be getting back to Dwight. I left in such a hurry that I didn't even tell him where I was going." She kissed Simone. "I had planned to skip the wedding, but if you think Sally might be there, I guess I can persuade Dwight to accompany me. So I'll be seeing you later on."

"*Planned to skip Anita's day in the sun?*" Simone asked with mock incredulity. "I can't imagine why. Isn't this what we came to New York for? Besides, if I were you I'd attend out of sheer gratefulness that Fingerhood isn't marrying Sally."

"That *is* a relief," Beverly said, thinking back. "Remember when we both were so crazy about him?"

"How can I forget? I tried to slash my wrists when he left me for you. I must have been out of my mind."

"We both were. I secretly used to hope that he would ask me to marry him. I mean, Fingerhood is all right. Actually, he's turned out to be a rather nice guy, but why did we think he was the earth, sun, and moon fifteen years ago? Was it just youth?"

"What else? Also, he came on like a big-time Casanova. Remember all those delicious meals he used to cook for us and how he drank champagne out of our shoes? Our shoes!" Simone giggled. "He really did that, and we fell for it hook, line, and sinker. I thought it was the most romantic thing that ever happened to me, despite the fact that my best pair of Charles Jourdan slings were soaked clear through."

"You too? My shoemaker used to ask me where I went on weekends to find so much rain. I wonder if he's drinking champagne out of Anita's shoes these days." Beverly shook her head. "I still can't believe that she's marrying the goofball, but I guess it's a big inducement knowing she'll never have to lift her little finger again."

"Not so long as she keeps lifting that ass of hers."

Beverly hugged her. "You always make me feel better, Simone. I'm sorry that Michael had to go back to London. I was looking forward to meeting him."

"You'll meet Jimmy Newton instead."

"Isn't that the movie director you've been living with? I read an article about the two of you, in *People*, I think."

"That's the one." Simone couldn't imagine where he had

gone so early in the day. "I've roped him into being my escort."

"Doesn't Michael object? Steve Omaha would have had a fit." Beverly vividly remembered Simone's possessive, hot-tempered ex-husband.

"Michael and Stevie are nothing alike. What about Dwight and Peter? Any resemblance?"

"None at all, thank God. It usually goes that way, doesn't it?"

"You mean, a complete reversal of types?"

Beverly nodded. "I think we tend to choose a total oppo-site the second time, in the hope that it will help ensure a successful marriage."

"Has it, in your case?"

"I'd be a liar if I said yes. But I'd be lying if I said no. There are problems, Simone."

*Career versus marriage, marriage versus career.* "Aren't there always?"

"What's the matter? Did you and Michael have a lovers' quarrel?"

"Worse than that," Simone said, turning morose.

"I'm sorry." Beverly realized that something serious was at stake. "What is it? Won't his wife give him a divorce?"

"*Au contraire*, she seems eager as hell to get rid of him. It's me. I'm getting cold feet about marrying him."

"How come? After that talk we had at Bendel's, I got the impression you were madly in love with the guy."

"I was. I mean, in a way I still am. But he wants me to give up acting and I'm not sure what I want to do. I'm being pulled in two directions at once. Also, I question my motives in both cases."

"What do you mean?"

"I wonder whether I'd be using marriage as an excuse to abandon my career and all the difficulties connected to it. Then I wonder whether I'd be using my career as an excuse to avoid making a commitment to marriage and all the difficul-ties connected to that. Either way I turn seems perilous."

"I don't know what to say," Beverly confessed.

"No one can help me. It's my problem, my future, my decision." The image of screwing Fingerhood on top of his desk came back to haunt her. "I don't want to take the path of least resistance. I've done enough of that over the years. I think it's about time that I started learning how to assume responsibility for my own actions, don't you?''

Beverly smiled. ''Hey, what happened to that silly scatterbrained screwball I used to know?''

Simone rolled her eyes, sucked in her lips, and made her imbecile face. ''Don't tell anyone, but she's trying to grow up.''

Jimmy got out of the cab in front of the Algonquin on West Forty-fourth Street and went directly to the house phone.

''I'd like to speak to Mr. Pierre deGaulle,'' he told the operator.

''Yes, Monsieur and Madame deGaulle just checked in. They're in room 402. You can dial them directly.''

''*Madame* deGaulle?''

''The lady in question.''

''Right. Sure. Thanks.'' He dialed and cupped his hand over his mouth. ''Hello, Fuckface. It's me. Should I come up, or are you making public appearances?''

''Did you bring the do-re-mi?''

''What else would I be doing in this neck of the woods at such an ungodly hour? Be right there.''

When he knocked on the door to room 402, it was opened by a tall thin brunette he had never seen before. ''Madame deGaulle?'' he said, frowning. As far as he was concerned, this cloak-and-dagger stuff was for the birds.

''It was the only French name Colin could think of. Come in, come in!'' She was ten feet off the ground. ''Are we ever glad to see you!''

Jimmy entered the modest room where one suitcase lay on the double bed, unopened. In a far corner was Colin's Yamaha, now dyed bright red, its license plate changed from the instantly recognizable ARIZ PETE to nondescript numbers. Jimmy wondered where he'd had it done and how much he paid to shut the person up. Just as he was about to ask the girl, the door to the bathroom opened and Colin emerged. He wore a curly gray wig, gray mustache, small gray beard, round glasses, and if Jimmy hadn't known better, he would have guessed him at fifty.

'' *'Allo, mon ami*,'' Colin said in a deep French accent before switching to his regular breezy voice. ''That's all the

Frog I know. Said it once in a minus-B flick I made prior to *Arizona Pete*. Sit down, old buddy, sit down!''

Jimmy remained standing, frowning, wondering why Colin continued to do drugs. Eventually they would catch up to him. But he never criticized. The two of them had a pact: Colin didn't mention his gambling, and he didn't mention Colin's coke habit.

''What the hell are you doing in that ridiculous disguise?'' he said instead. ''How much longer do you think you can keep this crap up? Everyone and his brother is out looking for you. Eddie is frantic. He's in New York, you know. I think the FBI is on your case, you asshole.''

Colin hooted with glee. ''I fooled them all, didn't I? Even managed to check into the famous Algonquin without anybody spotting me. Always do the obvious, that's my motto.'' He turned to the girl, who'd been sitting quietly. ''How about a little Pernod, darling?''

''Should I call room service?''

''Hell, no. I stuck a bottle in your suitcase. Want to do the honors? There are some glasses in the john.'' Before she could comply with his wishes, he grabbed and kissed her, ran his hands up and down her hips a couple of times. ''If there's anything I love, it's young firm flesh. Drives me wild. Hey, add some water to my drink. Okay, darling?''

''Anything you want, Colin.''

''Is that a promise?''

''You bet.''  ·

''I'll hold you to it, you sweet thing.''

They seemed to have forgotten that Jimmy was there. They were locked in another embrace, murmuring endearments. He cleared his throat. ''This is all very touching, but I've got a hot screenplay in a typewriter uptown and I haven't had breakfast yet. Can you do the love scene later, folks?'' He reached into his pocket and handed Colin a thick wad of bills. ''How long are you planning to hang around New York?''

''Another day or two, but unfortunately Mr. deGaulle doesn't have any credit cards. I appreciate this, old buddy. I'll reimburse you when we get back to L.A.''

''*We?*''

''This charming young lady has agreed to fly back with me. I figure now that Simone and the twins are moving to London, there'll be plenty of room in the house.''

Jimmy was surprised. Colin liked to fuck them and forget them, not live with them. He wondered what this one had that the others didn't. As far as he could see, she was nothing special.

"Don't count on Simone moving anywhere. It looks like she's changed her mind about marrying that Englishman. But since I assume the two of you will be sharing a bedroom, I don't anticipate any space problems." He took another peek at the girl. A par-for-the-course cokehead, too thin, too flaky. Considering all the beautiful women there were in Los Angeles, this one didn't make any sense. "What I do anticipate, Colin, are mucho problems for you with the studio. They're suing the shit out of you, you know. Jesus, what made you drive away like that right in the middle of a scene? Are you nuts?"

"Could be. One minute I was going to follow directions and chase Arizona Pete's suspect, the next minute I decided to go to New York and visit you, old buddy. But I seem to have gotten sidetracked along the way." He gazed affectionately at the girl, who'd removed a Pernod bottle from her suitcase and was heading for the bathroom. "Isn't she terrific? Not like those self-centered narcissistic actresses who're always looking in the mirror to see if they've grown a new wrinkle overnight. And she's got class, Jimmy, breeding, background, education."

"How did you meet?"

"Over a dish of ice cream at the Gramercy Regency, would you believe? That's where I checked in when I got here. But we had to split on accounta complications I won't bore you with." Colin chuckled. "At first, when I tried to pick her up, she thought I was an aging French fart. Then I revealed my true identity and it's been a hoot and a toot ever since."

"So I've noticed," Jimmy said tersely.

"Nah, I'm not talking just about the coke. I could have three million snorting partners in L.A. if I lifted my little finger. That's not it. What I really dig about her is that unlike the vast population of chicks in Southern California, she's not ambitious. She doesn't want a career. She only wants me! Do you believe it? This woman has one goal in life: to make me happy."

Jimmy felt jealous. He wished that was all Simone wanted. The fact that she was vacillating about marrying Harding and yet at the same time refused to marry him meant he had really lost her. He should have proposed a long time ago; that was where he'd goofed.

"I'm happy for you, amigo," he said to Colin. "It sounds like you've got it made."

"You never know where you'll find happiness, do you, old buddy?"

He could have kicked himself for taking Simone for granted all those years. "Or where you *won't* find it."

When the girl emerged from the bathroom, she held two glasses with milky Pernod. She gave one to Colin and sipped from the other. "Do me a favor," she suddenly said to Jimmy. "Don't tell Simone that you've seen me. She'll only tell my mother, and I'd rather surprise her myself later on."

He was startled. "Do you know Simone?"

"I've met her. She and my mother are old friends. Didn't Colin explain who I am?"

"My oversight," Colin interjected. "This is Sally Northrop deGaulle, the last real woman left in the Western world."

They shook hands.

"We'll be seeing you at the wedding this afternoon," she said to him, a sly twinkle in her eye. "I've talked Colin into being my guest."

"Wait a minute." Jimmy was starting to put it all together. "Aren't you the lady who was originally supposed to *marry* Fingerhood?"

"That's right, but I thought it would be more amusing this way."

"Which way?"

"Instead of walking down the aisle with Dr. Sex, I plan to make a rather spectacular entrance with Arizona Pete."

Their laughter followed Jimmy out the door.

When Beverly left the King Croesus, depression engulfed her again and she felt tempted to stop somewhere for a drink. *Anywhere.* Just one drink to help her cope with Sally's disappearance. It was kind of Simone to suggest that instead of running away, Sally had been detained in a romantic rendezvous. She wished she could believe it, but now that she was out in the hot no-nonsense glare of New York—with

Park Avenue stretching somberly before her—she knew it was a pipe dream.

Just as her wish to have one drink was. Experience had clearly proven that unfeasible. She would progress to two drinks, then three, six before she realized what was happening, ending up smashed out of her skull and feeling even worse than she did right now (if that were possible). Resentment swelled up within her, bitter and acrid.

It wasn't fair that she couldn't drink.

It wasn't fair that Sally had turned into a drug addict.

It wasn't fair that Peter blamed her for their daughter's disappearance ("If she hadn't moved into that damned hotel with you and Dwight, she'd be safe this very minute," he unjustly accused her).

It wasn't fair that Dwight had spiked his coffee with bourbon that morning, claiming it was her fault he'd fallen off the wagon ("If I have to go through this shit with Sally again, I'll end up on skid row," he threatened).

It wasn't fair that she felt too old to start out all over again, because otherwise she would divorce Dwight, wash her hands of Sally, tell Peter to go fuck himself, move back to New York, and get a job at one of the many art galleries that flourished in the city.

Until this return trip, she didn't realize how much she missed the galleries and museums. They were truly magnificent, awe-inspiring, and she had spent most of her time wandering up and down Fifth Avenue, Madison Avenue, Fifty-seventh Street, and SoHo gorging herself on the treasures they housed. The only place she hadn't gotten around to yet was the Guggenheim, which was having an exhibit of four decades of the New York School of Painting. She'd been greedily saving that for today, but now with her concern over Sally . . . Well, how could she go museum hopping when her only daughter was missing again? Guilt and a sharp sense of deprivation tore at her, made her walk even faster, as though she could leave them behind. As she stopped for a light near the Waldorf, a couple who were obviously from out of town (double-knit polyester for her, too-short trousers for him) asked her which way Bloomingdale's was.

"You walk one block east," Beverly said, pointing toward Lex. "And then nine blocks uptown." She pointed north, pleased to be of help. "*Et voilà.*"

Their accent was twangy, far Western, Wyoming for all she knew. "Thank you so much, ma'am," they trilled like children, as hand in hand they trustingly wandered off.

Instead of feeling an affinity with them, Beverly felt superior. Hicks. They made her realize how tired she was of small-town life in Wyoming. Sick and tired. Bored out of her mind. Now that she no longer had to hide her drinking (since she was no longer drinking), she didn't need to live there anymore. She was sick of the sticks, she thought, laughing out loud at this unexpected bit of self-knowledge. A man in a conservative gray suit and dark tie glanced at her nervously. In response, she gave him a leering clown's grin. His eyelids fluttered and he skirted away to escape her craziness.

"Sick of the sticks!" she joyously called after him, letting go with another peal of laughter.

It felt good to laugh. It felt good to think of all the things she might do if she weren't too old for new beginnings. It felt even better to wonder whether she *was* too old. Did forty-four mean the end of the world? Why should it? She was still an attractive, inquisitive, intelligent woman. Catching her reflection in a windowpane, she noted that her pantsuit was hanging on her. She had lost weight in New York without trying, and if she put on some decent makeup, bought some clothes, and stopped leering at strangers, she could easily become assimilated into the people landscape of this strange but wonderful city. She'd done it once before, hadn't she?

"Maybe it's time for you to break out of that nice, safe, warm little cocoon you've been holed up in for the last ten years," Peter had said to her only a few days ago.

How remarkable that he should have anticipated her actions. How very prescient of him. *I'm going to do it*, she thought, feeling slightly dazed. By the time she reached the Gramercy Regency, it almost seemed like a *fait accompli*. She would live around Beekman Place in a light, plant-filled, two-bedroom, two-bathroom apartment. It would be lovely if she could find something with a little garden or terrace, so that she didn't feel hemmed in after the open spaces of Wyoming. The image of fixing up the apartment filled her with happy anticipation. She would throw out her present furniture and buy everything new. She could see it already: all chrome and glass and clean lines, bright primary colors, cheerful colors to match the cheerful mood she intended to start out in, and she would hang Steve Omaha's Don Ameche–Alice Faye painting over the long sleek sofa. She hugged herself with excitement.

*"Where the hell have you been?"*

A disheveled unshaven Dwight sat slumped in one of the hotel armchairs, a glass in his hand, a bottle of Jack Daniel on the floor next to him. Something inside Beverly snapped. She had read about moments like this, when, in a flash, the person you used to be suddenly got tired of being that person. And changed. She always thought those moments didn't exist in real life, but she was wrong.

"I said, where have you been?" he barked.

"To see the Wizard of Oz." She grabbed the Jack Daniel bottle, went into the bathroom, and poured its contents down the sink.

Dwight followed her, amazed. "What do you think you're doing?"

"Getting rid of your fix." She threw the empty bottle into the wastebasket. "And if you don't stop drinking this very second, I'm divorcing you. No ifs, ands, or buts, no nothing. Cold turkey, Dwight. I don't care how you do it, just *do* it."

He appeared stunned. "I've never seen you like this before. What's happened?"

"I'm taking charge of my life before I have no life left. And you had better do the same." She softened her tone slightly. "I want you to shower and shave. I'll lay out your clothes."

"Where are we going?"

She pushed him toward the shower. "I'll tell you when you clean yourself up."

As soon as she heard the sound of running water, she got out his summer suit, her two-piece linen with the cool boat neckline, and sat down at the makeshift dressing table. She tweezed her eyebrows, put on foundation, rouge, mascara, and lipstick, brushed her long red hair, got undressed, and slipped into the sexy robe she'd bought at Saks the other day in a moment of impulse. It was a flimsy turquoise thing that clung to her provocative curves exactly where she wanted it to. She sprayed herself (and the room) with another new purchase: Cinnabar.

"Okay," Dwight said when he emerged from the bathroom, damp and clean and looking like a different person. "What gives?"

"First, you're taking me to brunch at the Plaza. Then we're going to see the exhibit at the Guggenheim. Then we're going to come back here and make love. And then," she finished with a flourish, "we're going to that goddamned stupid wedding."

He started to smile. "I thought you were hell bent on avoiding that wedding."

"I've changed my mind."

"I thought you didn't want to make love."

"I've changed my mind about that, too."

His smile grew broader. "How come?"

"I've decided that I can't beat myself up over Sally forever."

"Is that why . . . last night . . . when I tried to. . . ?"

She nodded. "It wasn't that I didn't want to, Dwight. I've been punishing myself, punishing you too. Only I didn't realize it before. It will be different from now on, I plan to turn over a new leaf."

She had done all the grieving and worrying and self-inflicting of pain that she intended to do. Sally was twenty years old. If she felt like spending the rest of her life sticking dope up her nose, it was her problem. Beverly would help her in any way she could, but first Sally had to reach out and *ask* for help. She had to want to change. Other people couldn't do that for her; not even parents with the best of intentions could do it.

Beverly pulled her shoulders back. She had a life of her own to consider. She was not only Sally's mother, she was a woman, a wife, a person in her own right. She had a commitment to herself and it was about time she honored it. The long-term situation with Dwight was sticky, complicated. She had no idea whether or not she would stay with him, but he sure was an attractive man. A desirable one too, she thought, suddenly excited by his handsome good looks, those blazing dark eyes that were regarding her now with a mixture of curiosity and longing. What a fool she was to have denied herself the pleasure of his lovemaking. Did she think that abstinence could help hasten Sally's safe return?

"I thought we were going to brunch at the Plaza," he said, catching his breath as she removed the robe and languidly approached him. "You're sure full of surprises today."

"Am I?" she teased, pressing her naked body against his. "Am I, really?"

She felt like saying that he didn't know the half of it, but that could wait until later. When they were seated across from each other in the luxurious confines of the Edwardian Room, she would tell him that they were moving to New York. He would probably be shocked, resistant, and pronounce her insane. That was all right, they'd work it out somehow. Or they wouldn't work it out and she would move here alone. The Beekman Place apartment shone like a jewel in a hope chest; she had every intention of turning it into a reality—with him or without him. Thank God she had money of her own and wasn't financially dependent upon Dwight. Thank God she was healthy, competent, and could get a job. It would be nice if he moved to New York too, but as with Sally, she could only do so much to convince him, and then the decision was out of her hands.

She closed her eyes and felt her husband's mouth open hers, warm, exploring. She had never known how marvelous it was not to feel responsible for the actions of others, not to feel guilty if those actions led to less-than-desirable results. When all was said and done, she was only responsible for her own actions. Why hadn't she figured that out before?

The knowledge seemed to loosen her, free her. She suddenly felt strong and happy. Yes, *happy*!

She started kissing him back with more pleasure than she remembered herself capable of. She wanted him so much, she wanted him now, she didn't want to wait another second. She had waited too long already. She all but dragged him over to the bed and lay down on top of him, reveling in the pressure of her body smack against his, all that beautiful bare skin of theirs just pasted together. Then, looking into his dark eyes, kissing his dark chest, she told him exactly what she would like him to do.

Lou awakened late on Anita's wedding day, curled up in Keith's arms. After finishing work at the penthouse yesterday, they agreed to sleep at his apartment. Vanessa and the SUCK sous chefs were sleeping at West End Avenue so as not to lose precious time cooking the revised wedding dinner.

Lou turned her head now and observed him. His eyes were shut and he was breathing gently, rhythmically. Yet even in sleep he held her close, a smile of contentment on his face. He looked so innocent, so guileless, but was he? Last night he told her that he loved her. They made love for what seemed like hours, and each time she thought it was over, one of them would do something and the frenzy would reignite. Finally, every part of her throbbed with sweet delicious warmth.

"I can't go on," she confessed. "I'm done in."

He laughed softly. "That's a relief. So am I."

"Let's sleep now. We have a big day tomorrow."

And that's when he said it. "I love you, Deidre."

Her breath caught in her throat, yet she couldn't reply. She didn't know whether or not to believe him. If she did, she suspected she would feel like a gullible fool; if she didn't, she was possibly putting the lid on the most compelling relationship that had come along in years. It seemed that either way, she couldn't win.

Maybe she had to stop thinking about winning and start thinking about being happy. Because in spite of all her ambivalence and paranoid fears, she felt happier than she remembered feeling in a long time. The truth was, she adored him. The other truth was, she didn't trust him for one minute. How could she?

Keith Winston (yes, Winston) Rinehart, born in Highland Park, Chicago, educated at the University of, employed as a photographer-journalist by *Time* magazine, was a traveler, adventurer, gourmet cook, connoisseur of fine wines, lover of slender brunettes, and no doubt an accomplished con man. He had charged into her life like a person who didn't understand the meaning of the word no, and turned her life upside down. She didn't know what to do with him. She couldn't bear the thought of letting him go and she couldn't reconcile herself to making him a partner—despite the fact that she needed one.

If only business hadn't entered into it. If only love and romance were the issues at stake. How much easier it would be. She liked the fact that he was the first one to come to her free and emotionally unencumbered. Peter Northrop was married to Beverly when she met him. Fingerhood was still reeling from Anita. Zachary was recovering from his late wife. Even Vanessa was recovering—from Zachary. But Keith had been divorced for seven years and his last serious affair ended too long ago to matter. Also, Zachary was so much older than she, and Vanessa so much younger, whereas she and Keith were only three months apart. She was born in August, he in November of the same year.

"Have some respect for your elders," she said to him last night when he scooped her up in his arms and deposited her on the bed. "That's the trouble with you kids, no goddamned respect."

"You want respect? I'll give you respect." He buried his face in her neck and kissed her senseless. "How's that? Is that enough respect? Do you want more? Where? How? Tell me. I'm not used to you demanding, critical, insatiable older women. I'll give you so much respect, you'll be sore for three weeks."

"Promise?"

When she thought of the rash of books and magazine articles that had been published in recent years advising women how to live alone and like it, how to be independent, how not to need or rely on a man, how to masturbate, fix your own car, install your own storm and screen windows, be your own grandma, she was glad she had met Keith. After Zachary's death she found herself bamboozled by one of those books and experienced a terrible sense of sadness as she turned the well-meaning, self-help pages. The more she read, the more depressed she became, until she felt utterly steeped in despair. But the clever author had anticipated such a reaction and warned it was indicative of women who were immature and refused to take responsibility for their own lives, women who still clung to the "knight-in-shining-armor" pipe dream.

*Prince Valiant is dead*, the author triumphantly declared. *A new age of self-reliance is upon us.*

Self-reliance wasn't Lou's problem. She threw the book down the incinerator, yet sections of it came back to haunt her. Such as the citing of grim urban statistics which proved there weren't enough men to go around and therefore women had better be prepared to do without if necessary. As if that weren't bad enough, the author further proposed a general across-the-board wartime philosophy of tightening one's belt. Joy, love, fun, and cuddling were suddenly dirty words. Maturity, solemnity, and taking care of numero uno were where it was at.

Lou bridled. She wouldn't mind fixing her own car or installing her own storm and screen windows, but she'd be damned if she would settle for auto-eroticism, that dubious gift of the Me Generation. And she'd doubly be damned if she would deprive herself of all those other goodies that made life worthwhile. Enter Vanessa, feminism's answer to grim urban statistics. . . .

"Good morning," he said, turning over beside her. "I have a great idea. It's about Some Like It Hot. After Vanessa leaves, let's expand."

"You're not a partner yet." But he had caught her interest. "Expand? How?"

"Go national with a chain of franchises. Like McDonald's and Kentucky Fried."

"Are you serious?"

"Sure, it's never been done with a catering company but I think it could work." He leaned on one elbow and looked at her intently. "There's a need for this kind of service right now, a big need. Home entertaining has always been popular, but with so many women currently in the work force, they don't have time to cook and bake and fuss for company. So we do it for them and bring it right to their homes, even serve it if they want us to. We could start off in major cities— Chicago, Dallas, San Francisco, Boston—lease the stores, supply the recipes, train the personnel, and take a percentage of the gross."

"The gross?" Lou asked with surprise.

"That's the way franchises work, which is why they just about never lose money. There's no waiting around for profits, you skim the cream right off the top. What do you think?"

"It sounds lucrative, but what advantage would we have over local catering companies that already exist? I mean, why would a hostess choose us rather than the friendly little caterer down the street whom she might have used before?"

"Because, for one thing, we'd be cheaper. We can afford to be, since this is a large-scale operation and we buy in bulk. We'd also offer a much wider and more imaginative selection of recipes than any local caterer could. But chances are we'd be preferred for the same reason that so many people continue to flock to McDonald's rather than the local beanery: McDonald's has eliminated the guesswork from eating out."

He emphasized his point. "In addition to offering tasty food at reasonable prices, chains like McDonald's are dependable, reliable, *consistent*."

"That's true," she concurred. "You know exactly what you're going to get."

He nodded. "There are no off-nights at McDonald's and that's how it would be with us. Some Like It Hot would eliminate the guesswork from eating *in*. Isn't that what a hostess wants? The assurance that she doesn't have to worry and fret about the dinner she's planning to serve? We'll give her that assurance in spades."

She observed him curiously. "When did you think of this?"

"It's been on my mind for a long time, way before I met you. Well? Does it have merit or doesn't it?"

"It has merit."

His face fell. "Is that all you're going to say?"

He didn't care about her, it was Some Like It Hot he was after. She'd been right all along, and yet going national was an intriguing, dazzling idea. Why the hell hadn't she thought of it herself? "I want to be president," she said.

He moved toward her. He needed a shave and smelled musky. "Would the president like to kiss the vice-president?"

Despite her antipathy toward early-morning sex, Lou felt aroused. But her mounting anger overcame that. "The president would like to do no such thing. She's too damned pissed off."

"Really? Why?"

"Because you've been using me." She got out of bed and started to throw on yesterday's clothes. She was seething now. "All you want to do is gain control of my company. You don't care beans about me."

"Hey, wait a minute. That's not true. You don't honestly think that, do you?" He followed her out of bed and tried to take her by the shoulders, but she shook him off. "That's a terrible thing to accuse me of, it's totally unwarranted. I'm crazy about you. I love you! How can you say that I'm using you?"

"Easily." She thought of how he had followed her all around New York, how hard he tried to meet her, how charming he was. "I should have known you had an ulterior motive all along."

"If you mean that I wanted to professionally align myself with Some Like It Hot, I won't deny it. I've always admired the operation. But if you think I have an unscrupulous underhanded takeover scheme in mind, you couldn't be more wrong. You're the one who conceived the company, you're the one who's made it what it is today, it's your baby and it always will be. I just want to be *part* of it, can't you understand that?''

"If that was all you wanted, you never would have thought of expanding on a national scale. You can't fool me.''

"That was only a suggestion," he said desperately. "We don't have to expand if you don't want to. Let's forget that I ever mentioned it and simply carry on as before.''

"I don't want to forget it. It's too brilliant an idea.''

"Then let's do it.''

"That isn't the point," she said, more furious than ever. His idea was a potential goldmine.

"What *is* the point?''

"Never mind." She cursed Fingerhood for having gotten in touch with her after all those years of silence. Without him as the link, she would never have spoken to Keith, never have found herself in this untenable position. "I'm leaving.''

"Why are you so angry? Tell me.''

"I already have.''

"There's more." He looked at her face. "Whatever I say, only seems to make you angrier. Why is that?''

"I don't owe you any explanations.''

The realization that she'd been used and manipulated filled her with outrage. The further realization that she would probably make him a partner and then risk losing her hold on the company she'd started from scratch filled her with panic. She wanted him, needed him, and was afraid of him. She had to get the hell out of there.

"I can't believe that a simple little suggestion of mine would drive a wedge between us," he said, bewildered.

"It's not a wedge, it's a Mack truck. And if you can't see that, you're not as ingenious as I think.''

He ran after her to the door. "I don't know what to say. I don't know what to do to make the president understand how silly she's being.''

Lou almost smiled. "The president is never silly.''

He longed to take her in his arms, but controlled himself. "Anything the president says goes.''

"Oh, yeah? In that case, how much of the gross do we skim off the top?''

"Twenty-five percent?"

"Forty."

"The president is greedy, I see."

"Very greedy," Lou said, walking out.

Anita sat at her dressing table wearing a plunging pink bra, matching scalloped tap pants, and an expression of grave disappointment. Fingerhood had flatly refused to disinvite the Northrops or go to Jamaica on their honeymoon. In fact, he refused to consider an imminent honeymoon at all.

"I don't know what you're thinking of," he admonished her earlier that morning. "I have patients scheduled for next week, patients with big problems. I can't just abandon them without warning."

"Why not?" She wondered how big those problems could be in view of his unusual specialty. "You said that most of them have never had an orgasm in their lives. Why can't they wait another week to have one? It's not as though they know what they're missing."

He looked at her with reproachful eyes. "We'll discuss this later. Meanwhile, cancel the Jamaican reservation and in the future don't go around committing us to anything unless you check with me first."

"You needn't sound so dictatorial."

"I don't like being manipulated, Anita. As for the Northrops, I wouldn't dream of telling them not to attend the wedding. I happen to be very fond of Beverly and Sally, and hopefully Peter won't show up of his own accord." He pecked her on the cheek. "See you later."

She felt frustrated as hell, but what could she do except grin and bear it? She had expected Fingerhood to be putty in her hands; instead he was firm and unrelenting. Was this how he intended to behave from now on? It did not augur well. She realized that she would have to think of strong counter-measures if she were ever to get her own way with him.

In front of her on the dressing table were two shades of foundation: Rose Indien and Ivory Coast. If she applied the former, she might look a little clownish; with the latter, she might look washed out. Just as she was wondering whether she should apply one on top of the other (but which one *first*?), her mother came racing into the room, clearly distraught.

"What is it this time?" Anita asked, not having recovered

from their earlier clash. "You're still not upset about the necklace, are you? Because I don't want to hear another word on the subject."

"*Gott im Himmel;* forget the necklace. I have just seen your wedding cake, such a disaster." Clad in a size-fifty-four peach silk A-line dress, Mrs. Schuler appeared ready to burst. Even her tightly curled hair stood at electrified attention. "*Tochter*, are you listening to me? Your wedding cake is sliding!"

Anita tried to retain what little patience she had left. "What do you mean, sliding? Where is it sliding? What are you talking about? Mother, don't you realize that you're upsetting me when you should be comforting and helping me?"

"But I *am* helping you. I am telling you that those people in the kitchen are ruining your beautiful cake." Mrs. Schuler wiped her brow with a peach handkerchief. "They have not used the proper size dowels for support, the *Dummkopfs*. Don't you understand plain English? Without the proper size, the cake slides!"

"So? What would you like me to do about it? Start carving dowels at this late date?" She knew that she shouldn't have let that diesel dike, Vanessa, talk her out of the Sacher Torte. Vanessa contended that the meal was too heavy to warrant an equally heavy dessert, adding that a traditional tiered white wedding cake was more romantic anyway. But how romantic would it be if it slid off its platter just as she was cutting the first slice, with Fingerhood's hand protectively over hers? "Mother, I suggest you go back in the kitchen and see if you can help correct the situation."

"They won't let me help them," Mrs. Schuler peevishly replied. "Those *Kochin* tell me to zip my lip, plus a few other words I cannot repeat. Are those women really *Kochin*? To me they behave more like lady wrestlers than cooks."

"I'll explain it to you some other time." She gazed at her exquisite gown and mantilla veil, which lay on the bed. They gave her the strength to go on despite insurmountable odds. "Meanwhile, try to get along with them, Mother. For my sake."

Mrs. Schuler sighed and left the kitchen, muttering, "What do wrestlers know about dowels?"

Anita loosened one of the rollers in her hair and tested to see how dry the clump felt. Pretty dry, she was pleased to note. The clump had a nice, thick, setting-lotion sheen and feel to it, which meant that once it and all the other clumps were combed out, they would turn into the smooth, wavy hairstyle she favored. Frizz was the last thing she needed on her wedding day. She turned to the well-thumbed magazine on the dressing table.

*Start getting dressed approximately two hours before the ceremony, with the assistance of your mother and the honor attendant.*

That was what *Today's Bride* advised in their latest issue, which she had been poring over ever since Fingerhood proposed. She didn't know what she would have done without the magazine, or whom she would have turned to for guidance. Who else would have told her how to keep her wedding gown looking fresh for years to come and suggested that the groom's flower be related to her bouquet?

Her mother had forgotten wedding etiquette a long time ago; Mrs. Fingerhood was still in shock from yesterday's events; Fingerhood, who'd never been married, was not only no help but needed help himself, having spent most of the afternoon throwing up in every bathroom in the penthouse (in later years, whenever Anita was asked what she remembered most vividly about today, she would say it was the sound of her future husband gagging and retching and then not disinfecting the toilet bowl afterward). As for her honor attendant being of assistance, that was a big joke. All Anita expected of Simone was to have her show up on time, which miraculously she did as the clock chimed three.

"Here I am, right on the dot," Simone said in a slurred voice, glancing at her watch, which she wore upside down. She smelled like a brewery. "Why are you staring at me? Do I have peanut butter on my dress? That's what I gave the twins for lunch. They'll be along soon with Jimmy."

"You're drunk." Anita thought of poor sweet Lucy Pickles, whom she'd always dreamed would serve as her matron of honor. Even speechless and half-paralyzed, Lucy would be an improvement. "How could you do this to me? You don't even *like* to drink."

"Now, don't get excited, Anita. I only had a few brandy alexanders to lift my spirits."

"Your spirits look pretty damned lifted to me." Simone's French-blue gown was even more overpowering than she feared, and neither the apricot cummerbund nor the garland of cymbidium orchids that she'd woven through her hair could detract from its vibrant color. "It's bad enough that you went to bed with Fingerhood yesterday. Do you have to try to outshine me today?"

Simone reddened. "Did Fingerhood tell you that?"

"No, Lou did."

*"Lou?"* She and Lou hadn't laid eyes on each other for fifteen years. "She must really hate me if she said that." Simone felt deeply ashamed of the incident, she felt more guilt-ridden than she had in a long time. "Would I do such a terrible thing to my best friend?"

*"Your best friend*? You fuck my future husband, try to hog the limelight, arrive here drunk, and you have the nerve to call yourself my best friend?"

"I'm the best friend you'll ever have. I love you in my own peculiar way."

*"Peculiar* is right, you French dingaling."

Simone's lower lip quivered. "Don't shout at me, Anita. I'm not feeling too wonderful. My life is in chaos again."

"You call marrying Michael and moving to London chaos? Most women would call it heaven. And what's this about Jimmy arriving with the twins? Where the hell is Michael?" She was looking forward to marrying Fingerhood in the presence of the man who had so callously thrown her over. "Don't tell me you two lovebirds had a fight already."

"Nothing so pedestrian." Simone hiccuped and flopped into a chaise, wishing she could decide what to do about her future. "Michael had to go back to England rather unexpectedly."

"What for? The Druid Festival at Stonehenge?"

"Don't be mean, just because he chose me over you."

"I can be as mean as I like, considering what you did with Fingerhood yesterday."

"I told you, I did not do it."

"Did."

"Didn't."

"Liar."

"Fool."

"Cunt!"

"Bitch!"

They glared at each other, then burst out laughing.

"Do you think we'll ever get along?" Anita asked.

"We get along. We just have an odd way of doing it. As for Michael, he had a crisis at home." Simone giggled. "A toucan bit off half his wife's nose, but fortunately she had an extra-large one to start with, so there was plenty left over for the plastic surgeon to work with." She glanced around the room. "Where's the champagne? I thought for sure you'd have a bottle in here while you got dressed."

"You thought wrong. Besides, the last thing you need is more booze."

"I meant for you. You look a little *fatiguée*."

"*Fatiguée* isn't the word for it. Do you have any idea what I've been through the last couple of days? It's no wonder I'm frazzled." Maybe she was stronger than she realized; a weaker woman would surely have collapsed by now. "In addition to all my other problems, my period is killing me. I've been bleeding through layers of Tampax, Kotex, Maxipads, Minipads, and Anyday panty liners like there's no tomorrow."

"That's why I suggested champagne. It will help you relax. Don't be so stoic."

"It has nothing to do with stoicism. It has to do with self-preservation. I want to keep my wits about me until after the ceremony; then I don't care what the hell happens."

"You mean, why take the chance of fucking things up now?"

"Exactly." She dusted over the Rose Indien and Ivory Coast with translucent powder, sprayed lightly with Evian, and decided she needed more blusher. Maybe the frosty terra-cotta would do the trick. "One of the reasons I'm so unnerved is my mother. She and I had a terrible fight this morning. I'd forgotten how provincial and puritanical she is."

Simone lit a cigarette, relieved to listen to someone else's problems. "What happened?"

"Please don't smoke in here."

"Jesus, I can't smoke, I can't drink. What *can* I do?"

"Sit there and try to sober up."

Simone extinguished the cigarette. "What did you and your mother fight about?"

"The necklace that Michael gave me." She dabbed Calandre (her perfume of the month) on all strategic pulse spots and then dabbed again for good luck. "My mother was shocked that I would consider wearing it today. She said only a whore would do a shameless thing like that. *Can you believe it?* My own mother! Is this why I good-naturedly flew her and my father here from Cleveland and have been waiting on them like a coolie ever since they arrived? So he could go around frightening the wits out of my future mother-in-law with his SS uniform and so that she could call me vile names after all the shit I've been through?"

"You never told me your father was in the SS."

"Oh, shut up." Anita felt a familiar pain threaten the right side of her face. "I tried to explain to my mother that the sapphire in the necklace would take care of the 'blue' part of 'something old, something new,' et cetera. But that failed to impress her. On and on she raved. It's not very pleasant listening to your own mother accuse you of being a materialistic, money-grabbing, jewelry-happy *Dirne* a few hours before the most glorious event of your whole life. That reminds me. You did bring the handkerchief, didn't you?"

"Sure. What's a *Dirne*?"

" 'Prostitute' in German. I've never been so insulted. It's a miracle I didn't have a liver attack on the spot."

"Here's your 'something borrowed.' " Simone took the delicate lace square out of her purse. "I didn't know that Michael gave you a sapphire necklace."

"Cartier's best, easily worth fifteen grand. It's eighteen-karat gold with diamonds and I plan to wear it today, no matter what my mother thinks. Why shouldn't I wear it? I worked my tail off for that necklace, being nice to creeps like Dickie Wembley."

"Who's Dickie Wembley?"

"You'll find out soon enough," Anita said with a smirk.

"Is he part of those threesomes you mentioned the other day?"

"I'm afraid so, but you could have worse things to contend with. Poverty and impotence, for example. At least Michael isn't cursed with those."

"I don't consider threesomes a curse. I like sex with two men—it means I get that much more attention."

"You always were weird."

"You call *me* weird? You're the one who's marrying Dr. Kronkeit in two more hours. What do you call yourself?"

"There's no need to denigrate my future husband just

because you didn't come—for a change—when he fucked you yesterday.''

"For the last time, I tell you that Fingerhood did not fuck me.''

"Oh, really? Then what did he do? Go down on you?''

"He didn't do anything because I wasn't with him, you foolish suspicious paranoid woman.''

"I admire you for sticking to your story, Simone, but you can't make a monkey out of me.''

"I don't have to. You're making a monkey out of yourself!''

"Kindly lower your voice, darling. My facial pain is returning.'' Maybe a glass of champagne wouldn't be a bad idea at that, Anita decided. She stuck her head out the door. "Jeeves! Champagne for two, please. On the double.''

Simone couldn't wait to have a glass of the bubbly. After Beverly left the King Croesus that morning, she had canceled her all-chocolate breakfast and begun drinking brandy alexanders in an attempt to blot out her uncertain future. Unfortunately, they hadn't worked.

"I'm sorry I screamed at you,'' she said to Anita. "But the truth is, I'm having second thoughts about marrying Michael. And believe me, it has nothing to do with threesomes.''

"What does it have to do with? I can't wait to hear.''

"Don't be sardonic. This is my life we're talking about.''

"So tell me.''

Simone took a deep breath. "If you must know, I'm afraid to marry him.''

"Afraid?'' Anita went rigid with alarm. "He doesn't have herpes or AIDS, does he? Because if so, I want to go on record as saying that he didn't get them from me.''

"You and your disease phobias,'' Simone scoffed. "It's nothing like that. It's worse. AIDS would be simple.''

"Sure, he'd die. But I don't understand. If it's not some fatal illness, what are you so afraid of?''

"Copping out. Avoiding self-commitment. Taking the easy path.''

"Would you like to translate that into plain English?''

"I'm trying to grow up, Anita. I think it's time that I became a responsible member of the human race.''

"You call that English?'' Anita applied a beauty mark next to her left eye, then looked at Simone shrewdly. "I get it.

Michael has dropped you. That's what this is all about, isn't it?''

"*Pas de tout*. I'm thinking of dropping him."

"What? I don't believe my ears." Anita whirled around, an eyebrow pencil in each hand. "I always knew you were impractical, now I'm beginning to think you're insane. Don't you realize what a catch Michael is? He's rich rich rich. He owns land, horses, stables, an ancestral home, a thriving aeronautics company. What's the matter with you? You don't even mind screwing his chums from Eton. I had to close my eyes and count my gold jewelry. How can you *consider* dropping him? Does he hate the twins? Is that it? It's not the end of the world, you just ship them off to boarding school.''

"He loves the twins. It's my career he hates." The brandy alexanders made her feel lugubrious. "He said I had to choose between him and acting, because I couldn't have both.''

"Is that all?" Anita laughed easily, freely for the first time since she opened her eyes that morning. "Boy, you had me scared for a minute. I thought it was something serious.''

"It *is* serious," Simone indignantly replied. "You may not be interested in a career, but that doesn't mean everyone else feels the same way. Acting has come to be important to me, it gives me a sense of myself. At times I loathe it, but I'm not sure I could survive without it.''

"So who's saying you should?''

"You are. You're saying I should marry Michael.''

"For a smart woman, you sure are stupid. Use your head, darling. You tell Michael that you'll give up your lousy career. You marry the man. Then, if you want to act afterward, you act. What can he do about it? He's trapped.''

Simone's lower lip started trembling. "I don't want to trap him. That's not the way I want to live. Don't you understand? Beneath this frivolous facade lurks a noble nature.''

"What lurks is a schmuck." Anita stroked her brows with Light Sable followed by Medium Sable, then dabbed a little Midnight Kohl around her inner lids. Good. Her face was starting to perk up. "Forget all that nobility crap, it won't get you anywhere. Life is a compromise, don't you know that by now? Look at me. It's true that I love Fingerhood—just as I'm sure you love Michael—but I have to make concessions just the same. Everyone does. That's the way it goes.''

"What kind of concessions?"

"You want a list? I'll give you a list. I have to sacrifice my Jamaican honeymoon, let the Northrops attend my wedding, act nice to Fingerhood's mother even though she calls me 'a dumb shiksa' behind my back, agree to be married by a Unitarian minister despite the fact that I was raised a Lutheran, agree to let Mink & Sable play 'When the Saints Go Marching In' as a processional, instead of 'Here Comes the Bride,' I have to give blow-jobs when I'm not in the mood, cope with a man who never disinfects, and there's plenty more where those came from, but so the hell what? In exchange, I'll never have to work or worry about money again."

She waited for Simone to absorb the immense significance of this last statement before continuing. "After today, I'll have charge accounts everywhere, I can redecorate this apartment to my heart's content, hire servants to wait on me hand and foot, go to lunch at Le Cirque, join the most fashionable gym, give smashing little dinner parties, be invited to more of the same, fly to Hollywood when Fingerhood's movie comes out, holiday in Cannes if it's accepted at the festival, travel the world with my charming, successful, devoted husband, I can even have children if that's what makes me happy. And 'happy' is the important word here. So I ask you, what's an occasional blow-job in the vast scheme of things?"

"It sounds like you'll still be a kept woman, only now it's legal."

Anita beamed at this succinct deduction. "That's what marriage is all about. For women, anyway. It's protection. And you could have it too if you grew up and started using your noodle. Just remember that Michael is your number-one priority. First you marry the son of a bitch, then you figure out the rest. A woman alone is a sorry sight, especially at our age. Screw those crazy feminists, they're all dikes."

"I envy you your clarity of vision," Simone said wistfully, remembering the days when she thought nothing of being supported. If only she could feel that way again. "But somehow I don't find it so simple."

"*Dimple, pimple, does Wimbledon rhyme?*" Miguel flew into the room, flapping his feathers and shrieking at the top of his lungs. "*Dime, chime, get me to the church on time!*"

"The only place you're getting is out of this room," Anita cried, chasing him with a hairbrush. "And after today, it will be out of our lives forever. I suppose you think you were pretty cute shitting all over my mother's new dress. You'll find out how cute that was when you're sitting in the window of a bird shop, you miserable disease-laden vulture.''

"I'm not a vulture, Thunder Thighs. I'm of the order Psittaciformes.''

*"OUT!"*

*"Shout, pout, without a doubt you're a pain in the ass! Sassy, brassy, but definitely not classy!"*

"Getting rid of Miguel will be the first big change I make around here,'' Anita told Simone after the parrot was gone. "And I can effect that change because I'll be Mrs. Robert Fingerhood. Wives have clout, and don't you forget it. Do you think Michael liked the idea of Lady Philippa keeping those filthy birds of hers? He hated it, but he felt powerless to stop her. And he'll feel just as powerless to stop you from pursuing an acting career, if that's what you want. Trust me, Simone, I know what I'm saying.''

Simone wished she had a smidgen of Anita's hard-eyed practicality. "I'll think it over,'' she promised.

"Just invite me to the wedding, darling, that's all I ask.'' There was a knock on the door. "Who is it?''

"Jeeves, madam.''

"Enter.''

The robot carried a silver tray that held a bottle of Dom Perignon chilling in a wine cooler, and two fluted glasses. "Shall I do the honors, madam?''

"Please,'' Anita said, opening her electronic pillbox.

He poured expertly and handed one glass to each of the women. Anita used hers to wash down a cortisone pill for her liver, Simone downed her champagne in two gulps and motioned for a refill.

"May I take this opportunity, madam, to wish you every happiness in the world?'' the robot said to Anita.

"Thank you, Jeeves. That's very kind of you.''

"May I also say that I don't wish to be replaced by a staff of three? I've grown very attached to Dr. Fingerhood and his nonorgasmic patients and I'm sure that, in time, I'll grow equally attached to you, madam. If you give me a chance, I can learn to disinfect and do all the other household chores you wish. All I need is a little encouragement and reprogramming.''

"I'll consider it, Jeeves. Have you seen Dr. Fingerhood? Is he getting dressed?"

"Slowly. In between purges. With the assistance of his best man. But don't concern yourself, madam. I called Gristede's and ordered every disinfectant they stock. Unlike Miguel, I'm very sensitive to smelly matters. I'll take care of the bathrooms. Just leave them to your faithful servant, Jeeves."

As he deferentially backed out of the room, three women entered. They were tall, muscular, and fit Mrs. Schuler's description of lady wrestlers despite the aprons they wore. The tallest and most menacing addressed Anita.

"Get that meddling mother of yours out of the kitchen or we won't be responsible for what happens to your wedding dinner, dig?"

"She's only trying to help." Anita suddenly felt naked in her bra and panties. "She told me that the cake is a bit wobbly. Is that true?"

The wrestler regarded her with a mixture of contempt and lust. "You don't need to worry about the cake. We've corrected the dowel situation. If you want to worry, think about your life."

The two other women chanted, "Right on, sister! Storm the locker rooms!"

"I have thought about my life." Anita decided that after today she would never again deal with Lou or that crazy catering company of hers. "And for your information, it's going to be just dandy."

"Victimization and exploitation are never dandy," the lead wrestler snapped. "They're tools of the Male Reich, the boot of which you will be under the second you say 'I do.' You know what a wife is, don't you?"

"I certainly have my private feelings on the matter."

"According to SUCK's dictionary, a wife is an over-worked and underpaid cleaning woman, nurse, cook, waitress, seamstress, laundress, child raiser, dog walker, ass wiper, cocksucker, and one hell of a cheap fuck." She stared at Anita condemningly. "It's not too late to change your mind, you know. You can still call off this medieval farce of a wedding."

"Call it off? That's hilarious. It's taken me forty years to get to this point. You must be kidding!"

"We never kid about sexism, misogynism, or the fact that

you will change the bed sheets four thousand times before you die. Minimum. Not to mention the seven thousand meals you'll prepare, the eight thousand fellatios you'll perform, or the nine thousand fucks you'll spread your legs for—whether you want to or not.''

"You should be so lucky."

"She wears the uniform of the female slave," the shortest woman said. She was about five-feet-nine and sported a punk-rock haircut. "We're wasting our time, she'll never be a sister."

"How about me? Can I be a sister?" Simone, who had been guzzling champagne, stood up and extended her hand to the lead wrestler. "Despite the fact that I've been recruited as matron of honor, I'm seriously thinking of calling off my own wedding. To whom do I have the pleasure of speaking?"

Anita ran over to her. "Don't encourage them," she hissed.

"We are representatives of the Society to Undermine Cock as King, reduced to cooking a sexist meal in order to raise funds for our organization," the lead wrestler explained, making a revolutionary gesture. "Lady, love your cunt!"

Simone giggled drunkenly. She hadn't had this much fun in years. "Excuse me?"

"That's the slogan of SUCK."

"It sounds kind of familiar. Where have I heard it before?"

"Germaine Greer may have said it first, but what the hell? We're all in this together, aren't we?"

"In what? I don't quite understand your position." She ignored the admonitory pinch that Anita gave her. "I've been doing a lot of soul-searching lately and I'm not sure if I can justify another marriage. Not if I want to live with myself in peace and harmony. Is that what you're talking about?"

*"Have you lost your mind?"* Anita whispered.

"If I become a sister, I won't have to think about whether or not to marry Michael," she whispered back.

The lead wrestler bestowed a congratulatory smile upon Simone. "That's the spirit, sister. The goal of SUCK is to banish matrimony, reexamine the genetic code, establish a new female hierarchy, and sanctify the vibrator."

"Can I shave under my arms?" Simone asked, hiccuping. "Or is that out, too?"

"Why are you asking *them*?" Anita said in exasperation.

"They're a bunch of bull dikes. The only place they shave is their faces."

The leader dug into her pocket and handed Simone a booklet entitled: *SUCK (or) If Cunt Tastes Like Truffles, Why Should Men Have All the Fun?* "If you read our Feministo, it will answer all your questions, sister."

Then the three women burst into an impassioned chant:

*Men are nerds*
*Men are turds*
*Their piggish words mean zilch to us*
*Y-e-y, SUCK!*

Simone wished she hadn't drunk so much champagne; she suddenly felt woozy. "I didn't know that cunt tasted like truffles, did you?" she asked Anita after the three women had trooped out singing another inflammatory song. "It explains an awful lot of behavior I never understood before."

"What bothers me is how I'm going to eat one bite of my own wedding dinner. Who knows where those women's hands have been?" She began taking the rollers out of her hair. "Ouch!" One of the rollers in back was stuck. "Simone, would you help me with this? Simone? Simone!"

To Anita's disgust, her matron of honor had passed out cold.

# 13

With the exception of Sally and Peter Northrop, all the wedding guests had arrived and were seated on the landscaped terrace—friends and relatives of the bride to the left, those of the groom to the right. Several large floor fans whirred silently, producing a pleasant breeze. The sky was cloudless, the atmosphere one of joyous anticipation.

Reverend Freshwater shook Fingerhood's clammy hand, checked the marriage license, pocketed his fee, tickled Prince under the chin after making sure he had the matching rings, and took his place beneath the arbor; Fingerhood and Keith positioned themselves beside him; Rima asked her mother why she looked so funny, to which Simone (who'd been revived with endless cups of black coffee) replied that if she started that question routine she would kill her; Mrs. Schuler and Mrs. Fingerhood exchanged guarded greetings and stealthily examined each other's dresses; Anita and her father hovered in the air-conditioned living room awaiting their muscial cue; Jeeves unrolled the long white canvas liner leading from the living room to the arbor; Mink & Sable, who had been playing selections from their own repertoire, now sounded the first stirring notes of "When the Saints Go Marching In," and all eyes turned to the entranceway wreathed in multicolored zinnias.

Simone took a deep breath, placed her left foot firmly in front, and started the processional in time with the beat. Rima followed her, scattering rose and dahlia petals for the bride to walk on; then came Prince in his knicker-and-vest outfit proudly carrying the velvet ring pillow; and at last Anita appeared on her father's arm, resplendent in her high-necked gown of antique lace and rose silk. A gasp of admiration swept the terrace as words like "exquisite" and "breathtaking" filled the air.

From her second-row seat on the groom's side, Beverly couldn't have agreed more. Despite her personal antipathy toward Anita, she found it hard to remember when she had seen a more beautiful bride. Anita's hair caught the sun's rays and shimmered like gold as it fell in soft waves over her shoulders, the sapphire-and-diamond necklace picked up the sparkle from the seed pearls woven throughout her bodice, and the long sweep train gave her the demeanor of royalty. Anita didn't walk, she floated toward Fingerhood on gossamer pumps holding a bouquet of pink tea roses (individually wired, like Princess Diana's) demurely close to her bosom.

When she reached the arbor, she let go of her father's arm, switched the bouquet to her left hand, and gave her right one to Fingerhood, who looked as if he were about to faint. She pressed his hand for reassurance, but he didn't seem to notice. Instead he gingerly touched his nose where he'd hurt himself yesterday. The bandage was gone and only a thin crusty brownish line marred his otherwise impeccable appearance. Anita felt proud, pleased that she'd talked him into buying "The Southampton." In the future, she would select all his clothes.

"Dearly beloved," Reverend Freshwater said in clear, ringing tones. "We are gathered here today in the sight of God and man . . ."

Dwight Kirby leaned over toward his wife. "Are you glad it's not Sally standing up there?"

"I'm not glad and I'm not sorry. I've stopped trying to decide who my daughter should marry, or how she should live her life."

"That's a new one. Since when?"

"Since today." Peter Jr., on her other side, was a mature responsible boy. At least one of her children had turned out admirably, perhaps she couldn't ask for more. "Whatever Sally does, I wish her well, but I'm through making the two of us sick over it."

"You sound like you mean that."

"I *do* mean it. I'm not even going to worry about whether she shows up today. If she does, fine. And if she doesn't, I'll survive without her."

He took her hand. "Have I told you lately that you not only are sensational, but that you look sensational?"

She felt pleased that her old turquoise chiffon was still

flattering. Because of the heat, she'd piled her long red hair on top of her head and at the last minute decided to wear her mother's drop earrings in brushed gold. She'd forgotten how much fun it was to dress up and be admired; she rarely had the opportunity to do so in Williams.

"You should deck yourself out like this more often," he said, pressing his lips to her ear. "It reminds me of what a gorgeous woman I'm married to, not to mention what a generous one. You and me living in New York! I still can't get over it."

Beverly smiled, thinking of the conversation they'd had during lunch in the Plaza's Edwardian Room. It was one of the most important conversations of her life, and she hoped she had done the right thing. . . .

*'New York?''* Dwight had just ordered two Perriers and was starting to look at the menu, when she announced her intentions. "I can't move to New York. Are you crazy? It's out of the question."

"I guess you'll have to stay in Wyoming, then."

"You mean, you'd move without me?"

"Yes, if I had to."

"I don't believe this." He was stunned by her cool self-confidence. "Oh, I get it. This is your way of getting back at me for all those times I was drunk and abusive, right?"

"Wrong. I'm not trying to spite you, nor am I trying to run away from you. The fact is, I'm not putting you first any longer. I feel the same way about you that I feel about Sally: either you'll shape up or you won't. It's your decision. As for New York, I'm doing that for me. It's where I want to live, and if you won't come, I'll go by myself."

He was at a loss for words. Was this the dependent, clutchy, punching bag of a woman he'd taken for granted? "I can't believe you would move to New York on your own. Despite all our problems, I thought you cared about me."

"I do care about you, Dwight, but I'm sick of living in a small town. I'm tired of the provinciality and lack of stimulation. I want to broaden my horizons."

"I'd like to broaden mine too, but I have a newspaper to run—or have you forgotten? I own twenty-five percent of the *Herald* and there's more to come, if I can ever increase that damned circulation. How can I just walk away?"

"Do you like living in Williams?"

"I'm not wild about it, but how many people get to live in places they are wild about? You know that it took my aunt's death to get me back there in the first place. Still, now I'm back, I'm settled, and I'm not a spring chicken any longer." He looked at her sharply. "Neither are you, for that matter."

"Are you saying that I'm too old to make a major move? Because if so, I disagree. I never intend to get too old for that. I'd rather be dead than feel I had to stay put just because I'm forty-four. What does age have to do with it, anyway?"

"It's harder to make adjustments as we get older. Whether we like it or not, we tend to get set in our ways. Besides, how am I going to make a living? Do you think the New York *Times* is out looking for aging reporters with small-town experience and a modicum of sophistication?"

"There's always that book you've dreamed of writing."

"Sure, but how would I support myself while I wrote it?"

"You wouldn't. I'd support you for the duration. It wouldn't be forever. A couple of years and you'd find out if you were any good at it. Maybe you'd find out that you didn't even enjoy writing it, that it wasn't what you had imagined. But if you don't try, you'll never know and it will always be a thorn in your side."

"I'm stunned that you would do this after the way I've treated you," he said after a long pause. "Are you serious, Beverly?"

She nodded. "A lot of people would say I was mad, but despite everything that's happened, I'm still very much in love with you. And when you love someone, you want what they want."

"I'm overwhelmed."

"Look, Dwight, deep down you hate the *Herald* and you know it. The paper is little more than a weekly gossip sheet paid for by those jerk advertisers you have to kowtow to every day of your life. You can do better than that. You've worked all over the country, you used to tell me how happy you were in larger cities, how much more alive you felt. Well, New York is the largest of them all and writing that book should give you a taste of the ultimate in aliveness, so why not take a chance on yourself?"

Tears came to his eyes. "Jesus, I love you. . . ."

Reverend Freshwater was reading solemnly from the book of Ruth.

" 'And Ruth said, Intreat me not to leave thee, or to return from following after thee: for whither thou goest, I will go; and where thou lodgest, I will lodge. . . .' "

Two rows behind Beverly, Lou removed her white sequined jacket and tried not to listen to the words from the Old Testament. She was glad that she'd dressed practically, as well as elegantly, for today's occasion. Her sleeveless navy top and flowing white crepe trousers felt comfortable in the heat of the afternoon sun.

" '. . . thy people shall be my people, and thy God, my God: where thou diest, I will die. . . .' "

The reason she didn't want to listen was that they were the same exact words that had been intoned at her wedding to Zachary. The emotion of that day returned to haunt her now. She had been so tremulously happy to be marrying him, as happy as Anita appeared to be marrying Fingerhood. All the trouble that Anita had put her and Vanessa to over the wedding dinner faded in light of her glowing radiance. The minute Lou saw her walk down the aisle, she forgave her everything. Anita was special today, she was a bride.

Cynics often asked what the big deal was in a piece of paper stating that two people were legally man and wife, but to Lou's mind they didn't understand. It *was* a big deal; the commitment to stay together forever made it so. Those same cynics said that it was an unrealistic commitment, naive and doomed to failure. Again, they didn't understand. Because it was so unrealistic (given the pressures and temptations of today's world), its goal was all the more noble. It lifted those who tried to accede to it to a level far above humdrum life. She herself had felt exalted when she heard those stirring words ("whither thou goest, I will go . . . where thou diest, I will die"), she had felt a sense of honor in taking such a sacred permanent vow.

True love. It was what everyone secretly longed to believe in, it was what made the madness of the world tolerable. It was why fifty guests were seated on the terrace this warm June afternoon: because Anita and Fingerhood had decided they shared true love. Just before the ceremony started, Joan confided that she and Cooley (the vibraphone player) shared it too.

"He's asked me to marry him," she excitedly told Lou.

"What did you say?"

"What do you think, Mom? Yes!"

"Oh, darling." Lou embraced her. "I'm so happy for you."

"I'm happy, too, happier than I've ever been in my entire life. In fact, I'm ecstatic." Joan's eyes were shining. "Don't get upset, Mom, but we're planning to be married within the next few days. We've already gotten our blood tests and marriage license, so we're all set."

*"The next few days?"* Lou felt a rush of alarm. "How can I arrange anything so quickly?"

"I don't want you to arrange anything. That's what I'm trying to tell you. We plan to dash down to City Hall and have a simple civil ceremony, then invite a few friends back to the flat for champagne, and that's it. Cooley has to go on tour with the Weirdos next week and we want to be married by then." Joan smiled self-consciously. "Maybe that way, I won't miss him so much."

Even hip, independent, rock-'n'-roll Joan believed in true love. It made Lou feel closer to her than she had in years. "So what you're saying is that the caterer doesn't get to cater her own daughter's wedding."

"You don't mind too much, do you?"

"Of course not," Lou lied. "It's up to you and Cooley to have the kind of wedding you want. Am I invited to the champagne celebration?"

"What a question. You. Vanessa. Keith." Joan looked at her curiously. "What's with you and Keith, anyway?"

After Lou left his apartment that morning, she went home and considered never seeing him again. She would break it off before the going got rough. That way, she would be safe and invulnerable to threat. But she also knew she would be miserable. In the short time she'd known Keith, he had managed to get a grip on her.

"What does it look like?" she asked Joan.

"It looks like romance. Am I right?"

Lou wished that's all it was. How much more simple the relationship would be, how fewer the problems. "You're half-right," she replied. "It's also business. Keith and I are going to be partners. He has an expansion scheme that will probably make your mother a very rich woman."

"That's sensational, but what about Vanessa? The two of

you were together for years. Now all of a sudden she's going to Paris and you're with Keith. What happened?''

''Vanessa wants to study at Cordon Bleu, so I agreed to buy her out. Why are you looking at me like that?''

''I meant, what happened to the two of you *personally?*''

''Personally?''

''Honestly, Mom.'' Joan groaned. ''Romantically? Sexually?''

Lou felt a stab of surprise. ''I didn't realize you knew.''

''Are you kidding? What am I—deaf, dumb, and blind?'' Joan was astonished. ''Did you think I had no idea that you and Vanessa were lovers all these years? I can't believe it.''

''I didn't want you to know, so I assumed that you didn't,'' she offered lamely. It felt strange to have her deep dark secret out in the open at last, now that it no longer was of any importance. ''Did it bother you?''

''You mean, that you and Vanessa were making it?''

She nodded, offended even now by the sexual allusion.

''Why should it bother *me*?'' Joan laughed. ''I wasn't the one in bed with another woman. I don't happen to go for women, it's not my scene. But I saw that it had become yours, so okay.''

''And that's it?''

''That's what?''

''The extent of your feelings on the matter?''

''I'm not sure I understand you. Are you asking whether I was prejudiced against the relationship because it was a lesbian one?''

Lou cringed. ''Yes, that's exactly what I'm asking.''

''The lesbian part didn't bother me at all.''

''You sound as though something else did.''

''There was a great deal of tension between you and Vanessa. I had the feeling you argued a lot, even though you put on a pretty good front when I was around. What bothered me was the fact that you didn't seem happy.''

How groundless her fears had been, how stupid and unnecessary. Joan knew the truth all along and it didn't shock, alarm, or mortify her. She'd only felt sorry that her mother wasn't happier!

''This is quite a wedding,'' the young man beside her now said. ''She looks beautiful, doesn't she?''

Lou thought he meant Anita. "Yes. Glowing."

"She's a fabulous musician, you know." Cooley was slim, hawk-nosed, in his early thirties, with a neatly clipped dark beard and large dark eyes. "Usually I steer clear of women in rock 'n' roll. They're either ballbreakers, crazies, or dikes. But Joan is something else, a superior human being all around."

"I think so too. I understand that you're going on tour as soon as you're married."

"What can I do?" he said with a regretful shrug. "It was arranged before I met Joan. It's only for a month, though."

"I know she's going to miss you."

"Not as much as I'll miss her," Lou's future son-in-law said, giving her a surprisingly bashful grin.

Reverend Freshwater put aside the Old Testament and picked up a copy of *The Prophet* by Kahlil Gibran. He began to read: "Love gives naught but itself and takes naught but itself. Love possesses not, nor would it be possessed; For love is sufficient unto love. When you love, you should not say, 'God is in my heart,' but rather, 'I am in the heart of God. . . .'"

Simone looked over her shoulder at Rima, who was gazing at Anita with awe and curiosity. It was Rima's very first wedding, she had never seen a bride in the flesh. Neither had Prince. He stood directly behind Fingerhood, holding his ring pillow with the solemnity the occasion demanded. Neither he nor Rima had faltered today, not for a second, neither had made the tiniest mistake. The twins were born troupers, Simone thought, her heart swelling with pride.

She and Michael hadn't discussed the possibility of having children and she wondered how he felt about it. She missed him, she realized with a pang of alarm (did that mean she loved him?). She missed his arms around her, the look of adoration in his eyes, the knowledge that she belonged to someone. She didn't want to face the future adrift, as she'd been with Jimmy. Was that sufficient reason to get married?

*"El sexo en vuelo,"* Reverend Freshwater said, starting to read from his translation of *The Fingerhood Position*, much to the confusion of the assembled guests, who couldn't understand a word he was saying. *"Todas las personas en el mundo quieren volar; ellas quieren ir mas lejos de la gravedad de esta planeta; ellas quieren remontrarse! El movimiento de*

*la hamaca es igual al vuelo, porque la persona está suspendida
en el aire como un pájaro. . . ."*

Quoting from *The Fingerhood Position* (and in Spanish
yet) was one of the nuttiest ideas Simone had ever heard of.
She couldn't help it, she giggled. No one seemed to notice
except Anita, who shot her a menacing look. She promptly
clamped her lips shut and tried to think dismal depressing
thoughts, but it didn't work. Unfortunately, she could understand many of the Spanish words because of their similarity
to French, and that brought forth another strangulated giggle.

*"Entonces, las aventuras sexuales en la hamaca están
iguales a transcender los límites de esta planeta. Es necesario
que las amantes tengan el mejor coordinación, visto que . . ."*

Simone wondered if anyone besides herself, Anita, and
Fingerhood realized that Reverend Freshwater was talking
about fucking in hammocks. Earlier Anita had confided that
if her future husband wanted to have part of his best-seller
read at the wedding, who was she to object? It was another
one of those famous concessions she was so willing to make.

"Why is it the women who always seem to be making
concessions, and not the men?" Simone had finally asked
her. "I don't think it's fair."

"Of course it's fair, dope. We're not in the driver's seat,
that's why we have to give in. We need them more than they
need us."

"We do?"

"Don't be a jerk all your life. It's known as upward
mobility. Why did you marry Steve Omaha?"

"Because I loved him."

"And why else?"

"I don't know what you mean."

"I mean, when you married that nut, you didn't have a pot
to piss in and he was able to support you. Not brilliantly, I
might add, but it was an improvement over your current
life-style. And Michael is more than an improvement, he's a
trip to the moon—first class all the way."

Having concluded from the book of Ruth, *The Prophet*,
and *The Fingerhood Position*, Reverend Freshwater turned to
the standard service offered by the Community Church of
New York.

"We are gathered together to unite this man and this

woman in marriage, which is an institution founded in nature, ordained by the state, sanctified by the church or synagogue, and made honorable by the faithful keeping of good men and women in all ages. . . .''

A strange truth suddenly dawned on Simone. As much as she loved Michael, she didn't want a first-class trip to the moon. She didn't need it, she didn't care to give up her career for it. It wasn't worth it. Not all the Bob Mackie gowns in the world could make it worthwhile. For the first time in her life, she felt like making her own way and taking her chances. If worst came to worst, she would put the twins in public school. They'd survive and so would she. Her earning power changed everything. Marriage was no longer the dire necessity that it remained for Anita, who had no trade, no occupation, nothing to fall back on except a man. Simone sighed. She wished that she'd never become an actress, never become independent, never become able to turn down a marriage proposal.

"You have major transits in your house of career," Kate had warned. "There's no going back to the way you used to be, Libra."

Maybe there wasn't, maybe she had reached the point of no return. It made her feel unfeminine and anxious to find herself at that point. It made her wonder what kind of woman she was turning into. Certainly it was not a woman she had ever set out to be. Perhaps that was the hardest thing of all to accept, she thought, swallowing hard.

". . . a union created by your loving purpose and kept by your abiding will. Into this estate these two people come to be united," Reverend Freshwater said, turning to Fingerhood. "Is it in this spirit and for this purpose that you have come hither to be joined together?"

"It is," Fingerhood said, in tones that were barely audible.

"Do you, Robert Alan Fingerhood, take Anita Marthe Schuler to be your wife, to love and to cherish, to honor and to comfort, in sickness and in health, in sorrow or in joy, in hardship or in ease, to have and to hold from this day forth?"

"I do," he mumbled.

"And do you, Anita Marthe Schuler, take Robert Alan Fingerhood to be your husband, to love and to cherish. . . ?"

Anita's "I do" was spoken in a clear, firm, exuberant

voice. Then she and Fingerhood exchanged gold rings and each repeated the same vow.

"With this ring, I thee wed and pledge my faithful love. Amen."

Simone couldn't keep her eyes off Anita's face, which was positively luminescent, as though lit by a secret source of gratitude. Yes, that was it. Anita felt *grateful* to Fingerhood for marrying her, for rescuing her. Simone would never be grateful to Michael, she would be resentful, thinking about all the movies she might have starred in. Moviemaking was dicey, chancy, subject to overnight change, which was probably why it appealed to the gambler in her. She might star in a hit tomorrow, be nominated for another Academy Award, form her own production company, perhaps even direct one day. Women in Hollywood were doing that more and more. The possibilities were dazzling, tempting, too irresistible to turn her back on.

"With the power invested in me, I now pronounce you husband and wife," Reverend Freshwater concluded in ringing tones. "You may now kiss the bride."

Fingerhood didn't move, he appeared frozen. So Anita pulled back her veil, flung her arms around him, and planted a long ardent kiss on his mouth. When they drew apart she was smiling the biggest, happiest, most triumphant smile Simone had ever seen. It was hard to believe that this was the same woman who, only a few days ago, had crept into her bedroom in the middle of the night and pretended to shoot her with a fake gun.

The silence of the terrace was broken as guests rose, chatted, collected themselves. Simone wiggled her toes. Mink & Sable burst into a lively rendition of the Beatles' song "I'm Happy Just to Dance with You" and the newlyweds marched up the aisle and into the air-conditioned living room, followed by their attendants and guests. Murmured reactions to the wedding abounded.

"Most unusual ceremony."

"Exquisite bride, fabulous gown."

"Nervous bridegroom, so touching."

"So nice to see two people deeply in love."

"And in these cynical times yet."

Simone took Rima and Prince by the hand, told them how

well they had done and how proud she was of them. She beckoned to Jimmy to join them. She caught a passing glimpse of a highly emotional Mrs. Fingerhood being comforted by a highly distraught Mrs. Schuler. She looked around for Sally, but the girl was nowhere to be seen. She waved at a surprisingly radiant Beverly, flanked on one side by her handsome son and on the other by her sexy husband. Where was Peter? Then she spotted that tattletale, Lou, heading toward the bridal table. Simone whisked her aside.

"Why the hell did you tell Anita about me and Fingerhood?" she asked accusingly. "She hasn't stopped badgering me about it since. You must really hate me."

"Of course I don't hate you, but you shouldn't have done it. As impossible as Anita is, you're supposed to be her friend. It's not the sort of thing a friend does."

"You're right. I'm so ashamed." The anger drained out of her. "I've denied it, Lou, and I intend to go on denying it. That way, she'll never know for sure."

"Good for you." Lou pecked her on the cheek. "We all have enough problems as it is, without adding to each other's burdens."

"You've just said a mouthful," Simone agreed.

As they began walking toward the bridal table, Lou caught the expression on Beverly's face. Aimed at her, it was one of suspicion and dislike. Beverly still resented her because of the affair with Peter, she realized, thinking of the advice she had just given Simone about not adding to each other's burdens. She wished that she hadn't added to Beverly's fifteen years ago. Maybe she would get a chance to tell her that when they were seated.

"Mommy," Rima said, tugging at Simone's gown. "I have to go to the bathroom."

"Then go."

"I forgot where it is."

"Walk through that archway. It's the first door on your right."

"Mommy, why are you crying?"

"Because it's a happy occasion."

"I thought people only cried on sad occasions."

"It's sad, too."

Rima cocked her head to one side. "Why is it sad, Mommy?"

"Because I'm not going to marry Mr. Harding."

"Are you going to marry Jimmy?"

"No, darling, I'm not going to marry anybody."

"Why not, Mommy?"

"Shut up and go pee."

# 14

*"Don't the tables look lovely?"* guests murmured as they found their place cards among the seven round dining tables that Lou had set with dusty-pink linen cloths, white bone china, Fingerhood's crystal, and his mother's best silver. In the middle of each table were huge hollowed-out cabbages filled with stalks of crisp raw vegetables, a creamy onion dip next to them. Straw baskets of flowers hung from the ceiling, their bright satin ribbons fluttering in the air. *"So summery, so colorful!"*

The eighth table, strategically placed, was the bridal table, with Anita reigning supreme smack in the center. Rectangular and larger than the others, it seated ten. Traditionally that number was limited to members of the wedding party, but Fingerhood had insisted that Beverly and Dwight be included as well, and Anita graciously complied. What was one concession more or less? she thought at the time.

Now she felt glad that she hadn't kicked up a fuss. Even though Beverly looked wildly sexy in her turquoise chiffon, with all that cleavage showing, Anita refused to be intimidated. Not today, not by anyone. She didn't care if Sophia Loren walked in stark naked, she wouldn't bat an eyelash. This was *her* moment of glory, *her* time to shine. Not even the profusion of flowers—orchids, asters, celosias, zinnias, daisies, freesias, roses, pansies, carnations, artemisias, dahlias, daffodils, and marigolds—could overshadow her own special bloom. She turned toward Fingerhood as champagne corks popped all around them.

"Happy, darling?"

The color had come back to his face and he looked almost human again. "I think I'm slightly delirious. I can't believe I've gone and done it."

"But you're glad, aren't you?"

He patted her hand consolingly. "Of course, of course."

"We're going to have a wonderful life. Don't doubt that for a second."

"I won't. I mean, I don't." His assurances felt as though they were coming from another man. "I know we will."

"I love you."

He smiled weakly and kissed his bride on the forehead. He was married! He couldn't get over it. It didn't seem real. How had this happened to him? He loved Anita (he sharply reminded himself), he wanted to spend the rest of his life with her. *The rest of his life?* It sounded like a prison sentence.

"You look beautiful," he said to her, trying to put some conviction into his voice.

She nestled closer. "Thank you, sweetheart."

Then he noticed that Beverly didn't look half bad either. Not to mention Simone seated directly to his left, delectable as always in her own unique tousled way. Even Lou seemed to hold a special chic appeal, as she glittered in her gold-and-white sequined pants outfit. Suddenly he wanted to fuck them all: Simone, Beverly, Lou. Separately. Together. On a bed, on the floor, in a hammock, standing up, upside down, he didn't care. Orgy visions flew before him, exciting, throbbing, tantalizing. He felt deranged with lust. He couldn't bear the idea that any of these beautiful women was off limits to him just because some lapsed Catholic of a minister had declared him legally wed.

Who ever heard of the Unitarian church anyway? He recalled his mother's dire warning about not being married by a rabbi, under a *huppah*, in the Hebrew faith. According to her, any other kind of marriage was no marriage at all. At the time, he'd cautioned her against being so narrow-minded, but now he wondered. Maybe she was right in her infinite wisdom, maybe he wasn't married—at least not in the official eyes of God.

And if he weren't married, then the prohibition against making love to other women didn't apply. That prohibition wasn't fair, it wasn't reasonable, it went against human nature. *Male* nature, anyway. Fingerhood bristled just thinking about it. Why the hell hadn't he thought about it before? Then he remembered (to his dismay) that he had, and decided he was mature enough to handle monogamy. Guess what, folks? He was wrong. One hundred percent misguided and demented wrong, no question of it.

A waiter filled his wineglass with champagne and Keith stood up, tapping for silence. The room grew still. "To Anita and Fingerhood," Keith said in a hearty booming voice. "May they always be as joyful as they are today!"

"Hear, hear," someone shouted.

"I'll drink to that," someone else added.

Fingerhood sourly looked out upon a sea of smiling faces. It seemed to him that every friend, relative, and woman he had ever screwed was there sipping champagne, wishing him well, drowning him in their good cheer and happiness. They made him feel like a total fraud. He had never wanted to get laid so badly; the urge was overpowering in its intensity and his only consolation was that no one could guess his feverish thoughts. He shouldn't have let Anita sleep alone last night, what a fatal mistake. If he'd been able to bang her brains out as usual, he wouldn't be feeling so horny right now.

He put his hand on her thigh beneath the table, and the touch of silk—soft, sensuous—increased his desire. He swiftly moved his hand toward the fold in her legs, calculating rapidly. If he weren't married (in the eyes of God), then he was entitled to a little fun. And if he were married (in the eyes of the law), then he was surely entitled, since the lady happened to be his wife. Fingerhood grinned for the first time that day, pressing flesh against silk.

"Not now," Anita hissed, pushing his hand away. "Later."

"I want to," he said. "Let me."

"No."

"I *have* to."

She looked at him curiously. "What's the matter with you? We're married, there'll be plenty of time for that." She laughed in a mocking manner. "The rest of our lives, in fact."

That prison sentence again. "I don't care about the rest of our lives. I have to do it now. This very second. If I don't, I won't be responsible for what happens. Do you understand?"

Her face darkened. "I have my period."

"I don't give a shit."

"But *I* do."

Undaunted, he began to slide her dress up her leg. She squirmed, but it didn't stop him. What the hell did she have on under there? Not pantyhose, thank God, but a garter belt, silk stockings, panties, even an old-fashioned garter. He promptly got a huge hard-on. Oh, oh, there was something else, something padded. Kotex? Yes. Then he felt a string. Tampax too? He had married a very thorough woman, he could see that. The implications were disturbing. He pulled the Tampax out and tossed it on the floor beneath the table, inched his hand up inside her Kotex-lined panties, and began to caress her. She was wet, probably with blood, but he didn't care. It felt good, comforting, familiar. She tried desperately to pull away, detach herself from him, but she had nowhere to go and was too intimidated to make a scene.

"You're trapped," he said gleefully.

"Don't do this to me!"

"Relax. Enjoy it."

"I'll bleed all over you and all over my wedding gown." She seemed frightened now. "What's the matter with you? Have you gone crazy?"

"I love your cunt," he said in her ear, thinking of Simone's cunt, Beverly's, Lou's. He loved them all. Would he never see them again? "I can't help myself. Things are beyond my control."

"This isn't the time or place," she pleaded.

"It is for me."

"Can't you wait until later?" She tried to appeal to the civilized side in him. *Quelle* mistake. "It will be nicer when we're alone, just the two of us. Then we can do anything we want."

His civilized side had left town and made room for his lusty primal side—that was what she failed to comprehend. "I don't want to wait." He dug deeper. "I can't wait. I've got to do this now."

"Jesus, you're an animal."

"I guess so."

"I can't believe this is happening to me. At my own bridal table, on my own wedding day," she said in his ear, all the while keeping a frozen smile on her lips. "It's obscene."

"Call it what you will. I'm enjoying myself."

"And what about *me*? Don't you care about *me*? How am I going to stand up after this? Keith will be taking pictures of us. We're supposed to dance the first dance, it's customary.

There'll be blood all over my gown. What will people think? What will I say? I'll die of shame!''

"No, you won't. I'm holding the blood back with my hand. I'm taking the place of a Tampax."

She shuddered. "That's disgusting, revolting, sick."

"Maybe, but it feels damned good."

"You're perverted. I've married a sick, perverted, depraved man."

"Possibly."

There were tears in her eyes. "Don't you respect me?"

"You bet I do. I have more respect for you than you'll ever know."

"You call this *respect*?"

He dug deeper into that mysterious land of folds, hills, and curves. "No one will ever respect your cunt like I do, Anita, just remember that."

Across the room at the parents-minister table, he saw his mother, still misty-eyed from the ceremony, starting to unwind at last. His gallant, patient, long-suffering mother. She had been so afraid he would never get married, she had lectured him endlessly on the perils of ending up a lonely old man with nobody to care for him, and today she had seen her worst fears overthrown. He was glad for her. He wished his father were alive to share her joy. Instead, she was flanked by Reverend Freshwater (né Aguafresca).

Fingerhood wondered what the good minister would think if he knew the man he'd just married had his hand up his wife's bloody cunt. Maybe as a fellow lech, he would understand. Probably all men would understand, while women would be shocked and revolted. From the expression on Anita's face, something told him that he was going to pay dearly for this later on. How quickly he'd accommodated himself to married life, he thought. She already had the power to make him pay; he had given her that power by marrying her. Unfortunately, his dear mother was wrong about no rabbi and no *huppah* adding up to no marriage. They added up in the eyes of New York State, he had the piece of paper to prove it.

"I'm especially pleased to make this toast," Keith continued, winking at the assembled guests as though they were conspirators, "because having been friends with the bridegroom for more years than I care to remember, I never thought I'd live to see the day he would relinquish his precious bachelorhood, choose one woman, and stop playing Casanova. Apparently miracles still happen." A tinkle of laughter spread across the room. Keith grinned, raised his champagne glass high. "Anita, you did the impossible. You conquered the unconquerable. You tamed the untamable. Let us drink to a very beautiful bride and a very lucky groom. Health! Happiness! Long life!"

Everyone drank and everyone beamed. Anita nudged Fingerhood. "You're supposed to get up now and say a few words."

"I am?"

"Wipe your hand off first."

He remained seated. "I'm too weak to stand," he told the roomful of guests, with an ingratiating laugh. "I'm pooped. Is this what marriage does to a man? And so soon, too!" They tittered. "But seriously, folks, on behalf of my lovely bride and myself I'd like to thank Keith for those kind words. At least, I think they were kind." He registered a quizzical expression. "Keith, let me put it this way: I plan to say the same exact thing at *your* wedding, buddy. How does that grab you?"

More laughter followed, more toasts, more drinking, more goodwill filled the air. Then Mink & Sable struck up the romantic song Anita and Joan had discussed. "I'll Always Love You."

"This is it," she told Fingerhood, stealthily pulling up her panties, relieved to find that the Kotex pad was still inside, not daring to wonder what had happened to the Tampax he discarded. "What are you waiting for?"

He couldn't imagine what she wanted. "Am I supposed to do something else now?"

"Yes, you pervert, you're supposed to dance with me."

He saw that she was right. Lou had arranged the tables in such a way that they made a circle around a good-sized opening of space, clearly meant to be the dance floor. All faces turned toward him and Anita. Lou's daughter picked up the mike and began to soulfully sing one of her own compositions:

> I'll always love you
> I'll always care

She was too short, too angular, too feral-looking for Fingerhood's taste, but he'd fuck her anyway, he thought as he surreptitiously wiped his bloody hand on the tablecloth and arose.

"Darling," he said loud enough for the wedding party to hear. "May I have the honor?"

"My pleasure, sweetheart."

Smiling, they stepped out onto the floor and he took her in his arms. They danced slowly, gracefully, round and round, Fingerhood's erection jutting into the soft folds of her skirt and hitting the top of her thigh in a way that no one else could see, only she could feel.

"Stop it immediately," she said between clenched teeth.

"Stop what?"

"You know."

His only response was to hold her tighter, closer, in a seemingly more loving embrace. People commented on what a devoted couple they made and what a handsome one, with his dark good looks highlighting her blond blue-eyed beauty. Both their mothers sobbed. Reverend Freshwater glowed. Even Miguel, who was perched on top of one of the straw flower baskets, felt reduced to respectful silence. Anita's father lit a cigar and asked the waiter for schnapps, relieved that his daughter had finally made him a proud man. Women sighed nostalgically, remembering their own weddings.

"If you don't put your damned prick away, I'll never let you touch me again," Anita threatened, furious by now. "And when I say *never*, you know that I mean it."

"Where would you like me to put it?"

"Back where it belongs. Look, Keith is coming over to take pictures of us. Oh, Jesus!"

"What's the matter?"

"Do you want our wedding photos to show you with a hard-on? Is that what you'd like our children to see?"

"I can think of worse things. Besides, it doesn't seem to want to go anywhere." He shrugged innocently, as a flash bulb popped. "It has a mind of its own."

"That's more than you have," she said, stepping on his foot as hard as she could. "Smile, sweetheart, it's for posterity."

His cry of pain was drowned out, as Joan leaned closer to the mike:

> I'll always want you
> I'll always be there

\*     \*     \*

Sally and Colin had managed to get into Fingerhood's fortress of a building by sneaking through the service entrance at an unguarded moment. But the man running the elevator looked at them and the red Yamaha with suspicion.

"Where you people going with that motorcycle?" he demanded. "And why you dressed so funny?"

Still in his Frenchman's disguise, Colin wore the exotic black Zandra Rhodes dress that Sally had bought at Bendel's. In order for him to fit into it they had to slit it down the back, safety-pin it together, and tie it with a black belt. Sally wore a white jumpsuit, with nothing underneath.

"We're the entertainment for Dr. Fingerhood's wedding," Colin explained in his deep French accent. "My partner and I are gymnasts."

"We've been hired to perform stunts on this motorcycle," Sally added with a pleasant smile.

"I'd better check with Dr. Fingerhood," the operator said dubiously. After several tries, he gave up. "Maybe they can't hear me, must be a lot of noise up there. You say you're *entertainers*?"

"Mr. Black and Mrs. White," Colin replied, indicating the color of their clothes. He slipped a ten-dollar bill into the man's hand. "And we're going to be late if you don't take us up there right now."

"Okay, okay." Having seen the three sous chefs and skimmed through *The Fingerhood Position*, the operator knew that the penthouse was not occupied by the most conventional of tenants. "Get in."

They slid the motorcycle into the elevator and grinned at each other behind the operator's back. They were stoned on a combination of coke, Pernod, Quaaludes, and amyl nitrite. Thanks to the poppers that Colin provided, Sally had just experienced the greatest orgasm of her life and was feeling sensational, invulnerable, as well as madly in love with America's missing TV star. She shuddered to think that had she married Dr. Sex, she never would have met Colin. What a close call! She couldn't wait to see the expression on her mother's face when the two of them made their grand entrance.

The elevator came to a stop. "Penthouse," the operator said.

*          *          *

Waiters were bringing out the *Schweinsulze* on graceful oval platters, attractively garnished with watercress and gherkins. Mrs. Schuler nudged her husband.

"Look, Fritz. Your favorite."

"*Ja*, I see." He cut off a large slice and dug in, alternately chewing and smoking his cigar. "*Es ist gut.*"

Mrs. Fingerhood, seated beside him, raised her chin, delicately sipped her champagne, and tried not to think about her in-laws. So gross, so crude, so boorish. At least they lived in Cleveland, she assured herself, meaning she wouldn't have to see them too often.

"You don't eat?" Mr. Schuler asked, poking her in the arm.

"I'm afraid my digestion is a bit too delicate to deal with this."

"*Es ist gut.*"

"So you've already said. I wonder. Would you mind putting out your cigar? I find the odor offensive."

He winked at her. "I put out cigar if you try delicious *Vorspeise.*"

To her surprise, she understood the German word; it was almost identical to the Yiddish word for "appetizer." She answered tentatively, "Maybe I will have a tiny little bite."

He extinguished the cigar and waited for her to fulfill her part of the bargain. Mrs. Fingerhood broke off a piece of the *Schweinsulze* and popped it into her mouth. It wasn't terrible, it wasn't even bad. Of course it wasn't as good as Chopped Liver Swans (lost forever to eternity), but it was nowhere near as distasteful as she had feared. Maybe her fears about her son's future were also exaggerated. Maybe, God willing, he would find happiness with that dumb blond *shiksa* who seemed to be crazy about him.

"So?" Mr. Schuler asked, waiting for her reaction. "You like?"

She honored him with her first smile, wondering how soon they would become grandparents. "*Es ist gut.*"

At the bridal table, Rima and Prince also had their doubts about the *Schweinsulze*. When Simone explained that it was jellied pork loaf, they gagged and refused to eat a bite. For once, she didn't blame them. She was abstaining, too. Not so Jimmy. She watched him gorge himself, then accuse her (with his mouth full) of making a terrible mistake by not marrying him.

"You could do a lot worse," he said, jealous of how happy Colin was with his new girlfriend. Although he'd been tempted to tell Simone that he knew where Sally Northrop and Arizona Pete were, he'd promised Colin not to say anything. Besides, they would be here soon enough. "If you marry me, I'll turn over a new leaf. No more gambling. I swear it."

"It's too late, Jimmy."

She would wait until tomorrow before announcing that she was moving out of the house in Malibu. There was no point in bringing it up now and disturbing the twins. Strangely enough, she didn't feel disturbed about the future. She felt good. Maybe one day she would find a man to love, someone who didn't gamble or ignore her (like Jimmy), or insist that she give up acting (like Michael). It had taken this trip to New York to make her realize not only how important her career was, but how important *she* was as a human being. In the past she'd undervalued herself with all that yearning and craving to be appreciated as a femme fatale. It was a dopey goal. Yes, her dingaling days were over, and good riddance, Simone thought. By inviting her to his wedding, Fingerhood had helped her sort out her priorities, the dear sweet nut.

"Mommy, why are you smiling?" Prince asked.

"Because I feel optimistic."

"What does 'optimistic' mean?"

"It means I expect the best to happen."

"What's the best, Mommy?"

"I'm not sure." She hugged him tight. "It's still to come. . . ."

Beverly fed a forkful of the *Schweinsulze* to Dwight, who had told her only a few minutes ago that he'd never been happier in his life. Beverly's own feelings were mixed. She wasn't sure that when they moved here, things would work out the way they planned. So much could go wrong. He could start drinking again, become abusive, be unable to write his book. Their marriage could collapse once and for all.

In addition, she had her own drinking problem to consider. After she got out of Smithers, she would have to work on staying sober for the rest of her life. It was an awesome prospect.

But at least she was no longer obsessed with Sally to the exclusion of everyone and everything else. The discovery that Sally had packed a suitcase and checked out of the Gramercy Regency, while she'd been visiting Simone, hadn't thrown her into a state of hysteria. Instead, she felt regretful but resigned. She might not see or hear from her for a long time to come. Maybe never. It was a bitter pill to swallow, but what could she do? She only wished that Peter hadn't reacted so violently to their daughter's second disappearance. She had never seen him so outraged.

"If she wants to pull this stupid Houdini act one more time, I've got news for her: she's bloody well succeeded!" he exploded yesterday. "I wash my hands of the entire business. I'm going back to Paris on the next plane."

"Please wait and come to the wedding. Your son would love to spend more time with you."

"He'll be in Paris in August. He'll spend more time with me then."

Some demon made her add, "Lou will be there, you know."

"Is that supposed to be an inducement?" Peter snapped.

"You certainly seemed pleased to see her the other evening."

"I *was* pleased. I was crazy about her once. But if you recall, that was a long time ago."

Strange how his admission still hurt. He'd been crazy about Lou when he was married to her. He'd cheated on her with Lou, repeatedly. He'd spent nights lying in Lou's arms while she lay alone wondering if he would come home and ask for a divorce. Even though he didn't (when the divorce happened, it was much later and had nothing to do with Lou), Beverly continued to resent her old rival. It was probably silly, but she couldn't help it. She didn't know if Lou was a lesbian, a switch hitter, or what. She only knew that she still felt jealous of her after all these years. Maybe some wounds never healed, maybe they weren't supposed to.

"Have a safe trip," she said to Peter. "And take care of yourself."

She hated to see him go. He was the first man she had ever loved, and part of her would always belong to him, no matter where he was or who he was with. . . .

Lou pushed her plate of *Schweinsulze* aside, untouched. She was thinking of Peter too. He had called her yesterday.

"I wanted to say good-bye, Lou. I'm going home."

"I'm sorry to hear that. I thought for sure you'd be at the wedding."

"Spare me!" he groaned. "Actually, Sally has run off again and it's all I can do to get out of here fast. I'm glad I saw you, though. You look wonderful. You *seem* wonderful."

"So do you, Peter, and I'm sorry about Sally. I know what her problem is."

"You do?" He was startled. "How?"

She explained the whole story, adding: "I like Sally. I think she's going to straighten out eventually."

"You're kind." A funny note came into his voice. "But then, you always were."

"What do you mean?"

"Years ago when we were together, you never pushed me into leaving Beverly. I probably would have done it and married you, if you'd insisted. But you didn't. Not once. You always seemed so concerned about my family. You still are."

She didn't say that the reason she hadn't pushed was that she'd been too involved with her career to make a personal commitment. Let him go away thinking she was noble and self-sacrificing. But as she watched Keith on the sidelines of the dance floor, snapping pictures of the bridal couple, she wondered whether her involvement with Some Like It Hot was stopping her from making another personal commitment.

"If you ever come over to Paris, give me a call," Peter had said. "Georges and I will show you around."

"Thank you. I will."

She knew she wouldn't. She preferred to remember him when they were crazily in love and couldn't get enough of each other. Yes, she had missed the boat with Peter, but by a stroke of luck romance was beckoning once more.

"What color do you think the franchises should be?" she asked Keith when he returned to the table.

"Terra-cotta with white trim?"

"Red with white trim. Red makes people hungry."

"Whatever the president says."

"I think we should cater three types of meals: American, international, and regional. That last category would make every franchise slightly unique, while in the other two categories it would remain identical to franchises all over the country. What do you say?"

"It sounds like the president has been doing some heavy thinking."

Lou smiled and reached for his hand. "That's because she realizes how much she cares for the vice-president."

He kissed her on the lips. She kissed him back, pleased by her own decision. She would make him a partner. She would take her chances. If the son of a bitch turned out to be a son of a bitch, she would see to it that her lawyer protected her as best he could. She didn't want to wake up fifteen years from now and feel that she had missed the boat again.


The bridal couple were still on the dance floor.

"Isn't that thing of yours ever going to go down?" Anita was crazed by now with fury, resentment, rage, humiliation, and disgust.

"Why should it?" Fingerhood felt proud that it had stayed hard this long without any encouragement. "It's a token of my affection and esteem."

"Some esteem."

"Put your hand on it."

She bristled. "I will not."

"Come on," he said, playfully pinching her nipple. "Give me a cheap thrill."

"Don't do that again," she cautioned him.

"I thought you liked your nipples touched."

"Not in public, you fool."

"Nobody can see. We're pressed too close together."

"Of course they can see. They're not blind. Why are you purposely trying to embarrass me on what's supposed to be the happiest day of my life? Why? Why?"

"Take it easy. I was only having a little fun."

"*Fun?*" she said in a low screech. "It is not *fun* to me. I don't find anything the least bit funny or amusing about your behavior. I find it degrading and disgusting, do you understand?"

He merely laughed. "Temper, temper."

She would never forgive him for treating her like this. That he dared behave so brazenly during the bride and groom's first dance was an outrage. She held her head even higher and thought of how she would get back at him. She was through making concessions, she was through being sweet, reasonable, and accommodating. From here on in, he would dance to *her* tune. Wives had clout, she reminded herself, trying to loosen his stranglehold grip. She did not succeed. Instead, he clasped her even tighter and tweaked her other nipple.

"Now they're even," he said with a maniacal grin.

That did it. She kicked him in the groin as hard as she could and he went white, gasped, cursed, faltered, started to double over in pain. She pulled him back up before anyone could notice. She placed his arms firmly around her. She looked into his eyes, enjoying the expression of stark agony they reflected.

"Dance, you asshole," she said.

Fingerhood danced. Anita's assault had stunned him into feeling a new respect for her. She possessed gumption and spunk, after all. Good. He liked the fact that he had married a woman who wasn't going to lie down, play dead, and let him walk all over her. He'd done that to too many women in the past and the majority had taken it without a whimper, which only decreased their value in his eyes. Maybe he was a bastard, but he was a *fair* bastard. If someone stood up to him, he applauded her for it.

"You're smiling," Anita said, seconds later. "You look happy."

"I am, sweetheart. I am."

*This is marriage*, Fingerhood told himself. And strangely enough, after those first few stabs of pain, it didn't hurt half as much as he thought it would. He might even get to like it. Actually, he was starting to feel certain that he would. He held his wife much more gently now, while off in the distance Simone, Beverly, and Lou blurred into a sea of amicable faces. He had begun to resign himself to never seeing their cunts again, and it didn't seem so bad. He still had Anita's cunt for consolation. No. He corrected himself. He had Anita, period. That knowledge warmed him and he began to dance in a more spirited fashion, making wider circles, nodding to friends and relatives whose faces radiated good cheer. Even Jeeves, stationed in the rear of the room, wore a wiry smile of approval. Only Vanessa and the SUCK sous chefs, who'd emerged from the kitchen, scowled in contempt. Fingerhood playfully waved to them, and their scowls deepened. He took Anita's hand, kissed it, enfolded it in his own with a sudden feeling of tenderness he didn't know he was capable of.

"I'm sorry about the way I've been acting," he said, meaning it. "I don't know what got into me."

She breathed her first sigh of relief, closed her eyes, and rested her head on her husband's shoulder. "You're forgiven."

"Thank you."

It was going to be all right. She would make it all right. Wives had clout. Just as she was starting to enjoy her wedding and relish her rosy future, the screech of tires made her head jerk up as though she'd been awakened by a bad dream.

"No," she said. "I don't believe it."

Some lunatic had driven a motorcycle smack into the middle of the living room, upsetting tables, china, crystal, loaves of *Schweinsulze*, and frightened guests who ran scurrying out of the way. Miguel began to screech and flap his feathers, all of Jeeves's lights turned on and blinked furiously, while Simone, Beverly, and Lou gasped in horror. Anita saw her mother go white with fear and her father pull her back, as two bodies tumbled off the bike and landed on the floor with a thud. The man ripped off a curly gray wig and fake gray beard and smiled triumphantly at his audience

"*Mon Dieu!*" Simone cried. "It's Arizona Pete!"

Anita stared. It was. To her astonishment, he wore the black Zandra Rhodes dress that Simone had described in such painstaking detail. She shook her head mutely. No, this couldn't be happening to her. It wasn't possible, not after all she'd been through already. It wasn't fair. Where had Colin come from? The son of a bitch wasn't even *invited*.

Then she saw that the woman with him was Sally Northrop, naked as a jaybird. Anita swayed and nearly fainted, but the realization that Sally was more flat-chested than she gave her the sustenance to remain standing. Suddenly she heard sounds of laughter. At first she couldn't believe her ears. She looked. To her horror, all the guests (even her own parents) had started laughing, chuckling, pointing at the pair of stoned intruders with uncontrollable glee. *Arizona Pete in a black dress*. Ha ha ha. *A skinny naked woman alongside him*. Ha ha ha. Laughing! At her wedding!

Anita regained her voice. "*Don't just stand there!*" she screamed at Fingerhood, who, to her chagrin, was laughing also. "*Do something!*"

"What would you like me to do?"

"*Something! Anything!*" Only Simone, Beverly, and Lou seemed horrified by the spectacle before them. Lou had put her arm around Beverly's shoulder, steadying and consoling her. Everyone else was in stitches. "*This is a disgrace!*"

In compliance with his wife's wishes, Fingerhood motioned to Mink & Sable, who'd broken off in the middle of their song. Joan motioned back and turned up the mike.

> I'll always love you
> I'll always be there

It was wonderful writing about "The Crazy Ladies" after fifteen years. It was like running into four old friends and finding out what they'd been up to since we last met, whom they were in love with, and how they had changed. Strange as it may sound, Simone, Beverly, Anita, and Lou are real people to me—not just characters in a book. Every so often while I was writing *Return of the Crazy Ladies*, I would decide upon a course of action for one of the women, only to find her going her own sweet way and doing something quite dramatically different. Yes, they gave me a few surprises as well as a few laughs. I hope they do the same for the reader. *The Crazy Ladies* is also available in a Signet edition.

## SIGNET Fiction by John Colleton

Ø

---

Fabulous Fiction by June Lund Shiplett from SIGNET